Robert Tannahill, David Semple

The Poems and Songs of Robert Tannahill

Robert Tannahill, David Semple

The Poems and Songs of Robert Tannahill

ISBN/EAN: 9783337007973

Printed in Europe, USA, Canada, Australia, Japan

Cover: Foto ©Andreas Hilbeck / pixelio.de

More available books at **www.hansebooks.com**

CENTENARY EDITION.

THE

POEMS AND SONGS

OF

ROBERT TANNAHILL.

WITH LIFE, AND NOTES

BY DAVID SEMPLE, F.S.A.

"I would I were a weaver, I could sing all manner of songs."
Shakespeare.

PAISLEY: ALEX. GARDNER.

1874.

THE present edition of the works of ROBERT TANNAHILL has
been prepared with considerable care. The notes, kindly
supplied by David Semple,' Esq., F.S.A.,—than whom
no more zealous and accomplished antiquary can be found
in any county in Britain—add to the value of the volume.
The notes on pages 26 and 36 are by the late James J.
Lamb, Esq., who originally undertook to edit the book.
A few additional notes, and other matter, will be found in
an Appendix.   The holograph letter of the author, reproduced by photo-lithography, has been kindly lent for that
purpose by Provost Murray before being deposited in the
Paisley Museum.   How the Weaver-Poet of Paisley will be
regarded on the 3d of June, 1974, is matter for curious
speculation.   Will his bi-centenary be held with even
greater demonstration than his centenary, or will
Time's "sharp-nailed, nibbling elves" have so changed
the tastes of Scotsmen that TANNAHILL'S "darling
verses" will no more be sung? Few bi-centenaries
are observed.   A century of Fame is more than most poets
enjoy ; but we here place our belief on record that after the
next three generations shall have passed away, the name and
the fame of ROBERT TANNAHILL will be as green in the
memories of Scotsmen as at this day.

3d JUNE, 1874.

CONTENTS.

EPIGRAMS.

EPITAPHS.

SONGS.

CONTENTS.

MEMOIR.

FIVE years after the suppression of the Rebellion of 1745, the staple trade of textile manufactures in Paisley was expanding and becoming a prosperous business. The population at that period would not exceed 4117. The ancient town had begun to exhibit symptoms of vitality, public buildings were erected, suburbs commenced in the south, west, and north quarters, and strangers were arriving from Ayrshire, and other localities, expecting to participate in the general prosperity of trade. Among them came four brothers from Kilmarnock, bearing the name of TANNAHILL. Sometime afterwards, the youngest two of these brothers emigrated to America, while the eldest two remained in their adopted town. James Tannahill, the eldest, followed the trade of a weaver—"a gallant weaver," as the Ayrshire bard, in the plenitude of his heart, called those living in the town "where Cart rins rowin' to the sea." In the process of time, James Tannahill became acquainted with Janet Pollock, and whether the intimacy commenced in Beith, Lochwinnoch, or Paisley, matters not, for it ripened into love, and Janet gave her heart and hand to the gallant weaver. She was the daughter of Matthew Pollock, the owner of a small mailing named Boghall, near Beith, Ayrshire—a " bonnet laird "—a class of farmers who cultivated their own lands, and received the distinctive name from their wearing large, broad Kilmarnock bonnets. James Tannahill and Janet Pollock were married at Lochwinnoch on Monday, 29th August, 1763. In their own sphere of life they were highly respected. They took up house in the property of William Gibb, popularly called Laird Gibb, in the Townhead of Paisley, the old ecclesiastic town then only extending to the passage leading to the Overcommon, now called Lady Lane. James Tannahill was a man superior in intelligence to the weavers and mechanics of that period, and his wife, gifted with natural talents and shrewdness, was remarkable for the extent of her information. She had passed a considerable part of her " youthful happy days " under the roof-tree of her uncle, Hugh Brodie, of Langcraft, in the parish of Lochwinnoch,—Langcraft, Calderwood Glen, and the woods of Balgreen (popularly pronounced Bowgreen), the scenes of her childhood, would be happy memories in the mind of that intelligent woman.   They had eight children, ROBERT or THOMAS,* who died on 27th September, 1765, THOMAS, JANET, JAMES, ROBERT, MATTHEW, HUGH, and ANDREW TANNAHILL.

A hundred years ago, on 3d June, 1774, their fifth child, a son, was born in Paisley, between the hours of nine and ten o'clock forenoon, and he was named

ROBERT TANNAHILL.

---

* He is named ROBERT in the Register, and THOMAS in the private note-book of the Parents.

From birth, ROBERT, like some other gifted poets, was afflicted with lameness ; but the anxious care and attention of his mother to her son, while yet in infancy, considerably alleviated natural defects. He was sent at an early age to school ;* but it is not on record that he there distinguished himself by any special genius. His latest biographer,—the late JAMES J. LAMB,—whose work, alas ! was so suddenly and unexpectedly cut short by death, relates that "his talent for rhyme early appeared, for, while yet a boy, he wrote verses. He wrote when he was a schoolboy, ten years old. His verses, then, were little more than doggerel, however ; and generally some odd character or circumstance, that had been under his own observation, was the subject of his boyish rhymes. An anecdote is thus told of his schoolboy versification. It was the custom among school boys—then as now—to ask riddles of each other, in Scottish phrase, to 'speir guesses.' ROBERT gave his in rhyme usually. This was one of them :—

> My colour's brown, my shape's uncouth,
> On ilka side I hae a mouth ;
> And, strange to tell, I will devour
> My bulk of meat in half-an-hour.

One may well conceive what excitement there would be in the playground when the grey-eyed boy propounded this wonderful riddle, and how many faces would brighten up when the solution was the big, brown, unshapely nose of a local character, who snuffed largely ! "

---

* The English School, taught by Mr. Eadie, and which met in the " Wee Steeple," which was afterwards occupied by a congregation of Baptists, whose memories have lately been immortalised as the " Pen Folk."

ROBERT TANNAHILL would seem to have gained the greater part of his education not so much at school,—although, no doubt, he there laid the foundation of his knowledge,—as from private study.   With the aid of a pocket dictionary and grammar, he studied, during his leisure hours, the best authors accessible to him, and made himself well acquainted with the literature of his time.   The fabrics of TANNAHILL's day were of a light description, and looms did not require much strength to work them, and at the early age of twelve years, the young poet was sent to learn what was the staple trade of Paisley at that time.   The occupation of a weaver, about the year 1786, was very remunerative,—wages being high and work plentiful,—so that a steady, well-behaved workman did not require to work more than four or five days a-week, and had thus considerable spare time to devote to the pursuit most congenial to his taste.   ROBERT TANNAHILL's leisure hours in the long summer evenings and short winter afternoons were most likely spent in the retreat of the "Bonnie wood o' Cragielea," or in roaming over Gleniffer Braes and by "the birks o' Stanely Shaw." Hardly a spot within Renfrewshire but seems to have been visited by him, either alone or in company with some chosen companion.   His songs are full of the praises of the sweet romantic scenes around Paisley.   Many of these localities are now almost unknown to the present genera-tion, and on that account the notes which accompany the poems and songs will enhance the interest of the present edition of the works of the sweetest singer of Paisley.

Long before the term of his apprenticeship had expired, TANNAHILL began to cultivate the Muse with avidity; but his first attempts gave little promise of what he afterwards accomplished. The better taste of the poet rejected what he himself had written, and many of his earlier effusions never saw the light. This anxious care of his reputation is a striking feature of the poet's character. When his apprenticeship was completed, he became master of his own fortunes, and had many opportunities of enlarging the circle of his acquaintance. The geniality and kindness of his disposition was rewarded by their warm attachment, and, as one of his biographers remarks, his friends " seemed to cherish his remembrance with a degree of fondness that could only arise from having found in him the valuable qualities of a sound head and a good heart." In pleasant intercourse with his companions, the happiest period of the poet's life passed away, till he reached the age of about twenty-one.

About the year 1795, several of his pieces appeared in the *Glasgow Courier;* but his chief composition was that on the emigration of his distinguished fellow-townsman, Alexander Wilson, better known afterwards as the " American Ornithologist." About this time the poet would seem to have fairly succumbed to Cupid's darts, and to this episode in his life we are most probably indebted for many of his sweetest songs. His intimate friend and companion, William Maclaren,* gives the following account of this

---

* William Maclaren was closely associated with TANNAHILL in the formation of the Paisley Burns' Club. The argument for the formation of the society was written by the poet, as secretary; while the chair was taken by Maclaren, as first president. The argument will be found in the Appendix.

affair :—" It was customary for the young people of both sexes, in the town where he lived, to meet at particular times in little convivial bands, where the song, the banter, and the jest, wore away the tedious winter night. At one of those meetings, ROBERT first saw her who afterwards became the subject of so many of his songs. His rank in life being equal to hers, he found no difficulty in communicating to her the wishes of his heart, and felt with rapturous exultation that he needed no advocate in his favour, but the warm emotions of his own soul. Often when the labours of the day were done, and the 'plantin' taps were ting'd wi' goud' by the setting sun, the happy lovers wandered in mutual bliss through those delicious scenes which the poet has himself so beautifully described. Their hearts beating with fond and endearing affection, they proudly anticipated the joyous days when, undisturbed by jealous doubts and fears, they would bo united in the tender ties of conjugal bliss. In the ardour of youthful imagination, the enraptured bard pictured the joys of other times, when, loving and beloved, they would steal through life without one care to wrinkle their brows—without one sorrow to sadden their hearts. Prophetic imagination wandering through the mists of futurity, guided them in unrepining felicity to the winter of life, where, weary with age and withered with decay, they would sink into the same grave, lamented and esteemed by a crowd of weeping friends. Such were the dreams that delighted the fancy of the bard. But the lady, seeing nothing done to promote the consummation of these wishes, began to repine. She was wise enough to know that the brightest face is subject to decay, and that Time plants wrinkles on the smoothest brow. Youth may be the season of love, but it is likewise that delicious period on the judicious management of which frequently depends the happiness or misery of our future lives. Another suitor came, whose addresses were not rejected. The pride of the bard was stung, and spoke in loud and angry reproach. The fair began to relent ; but it was too late. The vulture Jealousy had fixed her talons so firmly in her injured lover's heart, that promises were vain, and repentance useless. Although a man of no resentment, he was equally jealous of his honour and fame, and anything which he considered injurious to either was calculated to make a strong and lasting impression on his imagination. His bosom was the centre of contending passion ; but the pride of his soul rose superior to every other emotion, and, after a few extravagant follies, he sought refuge for his distempered imagination in song, and with these verses he sent her an eternal farewell,—

> ' Accuse me not, inconstant fair,
>   Of being false to thee,
> For I was true, would still been so,
>   Hadst thou been true to me.'

This was the only amour in which our bard was engaged, and his Muse was ever after destined to sing of loves which he never felt, and of beauties which he never saw."

Thus ended the only love passage in the poet's life. Henceforth, ROBERT TANNAHILL spent his leisure hours in solitary rambles through the country, gently rousing the echoes of every glade and sweet rural scene with his flute, and moulding his sweet strains under the inspiration of their influences.

When twenty-six years of age, ROBERT TANNAHILL and his younger brother went to Bolton. Trade was then dull in Paisley, and they expected easily to obtain employment in England. Perhaps the idea of seeing how the world looked beyond their own immediate neighbourhood, had something to do with this somewhat venturesome step on the part of these two quiet Paisley youths. The brothers soon repented their rash step, as they found, like many more dreamers, that "there's no place like home." A very slight occurrence at this time would seem to have been the means of turning our poet's career. The little store of money the travellers had with them when they arrived in England was soon exhausted, and finding no employment in Bolton or the vicinity, the two brothers set out on a weary tramp for the nearest seaport, resolving to enlist in the Royal Navy. Good fortune, however, did not utterly desert them, and an incident occurred which, we believe, saved to the world the Songs of ROBERT TANNAHILL. His friend previously mentioned relates how, while stopping for refreshment at a country ale-house, they were conducted into the parlour, where sat a cheerful-looking fellow, whose one hand held a tankard of ale, and the other supported a pipe from which he discharged large volumes of smoke into the chimney. After eyeing them for some time with more than ordinary attention, he, as a prelude to conversation, offered them his pot, and, in the language of a friend, asked them whence they came, and whither they were bound. Curiosity being satisfied, he discovered himself to be a countryman of their own,—a native of Paisley,—and, like themselves, a weaver by profession. With the partiality of a countryman, and

the sympathy of a friend, he offered them accommodation
for the night, and a promise of his influence and exer-
tion to procure them a comfortable situation in the morning. As the journey to the coast was undertaken at the
instigation of Despair, the reader will easily believe that
no great objections were made to the offers of their generous
friend. His promises were listened to with eagerness. In
the cheerful anticipation of better times, their miseries were
forgotten and the mirth-inspiring ale moved round, till drowsy
Morpheus warned them to repose. Morning told that
their hopes were not to be disappointed. After a cheerful
breakfast they were each provided with employment so
suitable to their wishes that they had both the pleasurable
satisfaction of earning their supper before it was eaten.
Who ever remembers the miseries that are past ? The bard,
now merry and contented, laughed at the capriciousness of
Fortune, who, from starving misery, permitted him to eat
roast beef upon Sundays, exercise the offices of humanity,
and occasionally toast a bumper with a friend. During his
stay in England, the poetic fire would seem never to have
been sufficiently kindled to produce anything remarkable.
This may have been owing to the dull and uninspiring nature of the country, or it may have been that he felt his
Muse could only be appreciated by Scotchmen.

After a stay of two years the brothers were called home
by the sudden illness of their father, who earnestly desired
to see his children's faces ere his eyes closed ; but they
they arrived only in time to see him die.

Writing in March, 1802, to William Kibble, a Scotch
friend in Bolton (probably the person he so opportunely

met), he thus feelingly relates the death of an acquaintance and the position of affairs at home :—"Alek, poor Alek, is gone to his long home! It was to me like an electric shock. Well, he was a good man ; his memory shall be dear, and his worth held in remembrance by all who knew him. Death, like a thief, nips off our friends, kindred, and acquaintances, one by one, till the natural chain is broken, link after link, and leaves us scarce a wish to stop behind them. My brother Hugh and I are all that now remain at home with our old mother bending under age and frailty, and but seven years back, nine of us used to sit at dinner together. (I still moralise sometimes.) I cannot but remember that such things were, and those most dear to me."

Hugh having married, his mother was left dependent on ROBERT, and he did not shirk the duty of supporting and comforting her widowhood as long as he lived. "The Filial Vow" attests to his anxiety to "soothe her every care," and gently "hand her down life's rugged steep." This filial love, one of the finest traits in our poet's character, was not confined to one member of the family, as we know that after ROBERT'S death, his mother was still maintained in comfort and independence by her remaining sons. TANNAHILL never left Paisley again, but pursued the even tenor of his way, undisturbed by thoughts of worldly gain. He is even said to have refused the offer of an overseership in the warehouse of a manufacturer in town, preferring to remain master of his own time. There, in that dainty little cottage in Queen Street, the poet who could sing of the beauties of Nature in the sweetest and most pathetic strains, was content to pass the best days of his existence. With an old German flute, cracked and bound with waxed thread in many places, he varied the dull click-click of the shuttle with simple tunes. An earthen ink pot hung by the loom post, and paper lay conveniently at hand that he might jot down ideas as they occurred, and thus the Weaver-poet, of whom Paisley is now so proud, composed the greater number of those songs which have made his name immortal.

Although his thoughts must have wandered away to the green fields or "streamlet skirted woods," he nevertheless wrought industriously at his occupation, not spending foolishly his gains, but laying up a little store in the bank against the day of scarce work or illness. Indeed, so far from the poet being in poor circumstances, as many have supposed, he was really very comfortable. The house in which he resided was the property of his mother, and he probably earned what would be equal to two pounds a week in these days of high prices. Those who remember the cottage as it was fifty years ago say it had every appearance of comfort and respectability. At his death a sum of twenty pounds was at his credit in the bank—a great comfort to his widowed and bereaved mother, as well as a provision for his funeral.

R. A. Smith was one of the poet's most constant and intimate companions. Indeed, but for the friendship of the composer, it is possible TANNAHILL's fame might never have reached the height it did. His hearing "Blythe was the time" sung, while yet in manuscript, was the occasion of Smith's seeking an introduction to the author. He says in reference to this and their future intimacy:—"I was so much struck with the beauty and natural simplicity of the language, that I found means, shortly afterwards, of being introduced to its author.   The acquaintance thus formed between us gradually ripened into a warm and steady friendship, that was never interrupted in a single instance till his lamented death. . . .   For several years previous to his death, we commonly spent the Saturday afternoons in a walk to the country ; but if the badness of the weather prevented us from enjoying this weekly recreation, the afternoon was spent in my room, reading and reviewing what pieces he had composed through the week, or if 1 had any new music, I played or sang it over to him."

TANNAHILL at this time (1805) was very happy.   The wound of Cupid's dart had been healed, and he dreamed of Fame.   He was asked to contribute to a London magazine of note, and he sent "The braes o' Gleniffer," "The Dirge," and some others.   These were accepted, and the poet then conceived the bold idea of publishing on his own account.   Arrangements were made, accordingly, with a local printer for the issue of a small volume, the author paying for the paper in advance, and the printer taking the risk of the workmanship.   From the well-composed, neatly written and punctuated letter to William Thomson, reproduced in this volume, it would appear that the poet's friends in various parts interested themselves in procuring subscribers.   The volume soon appeared, with the title of " The Soldier's Return ; a Scottish Interlude in Two Acts, with other Poems and Songs, chiefly in the Scottish Dialect."   The imprint bore that it was " Printed by Stephen Young, Bowling Green, 1805."   It consisted of 176 pages, and the impression was 900 copies.   This was a large edition, but every copy was sold within a few weeks, thanks to the energy of his friends. The profits must have been considerable. The volume was dedicated to his friend, William Maclaren, in remembrance of the happy hours they had spent together, and in testimony of the high regard he had for his many amiable qualities. The author seems to have had a great regard for this friend, and on that account we are inclined to place reliance in the tribute to the poet he published.* The prefatory advertisement to the "Soldier's Return" is worthy of preservation. It is as follows :—"The Author of the following Poems, from a hope that they possess some little merit, has ventured to publish them ; yet, fully sensible of the blinding partiality with which writers are apt to view their own productions, he offers them to the Public with unfeigned diffidence. When the man of taste and discrimination reads them, he will no doubt find many passages that might have been better, but his censures may be qualified with the remembrance that they are the effusions of an unlettered mechanic, whose hopes, as a poet, extend no further than to be reckoned respectable among the minor Bards of his country. Several of the songs have been honoured with original Music by Mr. Ross of Aberdeen, and others by Mr. Smith, Paisley ; the remainder were mostly written to suit favourite Scotch and Gaelic Airs that particularly pleased the author's fancy. The Interlude was undertaken by desire of the late Mr. Archibald Pollock, Comedian ; but, alas ! ere it was

---

* The Life of the Renfrewshire Bard, ROBERT TANNAHILL, author of "Jessie, the Flower o' Dunblane," &c. Paisley : J. NEILSON. 1815.

well begun, his last ACT was played. He was a worthy
man, and died deeply regretted by all who knew him.
The Author returns his sincere thanks to his numerous
Subscribers, particularly to those Friends who have so
warmly interested themselves in promoting the present publication ; and, with a due sense of their favours, he has, only
further, to solicit their indulgence in the perusal of his
volume, assuring them that their kindness, in the present
instance, shall long be felt with gratitude, and ever esteemed
among the first pleasures of his memory.—THE AUTHOR."

The work was well received by the critics, but specially
so by the public.   Whatever company TANNAHILL entered,
he was sure to hear his songs sung, and nothing could have
been more grateful to his feelings.   He was exceedingly
sensitive to praise or blame, too much, so, indeed, for his
mental comfort.   Writing to his friend, James King, he relates an incident of hearing, while walking home one night,
a girl within doors, " rattling away at one of them," and
this, he says, was " perhaps the highest pleasure ever I derived from these things."   On another occasion he heard a
country lassie in the fields singing to herself, " We'll meet
beside the dusky glen, by yon burn side."   This circumstance so elated him that, with honest pride, he declared it
to be the happiest moment of his life.   Specially anxious to
have the opinion of his brother-poets, he sent a copy of his
volume to Robert Allan of Kilbarchan, and the following
shows how grateful he felt for the meed of praise awarded :—

> " When I read o'er your kind epistle
> I didna ' dance,' nor ' sing,' nor ' whistle,'
> But jump'd and cried, Huzza, huzza !

Like Robin Roughhead in the play,—
But to be serious—jest aside,
I felt a glow o' secret pride,
Thus to be roos'd by ane like you,
Yet doubted if sic praise was due,
Till self thus reason'd in the matter :
    Ye ken that Robin scorns tae flatter,
    And ere he'd prostitute his quill,
    He'd rather burn his rhyming mill—
Enough ! I cried—I've gain'd my end,
Since I ha'e pleased my worthy friend.
My sangs are now before the warl',
And some may praise, and some may snarl ;
They ha'e their faults, yet I can tell
Nane sees them clearer than mysel' ;
But still I think they, too, inherit
Amang the dross some sparks o' merit."

He was jealously anxious that his name should be handed
down to posterity untarnished.   In an epistle to James
Buchanan, dated August, 1806, he thus pathetically appeals
to Time for mercy:—

" O Time, thou all-devouring bear !
  Hear—' List, O list ' my ardent prayer !
  I crave thee here, on bended knee,
  To let my dear-lov'd pages be !
  O take thy sharp-nail'd, nibbling elves,
  To musty scrolls on college shelves !
  There, with dry treatises on law,
  Feast, cram, and gorge thy greedy maw ;
  But grant, amidst thy thin-sown mercies,
  To spare, O spare my darling verses ! "

Poetry was now his constant pursuit. He could not patiently
study anything else—history and biography were tried as a

change, but in vain.   He constantly wandered into the country, finding there inspiration for fresh themes, and "building castles in the air" of fame and greatness.

Desirous of becoming a contributor to Thomson's *Select Melodies*, he wrote to a friend on the subject,—"I am now going to beg of you, as a very particular favour, that you would send me, as soon as you can, any fine Irish airs of the singing kind which you may chance to have. . . What makes me so importunate with you is, that if I can accomplish songs worthy of being attached to them, I shall have the pleasure of seeing them printed in, perhaps, the most respectable work of the kind that has ever been published in Britain.   Now, dear Jamie, as this is placing me on my very soul's hobby, do try to oblige me."   His friend seems to have obliged him, and he wrote a number of songs to Irish airs ; but none of these were considered worthy of a place in the *Select Melodies.*   This was poor TANNAHILL's first great disappointment, although he continued to write songs to Irish airs.   He now thought the time had arrived when he might give to the world something more ambitious than his former publication.   He prepared to publish his songs, set to their appropriate tunes,—his friend R. A. Smith agreeing to arrange his compositions, and another friend, Andrew Blaikie, undertaking to engrave the work ; but this idea was likely to prove too expensive, and had to be abandoned.

TANNAHILL had now acquired a local fame ; and his more congenial quiet country rambles were often interrupted by the solicitations of his admirers, who invited and led him too frequently into jovial company.   His most sincere friend,

R. A. Smith, says in regard to this period of his life :—"Unfortunately, his celebrity as a song writer led many an idle person, through vanity or curiosity, to see him, which was too frequently effected by sending for him to an inn ; and he has often lamented bitterly to me in private his want of fortitude to withstand those intrusions. Such deviations from prudence always produced the most agonising reflections, and I fear formed one of the causes which accelerated his unhappy fate. That this was the case is obvious from a letter which he wrote about this time to a friend in Glasgow, in which he says—'Scribbling of rhymes hath positively half ruined me. It has led me into a wide circle of acquaintance, of course into an involuntary habit of being oftener in a public-house than can be good for anybody ; although I go there as seldom as possible, yet how often have I sat till within my last shilling, and, unlike some of our friends who are better circumstanced, had to return to my loom sick and feverish. This often makes me appear sullen in company, for if I indulge to the extent we have both seen in others, I am in —— for two or three days afterwards.'"

This unnatural excitement produced the usual result, depression of mind ; and then, the censure of a portion of the press coming at the same time deepened his distress. Afraid lest his name should thus early be tarnished, he prepared to win fresh laurels, and retrieve past shortcomings. With confidence in his talent, he resolved to publish a corrected and carefully revised edition of his songs, and to offer them to some respectable publisher. A Greenock bookseller commissioned R. A. Smith to treat with him for the copyright, and received a portion of his proposed volume as a specimen. TANNAHILL was too impatient, however, to wait the Greenock bookseller's leisure, and sent his complete manuscript to Mr. Constable, the Edinburgh publisher. Here, again, was the poor author grievously disappointed. Mr. Constable happened to be in London when TANNAHILL sent his MS., and, when he did return, he sent the packet unopened to its author, with the chilling reply that he had more work on hand than he could undertake. This was a heavy blow to poor TANNAHILL. He had looked forward with eager expectation to the appearance of this edition of his poems as a vindication of his right to a place on the roll of fame among the poets of his country; and to have the result of all his pains-taking and care thus rudely ignored as unworthy of con-sideration, was almost more than he could bear. Other real or imaginary slights followed, and he gradually sunk into despondency and gloom. He was not altogether forgotten, however, for just at this time James Hogg, the Ettrick Shepherd, visited him; and had he not been too far sunk in despondency, this visit might have been the means of afford-ing him great pleasure and pride. Mr. Motherwell states that they passed a night together; but we have the testimony of James Barr ("Blythe Jamie Barr of St. Barchan's toun") that James Hogg came to Paisley in the morning and left in the evening. He says, in a letter to Mr. William Porteous, dated "Govan, June, 1859," after giving an account of the origin of the song, "The Five Frien's":—"Some time after this I was in Paisley, and spent the evening with TANNAHILL alone, (as was often the case).

It was late, and so dark that he would not allow me to take the road, but insisted on me taking a share of his bed. I did so, and next morning after breakfast, and at parting, he saw at a distance Smith and Stewart coming in our direction with three stranger gentlemen, he said 'there is something in the wind,' and wished me to stop and see. We kept out of their sight, but saw them go into a public house near the place. In a short time he was sent for. He desired me to wait, and he would let me know. He came for me, and, on entering the company, he introduced me to Hogg, the Ettrick Shepherd ; the meeting being so sudden and unexpected, I was for a moment stunned. The other two gentlemen, having business in Glasgow, left, promising to have a ticket for him by the evening coach with them to Edinburgh. We then went down town, as Hogg wished to see Mr. Blaikie, the engraver, an old acquaintance and a musical enthusiast, a good voice-reader, who played several instruments, and succeeded R. A. Smith in conducting the music of the Abbey Church. The forces were now collected, and such a congenial meeting I never beheld. Hogg was enraptured with our company, and it was a treat to see the friendship of the two bards. The contrast was striking, the one lively, healthy, and off hand ; the other delicate and unassuming. The only regret felt by all was the limited time. As my destination was Glasgow, I took the road with Hogg. We were convoyed by the whole company till necessity urged a parting. Soon after this Hogg spied an empty coal cart lolling on the road ; and asked me if we might get the cart to drive us in. I agreed, and Hogg cries, 'My lad, are you going to Glasgow ?' 'Ay man !' 'Will you gie us a smart drive, and we'll pay you for't ?' 'Ou ay man.' In we went, and at the half-way house primed him wi' a half-o'-mutchken, and galloped to the key-stane of the Broomielaw Bridge, where we came off—Hogg saying it would not do to be seen galloping through the streets of Glasgow in a coal cart. He hurried on to the Tontine—the coach had been waiting about five minutes, and was just starting. When we were observed running it stopped—we shook hands, and, in an instant, all disappeared in the shadow of the Gallowgate. These gentlemen had been on a tour through the Highlands, and came round by Paisley purposely to see ROBERT TANNA-HILL."

Motherwell relates that the parting of TANNAHILL with Hogg was very affecting. Grasping his hand, with tears in his eyes, in gratitude for his kindly visit and sympathy, TANNAHILL exclaimed, "Farewell, we shall never meet again ! Farewell, I shall never see you more ! "

He spoke at this time to a friend of travelling through the country to see for himself what the world said of his poems ; he continually laboured under the impression that his best friends were his enemies, even R. A. Smith found it impossible to convince him to the contrary. This showed plainly his failing mental power. That not a scrap of his writings might be left to futurity, he diligently collected all he could lay hands on, and consigned them to the flames.

Anxious to become a member of the Masonic brother-hood, he collected a number of friends for the purpose of being initiated into the mysteries of the Order. His friend, William Maclaren, was present by the poet's special request, and he relates that, during the performance

of that most uninteresting ceremony, the big tears rolled down his cheeks, to the utter amazement of the company and the grief of his friends ; but the poet seemed insensible to either. What was his object in joining this fraternity was never known. On the morning of 16th May, 1810, he visited his friend, Alexander Borland, then in Glasgow. His wild eye and evident mental agitation, and his complaints as to the decay of his fame, and the insupportable misery of life, were very painful to his friend. He endeavoured to calm him ; but his evident desire to quit the world was so apparent, that he accompanied him to Paisley, and informed his relatives of his state. Apparently soothed, his friend left him, promising to see him in the morning; but he seems never to have lain down, for, an hour after, his mother was aroused by the barking of a favourite dog, and went to see if anything was wrong, when she found to her consternation that her son had left the house. Fearing the worst, she anxiously waited for daylight, when his friends were alarmed, and search was immediately instituted. Little was needed ; for not many hundred yards from his dwelling, his coat was found by the side of the culvert of Maxwellton Burn, which passes under the Canal. His remains are buried in the Churchyard of the West Relief Church, now known as Canal Street United Presbyterian Church. Over his grave, an elegant monument has been erected by a number of his admirers.

THE

𝕾𝖔𝖑𝖉𝖎𝖊𝖗'𝖘 𝕽𝖊𝖙𝖚𝖗𝖓:

A

SCOTTISH INTERLUDE, IN TWO ACTS;

WITH OTHER

Poems and Songs,

CHIEFLY IN THE SCOTTISH DIALECT.

———————

BY ROBERT TANNAHILL.

———————

⊰•❂•⊱

PAISLEY:

PRINTED BY STEPHEN YOUNG, BOWLING GREEN.

··········

1807.

Dedication.

TO Mr. WILLIAM M'LAREN.

Sir,

WITH gratitude I reflect on the happy hours we have spent together, and in testimony of the high regard I entertain for your many worthy and amiable qualities, I take the liberty of INSCRIBING to you this little volume: several of the pieces contained in it you have already seen, and if the others afford you any pleasure, it will add much to the happiness of,

Dear Sir,

With true respect and sincerity,

Your Friend,

ROBERT TANNAHILL.

ADVERTISEMENT.

THE Author of the following Poems, from a hope that they possess some little merit, has ventured to publish them ; yet, fully sensible of that blinding partiality with which writers are apt to view their own productions, he offers them to the Public with unfeigned diffidence. When the man of taste and discrimination reads them, he will no doubt find many passages that might have been better, but his censures may be qualified with the remembrance that they are the effusions of an unlettered Mechanic, whose hopes, as a poet, extend no further than to be reckoned respectable among the minor Bards of his country.

Several of the Songs have been honoured with original Music by Mr. Ross of Aberdeen, and others by Mr. Smith, Paisley ; the remainder were mostly written to suit favourite Scotch and Gaelic Airs that particularly pleased the Author's fancy.

The INTERLUDE was undertaken by desire of the late Mr. Archibald Pollock, Comedian ; but, alas ! ere it was well begun, his last ACT was played. He was a worthy man, and died deeply regretted by all who knew him.

The Author returns his sincere thanks to his numerous Subscribers, particularly to those Friends who have so warmly interested themselves in promoting the present Publication ; and with a due sense of their favours, he has, only further, to solicit their indulgence in the perusal of his volume, assuring them that their kindness, in the present instance, shall long be felt with gratitude, and ever esteemed among the first pleasures of his memory.

THE AUTHOR.

Soldier's Return.

THE PERSONS.

MEN.

THE LAIRD, *Colonel of a Scotch Regiment.*
GAFFER, *the* LAIRD'S *Tenant.*
MUIRLAND WILLIE, *an old rich dotard.*
HARRY, *in love with* JEAN.

WOMEN.

MIRREN, GAFFER'S *Wife, a foolish old Woman.*
JEAN, *Daughter of* GAFFER *and* MIRREN, *beloved by* WILLIE,
but in love with HARRY.

SOLDIER'S RETURN.

ACT I.

SCENE I.

A range of hills, o'erhung with waving woods,
That spread their dark green bosoms to the clouds,
And seem to crave the tribute of a show'r,
Grateful to woodland plant and mountain flow'r ;——
A glen beneath, frae whilk a bick'rin' burn
Strays round the knowes, wi' bonny wimplin' turn,
Syne trottin' downwards thro' the cultured lands,
Runs by whare Gaffer's humble biggin' stands ;
His wife an' him are at some family plea,
To hear what ails them, just step in and see.

GAFFER *and* MIRREN.

Mirren.

" LOVE should be free ! "—My trouth, but ye craw crouse,
You a Gudeman, an' canna' rule your house !
Had I a father's pow'r, I'd let her see,
Wi' vengeance, whether or no that love be free.
She kens right weel Muirland has ilk thing ready,
An's fit to keep her busket like a lady:

Yet soon's she hears me mention Muirland Willie,
She skits an' flings like ony towmont filly——
Deil, nor ye'd broke your leg, gaun cross the hallan,
That day ye fee'd the skelpor Highland callan ;
We've fed him, clad him—what's our mense for't a'?
Base wretch, to steal our Dochter's heart awa'!
"Love should be free!" gude trouth, a bonny story!
That *Muirland* maun be lost for *Highland Harry*.
Muirland comes down this night—to tauk's nae use,
For she shall gie consent or lea' the house.
Oddsaffs! my heart did never wallop cadgier
Than when the Laird took Harry for a sodger;
An' now she sits a' day, sae dowf an' blearie,
An' sings luve sangs about her Highland Harry.

Gaf. Indeed, Gudewife, the lad did weel enough,
Was eident ay, an' deftly hel' the pleugh;
But Muirland's up in years, an' shame to tell,
Has ne'er been married, though as auld's mysel';
His locks are lyart, an' his joints are stiff,
A staff wad set him better than a wife.
Sooner shall roses in December blaw,
Sooner shall tulips flourish i' the snaw,
Sooner the woods shall bud wi' winter's cauld
Than lasses quit a young man for an auld :
Yet, she may tak' him gin she likes, for me,
My *say* shall never mak' them disagree.

Mir. Ye hinna' the ambition o' a mouse;
She'll gie consent this night, or lea' the house.

Enter JEAN *in haste.*

Jean. Father, the sheep are nibblin' i' the corn,
Wee Saundy's chain'd auld Bawtie to the thorn,
An' bawson'd Crummock's broken frae the sta';
Och! a's gane wrang since Harry gaed awa'. (*Aside.*

Gaf. A house divided, a' gangs to the devil.— [*Exit.*

Mir. Dochter, come here;—now, let us reason civil.
Isn't siller mak's our ladies gang sae braw?
Isn't siller buys their cleuks an' bonnets a'?
Isn't siller busks them up wi' silks an' satins,
Wi' umbrellas, muffs, claeth-shoon, an' patons?
Our Lady,—what is't gars us curtsey till her,
An' ca' her *Mam?* why, just 'cause she has siller;
Isn't siller mak's our gentles fair an' sappy?
Whilk lets us see, it's siller mak's fouks happy.

Jean. Mither, ae simple question let me speir,—
Is Muirland fat or fair wi' a' his gear?
Auld croighlin' wight, to hide the ails o' age,
He capers like a monkey on a stage;

An' cracks, an' sings, an' giggles sae light an' kittle,
Wi's auld beard slaver'd wi' tobacco spittle.—

Mir. Peace, wardless slut—O, whan will youth be wise!
Ye'll slight your *carefu'* Mither's gude advice:
I've brought you up, an' made ye what ye are ;
An' that's your *thanks* for a' my toil an' care:
Muirland comes down this night, sae drap your stodgin',
For ye must gie consent or change your lodgin'.   [*Exit.*

Jean. E'en turn me out, Muirland I'll never marry:
What's wealth or life without my dearest Harry?

———

SONG.

Set to Music by Mr. Ross, *Organist, Aberdeen.**

Our bonny Scots lads in their green tartan plaids,
  Their blue-belted bonnets, an' feathers sae braw,
Rank't up on the green war' fair to be seen,
  But my bonny young laddie was fairest of a' ;
His cheeks war' as red as the sweet heather-bell,
  Or the red western cloud lookin' down on the snaw,
His lang yellow hair o'er his braid shoulders fell,
  An' the een o' the lasses war' fix'd on him a'.

My heart sank wi' wae on the wearifu' day,
  When torn from my bosom they march'd him awa',
He bade me farewell, he cried "O be leal."
  An' his red cheeks war' wet wi' the tears that did fa'.

* R. A. Smith also composed music for this song.

Ah ! Harry my love, tho' thou ne'er shou'dst return,
  Till life's latest hour, I thy absence will mourn,
An' memory shall fade, like the leaf on the tree,
  E'er my heart spare ae thought on anither but thee.

                                                  [Exit.

ACT I.

SCENE II.

Harry return'd, as servant to the Laird,
Finds, for a whyle, his presence may be spar'd,
An' here, his lane, he wanders o'er each scene,
Whare first he lov'd an' fondly woo'd his Jean ;
He sees her cot, an' fain wad venture in,
But weel he minds her mither's no' his frien'.

Harry.

Tir'd with the painful sight of human ills,
Hail CALEDONIA ! hail my native hills !
Here exil'd virtue rears her humble cell,
With nature's jocund, honest sons to dwell ;
And hospitality, with open door,
Invites the stranger and the wand'ring poor ;
Tho' winter scowls along our northern sky,
In hardships rear'd we learn humanity :

Nor dare deceit here point her rankling dart,
A Scotchman's eye's the window of his heart.——
  When fate and adverse fortune bore me far,
O'er field and flood to join the din of war,
My young heart sicken'd, gloomy was my mind,
My love, my friends, my country all behind.
But whether tost upon the briny flood,
Or drag'd to combat in the scene of blood,
HOPE, like an angel, charm'd my cares away,
And pointed forward to this happy day.
Full well I mind yon breckan-skirted thorn,
That sheds its milk-white blossoms by the burn,
There first my heart life's highest bliss did prove,
'Twas there my Jeanie, blushing, own'd her love.
Yon dark green plantin's on the mountain's brow,
Yon yellow whins an' broomy knowes below,
Bring to my mind the happy, happy days,
I spent with her upon these rural braes——
But while remembrance, thus, my bosom warms,
I long to clasp my charmer in my arms.   [*Exit.*

ACT I.

SCENE III.

Now Mirren's to the burn to sine her kirn,
Here Jeanie waefu' sits an' reels her pirn,
While honest Gaffer ay for peace inclin'd,
Is ha'flins vext, an' freely speaks his mind.

Gaffer.

Thy Mither's gair an' set upon the warl',
It's Muirland's gear that gars her like the carl,
But nature bids thee spurn the silly tyke,
An' wha wou'd wed wi' ane they canna' like;
Just speak thy mind an' tell him ance for a',
That *eighteen* ne'er can 'gree wi' *sixty-twa;*
A mair disgusting sight I never knew,
Than *youthfu' folly* 'neath an' *auld grey pow.*

Enter Mirren *blythely.*

Mir. Here comes our nei'bour hurryin' frae the muir,
Mak' a' things snod, fey haste red up the floor;

The like o' him to visit you an' me,
Reflects an honour on our family;
Now lassie, mind my high comman' in *this*,
Whatever Muirland says, ye'll answer *Yes*.

Jean. Whatever Muirland says! it shall be so,
But soon as morning comes I'll answer *No*.   (*Aside.*

Enter MUIRLAND.

Muir. Peace to the biggin'—he, he, he.   (*Giggles.*) how's a'?

Mir. Gayly, a thank you—William come awa',
An' tell us how ye fen' this night yoursel'?

Muir. He, he! His name be praised! faith, unco weel,
I ne'er was ha'f sae strang in a' my days;
I'm grown sae fat, I'm like to burst my claise!
Nae won'er o't! I'm just now at my prime;
I'm just now five and thretty come the time!
Ho, ho, ho, ho; (*coughs*) I pity them wha're auld!
Yestreen I catch'd a wee bit croighle o' cauld.

Gaf. (disgusted) I might excuse a foolish, untaught *bairn*.
But second childhood, sure will never learn.   (*Aside.*
                                                                      [*Exit.*

MUIRLAND, *half-blind with age, slips on his Spectacles secretly, recognises* JEAN, *advances to her and sings.*

SONG.

Air.—" Whistle owre the lave o't."

O lassie will ye tak a' man,
Rich in housin', gear an' lan',
Deil tak' the cash ! that I soud ban,
    Nae mair I'll be the slave o't ;
I'll buy you claise to busk you braw,
A ridin' pouney, pad an' a',
On fashion's tap we'll drive awa',
    Whip, spur, an' a' the lave o't.

O Poortith is a winter day,
Cheerless, blirtie, cauld, an' blae,
But baskin' under fortune's ray,
    There's joy what e'er ye'd have o't ;
Then gie's your han', ye'll be my wife,
I'll mak' you happy a' your life,
We'll row in luve an' siller rife,
    Till death wind up the lave o't.

Mir. Nae toilin' there to raise a heavy rent,
Our fortune's made—O lassie gie consent !   *(Aside to J.*

Muir. Ye'll get a gouden ring an' siller broche,
An' now an' then we'll hurl in a coach ;

To shaw we're gentle, when we wauk on fit,
In passin' puir fouk how we'll flught and skit !

Jean. An' tho' ye're rather *auld*, I'm rather *young ;*
Our ages mix'd will stop the warl's tongue.

Muir. Auld, said ye ! No. Ye surely speak in jest.
Your Mither kens I'm just now at my best !

Mir. The lass is blunt; she means na' as she says :
Ye ne'er look'd ha'f sae weel in a' your days ! ! !
Wi' canny care I've spun a pickle yarn,
That honest-like we might set aff our bairn ;
If gang wi' me, we'll o'er to Wabster Pate's,
An' see him weavin' at the bridal sheets.

Muir. The bridal sheets ! he, he, he, he, what bliss !
The bridal sheets ! O, gie's an *erl-kiss !*

Mir. Fey ! come awa', and dinna think o' kissin'
Till ance Mess John hae gien you baith his blessin'.

[Exeunt.

JEAN, solus.

Alas ! my Mither's just like Whang the Miller,
O'erturns her house in hopes o' fin'ing siller !
For soon's I see the morning's first faint gleam,
She wakens sorrowing frae her gouden dream.

SONG.*

Air.—" Morneen I Gaberland."

Blythe was the time when he fee'd wi' my Father, O,
Happy war' the days when we herded thegither, O,
Sweet war' the hours when he row'd me in his plaidie, O,
An' vow'd to be mine, my dear Highland laddie, O ;

But ah! wae's me! wi' their sodg'ring sae gaudy, O,
The Laird's wys'd awa' my braw Highland laddie, O,
Misty are the glens, an' the dark hills sae cloudy, O,
That ay seem'd sae blythe wi' my dear Highland laddie, O.

The blae-berry banks, now, are lonesome an' dreary, O,
Muddy are the streams that gush'd down sae clearly, O,
Silent are the rocks that echoed sae gladly, O,
The wild melting strains o' my dear Highland laddie, O.

He pu'd me the crawberry, ripe frae the boggy fen,
He pu'd me the strawberry, red frae the foggy glen,
He pu'd me the row'n frae the wild steep sae giddy, O,
Sae loving an' kind was my dear Highland laddie, O.

Farewell my ewes! an' farewell my doggie, O,
Farewell ye knowes! now sae cheerless an' scroggie, O,
Farewell Glen-feoch!˜ my Mammie and my Daddie, O,
I will lea' you a', for my dear Highland laddie, O.

Thro' distant towns I'll stray a hapless stranger,

In thoughts o' him I'll brave pale want an' danger,

An' as I go, poor, weeping, mournfu' pond'rer,

Still some kind heart will cheer the weary wand'rer,

[*Exit.*

* R. A. Smith, in his *Scottish Minstrel*, calls the air to which this song is sung
" Mor nian a Ghibarlan."   The first, second, third, and last verses are those of
the Interlude ; the fourth verse appeared in the 1815 edition.

ACT II.

SCENE I.

GAFFER'S HOUSE.

JEAN, *her lane.*

SONG.

Set to Music by MR. R. A. SMITH.

Lang syne, beside the woodland burn,
  Amang the broom sae yellow,
I lean'd me 'neath the milk-white thorn,
  O nature's mossy pillow ;
A' round my seat the flow'rs were strew'd,
That frae the wild wood I had pu'd,
To weave mysel' a simmer snood,
  To pleasure my dear fellow.

I twin'd the woodbine round the rose,
  Its richer hues to mellow,
Green sprigs of fragrant birk I chose,
  To busk the sedge sae yellow.

The crow-flow'r blue, an' meadow-pink,
I wove in primrose-braided link,
But little, little did I think
    I should have wove the willow.

My bonnie lad was forc'd away,
    Tost on the raging billow,
Perhaps he's fa'n in bludy war,
    Or wreck'd on rocky shallow.
Yet, ay I hope for his return,
As round our wonted haunts I mourn,
And often by the woodland burn
    I pu' the weeping willow.

Enter MUIRLAND.

Muir. Faith ! Patie's spool jinks thro' wi' wondrous might,
An' ay it minds me o' " the bridal night ! "
I've rowth o' *sheets*, sae never fash your thumb—
O ! gie's ae kiss before your Minnie come.

Harry enters,—Jeanie kens him—
    Fast he grips her till his breast—
Willie gapes, an' glowrs, an' sanes him,
    Rins an' roars like ane possest ;
Wild, wilyart fancies revel in his brain—
They baith rin aff an' lea him a' his lane.

Muir. O, murder, murder !—O !—I'll die wi' fear !
O Gaffer, Mirren !—O, come here, come here !

Enter MIRREN, *in haste.*

Mir. The peesweep's scraighin' owre the *spunkie-cairn !*
My heart bodes ill—O, William, whare's my *bairn ?*

Muir. A great red dragon, wi' a warlock claw,
Has come, and wi' your Dochter flown awa' ! ! !

Enter GAFFER, *in haste.*

Gaf. What awfu' cry was yon I heard within ?
What mak's you glow'r, an' what caus'd a' yon din ?

Mir. A great big dragon, wi' a red airn claw,
Has come, an' wi' our Dochter flown awa' !   (*Crying.*

Muir. Its head was cover'd wi' a black airn ladle !
Black legs it had, an' tail as sharp's a needle !
A great red e'e stood starin' in its breast !
I'm like to swarf—O, 'twas a fearfu' beast !

Mir. The craw that bigged i' the stackyard thorn,
Scraigh'd an' forsook its *nest* when she was born;
Three pyats crost the *kirk* when she was christen'd,
I've heard it tauld, an' trembl'd while I listen'd.
O, dool an' wae ! My dream's been rede right soon !
Yestreen I dream'd twa mice had hol'd the *moon.*

Gaf. The swurd o' Justice never fa's unwrought for !
But come,—alive or dead, let's seek our Dochter.

Muir. I'll no' be weel this month—O, what a fright!
I'll no gang owre the Muir, my lane, this night.   [*Exeunt.*

ACT II.

SCENE II.

A briery bank, ahint a broomy knowe,
Our youthfu' loving Couple hid frae view,
Their vows renew, an' here wi' looks sae sweet,
They set their tryst whare neist again to meet.

Jean.

My heart shall, ever-gratefu', bless the Laird,
Wha shew'd my dearest Harry such regard,
Restor'd you to our hills an' rural plain,
Frae war's fatigues safe to my arms again.

Harry. Remote from bustling camps and war's alarms,
Thus, let me ever clasp thee in my arms.

Jean. But here, my Lad, we darna' weel be seen ;
Dear Harry ! say, whare will we meet at e'en ?

SONG.*

Set to Music by Mr. Ross, *of Aberdeen.*

Harry.

We'll meet beside the dusky glen, on yon burn side,
Whare the bushes form a cozie den, on yon burn side,
     Tho' the broomy knowes be green,
     Yet, there we may be seen,
But we'll meet—we'll meet at e'en, down by yon burn side.

I'll lead thee to the birken bow'r, on yon burn side,
Sae sweetly wove wi' woodbine flow'r, on yon burn side,
     There the busy prying eye,
     Ne'er disturbs the lovers' joy,
While in ithers' arms they lie, down by yon burn side.

Awa', ye rude unfeeling crew, frae yon burn side,
Those fairy scenes are no' for you, by yon burn side,—
     There Fancy smoothes her theme,
     By the sweetly murm'ring stream,
An' the rock-lodg'd echoes skim, down by yon burn side.

Now the plantin' taps are ting'd wi' goud, on yon burn side,
An' gloamin' draws her foggy shroud o'er yon burn side,
     Far frae the noisy scene,
     I'll through the fields alane,
There we'll meet—My ain dear Jean! down by yon burn side.

Jean. I'll jeer my *ancient wooer* hame, an' then
I'll meet you at the op'ning o' the glen.   [*Exit, separately.*

* For this fine song R. A. Smith arranged the air of "There grows a bonnie brier bush," or, as he has it in his *Scottish Minstrel*, "The Brier Bush," second set. This is the song which Tannahill heard a country lass lilting in a field when he was taking a lonely walk one evening. The incident was one of the happiest the poet ever experienced. Two localities in the neighbourhood of Paisley are named as the scene of this song. One, the lower portion of Gleniffer, the other a beautiful spot on the Alt-Patrick Burn, near Elderslie. Mr. Matthew Tannahill, the poet's brother, held to the former locality, and he gave as his reason, as Mr. Hugh Macdonald reports, that Robert and he were walking along the Braes

ACT II.

SCENE III.

GAFFER'S HOUSE.

With unsuccessfu' search the ghaist-rid three,
Hae socht the boortree bank, an' hemlock lee,
The nettle corner, an' the rown-tree brae,
Sae here they come, a' sunk in deepest wae.

Gaffer.

Alas! Gudewife, our search has been in vain,
Come o't what will, my bosom's wrung wi' pain;
I ha'flins think his *een* hae him mislipen'd,
But, Oh! it's hard to say what may hae happen'd.

Enter MUIRLAND, *running.*

Muir. Preserve's! O, haste ye! rin,—mak' mettle heels!
I saw the dragon spankin' owre the fiel's!

> (*They stop from going out on seeing* JEAN *enter.*

Jean. What mak's you stare sae strange! what's wrang wi'
　　Willie?
He roars as loud's a horn, tho' *auld* an' *silly.*

of Gleniffer on a summer evening, when the valley of the Clyde was filled with the
radiance of the setting sun. On gazing on the play of the sunbeams upon certain
trees in the landscape, "Look here, Matthew," said Robert, "did you ever see
anything so exquisitely beautiful! Why, the very leaves glimmer as gin they were
tinged wi' goud." Soon after this song appeared, with its beautiful bit of
imagery, "Now the plantin' taps are tinged wi' goud." This fixed Gleniffer as
the "dusky glen" in Matthew's mind. Most of the local admirers of Tannahill,
however, believe in the Alt-Patrick picturesque ravine as "the dusky glen."

Muir. I'm no' sae auld!—my pith ye yet may brag on!
But Jeanie, love! how did ye match the *dragon?*

Jean. Auld bleth'rin' Wight! the gowk's possest I wean.—

Gaf. Come, Dochter, clear this riddle, whare hae ye been?

Jean. Father, rare news; our Laird's come hame this day.
His *Man* ca'd in to tell us by the way,
Dress'd in his sodger's claise, wi' scarlet coat,
He is a bonny lad fu' weel I wot!

Muir. The dragon! he, he, he.—I've been deliered,
I'll wear a scarlet coat, too, when we're married.

Gaf. Our Laird come hame! an' safe but skaith or scar?
I'll owre an' hear the history o' the war,
Us kintra fouk are bun' like in a cage up,
I'll owre an' hear about that place ca'd—EGYPT.
I lang to hear him tell a' what he's seen.
For four lang winters he awa' has been—
Wife—fetch my bonnet that I caft last owk,
Here, brush my coat,—fey, Jean tak' aff that pouk.

Mir. Toot, snuff! 'bout news ye needna be sae thrang,
Let's set the *bridal night* afore ye gang.

Muir. The bridal night! he, he, he, he—that's right!
The bridal night! he, he—the bridal night!

Jean. I'll hing as heigh's the steeple, in a wudie,
Before I wed wi' that auld kecklin' *body.*

Mir. Was mither e'er sae plagued wi' a Dochter !
O that's her *thank* for a' the length I've brought her !   (*Crying.*

Gaf. This racket in a house!—it is a shame,
I'll thank you, Muirland, to be steppin' hame.

Jean. Auld, swirlon, slaethorn, camsheugh, crooked Wight,
Gae wa', an' ne'er again come in my sight.

Muir.—That e'er my lugs were doom'd to hear sic words !
Whilk rush into my heart like pointed swurds—
Frae me let younkers warnin' tak' in time,
An' wed, ere dozen'd down ayont their prime !
O, me ! I canna' gang,—'twill break my heart,—
Let's hae ae fareweel peep afore we part.

(He puts on his Spectacles, stares at Jean,
roars ludicrously. Exit Crying.

Enter the Laird, attended by Harry.

Laird. Well—how d'ye do, my worthy tenants ; pray,
How fairs good Gaffer since I went away ?

Gaf. My noble Laird ! thanks to the lucky star,
That steer'd you hame, safe thro' the storms o' war.

Laird. Thanks, honest friend—I know your heart of truth,
But for my safety, thank this gallant youth :
He sav'd my life—to him I owe my fame,
And gratitude shall still revere his name.

Gaf. May heav'n's post-angel swift my blessin's carry !
He sav'd your life !—preserve me, it is Harry !
Thrice welcome, lad, here—gie's a shake o' your paw !
Ye've mended hugely since ye gaed awa'.

Harry. Yes, sodg'ring brushes up a person's frame,
But at the heart, I hope I'm still the same.

Gaf. Your promise to do weel, I see ye've keepen't.
He sav'd your life !   O tell me how it happen't ?

Laird. 'Twas March the eight, that memorable day,
Our sea-worn troops all weary with delay,
For six long days storm-rock'd we lay off shore,
And heard the en'mies' guns menacing roar,
At length the wish'd-for orders came, to *land*,
And drive the foe back from the mounded strand ;
Then, each a hero, on the decks we stood,
Launch'd out our boats and speeded all we could ;
While clouds of sulph'rous smoke obscur'd the view,
And show'rs of grape-shot from their batt'ries flew—
A brother Captain, seated by my side,
Receiv'd a shot—he sunk—he quiver'd—died ;

With friendly hand I clos'd his life-gone eyes,
Our sighs, our tears, were all his obsequies.
Then, as our rowers strove with lengthen'd sweep,
Back from the stern I tumbl'd in the deep,
And sure had perish'd, for each pressing wave
Seem'd emulous to be a soldier's grave ;
Had not this gallant youth, at danger's shrine,
Off'ring his life a sacrifice for mine,
Leap'd from the boat and beat his billowy way,
To where I belch'd and struggl'd in the sea ;
With God-like arm sustain'd life's sinking hope,
Till the succeeding rowers pick'd us up.

Gaf. Fair fa' your worth, my brave young sodger lad,
To see you safe *return'd* my heart is glad ;
Ilk cottar round will lang your name regard,
An' bless you for your kindness to the Laird.

Laird. And when the day's hot work of war was done,
Each fight-tir'd soldier leaning on his gun,
I sought my brave deliverer, and made
An offer, with what influence I had,
To raise his fortune ; but he shunned reward :
Yet warmly thank'd me for my kind regard ;
Then, as in warmth I prais'd his good behaviour,
He modestly besought me this one *favour*,

That if surviving when the war was o'er,
And safe return'd to Scotia once more,
I'd ask your will, for him to wed your Daughter ;
A manly, virtuous heart he home hath brought her.

Gaf. Wi' a' my heart, he has my *free consent*,
Wife, what say ye ? I hope ye're weel content.

Mir. A Mither's *word* stan's neither here nor there ;
Tak' him or no', I'm sure I dinna care.

Laird. Accept this trifle as young Harry's wife.

(Gives his purse to JEAN.

Money is no equivalent for *life;*
And take this ring,—good Mistress, here's another,
With this I 'nlist you for young Harry's mother.

Jean. Excuse me, Sir,—my lips cannot impart
The warm emotions of my grateful heart.

Mir. It's goud, it's goud ! O yes, Sir—I agree.
Gaffer, it's goud ! Yes, "LOVE *shou'd ay be free.*"

Gaf. Daft woman, cease.

Laird...............And as for you, good Gaffer,
My steward will inform what's in your favour.
Meantime, prepare the WEDDING to your wills,
Invite my tenants from the neighb'ring hills,
Then feast, drink, dance till each one tynes his senses,
And spare no cost, for I shall pay the expenses.

Harry. Most gen'rous Sir! to tell how much I owe,
I'm weak in words—let time and actions show.

Laird. My dearest friend—I pray, no more of this,
Would I could make you happy as I wish;
From him most *benefited* most is due,
And sure the debt belongs from *me* to you.—
Attend the mansion, soon as morning's light—
And now my friends, I wish you all good night.   [*Exit.*

Harry. Great is his soul! soft be his bed of rest,
Whose *only wish* is to make others blest!

Mir. I'll gang to kirk niest Sunday, odd's my life!
This gouden ring will vex Glen-Craigie's wife.

Gaf. Wife—fy! let pride an' envy gang thegither,
This house, I hope, will ne'er be fash't wi' either;
Ay be content wi' what ye hae yoursel',
An' never grudge to see a nei'bour's weel—
But Harry, man, I lang to hear you sing,
Ye wont to mak' our glens an' plantin's ring.

Harry. My heart was never on a cantier key,
I'll sing you one with true spontaneous glee.

SONG.

Air.—" My laddie is gane."

From the rude bustling camp, to the calm rural plain,
I've come, my dear JEANIE, to bless thee again;

G

Still burning for honour our warriors may roam,
But the *laurel* I wish'd for I've won it at home:
All the glories of conquest no joy could impart,
When far from the kind little girl of my heart ;
Now, safely return'd, I will leave thee no more,
But love my dear JEANIE till life's latest hour.

The sweets of retirement, how pleasing to me !
Possessing all worth, my dear JEANIE, in thee !
Our flocks early bleating will wake us to joy,
And our raptures exceed the warm tints in the sky !
In sweet rural pastimes our days still will glide,
Till time looking back will admire at his speed,
Still blooming in Virtue, tho' youth then be o'er,
I'll love my dear JEANIE till life's latest hour.

Enter MUIRLAND.

Muir. That's nobly sung, my hearty sodger callan!
I've heard you a', ahint the byre-door hallan;
I see my fa'ts, I've chang'd my foolish views,
An' now I'm come to beg for your excuse,
The sang sings true, I own't without a swither,
"*Auld age an' young can never gree thegither.*"
I think, thro' life I'll mak' a canny fen',
Wi' hurcheon Nancy o' the hazel-glen;
She has my vows, but ay I lat her stan',
In hopes to won that bonny lassie's han';
O foolish thought ! I maist cou'd greet wi' spite,
But it was sleeky *luve* had a' the wyte :

Nae mair let fortune pride in her deserts,
Her goud may *purchase han's*, but ne'er can *sowther hearts*.

Gaf. The man wha sees his fa'ts an' strives to men' 'em,
Does *mair* for virtue than he ne'er had haen 'em;
An' he wha *deals* in scandal only gains,
A *rich repay* of scandal, for his pains:
Ye hae our free excuse, ye needna' doubt it,
Ye'll ne'er, for us, mair hear a word about it.

Muir. That's a' I wish'd,—I cou'dna bide the thought,
To live on earth an' bear your scorn in ocht;
My heart's now hale—ye soon shall hear the banns
Proclaim'd i' the Parish Kirk 'tween me an' Nanse;
I'm no' the first auld chield wha's gotten a slight,—
I'll owre the muir,—sae, fareweel a' this night !   [*Exit.*

Gaf. Of a' experience, that bears aff the bell,
Whilk lets a body *rightly* ken' himsel'.

Jean. May lasses, when their joes are far frae hame,
Bid stragglin' wooers gang the gates they came,
Else, aiblins, when their moonshine courtships' past,
They'll hae to wed *auld dotards* at the last.

Mir. Gudewives shou'd ay be *subject* to their men;
I'll ne'er speak contrar to your will again.

Gaf. That's right, gudewife,—I'm sure I weel may say,
Glen-feoch never saw sae blest a day.
Young fouks,—we'll set the bridal-day the morn,—

But, Lucky, haste ! bring ben the Christmas horn,

Let's pour ae sacred bumper to the Laird,

A glass, to crown a wish, was never better wair'd.

Harry. While I was yet a boy, my parents died,

And left me poor and friendless, wand'ring wide,

Your goodness found me, 'neath your fost'ring care,

I learn'd those precepts which I'll still revere,

And now, to Heav'n, for length of life I pray,

With filial love your goodness to repay.

Gaf. This sacred maxim let us still regard,

That " *Virtue ever is its own reward.*"

And what we give to succour the distrest,

Calls down from Heav'n a blessing on the rest.

---

* In writing *The Soldier's Return*, Tannahill had evidently Ramsay's *Gentle Shepherd* closely in his eye, the construction of the one poem being quite like the other. Even the manner is closely observed in the way the *Dramatis Personæ* are stated, in the description of the scenes, and so on. Motherwell says of this dramatic composition that it was unsuccessful, and that it was wisely omitted in editions subsequent to the first. We do not leave it out in this edition—first, because we wish to make this a complete one ; and, second, because in *The Soldier's Return*, some of the poet's finest songs, including the delightful lyric, " We'll meet beside the dusky glen," appeared, and we do not desire to take them out of his own setting. As the volume containing *The Soldier's Return* is the only volume of his writings which was printed in his life-time, and the proof sheets of which, indeed, he doubtless revised, *The Soldier's Return* is printed now exactly as he printed it then, with capitals, italics, contractions, &c., save in a few trifling exceptions, where the spelling was evidently wrong. The original title page, dedication, and advertisement are also reprinted. Mr. Hugh Macdonald, who is a good authority, thinks, or, as he says, suspects, that the vicinity of the Alt-Patrick Burn is the scene of *The Soldier's Return*, in one of the songs of which he makes his *persone* allude to natural beauties, including wild fruits similar to those of this locality.

Poems.

Poems.

THE STORM.

WRITTEN IN OCTOBER.

N OW the dark rains of autumn discolour the brook,
   And the rough winds of winter the woodlands deform;
Here, lonely, I lean by the sheltering rock,
   A-list'ning the voice of the loud-howling storm.

Now dreadfully furious it roars on the hill,
   The deep-groaning oaks seem all writhing with pain.
Now awfully calm, for a moment 'tis still,
   Then bursting it howls and it thunders again.

How cheerless and desert the fields now appear,
   Which so lately in summer's rich verdure were seen,
And each sad drooping spray from its heart drops a tear,
   As seeming to weep its lost mantle of green.

See, beneath the rude wall of yon ruinous pile,
   From the merciless tempest the cattle have fled,
And yon poor patient steed, at the gate by the stile,
   Looks wistfully home for his sheltering shed.

Ah! who would not feel for yon poor gipsy race,
   Peeping out from the door of yon old roofless barn;
There my wandering fancy her fortunes might trace,
   And sour discontent there a lesson might learn.

Yet oft in my bosom arises the sigh,
   That prompts the warm wish distant scenes to explore;
Hope gilds the fair prospect with visions of joy,
   That happiness reigns on some far distant shore.

But yon grey hermit-tree which stood lone on the moor,
   By the fierce-driving blast to the earth is blown down;
So the lone houseless wand'rer, unheeded and poor,
   May fall unprotected, unpitied, unknown.

See! o'er the grey steep, down the deep craggy glen,
   Pours the brown foaming torrent, swell'd big with the rain;
It roars thro' the caves of its dark wizard den,
   Then headlong, impetuous it sweeps thro' the plain.

Now the dark heavy clouds have unbosom'd their stores,
   And far to the westward the welkin is blue,
The sullen winds hiss as they die on the moors,
   And the sun faintly shines on yon bleak mountain's brow.

THE AMBITIOUS MITE.
A FABLE.

WHEN Hope persuades, and Fame inspires us,
And Pride with warm ambition fires us,
Let *Reason* instant seize the bridle,
And wrest us frae the Passions' guidal ;
Else, like the hero of our fable,
We'll aft be plung'd into a habble.

'Twas on a bonny simmer day,
When a' the insect tribes war' gay,
Some journeying o'er the leaves o' roses,
Some brushing thrang their wings an' noses,
Some wallowing sweet in bramble blossom,
In luxury's saft downy bosom ;
While ithers of a lower order,
Were perch'd on plantain leaf's smooth border,
Wha frae their twa-inch steeps look'd down,
An' view'd the kintra far aroun'.

Ae pridefu' *elf*, amang the rest,
Wha's pin-point heart bumpt 'gainst his breast,
To work some *mighty deed of fame*,
That would immortalize his name ;
Thro' future hours would hand him down,
The wonder of an afternoon ;
(For ae short day wi' them appears,
As lang's our lengthen'd hunder years.)

H

By chance, at hand, a *bow'd horse-hair*
Stood up six inches high in air ;
He plann'd to climb this lofty arch,
Wi' philosophic deep research,
To prove (which aft perplex'd their heads)
What people peopl'd ither blades,
Or from keen observation show,
Whether they peopl'd were or no.

Our tiny *hero* onward hies,
Quite big with daring enterprize,
Ascends the hair's curvatur'd side,
Now pale with fear, now red with pride,
Now hangin' pend'lous by the claw,
Now glad at having 'scap'd a fa' ;
What horrid dangers he came thro',
Would trifling seem for *man* to know ;
Suffice, at length he reach'd the top,
The summit of his pride and hope,
And on his elevated *station*,
Had plac'd himsel' for observation,
When, puff !—the wind did end the matter,
And dash'd him in a horse-hoof gutter.

Sae let the *lesson* gi'en us here,
Keep each within his proper sphere,
And when our fancies tak' their flight,
Think on the *wee ambitious mite*.

THE TRIFLER'S SABBATH-DAY.

——

L OUD sounds the deep-mouth'd parish-bell,
   Religion kirkward hies,
John lies in bed and counts each knell,
   And thinks 'tis time to rise.

But, O how weak are man's resolves !
   His projects ill to keep,
John thrusts his nose beneath the clothes,
   And dozes o'er asleep.

Now fairy-fancy plays her freaks
   Upon his sleep-swell'd brain ;
He dreams—he starts—he mutt'ring speaks,
   And waukens wi' a grane.

He rubs his e'en—the clock strikes TWELVE—
   Impelled by hunger's gripe,
One mighty effort backs resolve—
   He's up—at last he's up !

Hunger appeas'd—his cutty pipe
   Employs his time till TWO,—
And now he saunters thro' the house,
   And knows not what to do.

He baits the trap—catches a mouse—
   He sports it round the floor—
He swims it in a water tub—
   Gets *glorious* fun till FOUR !

And now of cats, and mice, and rats,
   He tells a thousand tricks,
Till even dullness tires herself,
   For hark—the clock strikes SIX !

Now view him in his easy chair
   Recline his pond'rous head ;
'Tis EIGHT—now Bessie raiks the fire,
   And *John* must go to bed !

DIRGE.

Written on reading an Account of ROBERT BURNS'
Funeral.

LET grief for ever cloud the day
That saw our Bard borne to the clay ;
Let joy be banish'd every eye,
And nature, weeping, seem to cry,
     " He's gone, he's gone ! he's frae us torn !
     " The ae best fellow e'er was born."

Let shepherds from the mountains steep,
Look down on widow'd Nith, and weep,
Let rustic swains their labours leave,
And sighing murmur o'er his grave,
      " He's gone, he's gone ! &c.

Let bonny Doon and winding Ayr,
Their bushy banks in anguish tear,
While many a tributary stream,
Pours down its griefs to swell the *theme*,
      " He's gone, he's gone ! &c.

All dismal let the night descend,
Let whirling storms the forest rend,
Let furious tempests sweep the sky,
And dreary, howling caverns cry,
      " He's gone, he's gone ! he's frae us torn !
      " The ae best fellow e'er was born ! "

ODE TO JEALOUSY.

MARK what *demon* hither bends,
Gnawing still his finger-ends,
Wrapt in contemplation deep,
Wrathful, yet inclined to weep.

Thy wizard gait, thy breath-check'd broken sigh,
Thy burning cheeks, thy lips, black, wither'd, dry;
Thy side-thrown glance, with wild malignant eye,
Betray thy foul intent, infernal Jealousy.

Hence, thou self-tormenting *fiend*,
To thy spleen-dug cave descend,
Fancying wrongs that never were,
Rend thy bosom, tear thy hair;
Brood, fell Hate, within thy den,
Come not near the haunts of men.

Let *man* be faithful to his brother *man*,
Nor guileful, still revert kind Heaven's plan,
Then slavish fear, and mean distrust shall cease,
And confidence confirm a lasting mental peace.

BAUDRONS AND THE HEN-BIRD.
A FABLE.

SOME folks there are of such behaviour,
They'll *cringe* themselves into your favour,
And when you think their friendship staunch is,
They'll tear your *character* to inches.
T' enforce this truth, as weel's I'm able,
Please, reader, to peruse a *fable*.

Deborah, an auld wealthy maiden,
Wi' spleen, remorse, an' scandal laden,
Sought out a solitary spat,
To live in quiet with her cat,—
A meikle, sonsy, tabby she ane,
(For Deborah abhor'd a *he ane*),
And in the house to be a third,
She gat a wee hen *chucky bird*.

Soon as our slee nocturnal ranger,
Beheld the wee bit timid stranger,
She thus began, wi' frien'ly fraise,—
"Come ben, poor thing, an' warm your taes ;
"This weather's cauld, an' wet, an' dreary,
"I'm wae to see you look sae eerie,
"Sirs ! how your tail an' wings are dreeping !
"Ye've surely been in piteous keeping ;
"See, here's my dish, come tak' a pick o't,
"But, deed, I fear there's scarce a lick o't."
Sic sympathizing words o' sense,
Soon gain'd poor *chucky's* confidence,
An' while *Deborah* mools some crumbs,
Auld *baudrons* sits, an' croodlin', thrums ;
In short, the twa soon grew sae pack,
Chuck roosted upon *pussie's* back !

But ere sax wee short days war' gane,
When baith left i' the house alane,
Then thinks the *hypocritic* sinner,
Now, now's my time to hae a dinner,

Sae, wi' a squat, a spring, an' squal,
She tore poor *chucky* spawl frae spawl.

Then mind this maxim,—*Rash acquaintance,*
Oft leads to ruin and repentance.

ON INVOCATION.

LET ither *bards* exhaust their stock
Of heav'nly names, on heav'nly folk,
An' gods an' godesses invoke,
          To guide the pen,
While, just as well, a barber's block
          Would ser' their en'.

Nae muse hae I like guid *Scotch drink,*
It mak's the dormant saul to think,
Gars wit and rhyme thegither clink,
          In canty measure,
An' even tho' half-fou' we wink,
          Inspires wi' pleasure.

Whyles dulness stands for *modest merit,*
And impudence for *manly spirit;*

To ken what *worth* each does inherit,

          Just try the bottle,

Sen' roun' the glass, an' dinna spare it,

          Ye'll see their mettle.

O would the gods but grant my wish !

My *constant pray'r* would be for this,

That love sincere, with health an' peace,

          My lot they'd clink in,

With now-an'-then the social joys

          O' friendly drinkin'.

And when youth's rattlin' days are done,

An' age brings on life's afternoon,

Then, like a summer's setting sun,

          Brightly serene,

Smiling, look back, an' slidder down

          To rise again.

THE PARNASSIAD.

A VISIONARY VIEW.

COME, *fancy*, thou hast ever been,

In life's low vale, my ready frien',

    To cheer the clouded hour ;

Tho' unfledg'd with scholastic law,
Some *visionary picture* draw,
  With all thy magic pow'r;
Now to the intellectual eye
  The glowing prospects rise,
Parnassus' lofty summits high,
    Far tow'ring mid the skies,
      Where vernally, eternally,
        Rich leafy laurels grow,
      With bloomy bays, thro' endless days,
        To crown the *Poet's* brow.

Sure, bold is he who dares to climb
Yon awful jutting rock sublime,
  Who dares *Pegasus* sit,
For should brain-ballast prove too light,
He'll spurn him from his airy height,
  Down to oblivion's pit ;
There, to disgrace for ever doom'd,
  To mourn his sick'ning woes,
And weep that ever he presum'd,
  Above the vale of Prose ;
      Then, O beware ! with prudent care,
        Nor 'tempt the steeps of fame,
      And leave behind thy peace of mind,
        To gain a sounding name.*

---

* The career of genius is rarely that of fortune, and often that of contempt :

Behold !—yon *ready-rhyming carl,*
With flatt'ry fir'd, attracts the warl',
  By canker'd, *pers'nal satire;*
He takes th' unthinking crowd's acclaim
For sterling proofs of lasting fame,
  And deals his inky spatter ;
Now, see he on *Pegasus* flies,
  With bluff, important straddle !
He bears him midway up the skies,
  See, see, he's off the saddle !
    He headlong tumbles, growls and grumbles,
      Down the dark abyss:
    The noisy core that prais'd before,
      Now joins the gen'ral hiss.

Now, see another vent'rer rise,
Deep-fraught with fulsome eulogies
  To win his patron's favour—
One of those adulating things,
That, dangling in the train of kings,
  Give guilt a splendid cover ;
He mounts, well-prefac'd by *my Lord,*
  Inflicts the spur's sharp wound ;
Pegasus spurns the *great man's* word,
  And wont move from the ground ;

even in its most flattering aspect, what is it but plucking a few brilliant flowers from precipices, while the reward terminates in the honour.—*D'Israeli.*

Now, mark his face, flush'd with disgrace,
    Thro' future life to grieve on,
His wishes cross'd, his hopes all lost,
    He sinks into *oblivion*.

Yon *city-scribbler* thinks to scale
The cliffs of fame with *Pastoral*,
    In worth thinks none e'er richer,
Yet never climb'd the upland steep,
Nor e'er beheld a flock of sheep,
    Save those driv'n by the butcher;
Nor ever mark'd the gurgling stream,
    Except the common sew'r
On rainy days, when dirt and slime
    Pour'd turbid past his door.
        Choice epithets in store he gets
          From *Virgil, Shenstone, Pope*,
        With tailor-art tacks part to part,
        And makes his Past'ral up.

But see, rich clad in native worth,
Yon *Bard of nature* ventures forth,
    In simple *modest tale;*
Applauding millions catch the song,
The raptur'd rocks the notes prolong,
    And hand them to the gale.
Pegasus kneels—he takes his seat—
    Now, see, aloft he towers,

To place him, 'bove the reach of fate,
In Fame's ambrosial bowers :
To be enroll'd with *bards of old*,
In ever-honour'd station,—
The gods, well-pleas'd, see mortals rais'd
Worthy of *their* creation !

Now, mark what crowds of *hackney-scribblers*,
Imitators, rhyming dabblers,
Follow in the rear !
Pegasus spurns us one by one,
Yet, still fame-struck, we follow on,
And tempt our fate severe :
In many a dogg'rel *Epitaph*,
And short-lined, *mournful Ditty*,
Our " AHS !—ALASES ! " raise the laugh,
Revert the tide of pity,
Yet still we write in nature's spite,
Our last piece *ay the best;*
Arraigning still, complaining still,
The world for want of *taste !*

Observe yon poor *deluded* man,
With thread-bare coat and visage wan,
Ambitious of a name ;

---

* " Still restless fancy drives us headlong on,
With dreams of wealth, and friends, and laurels won;
On ruin's brink we sleep, and wake undone."

The nat'ral claims of meat and cleading,
He reckons these not worth the heeding,
  But presses on for fame !
The public voice, *touch-stone of worth*,
  Anonymous he tries,
But draws the critic's vengeance forth,
  His fancied glory dies ;
        Neglected now, dejected now,
          He gives his spleen full scope,
        In solitude he chews his cud—
          A downright *misanthrope.*

Then, *brother-rhymsters*, O beware !
Nor tempt unscar'd the specious snare,
  Which *self-love* often weaves ;
Nor dote with a fond father's pains,
Upon the offspring of your brains,
  For fancy oft deceives ;
To lighten life, a wee bit sang
  Is sure a sweet illusion !
But ne'er provoke the critic's stang,
  By premature intrusion :
        Lock up your piece, let fondness cease,
          Till *mem'ry* fail to bear it,
        With critic-lore then read it o'er,
          Yourself may judge its merit.

ODE.

ONCE on a time, almighty JOVE
Invited all the minor gods above,
To spend one day in *social festive pleasure;*
His regal robes were laid aside,
His crown, his sceptre, and his pride :
And, wing'd with joy,
The hours did fly,
The happiest ever time did measure.

Of love and social harmony they sung,
Till heav'n's high golden arches echoing rung ;
And as they quaffed the nectar-flowing can,
Their toast was,
" *Universal peace 'twixt man and man.*"
Their godships' eyes beam'd gladness with the wish,
And Mars half-reddened with a guilty blush ;
Jove swore he'd hurl each rascal to perdition,
Who'd dare deface his works with wild ambition ;
But pour'd encomiums on each patriot band,
Who, *hating conquest,* guard their *native land.*

Loud, thund'ring plaudits shook the bright abodes,
Till Merc'ry, solemn-voic'd, assail'd their ears,
Informing that a *stranger*, all in tears,
Weeping, implored an audience of the gods.

Jove, ever prone to succour the distrest,
A swell redressive glow'd within his breast,
He pitied much the stranger's sad condition,
And order'd his immediate admission.

The *stranger* enter'd, bowed respect to all,
Respectful silence reign'd throughout the hall.
His *chequer'd robes* excited their surprise,
Richly transvers'd with various glowing dyes;
A *target* on his strong left arm he bore,
Broad as the shield the mighty FINGAL wore;
The glowing landscape on its centre shin'd,
And *massy thistles* round the borders twin'd;
His brows were bound with yellow-blossom'd *broom*,
Green birch and roses blending in perfume;
His eyes beam'd honour, tho' all red with grief,
And thus heav'n's King spake comfort to the Chief.
" My son, let speech unfold thy cause of woe,
Say, why does melancholy cloud thy brow?
'Tis mine the wrongs of virtue to redress;
Speak, for 'tis mine to succour deep distress."
Then thus he spake: " O king! by thy command,
I am the guardian of that far-fam'd land

Nam'd CALEDONIA, great in arts and arms,
And every worth that social fondness charms,
With every virtue that the heart approves,
Warm in their friendships, rapt'rous in their loves,
Profusely generous, obstinately just,
Inflexible as death their vows of trust :
For *independence* fires their noble minds,
Scorning deceit, as gods do scorn the fiends.
But what avail the virtues of the North,
No *Patriot Bard* to celebrate their worth,
No heav'n-taught *Minstrel*, with the voice of song,
To hymn their deeds, and make their names live long !
And, ah ! should luxury, with soft winning wiles,
Spread her contagion o'er my subject-isles,
My hardy sons, no longer valour's boast,
Would sink, despis'd,—their wonted greatness lost.
Forgive my wish, O King ! I speak with awe,
Thy will is fate, thy word is sovereign law !
O, wouldst thou deign thy suppliant to regard,
And grant my country one true *Patriot Bard*,
My sons would glory in the blessing given,
And virtuous deeds spring from the gift of heaven !"

To which the god—" My son, cease to deplore ;
Thy name in song shall sound the world all o'er ;
Thy Bard shall rise full-fraught with all the fire
That heav'n and free-born nature can inspire.

Ye sacred Nine, your golden harps prepare,
T' instruct the fav'rite of my special care,
That whether the song be rais'd to war or love,
His soul-wing'd strains may equal those above.
Now, faithful to thy trust, from sorrow free,
Go, wait the issue of our high decree."—
Speechless the Genius stood, in glad surprise,
Adoring gratitude beam'd in his eyes;
The promis'd Bard his soul with transport fills,
And, light with joy, he sought his native hills.

'Twas in regard of Wallace and his worth,
Jove honour'd COILA with his birth,
   And on that morn,
   When BURNS was born,
   Each Muse with joy
   Did hail the boy;
And Fame, on tiptoe, fain would blown her horn,
But Fate forbade the blast, too premature,
Till worth should sanction it beyond the critic's pow'r.

His merits proven—Fame her blast hath blown,
Now Scotia's Bard o'er all the world is known;—
But trembling doubts here check my unpolished lays,
What can they add to a whole world's praise;
Yet, while revolving time this day returns,
Let Scotchmen glory in the name of BURNS.

ODE.*

In imitation of PINDAR.

———

THE similie's a very useful thing,
  This, priests and poets needs must own,
  For when the clock-work of their brains runs down,
A similie winds up the mental spring ;
  For instance, when a priest does scan
        The fall of man,
  And all its consequences dire,
He makes him first a little sportive *pig*,
So clean, so innocent, so trig,
And then an aged *sow*, deep wallowing in the mire !

    Yes, sure the *similie's* a useful thing;
    Another instance I will bring.

Thou'st seen a *cork* tost on the rain-swell'd stream,
Now up, now down, now whirl'd round and round,
        Yet still 'twould *swim*,
And all the torrent's fury could not drown't :
  So have I seen a forward, empty *fop*,
  Tost in wit's blanket, ridicul'd, &c.
  Yet, after all the banter, off he'd hop,
Quite confident in *self-sufficiency*.

———

* Dr. Wolcot's satirical works were popular when this "Ode" was written.

Ah ! had kind heaven,
For a defence,
Allow'd me half the brazen confidence
That she to many a *cork-brain'd fool* hath given.

THE PORTRAIT OF GUILT.

In imitation of LEWIS.

'TWAS night, and the winds thro' the dark forest roar'd,
From heaven's wide cat'racts the torrents down pour'd,
　And blue light'nings flash'd on the eye ;
Demoniac howlings were heard in the air,
With groans of deep anguish, and shrieks of despair,
　And hoarse thunders growl'd thro' the sky.

Pale, breathless, and trembling the dark villain stood,
His hands and his clothes all bespotted with blood,
　His eyes wild with terror did stare ;
The earth yawn'd around him, and sulph'rous blue,
From the flame-boiling gaps, did expose to his view
　A *gibbet* and *skeleton bare.*

With horror he shrunk from a prospect so dread,
The blast swung the clanking chains over his head,
　The rattling bones sung in the wind ;

The lone bird of night from the abbey did cry,
He look'd o'er his shoulder, intending to fly,
   But a *spectre* stood ghastly behind.

" Stop, deep, hell-taught villain! " the *ghost* did exclaim,
" With thy brother of guilt here to expiate thy crime,
   " And atone for thy treacherous vow.
"'Tis here thou shalt hang, to the vultures a prey,
" Till, piece-meal, they tear thee and bear thee away,
   And thy bones rot unburied below."

Now, closing all round him, fierce demons did throng,
In sounds all unholy they howl'd their death-song,
   And the vultures around them did scream ;
Now clenching their claws in his fear-bristled hair,
Loud yelling they bore him aloft in the air,
   And the Murd'rer awoke—'*Twas a Dream !*

THE HAUNTET WUD.

In imitation of JOHN BARBOUR, *an old Scotch Poet.*

QUHY screim the crowis owr *yonder wud,*
   Witht loude and clamourynge dynne,
Haf deifenynge the torrentis roare,
   Quhilk dashis owr yon linne ?

Quhy straye the flokis far outowr,
  Alang the stanery lee,
And wil nocht graze anear the wud,
  Thof ryche the pasturis be?

And quhy dis oft the sheipherdis dog,
  Gif that ane lamikyne straye,
Ay yamf and yowl besyde *the wud*,
  Nae farthir yn wil gaye?

" Marvil thee nocht at quhat thou seist,"
  The tremblynge Rusticke sayde,
" For yn that *feindis-hauntet wud*,
  Hath guyltiles blude been sched.

" Thou seist far down yon buschye howe,
  An eldrin castil greye,
Witht teth of tyme, and weir of wyndis,
  Fast mouldiryng yn decaye.

" 'Twas ther the jealous Barrone livit,
  Witht Lady Anne hys wyfe,
He fleichit her neatht that *wudis* dark glume,
  And revit hyr ther of lyffe.

" And eir hyr fayre bodye was founde,
  The flesch cam fra the bane,

The snailis sat, feistyng onne hyr cheikis,
  The spydiris velit her ein.

" And evir syne nae beist nor byrde
  Will byde twa nichtis *ther*,
For fearful yellis and screichis wylde
  Are heird throch nicht sae dreir."

'Twas thus dark ignorance did ween,
  In fancy's wizard-reign,
When minstrel-fiction won belief,
  O'er Scotland's wide domain.

THE CHOICE.

YE vot'ries of pleasure and ease,
  Proud, wasting in riot the day,
Drive on your career as ye please,
  Let me follow a different way.
The woodland, the mountain, and hill,
  With the birds singing sweet from the tree,
The soul with serenity fill,
  And have pleasures more pleasing to me.

When I see yon parade thro' the streets,
    With affected, unnatural airs,
I smile at your low, trifling gaits,
    And could heartily lend you my pray'rs.
Great Jove ! was it ever design'd,
    That man should his reason lay down,
And barter the peace of his mind,
    For the follies and fashions of town ?

I'll retire to yon broom-cover'd fields,
    On the green mossy turf I'll recline,
The pleasures that solitude yields,
    Composure and peace shall be mine.
There Thomson or Shenstone I'll read,
    Well pleas'd with each well-manag'd theme,
With nothing to trouble my head,
    But ambition to imitate them.

EPISTLE.

TO A. B—RL—D.

Feb. 1806.

RETIR'D, disgusted, from the tavern-roar,
Where strong-lung'd ignorance does highest soar;
Where silly *ridicule* is pass'd for *wit;*
And shallow laughter takes her gaping fit;

Here lone I sit, in musing melancholy,
Resolv'd for aye to shun the court of folly;
For, from whole years' experience in her train,
One hour of joy brings twenty hours of pain.
Now since I'm on the would-be-better key,
The muse soft whispers me to write to thee,
Not that she means a self-debasing letter,
But merely show there's hopes I may turn better;
That what stands bad to my account of ill,
You may set down to passion, not to will.

The fate-scourg'd exile, destin'd still to roam,
Thro' desert wilds, far from his early home,
If some fair prospect meet his sorrowing eyes,
Like that he owned beneath his native skies,
Sad recollection, murdering relief,
He bursts in all the agonies of grief;
Memory presents the volume of his care,
And " harrows up his soul " with " such things were."
'Tis so in life, when youth folds up his page,
And turns the leaf to dark, blank, joyless age,
Where sad experience speaks in language plain,
Her thoughts of bliss, and highest hopes were vain;
O'er present ills I think I see her mourn,
And, " weep past joys that never will return."

Then, come, my friend, while yet in life's gay noon,
Ere grief's dark clouds obscure our summer-sun,

Ere Winter's sleety blasts around us howl,
And chill our every energy of soul—
Let us look back, retrace the ways we've trod,
Mark virtue's paths from guilty pleasure's road,
And, 'stead of wand'ring in a devious maze,
Mark some few precepts for our future days.

I mind, still well, when but a trifling boy,
My young heart fluttered with a savage joy,
As with my sire I wander'd thro' the wood,
And found the mavis' clump-lodg'd callow brood,
I tore them thence, exulting o'er my prize.
My father bade me list the mother's cries :
"So thine would wail," he said, "if reft of thee."—
It was a lesson of humanity.
HUMANITY ! thou'rt glory's brightest star,
Out-shining all the conqueror's trophies far !
One individual act of generous pity
Is nobler far than ravaging a city.
Ev'n let the blood-stain'd ruffians call thee coward,
An Alexander sinks beside a Howard.

Not to recount our every early joy,
When all was happiness without alloy ;
Nor tread again each flow'ry field we trac'd,
Light as the silk-wing'd butterflies we chas'd ;
Ere villain-falsehood taught the glowing mind,
To look with cold suspicion on mankind—
Let's pass the valley of our younger years,
And further up-hill mark what now appears.

We see the sensualist, fell vice's slave,
Fatigu'd, worn out, sink to an early grave ;
We see the slave of av'rice grind the poor,
His thirst for gold increasing with his store;
Packhorse of Fortune, all his days are care,
Her burthens bearing to his spendthrift heir.

Next view the spendthrift, joyous o'er his purse,
Exchanging all his guineas for remorse ;
On Pleasure's flow'r-deck'd barge away he's borne,
Supine, till ev'ry flow'r starts up a thorn.
Then all his pleasures fly, like air-blown bubbles :
He ruin'd, sinks, " amidst a sea of troubles."

Hail, TEMPERANCE ! thou'rt wisdom's first, best lore,
The sage in ev'ry age does thee adore ;
Within thy pale we taste of ev'ry joy,
O'er-stepping that, our highest pleasures cloy :
The heart-enlivening, friendly, social bowl,
To rapturous ecstasy exalts the soul ;
But when to midnight hour we keep it up,
Next morning feels the poison of the cup.

Though fate forbade the gifts of schoolmen mine,
With classic art to write the polished line,
Yet miners oft must gather earth with gold,
And truth may strike, though e'er so roughly told,

If thou in aught would rise to eminence,
Show not the faintest shadow of pretence,
Else busy Scandal, with her thousand tongues,
Will quickly find thee in ten thousand wrongs,

Each strives to tear his neighbour's honour down,
As if detracting something from his own.
Of all the ills with which mankind are curst,
An envious, discontented mind's the worst :
There muddy spleen exalts her gloomy throne,
Marks all conditions better than her own :
Hence defamation spreads her ant-bear tongue,
And grimly pleas'd, feeds on another's wrong.
Curse on the wretch, who, when his neighbour's blest,
Erects his peace-destroying, snaky crest !
And he who sits in surly, sullen mood,
Repining at a fellow-mortal's good !
Man owns so little of true happiness,
That curst be he who makes that little less !
    Vice to reclaim join not the old cant-cry,
Of " Son of Sathan, guilt, and misery ;"
One good example, more the point will carry,
Than all th' abuse in *Scandal's* dictionary.
    The *zealot* thinks he'll go to heav'n direct,
Adhering to the tenets of his sect,
E'en tho' his practice lie in this alone,
To rail at all persuasions but his own.
    In judging, still let moderation guide ;
O'er-heated zeal is certain to mislead.
First bow to God in heart-warm gratitude,
Next do our utmost for the general good.
In spite of all the forms which men devise,
'Tis there where real solid wisdom lies ;

And impious is the man who claims dominion,
To damn his neighbour diff'ring in opinion.
  When suppliant Misery greets thy wand'ring eye,
Altho' in public, pass not heedless by;
Distress impels her to implore the crowd,
For that denied within her lone abode.
Give thou the trifling pittance which she craves,
Tho' ostentation called by prudent knaves;
So conscience will a rich reward impart,
And finer feelings play around thy heart.
  When Wealth with arrogance exalts his brow,
And reckons Poverty a wretch most low,
Let good intentions dignify thy soul,
And conscious rectitude will crown the whole.
Hence indigence will independence own,
And soar above the haughty despot's frown.
  Still to thy lot be virtuously resign'd;
Above all treasures prize thy peace of mind;
Then let not envy rob thy soul of rest,
Nor discontent e'er harbour in thy breast.
Be not too fond of popular applause,
Which often echoes in a villain's cause,
Whose specious sophistry gilds his deceit,
Till pow'r abus'd, in time shows forth the cheat:
Yet be't thy pride to bear an honest fame;
More dear than life watch over thy good name;
For he, poor man! who has no wish to gain it,
Despises all the virtues which attain it.

Of friendship, still be secrecy the test,
This maxim let be 'graven in my breast—
Whate'er a friend enjoins me to conceal,
I'm weak, I'm base, if I the same reveal :
Let honour, acting as a pow'rful spell,
Suppress that itching fondness *still to tell;*
Else, unthank'd chronicle, the cunning's tool,
The world will stamp me for a gossip fool.
Yet let us act an honest open part,
Nor curb the warm effusions of the heart,
Which, naturally virtuous, discommends
Aught mean or base, e'en in our dearest friends.
    But why this long unjointed scrawl to thee,
Whose every action is a law to me,
Whose every deed proclaims thy noble mind ;
Industrious, independent, just, and kind.
Methinks I hear thee say, " *Each fool may teach,*
Since now my whim-led friend's begun to preach !"
But this first essay of my preaching strain,
Hear, and accept for friendship's sake.   Amen.

THE BACCHANALIANS.

Encircl'd in a cloud of smoke,
  Sat the convivial core ;
Like light'ning flash'd the merry joke,
  The thund'ring laugh did roar ;

Blythe Bacchus pierc'd his fav'rite hoard,
　　The sparkling glasses shine :
" 'Tis this," they cry, " come, sweep the board,
　　Which makes us all divine !"

Apollo tun'd the vocal shell,
　　With song, with catch, and glee :
The sonorous hall the notes did swell,
　　And echoed merrily.
Each sordid, selfish, little thought,
　　For shame itself did drown ;
And social love, with every draught,
　　Approv'd them for her own.

" Come, fill another bumper up,
　　And drink in Bacchus' praise,
Who sent the kind, congenial cup,
　　Such heav'nly joys to raise ! "
Great Jove, quite mad to see such fun,
　　At Bacchus 'gan to curse,
And to remind they were but men,
　　Sent down the fiend REMORSE.

THE FILIAL VOW.

WHY heaves my mother oft the deep-drawn sigh,
Why starts the big tear glist'ning in her eye?

Why oft retire to hide her bursting grief?
Why seeks she not, nor seems to wish relief?
'Tis for my Father, mould'ring with the dead,
My Brother, in bold manhood lowly laid,
And for the pains which age is doom'd to bear,
She heaves the deep-drawn sigh, and drops the secret tear.
Yes, partly these her gloomy thoughts employ,
But mostly this o'erclouds her ev'ry joy :
She grieves to think she may be burthensome,
Now feeble, old, and tottering to the tomb.

Oh, hear me, Heav'n, and record my Vow,
Its non-performance let Thy wrath pursue !
I swear—Of what thy providence may give,
My Mother shall her due maintenance have.
'Twas hers to guide me thro' life's early day,
To point out virtue's path and lead the way;
Now, while her pow'rs in frigid languor sleep,
'Tis mine to hand her down life's rugg'd steep;
With all her little weaknesses to bear,
Attentive, kind, to soothe her ev'ry care.
'Tis nature bids, and truest pleasure flows
From lessening an aged parent's woes.

EILD.

A FRAGMENT.

———

THE rough hail rattles through the trees,
  The sullen lift low'rs gloomy grey,
The trav'ller sees the swelling storm,
  And seeks the ale-house by the way.

But, waes me ! for yon widow'd wretch,
  Borne down wi' years, an' heavy care,
Her sapless fingers scarce can nip
  The wither'd twigs to beet her fire.

Thus youth and vigour fends itsel' ;
  Its help, reciprocal, is sure,
While dowless Eild, in poortith cauld,
  Is lanely left to stan' the stoure.

══

STANZAS.

*Written with a pencil on the grave-stone of a departed
friend.*

———

STOP, passenger,—here muse a while :
  Think on his darksome, lone abode,

Who late, like thee, did jocund smile,
   Now lies beneath this cold green sod.

Art thou to vicious ways inclin'd,
   Pursuing pleasure's flow'ry road,
Know—fell remorse shall rack thy mind,
   When tott'ring to thy cold green sod.

If thou a friend to virtue art,
   Oft pitying burthen'd mis'ry's load ;
Like thee, he had a feeling heart,
   Who lies beneath this cold green sod.

With studious, philosophic eye,
   He look'd thro' Nature up to God,
His future hope his greatest joy,
   Who lies beneath this cold green sod.

Go, passenger—revere this truth ;
   A life well spent in doing good,
Soothes joyless age, and sprightly youth,
   When drooping o'er the cold green sod.

PRAYER, UNDER AFFLICTION.

Almighty Pow'r, who wings the storm,
  And calms the raging wind,
Restore health to my wasted form,
  And tranquillize my mind.

For, ah! how poignant is the grief
  Which self-misconduct brings,
When racking pains find no relief,
  And injur'd conscience stings.

Let penitence forgiveness plead,
  Hear lenient mercy's claims,
Thy justice let be satisfied,
  And blotted out my crimes.

But should thy sacred law of Right,
  Seek life, a sacrifice,
O! haste that awful, solemn night,
  When death shall veil mine eyes.

EPISTLE,

TO J. KING.

On receiving a Moral Epistle from him.   May, 1802.

P LEASE accept the thanks and praise
Due to your poetic lays,
Wisdom ay should be rever'd,
Sense to wit be ay preferr'd.
—Just your thoughts, in simple guise,
Fit to make frail mortals wise ;
Every period, every line,
With some moral truth doth shine.
—Like the rocks, which storms divide,
Thund'ring down the mountain's side,
So strides Time, with rapid force,
Round his unobstructed course ;
Like a flood upon its way,
Sweeping downward to the sea :
But what figure so sublime
As describe the flight of time ?
Yesterday is past an' gane,
Just as it had never been.
—Life's a dream, and man's a bubble,
'Compass'd round with care and trouble,
Like a ship in tempest tost,
Soon o'erwhelm'd, for ever lost ;

Like the short-liv'd passion-flow'r,
Blooming, dying, in an hour;
Like the tuneful bird that sings,
Flutt'ring high on sportive wings,
Till the fowler's subtle art
Drives Death's message to its heart,
While, perhaps, Death aims his blow
For to lay the wretch as low.
—Now since life is but a day,
Make the most of it we may;
Not in drinking to excess—
Drink the spirits will depress:
Calm and tranquil let us be,
Still resign'd to Fate's decree:
Let not poortith sink us low,
Let not wealth exalt our brow,
Let's be grateful, virtuous, wise,—
There's where all our greatness lies;
Doing all the good we can,
Is all that Heaven requires of man.
—Wherefore should we grieve and sigh,
'Cause we know that we must die?
Death's a debt requir'd by nature,
To be paid by every creature;
Rich and poor, and high and low,
Fall by death's impartial blow—
God, perhaps, in kindness, will
Snatch us from some coming ill;

Death may kindly waft us o'er
To a milder, happier shore.
—But, Dear Jamie! after a',
What I've said's not worth a straw;
What is't worth to moralize
What we never can practise?
As for me, wi' a' my skill,
Passion leads me as she will:
But resolves, laid down to-day,
Ere to-morrow, 're done away.—
—Then, let's ever cheery live,
Do our best, an' never grieve;
Still let Friendship's warmest tie
A' deficiences supply,
And, while favour'd by the Nine,
I your laurels will entwine.

STANZAS.

Written on ALEX. WILSON'S *Emigration to America.*

O DEATH! it's no' thy deed I mourn,
Tho' oft my heart-strings thou hast torn,
'Tis worth an' merit left forlorn,

        Life's ills to dree,
Gars now the pearly, brakish burn

        Gush frae my e'e.

Is there wha feels the melting glow
O' sympathy for ithers' woe?
Come let our tears thegither flow ;
                              O join my mane !
For *Wilson*, worthiest of us a',
                              For ay is gane.

He bravely strave 'gainst fortune's stream,
While hope held forth ae distant gleam,
Till dash'd, and dash'd, time after time,
                              On life's rough sea,
He weep'd his thankless native clime,
                              And sail'd away.

The patriot bauld, the social brither,
In him war' sweetly join'd thegither ;
He knaves reprov'd without a swither,
                              In keenest satire ;
And taught what mankind owe each ither,
                              As sons of nature.

If thou hast heard his wee bit wren,
Wail forth its sorrows through the glen,
Tell how his warm, descriptive pen
                              Has thrill'd thy saul,
His sensibility sae keen,
                              He felt for all.

Since now he's gane, an' Burns is dead,
Ah ! wha will tune the Scottish reed ?
Her thistle, dowie, hings its head ;
                              Her harp's unstrung ;
While mountain, river, loch, an' mead,
                              Remain unsung.

Fareweel, thou much neglected bard !
These lines will speak my warm regard,
While strangers on a foreign sward
                              Thy worth hold dear,
Still some kind heart thy name shall guard
                              Unsullied here.

ALLAN'S ALE.

Written in 1799.

COME a' ye friendly, social pack,
Wha meet wi' glee to club your plack,
Attend while I rehearse a fact,
                              That winna fail ;
Nae drink can raise a canty crack,
                              Like Allan's * Ale.

* All-n Br—n's.

It waukens wit, an' mak's as merry,
As England's far-fam'd Canterbury;
Rich wines frae Lisbon or Canary,
                      Let gentles hail,
But we can be as brisk an' airy,
                      Wi' Allan's Ale.

It bears the gree, I'se gie my aith,
O' Widow Dean's an' Ralston's baith,
Wha may cast by their brewin' graith,
                      Baith pat and pail,
Since Paisley wisely puts mair faith
                      In Allan's Ale.

Unlike the poor, sma' *penny-wheep*,
Whilk worthless, petty change-folk keep,
O'er whilk mirth never deign'd to peep,
                      Sae sour an' stale,
I've seen me joyous, frisk an' leap,
                      Wi' Allan's Ale.

Whether a friendly, social meetin',
Or politicians thrang debatin',
Or benders blest your wizzens weetin',
                      Mark well my tale,
Ye'll fin' nae drink ha'f worth your gettin',
                      Like Allan's Ale.

N

When bleak December's blasts do blaw,
And Nature's face is co'er'd wi' snaw,
Poor bodies scarce do work at a',
The cauld's sae snell,
But meet an' drink their cares awa'
Wi' Allan's Ale.

Let auld Kilmarnock mak' a fraise,
What she has done in better days,
Her *thri-penny* ance her fame could raise,
O'er muir an' dale.
But Paisley now may claim the praise
Wi' Allan's Ale.

Let selfish wights impose their notions,
And d—n the man wont tak' their lessons,
I scorn their threats, I scorn their cautions,
Say what they will ;
Let friendship crown our best devotions
Wi' Allan's Ale.

While sun, an' moon, an' stars endure,
An' aid wi' light "a random splore,"
Still let each future social core,
Its praises tell :
Ador'd ay and for evermore
Be Allan's Ale!

EPISTLE,

TO J. SCADLOCK,

*On receiving from him a small MS. volume of
Original Scottish Poems.   April, 1803.*

WHILE colleg'd Bards bestride Pegassus,
An' try to gallop up Parnassus,
  By dint o' meikle lear,
The lowe o' friendship fires my saul,
To write you this poetic scrawl,—
  Prosaic dull, I fear!
    But, weel I ken, your gen'rous heart
      Will overlook its failings,
    An' whare the Poet has come short,
      Let friendship cure his ailings;
        'Tis kin', man, divine, man,
          To hide the faut we see,
        Or try to men't, as far's we ken't,
          Wi' true sincerity.

This last observe, brings't i' my head,
To tell you here my social creed—
  Let's use a' mankind weel,

An' ony sumph wha'd use us ill,
Wi' dry contempt let's treat him still,
  He'll feel it warst himsel' :
    I never flatter—praise but rare,
    I scorn a double part ;
    An' when I speak, I speak sincere,
    The dictates o' my heart ;
      I truly hate the dirty gait
        That mony a body tak's,
        Wha fraise ane, syne blaze ane
          As soon's they turn their backs.

In judging, let us be right hooly ;
I've heard some fouks descant sae freely,
  On ither people's matters,
As if themsel's war' real perfection,
When had they stood a fair inspection,
  Th' abus'd war' far their betters :
    But gossips ay maun hae their crack,
      Though moralists should rail.
    Let's end the matter wi' this fact,
      That, *Goodness pays itsel'*.
        The joys, man, that rise, man,
          To ane frae doing weel,
        Are sican joys that harden'd vice
          Can seldom ever feel.

O Jamie, man ! I'm proud to see't,
Our ain auld muse yet keeps her feet,
    'Maist healthy as before ;
For sad predicting fears foretauld,
When Robin's glowing heart turn'd cauld,
  Then a' our joys war' o'er,
      (Ilk future Bard revere his name,
        Through thousand years to come,
      And though we cannot reach his fame,
        Busk laurels round his tomb :)
            Yet, though he's dead, the Scottish reed,
              This mony a day may ring,
            In L—v—st—n, in A—d—s—n,
              In Sc—dl—ck, and in K—g.

" The Tap-room "—what a glorious treat !
" Complaint and wish "—how plaintive sweet !
  " The Weaver's " just " Lament."
" The Gloamin' fragment "—how divine !
There Nature speaks in every line,
  The Bard's immortal in't !
      Yon " Epigram on Jeanie L—g,"
        Is pointed as the steel,
      An' " Hoot ! ye ken' yoursel's,"—a sang
        Would pleas'd e'en Burns himsel' !
            Let snarling, mean quarr'ling,
              Be doubly d—d henceforth,
            And let us raise the voice of praise,
              To hearten modest worth.

And you, my dear respected frien',
Your "Spring's" a precious evergreen,
  Fresh beauties budding still.
Your " Levern Banks," an' " Killoch Burn,"
Ye sing them wi' sae sweet a turn,
  Ye gar the heart-strings thrill.
      " October winds "—e'en let them rave,
        With nature-blasting howl,
      If in return kind heaven give
        The sunshine of the soul :
            The feeling heart that bears a part,
              In others' joys and woes,
            May still depend to find a friend
              Howe'er the tempest blows.

Yet, lang I've thought, and think it yet,
True friends are rarely to be met,
  Wha share in ithers' troubles,
Wha jointly joy, or drap the tear
Reciprocal—and kindly bear
  Wi' ane anithers' foibles ;
      Ev'n such a friend I once could boast,
        Ah ! now in death he's low—
      But fond anticipation hopes
        For such a friend in *you*.
            Dear Jamie, forgi'e me,
              That last presumptive line ;
            See—here's my hand at your command,—
              Ye hae my heart langsyne.

PROLOGUE

To THE GENTLE SHEPHERD, *spoken in a Provincial
Theatre.*

YE patronisers of our little party,
My heart's e'en light to see you a' sae hearty;
I'm fain, indeed, an' trouth! I've meikle cause,
Since your blythe faces half insure applause.
We come this night wi' nae new-fangl'd story
O' knave's deceit, or fop's vain blust'ring glory,
Nor harlequin's wild pranks, wi' skin like leopard,—
We're come to gie your ain auld " Gentle Shepherd;"
Whilk ay will charm, an' will be read, an' acket,
Till Time himsel' turn auld, an' kick the bucket.
I mind, langsyne, when I was just a callan,
That a' the kintra rang in praise o' Allan;
Ilk rising generation toots his fame,
And, hun'er years to come, 'twill be the same:
For wha has read, tho' e'er sae lang sinsyne,
But keeps the living picture on his min';
Approves bauld *Patie's* clever, manly turn,
An' maist thinks *Roger* cheap o' *Jenny's* scorn;
His dowless gait, the cause o' a' his care,
For, " Nane, except the brave, deserve the fair."
Hence sweet young *Peggy* lo'ed her manly *Pate*,
An' *Jenny* geck't at *Roger*, dowf an' blate.

Our gude *Sir William* stands a lesson leal,
To lairds wha'd hae their vassals lo'e them weel;
To prince an' peer this maxim it imparts,
Their greatest treasures are the people's hearts.

Frae *Glaud* an' *Symon* would we draw a moral,
The virtuous youth-time mak's the canty carle;
The twa auld birkies caper blythe an' bauld,
Nor shaw the least regret that they're turn'd auld.

Poor *Bauldy!* O, it's like to split my jaws!
I think I see him under *Madge's* claws:
Sae may Misfortune tear him spawl and plack,
Wha'd wrang a bonnie lass, an' syne draw back.

But, Sirs, to you I maist forgat my mission,
I'm sent to beg a truce to criticism;
We don't pretend to speak by square and rule,
Like yon wise chaps bred up in Thespian-school;
An' to your wishes should we not succeed,
Pray be sae kind as tak' the will for deed;

(An' as our immortal ROBIN BURNS *says,)*

" Aiblins tho' we winna' stan' the test,
" Wink hard an' say, The folks hae done their best."
An' keep this gen'rous maxim still in min',
" To *err* is human, to *forgive* divine! "

EPISTLE

TO WILLIAM WYLIE.   *Jan. 1806.*

———

DEAR kindred saul, thanks to the cause
  First made us ken each ither,
Ca't fate, or chance, I carena whilk,
  To me it brought a brither.

Thy furthy, kindly, takin' gait ;—
  Sure every gude chiel' likes thee,
An' bad-luck wring his thrawart heart,
  Wha snarling e'er would vex thee.

Tho' mole-e'et Fortune's partial hand
  O' clink may keep thee bare o't ;
Of what thou hast, pale Misery
  Receives, unask'd, a share o't.

Thou gi'est without ae hank'rin' thought,
  Or cauld, self-stinted wish ;
E'en winter-finger'd Avarice,
  Approves thee with a blush.

If Grief e'er make thee her pack-horse,
  Her leaden-load to carry't,
Shove half the burthen on my back,
  I'll do my best to bear it.

Gude kens we a' hae fauts enew,
  'Tis Friendship's task to cure 'em,
But still she spurns the critic view,
  An' bids us to look o'er 'em.

When Death performs his beadle part,
  An' summons thee to heaven,
By virtue of thy warm, kind heart,
  Thy fauts will be forgiven.

And shouldst thou live to see thy friend,
  Borne lifeless on the bier,
I ask of thee, for epitaph,
  One kind, elegiac tear.

═══

SONNET

TO SINCERITY.

───

PURE emanation of the honest soul,
  Dear to my heart, manly Sincerity !
Dissimulation shrinks, a coward foul,
  Before thy noble art-detesting eye.

Thou scorn'st the wretch who acts a double part,
  Obsequious, servile, flatt'ring to betray,

With smiling face that veils a ranc'rous heart,
Like sunny morning of tempestuous day.

Thou spurn'st the sophist, with his guilty lore,
Whom int'rest prompts to weave the specious snare ;
In independence rich, thou own'st a store
Of conscious worth, which changelings never share.

Then come, bright Virtue, with thy dauntless brow,
And crush Deceit, vile monster, reptile-low.

EPISTLE

TO J. BARR,

Wherever he may be found.   *March, 1804.*

GUDE Pibrocharian, jorum-jirger,
Say, hae ye turn'd an Antiburgher ?
Or lang-fac'd Presbyterian El'er ?
Deep read in wiles o' gath'rin' siller?
Or cauld, splenetic solitair,
Resolv'd to herd wi' man nae mair?
    As to the second, I've nae fear for't ;
For siller, faith ! ye ne'er did care for't,
Unless to help a needfu' body,
An' get an antrin glass o' toddy.

But what the black mischief's come owre you ?
These three months I've been speirin' for you,
Till e'en the Muse, wi' downright grievin',
Has worn her chafts as thin's a shavin'.
Say, hae ye ta'en a tramp to Lon'on,
In *Co.* wi' worthy auld Buchanan,*
Wha mony a mile wad streek his shanks,
To hae a crack wi' Josie Banks
Concerning " Shells, an' birds, an' metals,
Moths, spiders, butterflies, an' beetles."
For you, I think ye'll cut a figure,
Wi' king o' pipers, Malc. M'Gregor,
An' wi' your clarion, flute, an' fiddle,
Will gar their southron heart-strings diddle.

Or are ye through the kintra whiskin',
Accoutr'd wi' the sock an' buskin,
Thinkin' to climb to wealth an' fame,
By adding Roscius to your name ?
Frae thoughts o' that, pray keep abeigh !
Ye're far owre auld, an' far owre heigh ;
Since in thir novel-huntin' days
There's nane but bairns can act our plays.
At twal year auld, if ye had tried it,
I doubtna but ye might succeedet ;
But full-grown boordly chields like you—
Quite monst'rous, man, 'twill never do !

---

* A much respected Naturalist in the west country.

Or are ye gane, as there are few sic,
For teachin' o' a band o' music?
O, hear auld Scotland's fervent pray'rs,
And teach her genuine native airs!
Whilk simply play'd, devoid o' art,
Thrill through the senses to the heart.

Play, when ye'd rouse the patriot's saul,
True valour's tune, " The Garb of Gaul ;"
An' when laid low in glory's bed,
Let " Roslin Castle " soothe his shade.
" The bonnie Bush aboon Traquair,"
Its every accent breathes despair ;
An' " Ettrick Banks," celestial strain !
Mak's simmer's gloamin mair serene ;
An', O how sweet the plaintive muse,
Amang " The broom o' Cowdenknowes ! "

To hear the love-lorn swain complain,
Lone, on " The braes o' Ballendine ; "
It e'en might melt the dortiest she,
That ever sklinted scornfu' e'e.

When Beauty tries her vocal pow'rs
Amang the greenwood's echoing bow'rs,
" The bonnie birks of Invermay "
Might mend a seraph's sweetest lay.

Then, should grim Care invest your castle,
Just knock him down wi' " Willie Wastle,"
An' rant blythe " Lumps o' puddin'" owre him ;
And for his dirge sing " Tullochgorum."

When Orpheus charm'd his wife frae h—ll,
'Twas nae Scotch tune he play'd sae well;
Else had the worthy auld wire-scraper
Been keepet for his d—lship's piper.

Or if ye're turn'd a feather'd fop,
Light dancing upon fashion's top,
Wi' lofty brow an' selfish e'e,
Despising low-clad dogs like me;
Uncaring your contempt or favour,
Sweet butterfly, adieu for ever!
But, hold—I'm wrong to doubt your sense,
For pride proceeds from ignorance.

If peace of mind lay in fine clothes,
I'd be the first of flutt'ring beaux,
An' strut as proud as ony peacock,
That ever craw'd on tap o' hay-cock;
An' ere I'd know one vexing thought,
Get dollar buttons on my coat,
Wi' a' the lave o' fulsome trash on,
That constitutes a man o' fashion.
O, grant me this, kind Providence,
A moderate, decent competence;
Thou'lt see me smile in independence,
Above weak-saul'd pride-born ascendence.

But whether ye're gane to teach the Whistle,
Midst noise an' rough reg'mental bustle;
Or gane to strut upon the stage,
Smit wi' the mania o' the age;
Or, Scotchman-like, hae tramp't abreed,
To yon big town far south the Tweed;
Or dourin' in the hermit's cell,
Unblessing an' unblest yoursel'—
In gude's name, write!—tak up your pen,
A' how ye're doin' let me ken.
Sae, hoping quickly your epistle,
Adieu! thou genuine son of song an' whistle.

POSTSCRIPT.

We had a concert here short syne;   ·
Oh, man! the Music was divine,
Baith plaintive sang an' merry glee,
In a' the soul of harmony.
When Smith and Stuart leave this earth,
The gods, in token o' their worth,
Will welcome them at heaven's portals,
The brightest, truest, best o' mortals;
Apollo proud, as weel he may,
Will walk on tip-toe a' that day;
While a' the Muses kindred claim,
Rememb'ring what they've done for them.

SECOND EPISTLE,

TO J. SCADLOCK, then at Perth.   *June, 1804.*

———

LET those who never felt its flame,
Say Friendship is an empty name ;
    Such selfish, cauld philosophy
    For ever I disclaim :

It soothes the soul with grief opprest,
Half-cures the care-distemper'd breast,
    And in the jocund, happy hour,
    Gives joy a higher zest.

All nature sadden'd at our parting hour,
Winds plaintive howl'd, clouds, weeping, dropt a show'r,
    Our fields look'd dead—as if they'd said,
    " We ne'er shall see him more."

Tho' fate an' fortune threw their darts,
Envying us your high deserts,
    They well might tear you from our arms,
    But never from our hearts.

When spring buds forth in vernal show'rs,
When summer comes array'd in flow'rs,
    Or autumn kind, from Ceres' horn,
    Her grateful bounty pours ;

Or bearded Winter curls his brow—
I'll often fondly think on you,
    And on our happy days and nights
    With pleasing back-cast view.

If e'er in musing mood ye stray
Alang the banks of classic Tay,
    Think on our walks by Stanely Tow'r,
    And sage Gleniffer brae ;

Think on our langsyne happy hours,
Spent where the burn wild, rapid, pours,
    And o'er the horrid dizzy steep
    Dashes her mountain stores ;

Think on our walks by sweet Greenlaw,
By woody hill and birken shaw,
    Where nature strews her choicest sweets
    To mak' the landscape braw.

And think on rural Ferguslie,
Its plantin's green, and flow'ry lee ;
    Such fairy scenes, tho' distant far,
    May please the mental e'e.

Yon mentor, Geordie Zimmerman,
Agrees exactly with our plan,

That partial hours of Solitude
Exalt the soul of man.

So, oft retir'd from strife and din,
Let's shun the jarring ways of men,
　　And seek serenity and peace
　　By stream and woody glen.

But ere a few short summers gae
Your friend will mix his kindred clay,
　　For fell disease tugs at my breast,
　　To hurry me away.

Yet while life's bellows bear to blaw,
Till life's last lang-fetch'd breath I draw,
　　I'll often fondly think on you,
　　And mind your kindness a'.

Now, fare-ye-weel! still may ye find
A friend congenial to your mind,
　　To share your joys, and half your woes—
　　Warm, sympathising, kind.

LINES,

Written on reading THOMAS CAMPBELL'S " *Pleasures of Hope.*"

———

HOW seldom 'tis the Poet's happy lot
T' inspire his readers with the fire he wrote ;
To strike those chords that wake the latent thrill,
And wind the willing passions to his will.
Yes, Campbell, sure that happy lot is thine,
With fit expression, rich from Nature's mine,
Like old Timotheus, skilful plac'd on high,
To rouse revenge, or soothe to sympathy.
Blest Bard ! who chose no paltry, local theme,
Kind Hope through wide creation is the same ;
Yes, Afric's sons shall one day burst their chains,
Will read thy lines, and bless thee for thy pains ;
Fame yet shall waft thy name to India's shore,
Where next to Brahma thee they will adore ;
And Hist'ry's page, exulting in thy praise,
Will proudly hand thee down to future days :
Detraction foil'd, reluctant quits her grip,
And carping Envy silent bites her lip.

THE CONTRAST.

Inscribed to Mr. J. SCADLOCK.   *Aug. 1803.*

———

WHEN Love proves false, and friends betray us,
All nature seems a dismal chaos
  Of wretchedness and woe ;
We stamp mankind a base ingrate,
Half loathing life, we challenge Fate
  To strike the final blow.
    Then settl'd grief, with wild despair,
      Stares from our blood-shot eyes,
    Tho' oft we try to hide our care,
      And check our bursting sighs.
      Still vexed, sae wretched,
        We seek some lonely wood,
      There sighing, and crying,
        We pour the briny flood.

Mark the contrast—what joys we find,
With friends sincere and beauty kind,
  Congenial to our wishes ;
Then life appears a summer's day,
Adown Time's crystal stream we play,
  As sportive's little fishes.
    We see nought then but general good,
      Which warm pervades all nature ;

Our hearts expand with gratitude
    Unto the great Creator.
        Then let's revere the virtuous fair,
            The friend whose truth is tried,
        For, without these, go where we please,
            We'll always find a void.

EPISTLE

TO W. THOMSON.   *June, 1805.*

DEAR WILL, my much respected frien',
I send you this to let you ken,
That, tho' at distance fate hath set you,
Your frien's in Paisley don't forget you ;
But often think on you, far lone,
Amang the braes of Overton.

    Our social club continues yet,
Perpetual source of mirth an' wit ;
Our rigid rules admit but few,
Yet still we'll keep a chair for you.

    A country life I've oft envied,
Where love, an' truth, an' peace preside ;
Without temptations to allure,
Your days glide on, unstain'd an' pure ;

Nae midnight revels waste your health,
Nor greedy landlord drains your wealth,
Ye're never fash't wi' whisky fever,
Nor dizzy pow, nor dulness ever,
But breathe the halesome caller air,
Remote from aught that genders care.
 I needna tell how much I lang
To hear your rural Scottish sang;
To hear you sing your heath-clad braes,
Your jocund nights, an' happy days;
An' lilt wi' glee the blythsome morn,
When dew-draps pearl every thorn;
When larks pour forth the early sang,
An' lintwhites chant the whins amang,
An' pyats hap frae tree to tree,
Teachin' their young anes how to flee,
While frae the mavis to the wren,
A' warble sweet in bush or glen.
 In town we scarce can fin' occasion,
To note the beauties o' creation,
But study mankind's diff'rent dealings,
Their virtues, vices, merits, failings,
Unpleasing task, compar'd wi' yours;
Ye range the hills 'mang mountain flow'rs,
An' view, afar, the smoky town,
More blest than all its riches were your own.

A lang Epistle I might scribble,
But aiblins ye will grudge the trouble
Of readin' sic low, hamert rhyme,
An' sae it's best to quat in time;
Sae, I, with soul sincere an' fervent,
Am still your trustful frien' an' servant.

EPISTLE

TO J. BUCHANAN.

Aug. 1806.

MY gude auld friend on Locher-banks,
Your kindness claims my warmest thanks;
Yet, thanks is but a draff-cheap phrase
O' little value now-a-days;
Indeed, it's hardly worth the heeding,
Unless to show a body's breeding.
Yet mony a poor, doil't, servile body,
Will scrimp his stomach o' its crowdy,
An' pride to rin a great man's erran's,
An' feed on smiles an' sour cheese parin's,
An' think himsel' nae sma' sheep-shank,
Rich laden wi' his lordship's thank.
The sodger, too, for a' his troubles,
His hungry wames, and bluidy hubbles,
His agues, rheumatisms, cramps,
Receiv'd in plashy winter camps,

O blest reward! at last he gains
His sov'reign's *thanks* for a' his pains.

'Twas wisely said by "Queer Sir John,"
That "Honour wudna buy a scone."
Sae ane, of thanks, may get a million,
Yet live as poor's a porter's scullion:
Indeed, they're just (but, beg your pardon,)
Priest-blessing like, no' worth a fardin'.*

Thus, tho' 'mang first o' friends I rank you,
'Twere but sma' compliment to thank you;
Yet, lest you think me here ungratefu',
Of hatefu' names, a name most hatefu',
The neist time that ye come to toon,
By a' the pow'rs beneath the moon!
I'll treat you wi' a Highland gill,
Tho' it should be my hindmaist fill.

Tho' in the bustling town, the Muse
Has gather'd little feck o' news,
—'Tis said, the Court of Antiquarians,
Has split on some great point o' variance,
For ane has got, in gouden box,
The *spentacles* of auld John Knox;

---

* Alluding to the anecdote of the sailor who would not accept of the priest's
blessing, alleging that if it was worth one farthing he would not part with it.

A second proudly thanks his fate wi'
The hindmaist pen that Nelson wrate wi';
A third ane owns an antique rare,
A saip-brush made o' mermaid's hair!
But, niggard wights! they a' refuse 'em—
These precious relics, to the museum,
Whilk selfish, mean, illegal deeds,
Hae set them a' at loggerheads.

'Tis also said, our noble Prince,
Has play'd the wee-saul't loon for ance,
Has gien his bonny wife the fling,
Yet gars her wear Hans Carvel's ring;
But a' sic clish-clash cracks I'll lea'
To yon sculdudry committee.

Sure, taste refin'd and public spirit
Stand next to genius in merit;
I'm proud to see your warm regard
For Caledonia's dearest bard.
Of him ye've got sae guid a painting,*
That nocht but real life is wanting.
I think yon rising genius, Tannock,
May gain a niche in fame's heigh winnock;
There, with auld Rubens, placed sublime,
Look down upon the wreck of time.

---

* Portrait of Burns, painted by Mr. J. Tannock, for the Kilbarchan Burns'
Anniversary Society.

I ne'er, as yet, hae found a patron,
For, scorn be till't! I hate a' flatt'rin',
Besides, I never had an itchin'
To slake about a great man's kitchen,
An' like a spaniel, lick his dishes,
An' come an' gang just to his wishes ;
Yet, studious to give worth its due,
I pride to praise the like of you ;
Gude chiels, replete wi' sterling sense,
Wha wi' their worth mak' nae pretence.
Ay—there's my worthy friend, M'Math,
I'll lo'e him till my latest breath,
An' like a traitor-wretch be hang'd,
Before I'd hear that fallow wrang'd ;
His every action shows his mind,
Humanely noble, bright, an' kind,
An' here's the worth o't, doubly rooted,
He never speaks ae word about it !
—My compliments an' warm gude-will,
To Maisters Simpson, Barr, and Lyle.
Wad rav'ning Time but spare my pages,
They'd tell the warl' in after-ages,
That it, to me, was wealth an' fame,
To be esteem'd by chiels like them.
O Time, thou all-devouring bear !
Hear—" List, O list " my ardent pray'r !
I crave thee here, on bended knee,
To let my dear lov'd pages be !

O tak' thy sharp-nail'd, nibbling elves,
To musty scrolls on college shelves !
There, with dry treatises on law,
Feast, cram, and gorge thy greedy maw ;
But grant, amidst thy thin-sown mercies,
To spare, O spare my darling verses !

Could I but up thro' hist'ry wimple,
Wi' Robertson, or sage Dalrymple ;
Or had I half the pith an' lear
Of a Mackenzie, or a Blair !
I aiblins then might tell some story,
Wad shaw the Muse in bleezin' glory ;
But scrimp't o' time* an' lear scholastic,
My lines limp on in Hudibrastic,
Till Hope, grown sick, flings down her claim,
An' draps her dreams o' future fame.
—Yes, O waesuck ! should I be vaunty ?
My Muse is just a Rosinante,
She stammers forth, wi' hilchin' canter,
Sagely intent on strange adventure,
Yet, sae uncouth in garb an' feature,
She seems the Fool of Literature.
But lest the critic's birsie besom,
Soop aff this cant of egotism,

---

* "Time"—Scottish idiom for leisure.

I'll sidelins hint—na, bauldly tell,
I whyles think something o' mysel':
Else, wha the deil wad fash to scribble,
Expectin' scorn for a' his trouble?
Yet, lest dear self should be mista'en,
I'll fling the bridle o'er the mane,
For after a', I fear this jargon,
Is but a Willie Glassford bargain.

LINES,

To W. M'LAREN,

To attend a meeting of the BURNS' ANNIVERSARY SOCIETY.

KING GEORDIE issues out his summons,
To ca' his bairns, the Lairds an' Commons,
To creesh the nation's moolie-heels,
An' butter commerce' rusty wheels,
An' see what new, what untried tax,
Will lie the easiest on our backs.

The priest convenes his scandal-court,
To ken what houghmagandie sport,
Has been gaun on within the parish,
Since last they met, their funds to cherish.

But I, the servant of Apollo,
Whose mandates I am proud to follow,
He bids me warn you as the friend
Of Burns's fame, that ye'll attend,
Neist Friday e'en, in Lucky Wright's,
To spend the best, the wale o' nights ;
Sae, under pain o' half-a-mark,
Ye'll come, as signed by me, the CLERK.

ODE,

Written for, and Performed at the Celebration of ROBERT
BURNS' *Birth-day, Paisley, 29th Jan., 1807.*

RECITATIVE.

WHILE Gallia's chief, with cruel conquests vain,
Bids clanging trumpets rend the skies,
The widow's, orphan's, and the father's sighs,
Breathe, hissing through the guilty strain ;
Mild Pity hears the harrowing tones,
Mixed with shrieks and dying groans ;
While warm Humanity, afar,
Weeps o'er the ravages of war,
And shudd'ring hears Ambition's servile train,
Rejoicing o'er their thousands slain.

But when the song to worth is given,
The grateful anthem wings its way to heaven,
Rings through the mansions of the bright abodes,
And melts to ecstasy the list'ning gods ;
Apollo, on fire,
Strikes with rapture the lyre,
And the Muses the summons obey ;
Joy wings the glad sound,
To the worlds around,
Till all nature re-echoes the lay !
Then, raise the song ye vocal few,
Give the praise to merit due.

SONG.

Set to Music by MR. R. A. SMITH.

Tho' dark scowling Winter, in dismal array,
  Remarshals his storms on the bleak hoary hill,
With joy we assemble to hail the great day
  That gave birth to the Bard who ennobles our isle.
Then loud to his merits the song let us raise,
Let each true Caledonian exult in his praise ;
For the glory of genius, its dearest reward,
Is the laurel entwin'd by his country's regard.

Let the Muse bring fresh honours his name to adorn,
  Let the voice of glad melody pride in the theme,
For the genius of Scotia, in ages unborn,
  Will light up her torch at the blaze of his fame.
When the dark mist of ages lies turbid between,
Still his star of renown through the gloom shall be seen,
And his rich blooming laurels, so dear to the Bard,
Will be cherish'd for ay by his country's regard.

RECITATIVE.

Yes, Burns, thou " dear departed shade !"
When rolling centuries have fled,
Thy name shall still survive the wreck of time,
Shall rouse the genius of thy native clime ;
Bards yet unborn, and patriots shall come,
And catch fresh ardour at thy hallow'd tomb—
　　There's not a cairn-built cottage on our hills,
　　　Nor rural hamlet on our fertile plains,
　　　But echoes to the magic of thy strains,
　　While every heart with highest transport thrills :
　　　　Our country's melodies shall perish never,
　　　　For Burns, thy songs shall live for ever.
　　　　　Then, once again, ye vocal few,
　　　　　Give the song to merit due.

SONG.

Written to MARSH'S *National Air, " Britons who for freedom bled."*

Harmonized as a Glee by MR. SMITH.

Hail, ye glorious sons of song,
　Who wrote to humanize the soul !
To you our highest strains belong,
　Your names shall crown our friendly bowl :
　　But chiefly, Burns, above the rest,
　　　We dedicate this night to thee ;
　　Engrav'd in every Scotsman's breast,
　　　Thy name, thy worth, shall ever be !

Fathers of our country's weal,
  Sternly virtuous, bold and free !
Ye taught your sons to fight, yet feel
  The dictates of humanity :
    But chiefly, Burns, above the rest,
      We dedicate this night to thee ;
    Engrav'd in every Scotsman's breast,
      Thy name, thy worth, shall ever be !

Haughty Gallia threats our coast,
  We hear their vaunts with disregard,
Secure in valour, still we boast,
  '' The Patriot and the Patriot Bard.''
    But chiefly, Burns, above the rest,
      We dedicate this night to thee :
    Engrav'd in every Scotsman's breast,
      Thy name, thy worth, shall ever be !

Yes, Caledonians ! to our country true,

Which Danes or Romans never could subdue,

Firmly resolved our native rights to guard,

Let's toast, " The Patriot and the Patriot Bard."

PARODY.

Written on seeing the late MR. THOMAS WILLOUGHBY,
Tragedian, rather below himself.

PEACEFUL, slumb'ring in the ale-house,
See the god-like *Rollo* lie,

Drink outwits the best of fellows ;
   Here lies poor Tom Willoughby.

Where is stern *King Richard's* fury ?
   Where is *Osmond's* blood-flush'd eye ?
See these mighty men before ye,
   Sunk to poor Tom Willoughby.

Pity 'tis that men of merit,
   Thus such sterling worth destroy ;
O ye gods ! did I inherit
   Half the pow'rs of Willoughby !

THE POOR BOWLMAN'S REMONSTRANCE.

THROUGH winter's cold and summer's heat,
   I earn my scanty fare ;
From morn till night, along the street,
   I cry my earthen ware ;
Then, O let pity sway your souls !
   And mock not that decrepitude
   Which draws me from my solitude
To cry my plates and bowls !

From thoughtless youth I often brook
   The trick and taunt of scorn,
And, though indiff'rence marks my look,
   My heart with grief is torn :
Then, O let pity sway your souls !
     Nor sneer contempt in passing by ;
     Nor mock, derisive while I cry,
"Come, buy my plates and bowls."

The potter moulds the passive clay
   To all the forms you see,
And that same Pow'r that formed you
   Hath likewise fashion'd me.
Then, O let pity sway your souls !—
     Though needy, poor as poor can be,
     I stoop not to your charity,
But cry my plates and bowls.*

---

* When decrepitude incapacitates a brother of humanity from gaining a subsistence by any of the less dishonourable callings, and when he possesses that independency of soul which disdains living on charity, it is certainly refinement in barbarity to hurt the feelings of such a one. The above was written on seeing the boys plaguing little Johnnie the Bowlman, while some who thought themselves men were reckoning it excellent sport.

WILL MACNEIL'S ELEGY.

"He was a man without a clag,
His heart was frank without a flaw."
Willie was a wanton wag.

RESPONSIVE to the roaring floods,
Ye winds, howl plaintive thro' the woods,
Thou gloomy sky, pour down hale clouds,
          His death to wail,
For bright as heaven's brightest studs,
          Shin'd Will MacNeil.*

He every selfish thought did scorn,
His warm heart in his looks did burn,
Ilk body own'd his kindly turn,
          An' gait sae leal;
A kinder saul was never born
          Than Will MacNeil.

He ne'er kept up a hidlins plack
To spen' ahint a comrade's back,
But on the table gar'd it whack,
          Wi' free guid will:
Free as the win' on winter stack,
          Was Will MacNeil.

---

* A surgeon in Old Kilpatrick.

He ne'er could bide a narrow saul
To a' the social virtues caul';
He wish'd ilk sic a fiery scaul',
                              His shins to peel:
Nane sic durst herd in fiel' or faul'
                              Wi' Will MacNeil.

He ay abhor'd the spaniel art,
Ay when he spak' 'twas frae the heart,
An honest, open, manly part
                              He ay uphel':
"Guile soud be davel'd i' the dirt,"
                              Said Will MacNeil.

He ne'er had greed to gather gear,
Yet rigid kept his credit clear;
He ever was to Mis'ry dear,
                              Her loss she'll feel:
She ay got saxpence, or a tear,
                              Frae Will MacNeil.

In Scotch antiquities he pridet;
Auld Hardyknute, he kent wha made it;
The bag-pipe, too, he sometimes sey'd it,
                              Pibroch and reel;
Our ain auld language, few could read it
                              Like Will MacNeil.

In wilyart glens he lik'd to stray,
By fuggy rocks, or castle grey ;
Yet ghaist-rid rustics ne'er did say,
                              " Uncanny chiel' !"
They fill'd their horns wi' usquebae
                              To Will MacNeil.

He sail'd and trampet mony a mile,
To visit auld I-columb-kill ;
He clamb the heights o' Jura's isle,
                              Wi' weary speel ;
But siccan sights ay paid the toil,
                              Wi' Will MacNeil.

He rang'd thro' Morven's hills an' glens,
Saw some o' Ossian's moss-grown stanes,
Where rest the low-laid heroes' banes,
                              Deep in the hill ;
He cruin't a cronach to their manes,
                              Kind Will MacNeil.

He was deep-read in nature's beuk,
Explor'd ilk dark mysterious creuk,
Kent a' her laws wi' antrin leuk,
                              An' that right weel ;
But (fate o' genius) death soon teuk
                              Aff Will MacNeil.

O' ilka rock he kent the ore,
He kent the virtues o' ilk flow'r,
Ilk banefu' plant he kent its pow'r,
                    An' warn'd frae ill;
A' nature's warks few could explore
                    Like Will MacNeil.

He kent a' creatures, clute an' tail,
Down frae the lion to the snail,
Up frae the menin to the whale,
                    An' kraken eel;
Scarce ane could tell their gaits sae weel
                    As Will MacNeil.

Nor past he ocht thing slightly by,
But with keen scrutinizing eye,
He to its inmaist bore would pry
                    Wi' wond'rous skill;
An' teaching ithers ay gae joy
                    To Will MacNeil.

He kent auld Archimedes' gait,
What way he burnt the Roman fleet:
" 'Twas by the rays' reflected heat,
                    Frae speculum steel;
For bare refraction ne'er could do't,"
                    Said Will MacNeil.

Yet fame his praise did never rair it,
For poortith's weeds obscur'd his merit,
Forby, he had a bashfu' spirit,
    That sham'd to tell
His worth or wants; let envy spare it
    To Will MacNeil.

O Barra,* thou wast sair to blame !
I here record it to thy shame,
Thou luit the brightest o' thy name
    Unheeded steal
Thro' murky life, to his lang hame—
    Poor Will MacNeil.

He ne'er did wrang to livin' creature,
For ill, Will hadna't in his nature ;
A warm kind heart his leading feature,
    His main-spring wheel,
Ilk virtue grew to noble stature
    In Will MacNeil.

There's no a man that ever kent him,
But wi' their tears will lang lament him,
He hasna' left his match ahint him,
    At hame or fiel',
His worth lang on our minds will prent him—
    Kind Will MacNeil.

---

* The Laird of Barra, Chief of the MacNeil clan.

But close my sang ; my hamert lays,
Are far unfit to speak his praise ;
Our happy nights, our happy days,

           Fareweel, fareweel !

Now dowie, mute—tears speak our waes
           For Will MacNeil !

THE CONTRARY.

Get up, my Muse, an' sound thy chanter,
Nor langer wi' our feelings saunter;
Ilk true-blue Scot get up an' canter,

           He's hale an' weel !

An' lang may fate keep aff mishanter,
           Frae Will MacNeil.

THE
COCK-PIT.

The barbarian-like amusement of seeing two animals instinctively destroy each other certainly affords sufficient scope for the pen of the Satirist ; the author thought he could not do it more effectually than by giving a picture of the COCK-PIT, *and describing a few of the characters who generally may be seen at such glorious contests.*

"THE great, the important hour is come."
O Hope ! thou wily nurse !

I see bad luck behind thy back,
  Dark, brooding, deep remorse.

No fancied muse will I invoke,
  To grace my humble strain,
But sing my song in homely phrase,
  Inspir'd by what I've seen.

Here comes a " feeder " with his charge ;
  'Mong friends 'tis whisper'd straight,
How long he swung him on a string
  To bring him to his weight.*

The carpet's laid—pit-money drawn—
  All's high with expectation ;
With birds bereft of Nature's garb,
  The " handlers " tak' their station.

What roaring, betting, bawling, swearing,
  Now assail the ear !

---

* When a feeder has unluckily fed his bird above the stipulated weight, recourse is had to the ludicrous expedient of making poor chanticleer commence rope-dancing. Being tied on the rope, he flutters, and through fear loses part of his preponderancy. When this happens to be the case, the *knowing ones* who are up to it, will not bet so freely on his prowess, as the operation is supposed to have weakened him.

S

"Three pounds ! "—" four pounds, on Phillip's cock !"
  " Done !—done, by G—d, sir !—here !"

Now cast a serious eye around—
  Behold the motley group,
All gamblers, swindlers, ragamuffins,
  Vot'ries of the stoup.

But why of *it* thus lightly speak?
  The poor man's ae best frien'—
When fortune's sky lours dark an' grim,
  It clears the drumly scene.

Here sits a wretch with meagre face,
  And sullen, drowsy eye ;
Nor speaks he much—last night at cards
  A gamester drained him dry.

Here bawls another ven'trous soul,
  Who risks his every farthing ;
What d—l's the matter though at home
  His wife an' brats are starving.

See, here's a father 'gainst a son,
  A brither 'gainst a brither,
Wha, e'en wi' mair than common spite,
  Bark hard at ane anither.

But see yon fellow all in black,
    His looks speak inward joy ;
Mad-happy since his father's death,
    Sporting his legacy.

And, mark this aged debauchee,
    With red bepimpl'd face—
He fain would bet a crown or two,
    But purse is not in case.

But hark !—what cry !—" He's run !—he's run ! "—
    And loud huzzas take place—
Now, mark what deep dejection sits
    On every *loser's* face.

Observe the *owner*—frantic man,
    With imprecations dread,
He grasps his vanquish'd idol-god,
    And twirls off his head.

But, bliss attend their feeling souls,
    Wha nae sic deeds delight in !
Brutes are but brutes, let men be *men*,
    Nor pleasure in COCK-FIGHTING.

TOWSER,

A TRUE TALE.

" Dogs are honest creatures,
Ne'er fawn on any that they love not;—
And I'm a friend to dogs,—
They ne'er betray their masters."

IN mony an instance, without doubt,
The man may copy frae the brute,
And by th' example grow much wiser;—
Then read the short memoirs of Towser.

With def'rence to our great Lavaters,
Wha judge a' mankind by their features,
There's mony a smiling, pleasant-fac'd cock,
That wears a heart no worth a custock;
While mony a visage, antic, droll,
O'er-veils a noble, gen'rous soul.
With Towser this was just the case:
He had an ill-faur't tawtie face,
His mak' was something like a messin,
But big, an' quite unprepossessin',
His master caft him frae some fallows,
Wha had him doom'd unto the gallows,

Because (sae hap'd poor Towser's lot),
He wadna tear a comrade's throat;
Yet, in affairs of love or honour,
He'd stan' his part amang a hun'er,
An' whare'er fighting was a merit,
He never failed to shaw his spirit.

He never girn'd in neighbour's face,
Wi' wild, ill-natur'd scant o' grace,
Nor e'er accosted ane wi' smiles,
Then, soon as turn'd, wad bite his heels,
Nor ever kent the courtier art,
To fawn wi' rancour at his heart;
Nor aught kent he o' cankert quarlin',
Nor snarlin' just for sake o' snarlin';
Ye'd pinch him sair afore he'd growl,
Whilk ever shaws a magnanimity of soul.

But what adds maistly to his fame,
An' will immortalize his name—
(Immortalize!—presumptive wight!
Thy lines are dull as darkest night,
Without ae spark o' wit or glee,
To light them through futurity.)
E'en be it sae;—poor Towser's story,
Though lamely tauld, will speak his glory.

'Twas in the month o' cauld December,
When Nature's fire seem'd just an ember,

An' growlin' winter bellow'd forth,
In storms and tempests frae the north—
When honest Towser's loving master,
Regardless o' the surly bluster,
Set out to the neist borough town,
To buy some needments o' his own ;
An', case some purse-pest soud way-lay him,
He took his trusty servant wi' him.

His bus'ness done, 'twas near the gloamin',
An' ay the king o' storms was foamin',
The doors did ring—lum-pigs down tuml'd,
The strawns gush'd big—the sinks loud ruml'd ;
Auld grannies spread their looves, an' sigh't,
Wi' " O sirs ! what an' awfu' night ! "
Poor Towser shook his sides a' draigl'd,
An's master grudg'd that he had taigl'd ;
But, wi' his merchandizing load,
Come weel, come wae, he took the road.
Now clouds drave o'er the fields like drift,
Night flung her black cleuk o'er the lift ;
An' thro' the naked trees and hedges,
The horrid storm redoubl'd rages :
An', to complete his piteous case,
It blew directly in his face.
Whiles 'gainst the footpath stabs he thumped,
Whiles o'er the coots in holes he plumped ;

But on he gaed, an' on he waded,
Till he at length turn'd faint and jaded.
To gang he could nae langer bide,
But lay down by the bare dyke-side.
Now, bairns and wife rush'd on his soul—
He groan'd—poor Towser loud did howl,
An', mournin', couret down aside him ;
But, oh ! his master couldna heed him,
For now his senses 'gan to dozen,
His vera life-streams maist war' frozen ;
An't seemed as if the cruel skies
Exulted o'er their sacrifice,
For fierce the win's did o'er him hiss,
An' dash'd the sleet on his cauld face.

As on a rock, far, far frae land,
Twa ship-wreck'd sailors shiv'ring stand,
If chance a vessel they descry,
Their hearts exult with instant joy,
Sae was poor Towser joy'd to hear
The tread o' trav'llers drawing near,
He ran, an' yowl'd, and fawn'd upon 'em,
But couldna mak' them understan' him,
Till, tugging at the foremost's coat,
He led them to the mournfu' spot,
Where, cauld an' stiff his master lay,
To the rude storm a helpless prey.

Wi' Caledonian sympathy
They bore him kindly on the way,
Until they reach'd a cottage bien.
They tauld the case, war' welcomed in—
The rousin' fire, the cordial drop,
Restor'd him soon to life an' hope ;
Fond raptures beam'd in Towser's eye,
An' antic gambols spake his joy.

Wha reads this simple tale may see
The worth of sensibility,
And learn frae it to be humane—
In TOWSER's life he sav'd his ain.

THE RESOLVE.

" Him who ne'er listen'd to the voice of praise,
The silence of neglect can ne'er appal."

BEATTIE.

'TWAS on a sunny Sabbath day,
When wark-worn bodies get their play,
(Thanks to the rulers o' the nation,
Wha gi'e us all a toleration,
To gang, as best may please oursel's ;
Some to the kirk, some to the fiel's),

I've wander'd out, wi' serious leuk,
To read twa page on Nature's beuk;
For lang I've thought, as little harm in
Hearing a lively out-fiel' sermon,
Even tho' rowted by a stirk,
As that aft bawl'd in crowded kirk,
By some proud, stern, polemic wight,
Wha cries, " My way alone is right ! "
Wha lairs himsel' in controversy,
Then d—s his neighbours without mercy,
As if the fewer that were spar'd,
These few would be the better ser'd.
   Now to my tale—digression o'er—
I wander'd out by Stanely tow'r,
The lang grass on its tap did wave,
Like weeds upon a warrior's grave;
Whilk seem'd to mock the bloody braggers,
An' grow on theirs as rank's on beggars'—
But hold, I'm frae the point again.—
I wander'd up Gleniffer glen;
There, leaning 'gainst a mossy rock,
I, musing, ey'd the passing brook,
That in its murmurs seem'd to say,
" 'Tis thus thy life glides fast away :
Observe the bubbles on my stream:
Like them, Fame is an empty dream,
They blink a moment to the sun,
Then burst, and are for ever gone :

So Fame's a bubble of the mind ;
Possess'd, 'tis nought but empty wind,
No courtly gem e'er purchas'd dearer,
An' ne'er can satisfy the wearer.
Let them wha hae a bleezing share o't
Confess the truth, they sigh for mair o't.
Then let Contentment be thy cheer,
An' never soar aboon thy sphere ;
Rude storms assail the mountain's brow
That lightly skiff the vale below."

A gaudy *rose* was growing near,
Proud, tow'ring on its leafy brier ;
In fancy's ear it seem'd to say—
" Sir, have you seen a flower so gay ?
The poets in my praise combine,
Comparing Chloe's charms to mine ;
The sunbeams for my favour sue me,
And dark-brow'd night comes down to woo me ;
But when I shrink from his request,
He draps his tears upon my breast,
And in his misty cloud sits wae,
Till chas'd awa' by rival day—
That streamlet's grov'lling grunting fires me,
Since no ane sees me but admires me ;
See yon bit *violet* 'neath my view :
Wee sallow thing, its nose is blue !
An' that bit *primrose* 'side the breckan,
Poor yellow ghaist, it seems forsaken !

The sun ne'er throws't ae transient glow,
Unless when passing whether or no ;
But wisely spurning ane sae mean,
He blinks on me frae morn till e'en."

To which the *primrose* calm replied—
" Poor gaudy gowk, suppress your pride,
For soon the strong flow'r-sweeping blast
Shall strew your honours in the dust ;
While I, beneath my lowly bield,
Will live an' bloom frae harm conceal'd ;
An' while the heavy rain-draps pelt you,
Ye'll maybe think on what I've tell't you."
The *rose*, derisive, seem'd to sneer,
An' wav'd upon its bonny brier.

Now dark'ning clouds began to gather,
Presaging sudden change of weather ;
I wander'd hame by Stanely green,
Deep pond'ring what I'd heard an' seen,
Firmly resolv'd to shun from hence
The dangerous steeps of eminence,
To drap this rhyming trade for ever,
And creep thro' life, a plain, day-plodding weaver.

CONNEL AND FLORA.

A SCOTTISH LEGEND.

———

" THE western sun shines o'er the loch,
　And gilds the mountain's brow,
And what are Nature's smiles to me,
　Without the smile of you ?

"O will ye go to Garnock side,
　Where birks and woodbines twine !
I've sought you oft to be my bride,
　When ! when will ye be mine ? "

" Oft as ye sought me for your bride,
　My mind spoke frae my e'e ;
Then wherefore seek to win a heart
　That is not mine to gi'e ?

" With Connel down the dusky dale
　Long plighted are my vows ;
He won my heart before I wist
　I had a heart to lose."

The fire flash'd from his eyes of wrath,
　Dark gloom'd his heavy brow,
He grasp'd her in his arms of strength,
　And strain'd to lay her low.

She wept and cried—the rocks replied—
  The echoes from their cell,
On fairy-wing, swift bore her voice
  To Connel of the dale.

With vengeful haste he hied him up,
  But when stern Donald saw,
The youth approach, deep-stung with guilt,
  He, shame-fac'd, fled awa'.

" Ah ! stay my Connel—sheath thy sword—
  O, do not him pursue !
For mighty are his arms of strength,
  And thou the fight may rue."

" No !—wait thee here,—I'll soon return,—
  I mark'd him from the wood !
The lion-heart of jealous love
  Burns for its rival's blood !

" Ho ! stop thee, coward,—villain vile !
  With all thy boasted art,
My sword's blade soon shall dim its shine,
  Within thy reynard-heart ! "

" Ha! foolish stripling, dost thou urge
  The deadly fight with me ?

This arm strove hard in Flodden field,
   Dost think 'twill shrink from thee ! "

" Thy frequent vaunts of Flodden field,
   Were ever fraught with guile :
For honour ever marks the brave,
   But thou'rt a villain vile ! "

Their broad blades glitter to the sun—
   The woods resound each clash—
Young Connel sinks 'neath Donald's sword,
   With deep and deadly gash.

" Ah ! dearest Flora, soon our morn
   Of love is overcast !—
The hills look dim—Alas ! my love ! "—
   He groan'd and breath'd his last.

" Stay, ruthless ruffian !—murderer !—
   Here glut thy savage wrath !—
Be thou the baneful minister
   To join us low in death ! "

In wild despair she tore her hair,
   Sunk speechless by his side—
Mild Evening wept in dewy tears,
   And, wrapt in night, she died.

LINES

Written on the back of a Guinea Note.

Thou little badge of independence,
Thou mak'st e'en pride dance mean attendance;
Thou sure has magic in thy looks,
Gives p——ts a taste for tasteless books;
Makes lawyers lie, make courtiers flatter,
And wily statesmen patriots clatter;
Makes ancient maids seem young again,
At sixty, beauteous as sixteen;
Makes foes turn friends, and friends turn foes,
And drugmen brew the pois'ning dose,
And ev'n as common say prevails,
Thou mak'st e'en Justice tip the scales.

LINES

Written on seeing a Spider dart out upon a Fly.

Let gang your grip, ye auld grim devil!
Else with ae crush I'll mak' you civil—
Like debtor-bard in merchant's claw,
The fient o' mercy ye've at a'!
Sae spite an' malice (hard to ken 'em),
Sit spewin' out their secret venom—

Ah, hear !—poor buzzart's roaring " Murder : "
Let gang !—Na, faith !—thou scorn'st my order !—
Weel, tak' thee that !—vile ruthless creature !
For wha but hates a savage nature ?
Sic fate to ilk unsocial kebar
Who lays a snare to wrang his neighbour.

LINES

On seeing a Fop pass an old Beggar.

HE who, unmov'd, can hear the suppliant cry
  Of pallid wretch, plac'd on the pathway side,
Nor deigns one pitying look, but passes by,
  In all the pomp of self-adoring pride :
So may some great man vex his little soul,
  When he, obsequious, makes his lowest bow ;
Turn from him with a look that says, " Vain fool,"
And speak to some poor man whom he would shame to know.

LINES

On a country Justice in the South.

WHAT gars yon gentry gang wi' Jock,
  An' ca' him Sir and Master ?

The greatest dunce, the biggest block,
   That ever Nature cuist her ;
Yet see, they've plac'd this human stock
   Strict justice to dispense:
Which plainly shows yon meikle folk
   Think *siller* stands for *sense.*

THE MORALIST.

"BARB'ROUS!" cried John, in humanizing mood,
To Will, who'd shot a blackbird in the wood;
" The savage Indian pleads necessity,
But thou, barbarian wretch ! hast no such plea."
Hark !—click the ale-house door—his wife comes in—
" Dear, help's man, John !—preserve me, what d'ye mean !
Sax helpless bairns—the deil confound your drouth !
Without ae bit to stop a single mouth."
"Get hame," cried John, " else, jade ! I'll kick your ——! "
Sure such humanity is all ——.

A LESSON.

QUOTH gobbin Tom of Lancashire,
   To northern Jock, a lowland drover,
" Thoose are foin *kaise* thai'rt driving there,
   They've zure been fed on English clover."

" *Foin kaise !*" quoth Jock, " ye bleth'rin' hash,
   Deil draw your nose as lang's a sow's !
That tauk o' yours is queer-like trash ;
   Foin kaise ! poor gowk !—their names are KOOSE."
The very fault which I in others see,
Like kind, or worse, perhaps is seen in me.

LINES
On a Flatterer.

I HATE a flatt'rer as I hate the devil,
   But Tom's a very, very pleasing dog,
Of course, let's speak of him in terms more civil—
   I hate a flatt'rer as I hate a hog ;
Not but applause is music to mine ears—
   He is a knave who says he likes it not,
But when, in friendship's guise, deceit appears,
   'Twould fret a Stoic's frigid temper hot.

A RESOLVE.

Written on hearing a fellow tell some stories to the hurt
of his best friends.

As secret's the grave be the man whom I trust ;
   What friendship imparts still let honour conceal,
A plague on those babblers, their names be accurs'd !
   Still first to *enquire*, and the first to *reveal*.

As open as day let me be with the man
  Who tells me my failings from motives upright,
But when of those gossiping fools I meet one,
  Let me fold in my soul and be close as the night.

LINES
Written with a pencil in a Tap-Room.

THIS warl's a tap-room owre an' owre,
  Whare ilk ane tak's his caper,
Some taste the sweet, some drink the sour,
  As waiter Fate sees proper ;
Let mankind live, ae social core,
  An' drap a' selfish quar'ling,
An' when the Landlord ca's his score,
  May ilk ane's clink be sterling.

LINES.

RICH Gripus pretends he's my patron and friend,
  That at all times to serve me he's willing,
But he looks down so sour on the suppliant poor,
  That I'd starve ere I'd ask him one shilling.

THE PROMOTION.
For Mr. J. L.

WHEN the d-v-l got notice old Charon was dead,
He wish'd for some blockhead to row in his stead ;

For he fear'd one with int'lect discov'ries might make,
Of his tortures and racks, 'tother side of the lake ;
So for true native dulness and want of discernment,
He sought the whole world, and gave John the preferment.

ANTIPATHY.

I SCORN the selfish, purse-proud ——,
Who piques himself on being rich
With twoscore pounds, late legacied,
Sav'd by his half-starv'd father's greed—
To former neighbours not one word !
He bows obsequious to my Lord.
In public see him—how he capers !
Looks big—stops short—pulls out his papers,
And from a silly, puppish dunce,
Commences the great man at once.

LINES,
TO W. ——,
Noted for his assumed sanctity.

WHAT need'st thou dread the end of sin,
  The dire reward of evil ;
Keep but that black infernal grin,
  'Twill scar the vera d-v-l.

W. ————'S RECIPE
For attaining a character.

I F thou on earth wouldst live respecket,
In few words, here's the way to make it——·
Get dog-thick wi' the parish priest,
To a' his foibles mould thy taste ;
Wh'at he condemns, do thou condemn,
What he approves do thou the same ;
Cant scripture words in every case,
" Salvashion, saunt, redemshion, grace ;"
But controverted points forbear,
For thou may'st shew thy weakness there ;
Look grave, demure as any owl——
A cheerful look might damn the whole,
Gang rigid to the kirk on Sunday,
With face as lang's a gothic window ;
But from these maxims should'st thou sever,
Poor profligate ! thou'rt lost for ever.

LINES
On a man of CHARACTER.

W EE A —— ——, self-sainted wight,
  If e'er he won to heaven,
The veriest wretch, though black as pitch,
  May rest he'll be forgiven :

Wi' haly pride he cocks his nose,
An' talks of honest dealings,
For when our webs are at the close,
He nips aff twa three shillings.

EPIGRAMS.

CRIED Dick to Bob, " Great news to-day !"
" Great news," quoth Bob, " what great news, pray? "
Said Dick, " Our gallant tars at sea
Have gain'd a brilliant victory."
" Indeed !" cried Bob, " it may be true,
But that, you know, is nothing new."

" FRENCH threats of invasion let Britons defy,
And spike the proud frogs if our coast they should crawl on."
Yes, statesmen know well that our *spirits* are high,
The financier has rais'd them *two shillings per gallon.*

NATURE, impartial in her ends,
When she made man the strongest,
For scrimpet *pith* to mak' amends,
Made woman's *tongue* the *longest.*

EPITAPHS.

———

On seeing a ONCE WORTHY CHARACTER *lying in a state of inebriation in the street.*

———

IF loss of worth may draw the pitying tear,
Stop, passenger, and pay that tribute here—
Here lies, whom all with justice did commend,
The rich man's pattern, and the poor man's friend ;
He cheer'd pale Indigence's bleak abode,
He oft remov'd Misfortune's galling load :
Nor was his bounty to one sect confin'd,
His goodness beam'd alike on all mankind ;
Now, lost in folly, all his virtues sleep,—
Let's mind his former worth, and o'er his frailties weep.

———

FOR T. B., ESQ.,

A Gentleman whom Indigence never solicited in vain.

EVER green be the sod o'er kind Tom of the wood,
   For the poor man he ever supplied;

We may weel say, alas! for our ain scant o' grace,
    That we reck'd not his worth till he died:
Though no rich marble bust mimics grief o'er his dust,
    Yet fond memory his virtues will save.
Oft at lone twilight hour sad remembrance shall pour
    Her sorrows, unfeign'd, o'er his grave.

On a Crabbed Old Maid.

HERE slaethorn Mary's hurcheon bouk,
    Resigns its fretfu' bristles ;—
And is she dead !—no—reader, look,
    Her grave's o'ergrown wi' *thistles*.

On a farthing-gatherer.

HERE lies Jamie Wight, wha was wealthy an' proud,
Few shar'd his regard an' far fewer his goud ;
He liv'd unesteem'd, and he died unlamented,
The *kirk* gat his gear an' auld Jamie is *sainted*.

EPISTLE TO ROBERT ALLAN.

KILBARCHAN.—1807.

DEAR ROBIN,

The Muse is now a wee at leisure,
An' sits her down wi' meikle pleasure,
To skelp ye aff a blaud * o' rhyme,
As near's she can to true sublime;
But here's the rub,—poor poet-devils,
We're compassed round wi' mony evils;
We jerk oursel's into a fever
To give the world something clever,
An' after a' perhaps we muddle
In vile prosaic stagnant puddle.
For me—I seldom choose a subject,
My rhymes are oft without an object;
I let the Muse e'en tak' her win',
And dash awa' thro' thick and thin:
For Method's sic a servile creature,
She spurns the wilds o' simple nature,
And paces on, wi' easy art,
A lang day's journey frae the heart:—
Sae what comes uppermaist you'll get it,
Be't good or ill, for you I write it.

---

* " Blaud "—A large piece of anything.

How fares my worthy friend, the bard ?
Be peace and honour his reward !
May every ill that gars us fyke, *
Bad webs, toom pouches, and sic like,
An' ought that would his spirit bend,
Be ten miles distant from my friend.
Alas ! this wicked endless war,
Rul'd by some vile malignant star,
Has sunk poor Britain low indeed,
Has robb'd Industry o' her bread,
An' dash'd the sair-won cog o' crowdie †
Frae mony an honest eident body;
While Genius, dying through neglect,
Sinks down amidst the general wreck
Just like twa cats tied tail to tail,
They worry at it tooth and nail ;
They girn, they bite in deadly wrath,
An' what is't for ? for nought, in faith !
Wee Lourie Frank ‡ wi' brazen snout,
Nae doubt would like to scart us out,
For proud John Bull, aye us'd to hone him,
We'll no gi'e o'er to spit upon him ;
But Lourie's rais'd to sic degree,
John would be wise to let him be ;

---

* " Fyke "—Makes one uneasy.
† " Crowdie "—Oatmeal porridge.
‡ A personification of France.

Else aiblins, as his wearin' aul',
Frank yet may tear him spawl frae spawl, *
For wi' the mony chirts he's gotten,
I fear his *constitution's* rotten.

But while the bullying blades o' Europe
Are boxing ither to a syrup,
Let's mind oursel's as weel's we can,
An' live in peace, like man and man,
An' no cast out and fecht like brutes,
Without a cause for our disputes.

When I read o'er your kind epistle,
I didna dance, nor sing, nor whistle,
But jump'd, and cried, Huzza! huzza!
Like Robin Roughhead in the play :—
But to be serious—jest aside,
I felt a glow o' secret pride,
Thus to be roos'd † by ane like you;
Yet doubted if sic praise was due,
Till self thus reason'd in the matter :
Ye ken that Robin scorns to flatter,
And ere he'd prostitute his quill,
He'd rather burn his rhyming mill—
Enough ! I cried—I've gain'd my end,
Since I ha'e pleas'd my worthy friend.

---

† Limb from limb,
* "Roos'd"—Extolled.

My sangs are now before the warl',
An' some may praise, and some may snarl;
They ha'e their faults, yet I can tell
Nane sees them clearer than mysel';
But still, I think, they, too, inherit,
Amang the dross, some sparks o' merit.

Then come, my dear Parnassian brither,
Let's lay our poet heads thegither,
And sing our ain sweet native scenes,
Our streams, our banks, and rural plains,
Our woods, our shaws, and flow'ry holms,.
An' mountains clad wi' purple blooms,
Wi' burnies bickerin' down their braes,
Reflecting back the sunny rays:
Ye've Semple Woods,* and Calder Glen, †

---

* *Semple Woods.*—The lands of Castlesemple, under the various proprietors, have always been ornamented with thriving plantations, yielding a constant supply of very valuable timber. The policies of Castlesemple were the most beautiful and extensive in this district of country, and the aristocratic ancient trees, single and in clumps, were certainly worthy the laudation of a poet. The once potent house of Sempill were in possession of the estate in 1214, and it descended from generation to generation in that family till 1727, when Colonel William M'Dowall acquired it from Hew, 11th Lord Scmpill. This Lord Sempill, a Brigadier-General, was appointed Colonel of the *Black Watch*, or 42nd Foot, on 14th January, 1741, and during his command the regiment was called Lord Sempill's Highlanders. In 1743, the regiment was marched to London, reviewed on 14th May by General Wade, and dispatched to Flanders, where they made a gallant defence under their brave Colonel. In 1813, Castlesemple estate passed into the possession of John Rae or Harvey, and it has continued in that family till the present time.

† *Calder Glen.*—This romantic glen—sometimes called Calderwood Glen—in the romantic parish of Lochwinnoch, is worth visiting, with its sylvan scenery, and

And Locherbank, * sweet fairy den !
And Auchinames, † a glorious theme !
Where Crawfurd ‡ lived, of deathless name,
Where Sempill § sued his lass to win,
And Nelly rose and let him in ;

---

has been the theme of the American Ornithologist, Alexander Wilson, in his "Calder Banks." The author of "Watty and Meg" lived in the neighbourhood for several years, and Tannahill visited it frequently, and notices Calderwood Glen in his "Jessie, the Flower o' Dunblane."

* *Locher Bank.*—Another sweet place in the Parish of Kilbarchan. The scenery on the rivulet of Locher is beautiful, and on entering the policies of Craigends it becomes perfectly enchanting.

† *Auchinames.*—The old Barony of Auchinames, belonging to the ancient family of the Crawfurds, is also situated in the Parish of Kilbarchan, and has now been feued out to various proprietors.

‡ *Crawfurd.*—This is Robert Crawfurd, youngest son of Patrick Crawfurd of Auchinames, by his first marriage, He resided a considerable time in France, and on returning to Scotland was drowned in May, 1733. He was an elegant writer of pastoral poetry, and has found a first place in the ranks of lyric poets. He was the author of "The Bush aboon Traquair," "My dearie, an' ye dee," "Tweedside," and other songs.

§ *Sempill.*—This was Francis Sempill, one of the hereditary poets of Belltrees, and Sheriff of Renfrewshire. Francis Sempill, the son of Robert Sempill of Belltrees, author of the elegy on Habbie Simpson, was born about 1630, married on 3rd April, 1655, and died suddenly on 12th March, 1682, in his house in Paisley. He was the author of "Maggie Lauder," "The Blythesome Bridal," "She raise an' loot me in," and other poems. A *Nelly* was the heroine of the latter song, but there is no evidence that she was Helen Crawfurd of Auchinames, although our author Tannahill, according to the tradition of the period, without weighing dates, says the latter named place was

> " Where Sempill sued his lass to win,
> And Nelly rose and let him in."

Where Habbie Simpson * lang did play,
The first o' pipers in his day;
And though aneath the turf langsyne,
Their sangs and tunes shall never tyne.
Sae, Robin, briskly ply the Muse;
She warms our hearts, expands our views,
Gars every sordid passion flee,
And waukens every sympathy.

---

* *Habbie Simpson.*—He was a well-known piper, a wandering minstrel, who generally resided in the Parish of Kilbarchan, and attended weddings, merry-makings, and fairs. On the death of this celebrated piper, his fame became more extended from Robert Sempill of Belltrees, eldest son and third child of Sir James Sempill of Belltrees, having written the popular elegy—"The Life and Death of the Piper of Kilbarchan, or the Epitaph on Habbie Simpson." Robert Sempill was born in 1599, was educated at the Paisley Grammar School, and matriculated in Glasgow University in the kalends of March, 1613. He succeeded to the estate of Belltrees and other heritable properties on the death of his father, who died at his great lodging or tenement at the head of Saint Mirin's Wynd, Paisley, in 1625. In the rude days of the piper, common people with the christian name of Robert were vulgarly called Hob, Hab, Hobbie, and Habbie, according to the district of country in which they resided. In ancient criminal trials, persons were indicted both by their proper and popular names, and the names of Hob, *alias* Robert, frequently occur. Pitcairn, the learned editor of *Criminal Trials*, in reporting the cases of Robert Eldwalde, *alias* "Hob the King;" Robert *alias* Hob Ormeston; and Robert Turnbull, *alias* "Fabel Hob," in a note to the first of these cases, explains to his readers that "'Hob' is a familiar border abbreviation for Robert, not *Halbert*." The border names of Hob and Hobbie, and the west country softened names of Hab and Habbie, all represent Robert, and not Halbert. Habbie Simpson, under his proper name of Robert Simpson, piper, occasionally appears in the Council books of Paisley for rude manners or piper immorality. His true name would be well known

Now, wishing Fate may never tax you,
Wi' cross, nor loss, to thraw and vex you,
But keep you hale till ninety-nine,
Till you and yours in honour shine,
Shall ever be my earnest prayer,
While I've a friendly wish to spare.

---

to the Bailies and the whole inhabitants of that town, the population at the time not exceeding 915. Those names have been changed into Bob, Robin and Rabbie, and our author himself was called by his companions Robin Tannahill. The cleverly written elegy of Robert Sempill brought Robert Simpson, *alias* Habbie, into greater fame than the author himself of the elegiac poem, and the peculiar people of Kilbarchan to elevate the vulgar name of the parish piper erected a statue to the memory of Habbie Simpson instead of the gifted poet and famed author

ODE FOR BURNS' BIRTHDAY, 1810. *

AGAIN the happy day returns,
    A day to Scotchmen ever dear,
    Tho' bleakest of the changeful year,
It blest us with a BURNS.

Fierce the whirling blast may blow,
Drifting wide the crispy snow;
Rude the ruthless storms may sweep,
Howling round our mountain's steep;
While the heavy lashing rains,
Swell our rivers, drench our plains,
And the angry ocean roars
Round our broken craggy shores;
But, mindful of our poet's worth,
We hail the honoured day that gave him birth.

---

* Recited by the President at the celebration of Burns' Birthday, by the
Paisley Burns Club, 1810.   The minute of the meeting, taken from the official
record of the society, elsewhere referred to, is as follows :—" Paisley, 29th
January, 1810.—This evening the admirers of Scottish Poetry met to celebrate the birth of their favourite bard.   A most appropriate address was
delivered by the president, Mr. William Wylie, who filled the chair with
distinguished ability.   The following ode, written for the occasion by Mr.
Robert Tannahill, highly gratified the company when recited by the president."

Come, ye vot'ries of the lyre,
Trim the torch of heav'nly fire,
Raise the song in Scotia's praise,
Sing anew her bonnie braes,
Sing her thousand siller streams,
Bickering to the sunny beams;
Sing her sons beyond compare,
Sing her dochters, peerless, fair;
Sing, till Winter's storms be o'er,
The matchless bards that sung before;
And I, the meanest of the Muse's train,
Shall join my feeble aid to swell the strain.

Dear Scotia, though thy clime be cauld,
Thy sons were ever brave and bauld,
Thy dochters modest, kind, and leal,
The fairest in creation's fiel';
Alike inur'd to every toil,
Thou'rt foremost in the battle broil;
Prepar'd alike in peace and weir,
To guide the plough or wield the spear;
As the mountain torrent raves.
Dashing through its rugged caves,
So the Scottish legions pour
Dreadful in the avenging hour;
But when Peace, with kind accord,
Bids them sheath the sated sword,

See them in their native vales,
Jocund as the Summer gales,
Cheering labour all the day,
With some merry roundelay.
　　Dear Scotia, though thy nights be drear,
When surly Winter rules the year,
Around thy cottage hearths are seen
The glow of health, the cheerful mien;
The mutual glance that fondly shares,
A neighbour's joys, a neighbour's cares:
Here oft, while raves the wind and weet,
The canty lads and lasses meet.
Sae light of heart, sae full of glee,
Their gaits sae artless and sae free,
The hours of joy come dancing on,
To share their frolic and their fun.
Here many a song and jest goes round,
With tales of ghosts and rites profound,
Perform'd in dreary wizard glen,
By wrinkled hags and warlike men,
Or of the hell-fee'd crew combin'd,
Carousing on the midnight wind,
On some infernal errand bent,
While darkness shrouds their black intent;
But chiefly, BURNS, thy songs delight
To charm the weary winter night,
And bid the lingering moments flee,
Without a care unless for thee,

Wha sang sae sweet and dee't sae soon,
And sought the native sphere aboon.
Thy " Lovely Jean," thy " Nannie, O,"
Thy much lov'd "Caledonia,"
Thy " Wat ye wha's in yonder town,"
Thy " Banks and Braes o' Bonnie Doon,"
Thy "Shepherdess on Afton Braes,"
Thy " Logan Lassie's " bitter waes,
Are a' gane o'er, sae sweetly tun'd,
That e'en the storm, pleased with the sound,
Fa's lown, * and sings with eerie slight,
" O let me in this ae, ae night."
   Alas ! our best, our dearest Bard,
How poor, how great was his reward ;
Unaided he has fix'd his name,
Immortal, in the rolls of fame ;
   Yet who can hear without a tear,
   What sorrows wrung his manly breast,
To see his little, helpless, filial band,
Imploring succour from a father's hand,
   And there no succour near ?
Himself the while with sick'ning woes opprest,
   Fast hast'ning on to where the weary rest—
For this let Scotia's bitter tears atone,
She reck'd not half his worth till he was gone.

---

* " Lown "—Softly.

Songs.

SONGS.

THE MIDGES DANCE ABOON THE BURN.

THE midges dance aboon the burn,
　The dews begin to fa',
The paitricks * doun the rushy holm,
　Set up their evening ca'.
Now loud and clear the blackbird's sang
　Rings through the briery shaw,
While flitting gay, the swallows play
　Around the castle wa'.

Beneath the golden gloamin' sky,
　The mavis mends her lay,
The redbreast pours his sweetest strains,
　To charm the lingering day;
While weary yeldrins † seem to wail
　Their little nestlings torn,
The merry wren, frae den to den,
　Gaes jinking through the thorn.

---

* " Paitrick "—Partridge.
† " Yeldrin "—Yellow-hammer.

The roses fauld their silken leaves,
 The foxglove shuts its bell,
The honeysuckle and the birk
 Spread fragrance through the dell.
Let others crowd the giddy court
 Of mirth and revelry,
The simple joys that Nature yields
 Are dearer far to me.

GLOOMY WINTER'S NOW AWA'.*

Air—"Lord Balgownie's Favourite."

GLOOMY Winter's now awa',
Saft the westlan' breezes blaw ;
'Mang the birks of Stanley shaw
The mavis sings fu' cheerie, O ;

* R. A. Smith gives the following interesting account of the occasion of the composition of this piece :—" Miss ———— of ———— was particularly fond of the Scottish melody, 'Lord Balgownie's Favourite,' and had expressed a wish to see it united to good poetry. I accordingly applied to my friend, who produced his song, 'Gloomy Winter's now awa','in a few days. As soon as I had arranged the air, with symphonies and accompaniment for the pianoforte, I waited on the lady, who was much delighted with the verses, and begged of me to invite the author to take a walk with me to the house at any leisure time. I knew that it

Sweet the crawflower's early bell
Decks Gleniffer's * dewy dell,
Blooming like thy bonny sel',
    My young, my artless dearie, O.

---

would be almost impossible to prevail on Robert to allow himself to be introduced by *fair means*, so, for once, I made use of the only alternative in my power by beguiling him thither during our first Saturday's ramble, under the pretence of being obliged to call with some music I had with me for the ladies. . This, however, could not be effected, till I had promised not to make him known, in case any of the family came to the door ; but how great was his astonishment when Miss ———— came forward to invite him into the house by name. I shall never forget the awkwardness with which he accompanied us to the music room. He sat as it were quite petrified, till the magic of the music and the great affability of the ladies reconciled him to his situation. In a short time Mr. ———— came in, was introduced to his visitor in due form, and with that goodness of heart and simplicity of manner, for which he is so deservedly esteemed by all who have the pleasure of knowing him, chatted with his guest till near dinner time, when Robert again became terribly uneasy, as Mr. ———— insisted on our staying to dine with the family. Many a rueful look was cast to me, and many an excuse was made to get away, but, alas ! there was no escaping with a good grace, and finding that I was little inclined to understand his signals, the kind request was at length reluctantly complied with.

    *   *   *   *   After a cheerful glass or two, the restraint he was under gradually wore away, and he became tolerably communicative. I believe that, when we left the mansion, the poet entertained very different sentiments from those with which he had entered it. He had formed an opinion that nothing, save distant pride and cold formality, was to be met with from people in the higher walks of life, but on experiencing the very reverse of his imaginings, he was quite delighted, and when Mr. ————'s name happened to be mentioned in his hearing afterwards, it generally called forth expressions of respect and admiration. ' Gloomy winter's now awa' ' became a very popular song, and was the reigning favourite in Edinburgh for a considerable time.

    * *Glen-Iffer.*—There have been several definitions suggested of this compound word. One person stating it is derived from the Gaelic, *Glenn-Ibher*, the *adder* glen ; a second, from *Glenn-Uigher*, the *yew* glen ; a third, from *Glenn-Naither*,

Come, my lassie, let us stray
O'er Glenkilloch's * sunny brae,
Blythely spend the gowden day,
    Midst joys that never weary, O.

Tow'ring o'er the Newton † woods,
Lav'rocks fan the snaw-white clouds,
Siller saughs, wi' downy buds,
    Adorn the banks sae briery, O.

---

the *serpent* glen ; and a fourth, *Glean-Ifurin, hell of the Druids.*   In visiting Glen-Iffer when the Espedair is in full flood, and standing on the high projecting precipice, looking down into the dark, rugged, deep ravine, the impetuous mountain stream furiously dashing downwards from rock to rock with deafening din, causing the spray to rise in clouds of mist, at once realises the graphic description contained in the interpretation of the Gaelic words in the fourth definition.   Tannahill himself, in an epistle to his friend, James Scadlock, nearly in equally graphic words, realises the same description, when he asks his friend to

    " Think on our langsyne happy hours,
      Spent where the burn wild rapid pours,
        And o'er the horrid dizzy steep
        Dashes her mountain stores."

  * *Glenkilloch.*—The farm of Killoch is situated in Neilston parish, in the Fereneze portion of the mountainous range dividing that parish from the parish of Paisley, and, having a southern exposure, the lyric poet has described the place as "Glenkilloch's sunny brae."   In Killoch Glen there are a succession of beautiful cascades, or falls of water, before the Killoch burn sinks into the bosom of the Levern rivulet near Broadley Mill.

  † *Newton.*—The lands of Newton are situated at a short distance to the northwest of Stanely Castle.   These lands were acquired by Claud Alexander, and he and his descendants were the respected landlords for upwards of a hundred years. He was the ancestor and founder of the present Ballochmyle family of Alexander.

Round the sylvan fairy nooks,
Feath'ry breckans fringe the rocks,
'Neath the brae the burnie jouks,
  And ilka thing is cheerie, O.

Trees may bud, and birds may sing,
Flowers may bloom, and verdure spring,
Joy to me they canna bring,
  Unless wi' thee, my dearie, O.

LOUDON'S BONNIE WOODS AND BRAES. *

Air—" Earl Moira's Welcome to Scotland.

LOUDON'S bonnie woods and braes,
  I maun lea' them a', lassie ;
Wha can thole when Britain's faes,
  Would gi'e Britons law, lassie ?

Speirs of Elderslie acquired the lands of Newton about a century ago, and in the time of Tannahill it was a finely wooded estate.   The mansion house built by the Alexanders was sold by the Speirs, and the purchaser, about 1806, re-erected the old materials at the south-west angle of Saint James Street and Glen Lane, Paisley, and it still bears the name of "Newton House."

* *Loudon's bonnie woods and braes.*—The place here mentioned is the beautiful plantations and heights surrounding Loudon Castle in Ayrshire, that belonged to the Countess of Loudon, Flora Mure Campbell, who succeeded to the peerage at the age of six, on the death of her father on 28th April, 1786. The Countess was

Wha would shun the field o' danger?
Wha frae Fame would live a stranger?
Now when Freedom bids avenge her,
   Wha would shun her ca', lassie?
Loudon's bonnie woods and braes
Ha'e seen our happy bridal days,
And gentle hope shall soothe thy waes,
   When I am far awa', lassie.

Hark! the swelling bugle sings,
   Yielding joy to thee, laddie;
But the dolefu' bugle brings
   Waefu' thoughts to me, laddie.
Lanely I may climb the mountain,
Lanely stray beside the fountain,
Still the weary moments countin',
   Far frae love and thee, laddie.
O'er the gory fields o' war,
When Vengeance drives his crimson car,
Thou'lt maybe fa', frae me afar,
   And nane to close thy e'e, laddie.

---

married to Francis Rawdon Hastings, Earl of Moira (afterwards Marquess of Hastings), Commander of the Forces in Scotland on 12th July, 1804, and she was given away by the Prince of Wales (afterwards King George IV.) They spent their nuptial days at Loudon Castle, and his Lordship, having obeyed a call to foreign service, Tannahill composed this beautiful and popular song on his leaving Scotland,—

    " Loudon's bonnie woods and braes,
      I maun lea' them a', lassie."

Oh, resume thy wonted smile!
  Oh, suppress thy fears, lassie!
Glorious honour crowns the toil
  That the soldier shares lassie.
Heaven will shield thy faithful lover,
Till the vengeful strife is over,
Then we'll meet, nae mair to sever
  Till the day we dee, lassie:
Midst our bonnie woods and braes,
We'll spend our peaceful, happy days,
As blythe's yon lichtsome lamb that plays
  On Loudon's flowery lea, lassie.

CROCSTON CASTLE'S LANELY WA'S. *

THROUGH Crocston Castle's lanely wa's
  The wintry wind howls wild and dreary;
Though mirk the cheerless e'ening fa's,
  Yet I ha'e vow'd to meet my Mary:

* *Crocston Castle's Lanely Wa's.*—Crocston was named after Robert Croc, one
of the Anglo-Norman companions of Walter, first High Steward of Scotland, and
first Baron of Renfrew.   The Castle is one of the oldest baronial residences in
the Barony of Renfrew.   The heiress of the House of Croc married a younger
son of a High Steward, and her descendant, Lord Darnley, married Marie,
Queen of Scotland, the lineal descendant of the High Steward.   The tradition

Yes, Mary, though the wind should rave
  Wi' jealous spite to keep me frae thee,
The darkest stormy nicht I'd brave,
  For ae sweet secret moment wi' thee.

Loud o'er Cardonald's rocky steep,
  Rude Cartha pours in boundless measure ;
But I will ford the whirling deep,
  That roars between me and my treasure :
Yes, Mary, though the torrent rave
  Wi' jealous spite to keep me frae thee,
Its deepest flood I'd bauldly brave,
  For ae sweet secret moment wi' thee.

The watch-dog's howling loads the blast,
  And makes the nichtly wanderer eerie,
But when the lonesome way is past,
  I'll to this bosom clasp my Mary.
Yes, Mary, though stern Winter rave
  Wi' a' his storms to keep me frae thee,
The wildest dreary nicht I'd brave,
  For ae sweet secret moment wi' thee.

---

that either the courtship of Lord Darnley and Queen Marie, or the honeymoon of the royal pair, was passed at the Castle of Crocston, is entirely without foundation. Crocston Castle was abandoned by the Lennox family as a place of residence when they built their palace of Inchinnan in 1506. *Cardonald* is on the opposite side of the River Cart from the lands of Crocston. *Cartha* is the Latinised word of the Gaelic name *Cart*.

THE BRAES O' GLENIFFER. *

Air—"Saw ye my wee thing."

KEEN blaws the wind o'er the braes o' Gleniffer,
   The auld castle's turrets are covered wi' snaw ;
How changed frae the time when I met wi' my lover
   Amang the brume bushes by Stanely green shaw ;
The wild flowers o' Simmer were spread a' sae bonnie,
   The mavis sang sweet frae the green birken tree ;
But far to the camp they ha'e march'd my dear Johnnie,
   And now it is winter wi' nature and me.

---

* The places mentioned in this beautiful song are the Braes of Gleniffer, the Castle turrets, and Stanely green shaw. Gleniffer Braes was one of the favourite haunts of Tannahill. This mountainous range, lying east and west, is the boundary between Paisley and Neilston parishes. The forest of Passeleth was situated here. It was originally divided into three large portions, called Stanely, Thornly, and Fereneze. The north side of the ridge was afterwards called Paisley Braes, but now better known by the classic name of the Braes of Gleniffer. The south side of the ridge is called the Fereneze Braes. The lands of Stanely are the westmost part of the ridge of Paisley Braes, and were granted by King Robert III. to Sir Robert Danyelston in 1392. One of his two daughters and co-heiresses married Sir Robert Maxwell, laird of Calderwood, in the parish of East Kilbride, and these lands, along with others, were allocated to Lady Calderwood. In the middle of the 15th century the Maxwell family built a strong tower, a massive piece of masonry, 40 feet high, which became well known by the name of Stanely Castle. The Maxwells continued in possession of the estate for several generations, and John Maxwell, in 1629, with consent of his son John, sold the estate to Jean Hamilton, dowager of Robert, fourth Lord Ross. It has continued in the Ross-Boyle families till the present time. The roof was taken off in 1714, when the "auld castle's turrets" and the inside of the building were

Then ilk thing around us was blythesome and cheerie,

Then ilk thing around us was bonnie and braw ;

Now naething is heard but the win'. whistling dreary,

And naething is seen but the wide-spreading snaw.

The trees are a' bare, and the birds mute and dowie ;

They shake the cauld drift frae their wings as they flee,

And chirp out their plaints, seeming wae for my Johnnie ;

'Tis winter wi' them and 'tis winter wi' me.

---

exposed to the inclemency of the weather. The broom bushes, that indigenous shrub with the bright yellow blossoms, grow luxuriantly on the congenial soil "by Stanely green shaw." The contrast between the seasons of summer and winter are well pourtrayed—the bloom of the wild flowers with the sleep of the plants—the song of the mountain warblers with their silence ; but none of them are to be compared with the meetings of lovers and their forced separation.

R. A. Smith, in his sketch of Tannahill in the *Harp of Renfrewshire*, says:—

"Songs possessing great poetical beauty do not always become favourites with the public.—' Keen blaws the wind o'er the braes o' Gleniffer ' is perhaps Tannahill's best lyrical effusion, yet it does not appear to be much known, at least it is but seldom sung. It was written for the old Scottish melody, ' Bonnie Dundee,' but Burns had occupied the same ground before him. Mr. Ross, of Aberdeen, composed a very pretty air for it, yet, to use the phrase of a certain favourite vocal performer, it did not *hit*. The language and imagery of this song appear to me beautiful and natural. There is an elegant simplicity in the couplet,

> ' The wild flowers of summer were spread a' sae bonnie,
>   The mavis sang sweet frae the green birken tree ;'

And the dreary appearance of the scenery in winter is strikingly pourtrayed in the second stanza,

> ' Now naething is heard but the wind whistling dreary ;
>   And naething is seen but the wide-spreading snaw.'

Again,

> ' The trees are a' bare, and the birds mute and dowie,
>   They shake the cauld drift frae their wings as they flee,
>   And chirp out their plaints, seeming wae for my Johnnie,
>   'Tis winter wi' them, and 'tis winter wi' me.'

The birds shaking ' the cauld drift frae their wings ' is an idea not unworthy of Burns."

Yon cauld sleety cloud skiffs alang the bleak mountain,
  And shakes the dark firs on the stey rocky brae,
While down the deep glen bawls the sna'-flooded fountain,
  That murmur'd sae sweet to my laddie an' me.
'Tis no its loud roar, on the wint'ry win' swellin',
  'Tis no the cauld blast brings the tear to my e'e,
For, oh, gin I saw my bonnie Scots callan,
  The dark days o' Winter were Simmer to me !,

LANGSYNE BESIDE THE WOODLAND BURN.

LANGSYNE, beside the woodland burn,
  Amang the brume sae yellow,
I lean'd me 'neath the milk-white thorn,
  On Nature's mossy pillow ;
A' round my seat the flowers were strew'd,
That frae the wild wood I had pu'd,
To weave mysel' a Simmer snood,
  To pleasure my dear fellow.

I twin'd the woodbine round the rose,
  Its richer hues to mellow,
Green sprigs of fragrant birk I chose,
  To busk the sedge sae yellow.

The crawflow'r blue, an' meadow-pink,
I wove in primrose-braided link ;
But little, little, did I think
    I should have wove the willow. *

My bonnie lad was forc'd away,
    Tost on the raging billow ;
Perhaps he's fa'n in bludy war,
    Or wreck'd on rocky shallow :
Yet, ay I hope for his return,
As round our wonted haunts I mourn,
And often by the woodland burn,
    I pu' the weeping willow.

WE'LL MEET BESIDE THE DUSKY GLEN. †

WE'LL meet beside the dusky glen, on yon burn side,
Whar the bushes form a cozie den, on yon burn side,
    Tho' the brumy knowes be green,
    Yet, there we may be seen,
But we'll meet—we'll meet at e'en, down by yon burn side.

---

* The willow, or any green leaf, signifies sorrow or *forsaken*.
† *See note on page 26.*

I'll lead thee to the birken bow'r, on yon burn side,
Sae sweetly wove wi' woodbine flow'r, on yon burn side,
      There the busy prying eye,
      Ne'er disturbs the lovers' joy,
While in ithers' arms they lie, down by yon burn side.

Awa', ye rude unfeeling crew, frae yon burn side,
Those fairy scenes are no for you, by yon burn side,—
      There Fancy smooths her theme,
      By the sweetly murm'ring stream,
An' the rock-lodg'd echoes skim, down by yon burn side.

Now the plantin' taps are ting'd wi' goud, on yon burn side,
And gloamin' draws her foggy shroud o'er yon burn side,
      Far frae the noisy scene,
      I'll through the fields alane,
There we'll meet—My ain dear Jean! down by yon burn side.

JESSIE, THE FLOWER O' DUNBLANE. *

THE sun has gane down o'er the lofty Benlomond,
  And left the red clouds to preside o'er the scene,
While lanely I stray in the calm Simmer gloaming,
  To muse on sweet Jessie, the flower o' Dunblane.

---

* This flower of Scottish song was introduced by Tannahill in 1808, and many a
sweet, lovely, charming young Jessie has claimed to be the flower of Dunblane.
There are three places mentioned in this popular melody—*Dunblane*, a parish

How sweet is the brier wi' its saft faulding blossom,
    And sweet is the birk, wi' its mantle o' green ;
Yet sweeter, and fairer, and dear to this bosom,
    Is lovely young Jessie, the flower o' Dunblane.

She's modest as ony, and blythe as she's bonnie,
    For guileless Simplicity marks her its ain ;
And far be the villain, divested o' feelin',
    Wha'd blight in its bloom the sweet flower o' Dunblane.
Sing on, thou sweet mavis, thy hymn to the e'ening,
    Thou'rt dear to the echoes o' Calderwood glen ;
Sae dear to this bosom, sae artless and winning,
    Is charming young Jessie, the flower o' Dunblane.

---

in Perthshire, *Benlomond*, in the parish of Buchanan in Stirlingshire, and *Calderwood Glen*, in Lochwinnoch parish, Renfrewshire. Tannahill may have been in Dunblane, and may have seen the modest and blithe maiden in that village. The lofty Ben Lomond, 3192 feet high, can be seen from any little eminence in Renfrewshire. Tannahill, in his wanderings through Lochwinnoch village and Calderwood Glen, in the neighbourhood of Langcraft, the residence of his Brodie relations, may have spoken to an artless winning maid from Dunblane who bore the sweet name of Jessie; and this may have suggested the song.

The poet's friend, R. A. Smith, who composed the music for this song, says :—
"The third stanza of this song was not written till several months after the others were finished, and, in my opinion, it would have been more to the author's credit had such an addition never been made. The language, I think, falls considerably below that of the two first verses. Surely the Promethean fire must have been burning but *lownly*, when such common-place ideas could be coolly written, after the song had been so finely wound up with the beautiful apostrophe to the mavis,
    'Sing on, thou sweet mavis, thy hymn to the e'ening.'
"When I had composed the music, Jessie was introduced to the world with this clog hanging at her foot, much against my inclination and advice ; however, I feel confident that every singer of taste will discard it as a useless appendage."

How lost were my days till I met wi' my Jessie ;
  The sports o' the city seemed foolish and vain,
I ne'er saw a nymph I would ca' my dear lassie,
  Till charmed wi' sweet Jessie, the flower o' Dunblane.
Though mine were the station o' loftiest grandeur,
  Amidst its profusion I'd languish in pain ;
And reckon as naething the height o' its splendour,
  If wanting sweet Jessie, the flower o' Dunblane.

THE LASS O' ARRANTEENIE. *

Set to Music by Mr. Ross *of Aberdeen.*

FAR lone amang the Highland hills,
  Midst Nature's wildest grandeur,
By rocky dens, an' woody glens,
  With weary steps I wander.

---

* Ardentinny, popularly pronounced *Arranteenie*, is a romantic village on the shores of Loch Long, in the united parishes of Dunoon and Kilmun. Sixty years ago it was the opening to the Highlands, and Gaelic was the language of the locality. A friend of the poet, during an excursion to the Highlands, accidentally met a young lady amidst her native hills—the "sweet lass o' Arranteenie"—and Tannahill wrote this song in her honour. The writer of this note visited Ardentinny last year, roamed through the district, and found it still in the state so truthfully described by the poet—

" Far lone amang the Highland hills,
    Midst Nature's wildest grandeur."

The langsome way, the darksome day,
　　The mountain mist sae rainy,
Are naught to me when gaun to thee,
　　Sweet lass o' Arranteenie.

Yon mossy rose-bud down the howe,
　　Just op'ning fresh an' bonny,
Blinks sweetly 'neath the hazel bough,
　　An's scarcely seen by ony :
Sae, sweet amidst her native hills,
　　Obscurely blooms my Jeanie—
Mair fair an' gay than rosy May,
　　The flower o' Arranteenie. *

---

* The following anecdote is related in the London *Daily News* of May 6, 1874 :—

" Christopher North was challenged to say, on one occasion, whether Wordsworth's description of a girl as

> A violet by a mossy stone,
> 　Half hidden from the eye ;
> Fair as a star, when only one
> 　Is shining in the sky,

was not fairly met by Tannahill's verse :

> Yon mossy rose-bud down the howe,
> 　Just op'ning fresh and bonny,
> Blinks sweetly 'neath the hazel bough,
> 　An's scarcely seen by ony :

> Sae, sweet amidst her native hills,
> 　Obscurely blooms my Jeanie—
> Mair fair an' gay than rosy May,
> 　The flower o' Arranteenie !

He at once declared in favour of the latter, and added, ' Tannahill's will be sung in cottage and in hall, while that of Wordsworth will be read only by the few.' "

Now, from the mountain's lofty brow,
  I view the distant ocean,
There Av'rice guides the bounding prow—
  Ambition courts promotion;
Let Fortune pour her golden store,
  Her laurel'd favours many,
Gi'e me but this, my soul's first wish,
  The lass o' Arranteenie.

THE FLOWER O' LEVERN SIDE. *

YE sunny braes that skirt the Clyde,
  Wi' Simmer flowers sae braw,
There's ae sweet flower on Levern side,
  That's fairer than them a':

---

* The places mentioned are Levernside and "the braes that skirt the Clyde." The Levern rivulet has its source in the Long Loch, four miles above the village of Neilston, and after its noisy passage through the parish of that name, enriching the district by its valuable water for driving power, and receiving supplies from tributary streamlets, merges in the River Cart near Crocston Castle. Standing on the summit of Gleniffer Braes, 580 feet high, one of the most magnificent and varied scenes is opened up to view ;—the great valley of Strathgryffe, in the highest state of cultivation, dotted over with mansions and plantations lies at your feet, and in the distance the Kilpatrick Hills from Partick to Dumbarton—the "sunny braes that skirt the Clyde,"—where the great luminary, when he shines, always shines with freshness and brilliancy.

Yet aye it droops its head in wae,
Regardless o' the sunny ray,
And wastes its sweets frae day to day,
  Beside the lanely shaw.
Wi' leaves a' steep'd in sorrow's dew,
Fause, cruel man, it seems to rue :
Wha aft the sweetest flower will pu',
  Then rend its heart in twa.

Thou bonnie flower on Levern side,
  Oh, gin thou'lt be but mine ;
I'll tend thee wi' a lover's pride,
  Wi' love that ne'er shall tyne.
I'll tak' thee to my shelt'ring bower,
And shield thee frae the beating shower,
Unharmed by aught thou'lt bloom secure
  Frae a' the blasts that blaw :
Thy charms surpass the crimson dye
That streaks the glowing western sky ;
But here, unshaded, soon thou'lt die,
  And lone will be thy fa'.

WI' WAEFU' HEART.

Air—" Sweet Annie frae the sea-beach came."

———

Wi' waefu' heart and sorrowing e'e
  I saw my Jamie sail awa';
Oh ! 'twas a fatal day to me,
  . That day he pass'd the Berwick Law ; *
How joyless now seemed all behind !
  I lingering, strayed along the shore ;
Dark boding fears hung on my mind
  That I might never see him more.

The night came on with heavy rain,
  Loud, fierce, and wild the tempest blew ;
In mountains rolled the awful main :
  Ah, hapless maid ! my fears how true !
The landsmen heard their drowning cries,
  The wreck was seen with dawning day ;
My love was found, an' now he lies
  Low in the isle of gloomy May.

---

* The places mentioned here are the Berwick Law and the Isle of
May. Berwick Law is a hill in the county of Berwick, on the shore of the German
Ocean ; the Isle of May is on the opposite shore, near the mouth of the Forth,
and is in the parish of Crail, Fifeshire.

O boatman, kindly waft me o'er !
  The cavern'd rock shall be my home ;
'Twill ease my burdened heart, to pour
  Its sorrows o'er his grassy tomb ;
With sweetest flowers I'll deck his grave,
  And tend them through the langsome year;
I'll water them, ilk morn and eve,
  With deepest sorrow's warmest tear.

COMPANION OF MY YOUTHFUL SPORTS.

Air—" Gilderoy."

COMPANION of my youthful sports,
  From love and friendship torn,
A victim to the pride of courts,
  Thy early death I mourn.
Unshrouded on a foreign shore,
  Thou'rt mouldering in the clay,
While here thy weeping friends deplore
  Corunna's fatal day. *

---

* " Corunna's fatal day " is a memorable event in British history.
The battle of Corunna, in Spain, between the French and British, was
fought on Monday, 16th January, 1809. The British were victorious. The

How glows the youthful warrior's mind
  With thoughts of laurels won,
But ruthless Ruin lurks behind,
  "And marks him for her own."
How soon the meteor ray is shed,
  "That lures him to his doom,"
And dark Oblivion veils his head
  In everlasting gloom !

THE WANDERING BARD.

CHILL the wintry winds were blowing,
Foul the murky night was snowing,
Through the storm, the minstrel, bowing,
  Sought the inn on yonder moor.
All within was warm and cheery,
All without was cold and dreary,
There the wand'rer, old and weary,
  Thought to pass the night secure.

---

distinguished commander, General Sir John Moore, a native of Glasgow, and the gallant Lieutenant-Colonel Alexander Napier, of Blackston, of the 92nd Highlanders, both fell that day, and were buried at Corunna. Odes were written to the memories of each of them, and Tannahill did not forget a companion of his youth, who fell on the same bloody field.

Softly rose his mournful ditty,
Suiting to his tale of pity;
But the master, scoffing, witty,
    Checked his strain with scornful jeer:
"Hoary vagrant, frequent comer,
Canst thou guide thy gains of summer?
No, thou old intruding thrummer,
    Thou canst have no lodging here.'

Slow the bard departed, sighing;
Wounded worth forbade replying;
One last feeble effort trying,
    Faint, he sunk no more to rise.
Through his harp, the breeze sharp ringing,
Wild his dying dirge was singing,
While his soul, from insult springing,
    Sought its mansion in the skies.

Now, though wintry winds be blowing,
Night be foul with raining, snowing,
Still the trav'ller, that way going,
    Shuns the inn upon the moor.
Though within 'tis warm and cheery,
Though without 'tis cold and dreary,
Still he minds the minstrel weary,
    Spurn'd from that unfriendly door.

WHILE THE GREY-PINIONED LARK.

WHILE the grey-pinioned lark early mounts to the skies,
　And cheerily hails the sweet dawn,
And the sun, newly risen, sheds the mists from his eyes,
　And smiles over mountain and lawn,
Delighted I stray by the fairy Woodside,
　Where the dewdrops the crowflowers adorn,
And Nature, array'd in her midsummer's pride,
　Sweetly smiles to the smile of the morn.

Ye dark waving plantings, ye green shady bowers,
　Your charms ever varying I view ;
My soul's dearest transports, my happiest hours,
　Have owed half their pleasures to you.
Sweet Ferguslie, * hail ! thou'rt the dear sacred grove,
　Where first my young Muse spread her wing ;
Here Nature first waked me to rapture and love,
　And taught me her beauties to sing.

---

* *Ferguslie.*—This estate was feued by Abbot John Hamilton, of the Monastery
of Paisley, to the tenant, John Hamilton, in 1545.　The lands were bounded by
the Burgh of Paisley, Darskaith Wood, and the lands of Woodside on the east,
Candren Burn on the south and west.　The Abbot reserved a public way through
the lands of Ferguslie from the wood of Darskaith towards Candren Burn, with

THE BRAES O' BALQUHITHER.

Air—" The three carles o' Buchanan."

———

LET us go, lassie, go,
To the braes of Balquhither,
Where the blaeberries grow
'Mang the bonnie Highland heather;

———

power to quarry stones for building his place, his town, and millstones for his mill of Paisley. That public way became the high road to the west country from Paisley, and traces of it from Sandholes Street to the Candren Burn can be seen at the present day. On the opening of the new turnpike road to the south, in a line with Broomlands Street in 1750, the old carriage road was superseded, and became a private walk. In the days of Tannahill it was a quiet and retired spot, much frequented by meditative weavers of the west end. The quarrying of stones on the lands of Ferguslie for building the place and town of Paisley continued for 200 years. The estate remained in the Hamilton family till 1680. During that period the celebrated case of discipline between the Paisley Presbytery and the guidwife of Ferguslie, Margaret Hamilton, wife of John Wallace, factor for the Earl of Abercorn, which lasted for five years, from June, 1642, to August, 1647, occurred. John Cochran, nephew of William, first Earl of Dundonald, acquired the estate in 1680, the Corporation of Paisley in 1749, and Thos. Bissland, merchant, Paisley, in 1806. "Sweet Ferguslie," from the earliest times down to the death of Robert Tannahill, in 1810, was always adorned with waving plantations. In 1751 King Street was formed through Woodside lands, and the road to Blackston through Ferguslie estate opened. The fences on the road were low, dry stone dykes, and the ground on each side was planted with trees, principally Scots firs, and these plantations were popularly known by the name of the King Street woods. Wild plants and indigenous shrubs thrived luxuriantly amongst the many quarry holes, and on the heaps of accumulated quarry rubbish, and these, with the fir plantations, afforded shelter to the numerous feathered warblers that frequented the "dear sacred grove." Both the old wood road, the quarry road, and the new planting road, with their green shady bowers, were of easy access to Tannahill, who was brought up and resided at No. 6 Queen Street.

Where the deer and the rae,
  Lightly bounding together,
Sport the lang Simmer day
  On the braes o' Balquhither. *

I will twine thee a bow'r,
  By the clear siller fountain,
And I'll cover it o'er
  Wi' the flowers o' the mountain ;
I will range through the wilds,
  And the deep glens sae dreary,
And return wi' their spoils,
  To the bow'r o' my deary.

---

* *Balquhither.*—Listening to this song is among the earliest recollections of the writer of this note.   Mary M'Intyre or Wright, the Highland domestic, who took charge of him in his infant days, was continually crooning it.   She mentioned that she had been born in the parish of Balquhither, and when a lassie had gathered blaeberries on the braes among the Highland heather.   She frequently stated that she had assisted her mother in baking bannocks for the army of bonnie Prince Charlie on their march to Culloden.   Another theme of hers was the exploits of Rob Roy Macgregor, who lay buried in the churchyard of Balquhither.   This faithful domestic servant died in November, 1825, in the 84th year of her age. From the description of vegetation and animals of the mountain, mentioned in this song, and the names of " Benvoirlich " and " Fillan Glen " mentioned in the song of "Brave Lewie Roy," in the neighbourhood of the braes of Balquhither, but in the adjoining parish of Comrie, it may be inferred that Tannahill had visited these places.   In other songs the poet mentions the names of places he had evidently seen, and where circumstances may have occurred suggesting a subject for his Muse.

When the rude wintry win'
  Idly raves round our dwelling,
And the roar of the linn
  On the night breeze is swelling ;
So merrily we'll sing,
  As the storm rattles o'er us,
'Till the dear shieling ring
  Wi' the light lilting chorus.

Now the Simmer is in prime,
  Wi' the flowers richly blooming,
And the wild mountain thyme
  A' the moorlands perfuming ;
To our dear native scenes
  Let us journey together,
Whar glad innocence reigns,
  'Mang the braes o' Balquhither.

WHEN JOHN AN' ME WAR' MARRIED.

Air—" Clean pea-strae."

WHEN John an' me war' married,
  Our haudin' was but sma',
For my minnie, cankert carlin,
  Would gie us nocht ava' ;

I wair't my fee wi' canny care,
    As far as it would gae,
But, weel-I-wat, our bridal bed
    Was clean pea-strae.

Wi' workin' late an' early,
    We've come to what ye see,
For fortune thrave aneath our han's,
    Sae eident ay war' we ;
The lowe o' love made labour licht,
    I'm sure ye'll find it sae,
When kind ye cuddle down at e'en,
    'Mang clean pea-strae.

The rose blumes gay on cairny brae,
    As weel's in birken shaw,
An' love will lowe in cottage low,
    As weel's in lofty ha' :
Sae, lassie, tak' the lad ye like,
    Whate'er your minnie say,
Tho' ye soud mak' your bridal bed
    O' clean pea-strae.

BAROCHAN JEAN.

Air—" Johnnie M'Gill."

'TIS ha'ena ye heard, man, o' Barochan * Jean?
  An' ha'ena ye heard, man, o' Barochan Jean?
How death an' starvation cam' o'er the hale nation,
  She wrought sic mischief wi' her twa pawkie een.
The lads an' the lasses were deein' in dizzens,
  The tane killed wi' love, an' the tither wi' spleen;
The ploughin', the sawin', the shearin', the mawin'—
  A' wark was forgotten for Barochan Jean.

Frae the south an' the north, o'er the Tweed an' the Forth,
  Sic comin' and gangin' there never was seen;
The comers were cheerie, the gangers were blearie,
  Despairin' or hopin' for Barochan Jean.
The carlins at hame were a' girnin' and granin',
  The bairns were a' greetin' frae mornin' till e'en;
They gat naething for crowdie † but runts boiled tae sowdie, ‡
  For naething gat growin' for Barochan Jean.

---

* *Barochan.*—The seat of the Flemings, in the parish of Killellan, Renfrewshire—an old family, dating back to 1260. The well known Barochan Cross stands on the ancient site of the Castle of Barochan. It has been called a Danish stone by some persons, but this is doubtful. The stone has the appearance of the tombstone of a Maltese Knight, but is now very much wasted.

† " Crowdie "—Porridge.   ‡ " Sowdie "- -A mixture of refuse.

The doctors declared it was past their descrivin',
　The ministers said 'twas a judgment for sin;
But they looked sae blae, an' their hearts were sae wae,
　I was sure they were deein' for Barochan Jean.
The burns on road-sides were a' dry wi' their drinkin',
　Yet a' wadna sloken the drouth i' their skin;
A' roun' the peat-stacks, an' alangst the dyke backs,
　E'en the win's were a' sighin', sweet Barochan Jean.

The timmer ran dune wi' the makin' o' coffins,
　Kirkyairds o' their swaird were a' howkit fu' clean;
Deid lovers were packit like herrin' in barrels,
　Sic thousan's were deein' for Barochan Jean.
But mony braw thanks tae the laird o' Glenbrodie, *
　The grass owre their graffs† is now bonnie an' green:
He sta'‡ the proud heart o' our wanton young ladie,
　An' spoiled a' the charms o' her twa pawkie een.

---

* *Glen-Brodie.*—No such place can be found in the united parishes of Houston
and Killellan, or in the parish of Lochwinnoch.　Tannahill had a granduncle,
called Hugh Brodie of Langcraft, in the latter parish, with whom the poet's
mother was brought up.　Brodie was also a poet, and delivered a poetical speech
at a meeting of the Farmer's Society of Kilbarchan in 1769, which is given in
William Semple's continuation of Renfrewshire, page 116.　Brodie's wife may
have been Barochan Jean.

　　　† "Graffs "- Graves.　　　‡ "Sta "—Stale.

O ARE YE SLEEPIN', MAGGIE.

Air—"Sleepin' Maggie."

CHOR.—" O are ye sleepin', Maggie,
　　　　O are ye sleepin', Maggie!
　　　　Let me in, for loud the linn,
　　　　Is roarin' o'er the warlock craigie."

MIRK an' rainy is the nicht,
　　No' a starn in a' the carry,
Lightnin's gleam athwart the lift,
　　An' win's drive wi' Winter's fury.
　　　　O are ye sleepin', Maggie, &c.

Fearfu' soughs the boortree * bank,
　　The rifted wood roars wild an' dreary,
Loud the iron yett does clank,
　　An' cry o' howlets mak's me eerie.
　　　　O are ye sleepin', Maggie, &c.

Aboon my breath I daurna' speak,
　　For fear I rouse your waukrif' daddie.
Cauld's the blast upon my cheek,
　　O rise, rise my bonnie ladie !
　　　　O are ye sleepin', Maggie, &c.

She op'd the door, she let me in,
　　I cuist aside my dreepin' plaidie :

---

* "Boortree"—Elder tree.

Blaw your warst, ye rain an' win',
    Since, Maggie, now I'm in aside ye.

    Now since ye're waukin', Maggie,
    Now since ye're waukin', Maggie,
    What care I for howlet's cry,
    For boortree bank, or warlock craigie?

THE KEBBUCKSTON WEDDIN'.

Written to an ancient Highland Air.

AULD Wattie o' Kebbuckston brae, *
  Wi' lear an' readin' o' beuks auld farren',
What think ye! the body cam' owre the day,
  An' tauld us he's gaun tae be married tae Mirren.

---

* *Kebbuckston Brae.*—The only place known by the name of Kebbuckston is a small mailing at the west side of the estate of Ferguslie, near the Candren Burn, in Renfrewshire. Kebbuckston is a modern name, and cannot be found among the old names of mailings on the estate of Ferguslie, but is perhaps conferred from having been the site of the Laird's cheese press ;—Kebbuck, a cheese. The roads through the estate of Ferguslie have been greatly altered since the days of Tannahill. The ancient carriage road, leading from Sandholes through Ferguslie, and the Quarry roads, between that ancient road and Blackston road, have all been shut up. These quiet rural paths for walks of solitude were much enjoyed by the weaving population of the West-end of Paisley in the gloamings of summer and autumn evenings. The sonnets and songs of Tannahill testify that he took advantage of their benefits. The course of the *broose*, or the wedding race of Kebbuckston, would be some of these roads. The number of invited guests, and the weavers and school children always ready for enjoyment, would make a goodly gathering at the *broose*.

We a' gat a biddin'

Tae gang tae the weddin',

Baith Johnnie an' Saunie, an' Nellie an' Nannie;

An' Tam o' the Knows,

He swears an' he vows,

At the dancin' he'll face tae the bride wi' his grannie.

A' the lads ha'e trystet their joes;

Slee Wullie cam' up, an' ca'd on Nellie;

Although she was hecht tae Geordie Bowse,

She's gi'en him the gunk, an' she's gaun wi' Wullie.

Wee collier Johnnie

Has yoket his pony,

An's aff tae the toun for a ladin' o' nappy,

Wi' fouth o' gude meat

Tae ser' us tae eat;

Sae wi' fuddlin' an' feastin' we'll a' be fu' happy.

Wee Patie Brydie's * tae say the grace—

The body's aye ready at dredgies an' weddin's;

---

* *Patie Brydie.*—At the sale of books of the late Mr. Andrew Teas, on 21st April, 1874, a parcel of books was sold to a bookseller in town, and on his examining it, he found one of them to be "Gospel Sonnets or Spiritual Songs, 11th edition, by the late Reverend Mr. Ralph Erskine, Minister of the Gospel at Dumfermline; printed by John Gray and Gavin Alston." No date. On the fly-leaf, in the veritable handwriting of the chaplain of the wedding, "Peter Brydie, his book, bought in Paisley, price eight pence. Feb. 5, 1781." The original purchaser of that book being the person who said the grace at the wedding was quite characteristic; and it was a strange coincidence that the purchase made at the recent sale was by the Secretary to the Tannahill Centenary Committee just at the time required, and verifying the name of one of the principal guests at the nuptials of Auld Wattie and Mirren.

An' flunkie M'Fee, o' the Skiverton place,
  Is chosen tae scuttle the pies and th' puddin's.
        For there'll be plenty
        O' ilka thing dainty,
  Baith lang kail an' haggis, an' ilka thing fittin';
        Wi' luggies o' beer,
        Our wizzens tae clear,
  Sae the de'il fill his kyte* wha gaes clung† frae the meetin'.

Lowrie has caft‡ Gibbie Cameron's gun,
  That his auld gutcher§ bore whan he followed Prince Charlie;
The barrel was rusted as black as the grun',
  But he's ta'en't to the smiddy, an's fettled it rarelie.
        Wi' wallets o' pouther,
        His musket he'll shouther,
  An' ride at our head, tae the bride's a-paradin';
        At ilka farm toon,
        He'll fire them three roun',
  Till the hale kintra ring wi' the Kebbuckston weddin'.

Jamie an' Johnie maun ride the broose,‖
  For few like them can sit in the saddle;

---

* " Kyte "—Stomach.   † " Clung "—Unsatisfied.   ‡ " Caft "—Bought.
                § " Gutcher "—Grandfather.

‖ *To ride the broose*—To run a race on horseback at a wedding. A Scots custom, still preserved in the country. Those who are at a wedding, especially the younger part of the company, who are conducting the bride from her own house to the bridegroom's, often set off at full speed for the latter. This is called *riding the broose.* He who first reaches the house is said to *win the broose.*
—*Jamieson.*

An' Willie Ga'braith, the best o' the bows,
  Is trysted to jig in the barn wi' his fiddle.
          Wi' whiskin' an' fliskin',
          An' reelin' an' wheelin',
The young anes are like to loup out o' the body,
          An' Wullie M'Nairn,
          Though sair forfairn,
He vows that he'll wallop twa sets wi' the howdie.

Saunie M'Nab, wi' his tartan trews,
  Has hecht* tae come doon in the midst o' the caper,
An' gi'e us three wallops o' merry shantrews,
  Wi' the true Hielan' fling o' Macrimmon the piper,
          Sic hippin' an' skippin',
          An' springin' an' flingin',
I'se wad that there's nane in the Lawlands can waff it!†
          Faith! Wullie maun fiddle,
          An' jirgun an' diddle,
An' screed till the sweet fa' in beads frae his haffet.

Then gi'e me your han', my trusty guid frien',
  An' gi'e me yer word, my worthy auld kimmer,‡
Ye'll baith come owre on Friday bedeen,
  An' join us in rantin' and toomin' the timmer.§
          Wi' fouth o' guid liquor,
          We'll haud at the bicker,

---

* " Hecht "—Promised. †" Waff it "—In the least approach it. ‡" Kimmer "
—A Gossiping Matron. §" Timmer "—A Wooden Cup.

And lang may the mailin' o' Kebbuckston flourish ;

For Wattie's sae free,

Between you an' me,

I'se warrant he's bidden the ha'f o' the parish.

I'LL HIE ME TO THE SHEELIN' HILL. *

Air—" Gillie Callum."

I'LL hie me to the sheelin' hill,

And bide amang the braes, Callum ;

Ere I gang to Crochan mill,†

I'll live on hips and slaes, Callum.

Wealthy pride but ill can hide

Your runkl'd measl't shins, Callum ;

Lyart pow, as white's the tow,

And beard as rough's the whins, Callum.

---

* "Sheelin' hill "—The eminence near a mill where the chaff is winnowed from the grain.

† *Crochan-Mill.*—The writer of this note, in looking at this name, considered there had been a mistake. He never heard of such a place, but there may be still such a mill struggling for existence in an obscure district, or it may have sunk into oblivion since the time when Tannahill composed this song on Highland girlish pride, 70 years ago. The writer, after racking his brains to discover the locality of Crochan-Mill, concluded it was a misprint for *Barochan* Mill. He then measured the quatrain verse by the rule of prosody, the first and third lines rhyming with each other, and on scanning them found the first line to contain four feet, and the third line only three feet and a-half—

I'll hie me to the Sheelin'-hill,
And bide amang the braes, Callum ;
Ere I gang to Barochan mill
I'll live on hips and slaes, Callum.

Wily woman aft deceives,
  Sae ye'll think, I ween, Callum;
Trees may keep their withered leaves,
  Till ance they get the green, Callum.
Blythe young Donald's won my heart,
  Has my willing vow, Callum ;
Now, for a' your couthy art, *
  I winna marry you, Callum.

O LASSIE, WILL YOU TAK' A MAN?

Air—" Whistle owre the lave o't.

O LASSIE, will ye tak' a man,
Rich in housin', gear, an' lan'?
De'il tak' the cash! that I soud ban,—
  Nae mair I'll be the slave o't.

I'll buy you claise to busk you braw,
A ridin' pouney, pad an' a';
On fashion's tap we'll drive awa',
  Whip, spur, an' a' the lave o't.

Oh, poortith is a wintry day!
Cheerless, blirtie,† cauld, an' blae,
But baskin' under Fortune's ray,
  There's joy whate'er ye'd have o't.

---

* "Couthy "—Loving.   † " Blirtie "—Wet and gusty.

Then gie's your han', ye'll be my wife,
I'll mak' you happy a' your life;
We'll row in love and siller rife,
    Till death wind up the lave o't.

WINTER WI' HIS CLOUDY BROW.

Air—" Forneth house."

Now Winter, wi' his cloudy brow,
  Is far ayont yon mountains,
And Spring beholds her azure sky
  Reflected in the fountains.
Now, on the budding slaethorn bank,
  She spreads her early blossom,
And wooes the mirly-breasted birds
  To nestle in her bosom ;
But lately a' was clad wi' snaw,
  Sae darksome, dull, an' dreary,
Now lav'rocks sing to hail the Spring,
  An' Nature all is cheery.

Then let us leave the town, my love,
  An' seek our country dwelling,
Where waving woods, and spreading flow'rs
  On ev'ry side are smiling.

We'll tread again the daisied green,
   Where first your beauty mov'd me;
We'll trace again the woodland scene,
   Where first ye own'd ye lov'd me.
We soon will view the roses blaw,
   In a' the charms o' fancy,
For doubly dear these pleasures a',
   When shar'd with you, my Nancy.

MY MARY.

Air—"Invercauld's Reel."

My Mary is a bonnie lassie,
   Sweet as dewy morn,
When Fancy tunes her rural reed
   Beside the upland thorn.
She lives ahint yon sunny knowe,
Where flow'rs in wild profusion grow,
Where spreading birks and hazels throw
   Their shadows o'er the burn.

'Tis no' the streamlet-skirted wood,
   Wi' a' its leafy bow'rs,
That gars me wade in solitude
   Amang the wild-sprung flow'rs;

But aft I cast a langin' e'e,
Down frae the bank, out owre the lea,
There, haply, I my lass may see,
   As through the brume she scours.

Yestreen I met my bonnie lassie
   Coming frae the toun,
We raptured sank in ither's arms,
   An' press'd the breckans doun.
The paitrick sung his e'ening note,
The rye-craik * risp'd his clam'rous throat,
While there the heavenly vow I got,
   That erl'd her my own.

OH, ROW THEE IN MY HIGHLAND PLAID.

Arranged by Ross *of Aberdeen.*

LAWLAND lassie, wilt thou go
Whar the hills are clad wi' snow;
Whar, beneath the icy steep,
The hardy shepherd tends his sheep?
Ill nor wae shall thee betide,
When rowed within my Highland plaid.

---

* Probably Tannahill meant the "corn-craik," or landrail.

Soon the voice of cheery Spring
Will gar a' our plantin's ring;
Soon our bonnie heather braes,
Will put on their Simmer claes;
On the mountain's sunny side,
We'll lean us on my Highland plaid.

When the Simmer spreads the flow'rs,
Busks the glens in leafy bow'rs,
Then we'll seek the caller shade,
Lean us on the primrose bed;
While the burning hours preside,
I'll screen thee wi' my Highland plaid.

Then we'll leave the sheep an' goat,
I will launch the bonnie boat,
Skim the loch in canty glee,
Rest the oars to pleasure thee;
When chilly breezes sweep the tide,
I'll hap thee wi' my Highland plaid.

Lawland lads may dress mair fine,
Woo in words mair saft than mine;
Lawland lads ha'e mair o' art,
A' my boast's an honest heart,
Whilk shall ever be my pride:
Oh, row thee in my Highland plaid!

" Bonnie lad, ye've been sae leal,
  My heart would break at our fareweel ;
  Lang your love has made me fain :
  Tak' me,—tak' me for your ain !"

'Cross the Firth awa' they glide,
Young Donald and his Lawland bride.

MY HEART IS SAIR WI' HEAVY CARE.

Air—" The rosy brier."

M Y heart is sair wi' heavy care,
  To think on Friendship's fickle smile ;
It blinks a wee wi' kindly e'e,
  When warld's thrift rins weel the while.
But let Misfortune's tempests low'r,
It soon turns cauld, it soon turns sour;
  It looks sae high and scornfully,
It winna ken a poor man's door.

I ance had siller in my purse,
  I dealt it out right frank and free,
And hoped, should Fortune change her course,
  That they would do the same for me :

But, weak in wit, I little thought
That Friendship's smiles were sold and bought,
    Till ance I saw, like April snaw,
They waned awa' when I had nought.

It's no' to see my threadbare coat,
    It's no' to see my coggie toom,
It's no' to wair my hindmost groat,
    That gars me fret an' gars me gloom ;
But 'tis to see the scornful pride
That honest poortith aft maun bide
    Frae selfish slaves, and sordid knaves,
Wha strut with Fortune on their side.

But let it gang ; what de'il care I !
    Wi' eident thrift I'll toil for mair ;
I'll halve my mite with misery,
    But fient a ane o' them shall share :
With soul unbent I'll stand the stour,
And while they're flutt'ring past my door,
    I'll sing with glee, and let them see
An honest heart can ne'er be poor.

YE ECHOES THAT RING.

Set to Music by R. A. SMITH.

———

YE echoes that ring roun' the woods o' Bowgreen, *
  Say, did ye e'er listen sae meltin' a strain,
When lovely young Jessie gaed wand'rin' unseen,
  An' sung o' her laddie, the pride o' the plain?
Aye she sang, "Willie, my bonnie young Willie!
There's no' a sweet flow'r on the mountain or valley,
Mild blue spritl'd crawflow'r, or wild woodland lily,
  But tynes a' its sweets in my bonnie young swain.
Thou goddess o' Love, keep him constant tae me,
Else, with'rin' in sorrow, puir Jessie shall dee!"

Her laddie had stray'd through the dark leafy wood,
  His thoughts war a' fixt on his dear lassie's charms,
He heard her sweet voice, a' transported he stood,
  'Twas the soul o' his wishes—he flew tae her arms.

———

* *Bowgreen.*—This name may either apply to lands with an affix or prefix, such as *Bowfield*, or *Balgreen*, both situated in the parish of Lochwinnoch, Renfrewshire, the former lying in the south east, and the latter in the north west, of the parish. The writer is inclined for Balgreen, which at one time belonged to the Fultons, and lay to the south of the lands of Langcroft. It belonged to Andrew Brodie, cousin of the poet's mother, and there she had been partly brought up with his uncle, Hugh Brodie. The poet, in visiting his maternal relations at Langcroft, would hear the "echoes that ring roun' the woods o' Bowgreen." Calderwood Glen, Balgreen, and Langcroft, are in the neighbourhood of each other, and this song may be compared with "Jessie, the flow'r o' Dunblane."

"No, my dear Jessie! my lovely young Jessie!
Thro' simmer, thro' winter I'll daut an' caress thee,
Thou'rt dearer than life! thou'rt my ae only lassie!
Then, banish thy bosom these needless alarms:
Yon red setting sun sooner changeful shall be,
Ere wav'ring in falsehood I wander frae thee."

THE COGGIE.

Air—"Cauld kail in Aberdeen."

WHEN poortith cauld, an' sour disdain,
Hang owre life's vale sae foggie,
The sun that brightens up the scene,
Is Friendship's kindly coggie!
Then, oh! revere the coggie, sirs!
The friendly, social coggie!
It gars the wheels o' life run licht,
Tho' e'er so doilt an' cloggie.

Let Pride in Fortune's chariot fly,
Sae empty, vain, an' voggie;*
The source o' wit, the spring o' joy,
Lies in the social coggie!

---

* "Voggie"—Merry, cheerful.

Then, oh! revere the coggie, sirs!
The independent coggie!
An' never snool † beneath the frown
O' ony selfish roggie.

Puir modest Worth, wi' cheerless e'e,
  Sits hurklin' ‡ in the boggie,
Till she asserts her dignity,
  By virtue o' the coggie!
    Then, oh! revere the coggie, sirs!
    The poor man's patron coggie,
    It warsels care, it fechts life's faughts,
    An' lifts him frae the boggie.

Gi'e feckless Spain her weak snail-broo,
  Gi'e France her weel-spic'd froggie,
Gi'e brither John his luncheon too,
  But gi'e to us our coggie!
    Then, oh! revere the coggie, sirs!
    Our soul-warm kindred coggie;
    Hearts doubly knit in social tie,
    When just a wee thocht groggie.

---

† "Snool"—Be subdued or snubbed by underhand means.
‡ "Hurklin'"—Sitting in a slovenly manner. .

In days of yore our sturdy sires,
  Upon their hills sae scroggie, *
Glow'd with true Freedom's warmest fires,
  An' faught to save their coggie !
    Then, oh ! revere the coggie, sirs,
    Our brave forefathers' coggie ;
    It rous'd them up to doughty deeds,
    O'er whilk we'll lang be voggie.

Then, here's—May Scotland ne'er fa' doun,
  A cringin', coward doggie,
But bauldly stan' an' bang the loon,
  Wha'd reave † her o' her coggie !
    Then, oh ! protect the coggie, sirs,
    Our guid auld mither's coggie !
    Nor let her luggie e'er be drained
    By ony foreign roggie.

FRAGMENT OF A SCOTTISH BALLAD.

Air—" Fingal's Lamentation."

" WILD drives the bitter northern blast,
  Fierce whirling wide the crispy snaw,
Young lassie, turn your wand'ring steps,
  For e'ening's gloom begins to fa' :

---

* " Scroggie "—Covered with stunted bushes.
† " Reave "—Rob.

I'll tak' you to my father's ha',
   An' shield you frae the wintry air,
For, wand'ring thro' the drifting snaw,
   I fear ye'll sink to rise nae mair."

" Ah ! gentle lady, airt my way
   Across this langsome, lanely moor,
For he wha's dearest to my heart,
   Now waits me on the western shore ;
With morn he spreads his outward sail—
   This nicht I vow'd to meet him there,
To tak' ae secret, fond fareweel,
   We maybe part to meet nae mair."

" Dear lassie, turn—'twill be your dead !
   The dreary waste lies far an' wide ;
Abide till morn, an' then ye'll hae
   My father's herd-boy for your guide."
" No, lady,—no ! I maunna' turn,
   Impatient love now chides my stay,
Yon rising moon, wi' kindly beam,
   Will licht me on my weary way."

     *   *   *   *   *

Ah ! Donald, wherefore bounds thy heart ?
   Why beams wi' joy thy wistfu' e'e ?
Yon's but thy true-love's fleeting form,
   Thy true-love mair thou'lt never see ;

Deep in the hollow glen she lies,
   Amang the snaw, beneath the tree,
She soundly sleeps in Death's cauld arms,
   A victim to her love for thee.

MINE AIN DEAR SOMEBODY.

Air—" Were I obliged to beg."

WHEN gloamin' treads the heels o' day,
And birds sit courin' on the spray,
Alang the flow'ry hedge I stray
   To meet mine ain dear *somebody*.

The scented brier, the fragrant bean,
The clover bloom, the dewy green,
A' charm me, as I rove at e'en,
   To meet mine ain dear *somebody*.

Let warriors prize the hero's name,
Let mad Ambition tow'r for fame,
I'm happier in my lowly hame,
   Obscurely blest wi' *somebody*.

JOHNNIE, LAD.

Air—" The lasses o' the ferry."

Och, hey! Johnnie, lad,
  Ye're no sae kind's ye soud ha'e been;
Och, hey! Johnnie, lad,
  Ye didna keep your tryst yestreen:
I waited lang beside the wud,
  Sae wae an' weary, a' my lane;
Och, hey! Johnnie, lad,
  Ye're no sae kind's ye soud ha'e been.

I looked by the whinny knowe,
  I looked by the firs sae green,
I looked owre the spunkie howe,
  An' aye I thocht ye would ha'e been.
The ne'er a supper cross'd my craig,*
  The ne'er a sleep has clos'd my een;
Och, hey! Johnnie, lad,
  Ye're no sae kind's ye soud ha'e been.

Gin ye war waitin' by the wud,
  Then I was waitin' by the thorn,
I thocht it was the place we set,
  And waited maist till dawnin' morn;

* "Craig"—Mouth.

Sae be na' vex'd, my bonnie lassie,
   Let my waitin' stan' for thine,
We'll awa' to Craigton-shaw, *
   And seek the joys we tint yestreen.

FLY WE TO SOME DESERT ISLE.
Gaelic Air.

FLY we to some desert isle,
   There we'll pass our days thegither,
Shun the world's derisive smile,
   Wand'ring tenants of the heather;
Shelter'd in some lonely glen,
Far remov'd from mortal ken,
Forget the selfish ways o' men,
   Nor feel a wish beyond each other.

Though my friends deride me still,
   Jamie, I'll disown thee never ;
Let them scorn me as they will,
   I'll be thine, and thine for ever.
What are a' my kin to me,
A' their pride o' pedigree !
What were life, if wantin' thee,
   An' what were death, if we maun sever !

---

* Craigton is in the Abbey parish of Paisley, on Cochran land, near Johnstone Castle. .

OH, SAIR I RUE THE WITLESS WISH.

Arranged by R. A. SMITH.

———

OH, sair I rue the witless wish,
　That gar'd me gang wi' ye at e'en ;
An' sair I rue the birken bush,
　That screen'd us wi' its leaves sae green :
An' tho' ye vowed ye wad be mine,
　The tear o' grief aye dims my e'e ;
For, oh! I'm fear'd that I may tyne
　The love that ye ha'e promis'd me !

While ithers seek their e'ening sports,
　I wander, dowie,* a' my lane,
For whan I join their glad resorts,
　Their daffing gi'es me meikle pain.
Alas, it wasna sae shortsyne,
　Whan a' my nichts war spent wi' glee ;
But, oh! I'm fear'd that I may tyne
　The love that ye ha'e promis'd me !

———

* " Dowie "—Sad.

Dear lassie, keep thy heart aboon,
  For I ha'e wair'd my winter's fee;
I've caft a bonnie silken goun,
  Tae be a bridal gift for thee.
An' sooner shall the hills fa' doun,
  An' mountain high shall stan' th' sea,
Ere I'd accept a gouden croun,
  Tae change that love I bear for thee.

KITTY TYRELL.

Irish Air.

THE breeze of the night fans the dark mountain's breast,
And the light bounding deer have all sunk to their rest;
The big sullen waves lash the loch's rocky shore,
And the lone drowsy fisherman nods o'er his oar.
Tho' pathless the moor, and tho' starless the skies,
The star of my heart is my Kitty's bright eyes;
And joyful I hie over glen, brake, and fell,
In secret to meet my sweet Kitty Tyrell.

Ah! long we have lov'd in her father's despite,
And oft we have met at the dead hour of night,
When hard-hearted vigilance, sunk in repose,
Gave love one sweet hour its fond tale to disclose.

These moments of transport, to me, oh, how dear !
And the fate that would part us, alas, how severe !
Although the rude storm rise with merciless swell,
This night I shall meet my sweet Kitty Tyrell.

Ah ! turn, hapless youth ! see the dark cloud of death,
Comes rolling in gloom o'er the wild haunted heath ;
Deep groans the scathed oak on the glen's cliffy brow,
And the sound of the torrent seems heavy with woe.
Away, foolish seer, with thy fancies so wild,
Go, tell thy weak dreams to some credulous child ;
Love guides my light steps through the lone dreary dell,
And I fly to the arms of sweet Kitty Tyrell.

DESPAIRING MARY.

Set to Music by R. A. SMITH.

" MARY, why thus waste thy youthtime in sorrow ?
See a' aroun' you the flowers sweetly blaw ;
Blythe sets the sun o'er the wild cliffs o' Jura,*
Blythe sings the mavis in ilka green shaw !"

---

* *Jura.*—This is the island and parish of that name. It presents to the eye
a rough and rugged appearance, and the wild cliffs mentioned by the author will
be the conical mountains, called the "Paps of Jura,"—the landmarks that are

"How can this heart ever mair think o' pleasure,
  Simmer may smile, but delight I ha'e nane;
Cauld i' the grave lies my heart's only treasure,
  Nature seems deid since my Jamie is gane.

"This 'kerchief he gave me, a true lover's token,
  Dear, dear tae me was the gift for his sake!
I wear't near my heart, but this poor heart is broken,
  Hope dee'd wi' Jamie, an' left it tae break.
Sighin' for him I lie doun in the e'enin',
  Sighin' for him I awake in the morn;
Spent are my days a' in secret repinin',
  Peace tae this bosom can never return.

"Oft ha'e we wander'd in sweetest retirement,
  Tellin' our loves 'neath the moon's silent beam;
Sweet were our meetin's o' tender endearment,
  But fled are these joys like a fleet passin' dream.

---

seen at a great distance. The sun, in setting, referred to by him, sinks down behind them into the bosom of his ocean love.

Of the music of this piece the composer (R. A. Smith) relates :—
"The music published with this song was originally composed for other words, but Tannahill took a fancy to the air, and immediately wrote 'Despairing Mary' for it, which, being the better song, was adopted. The opening of the melody is too like the first part of 'The flowers of the forest' to lay claim to great originality, but after it was composed I never could please myself with any alteration I attempted to make, so it remains as it was first sketched."

Cruel Remembrancer, ah ! why wilt thou wreck me?
   Broodin' o'er joys that for ever are flown ;
Cruel Remembrance, in pity forsake me,
   Flee tae some bosom where grief is unknown !"

RAB RORYSON'S BONNET. *

Air—" The auld wife o' the glen."

YE'LL a' ha'e heard tell o' Rab Roryson's bonnet,
Ye'll a' ha'e heard tell o' Rab Roryson's bonnet ;
'Twas no for itsel', 'twas the heid that was in it,
Gar't a' bodies talk o' Rab Roryson's bonnet.

This bonnet, that theekit his won'erfu' heid,
Was his shelter in Winter, in Simmer his shade ;
An' at kirk, or at market, or bridals, I ween,
A braw gawcier bonnet there never was seen.

Wi' a roun' rosy tap, like a muckle blackbide,
It was slouch'd just a kennin' on either han' side ;
Some maintained it was black, some maintained it was blue,
It had something o' baith, as a body may trew.

---

* The last verse is from a letter to King, dated 9th May, 1809, and first appeared in Mr. Ramsay's edition.

But, in sooth, I assure you, for ought that I saw,
Still his bonnet had naething uncommon ava';
Tho' the haill pairish talk'd o' Rab Roryson's bonnet,
'Twas a' for the marvellous heid that was in it.

That heid, let it rest, it is noo in the mools,
Tho' in life a' the warld beside it war fools;
Yet o' what kind o' wisdom his heid was possess't,
Nane e'er kent but himsel', sae there's nane that will miss't.

There are some still in life wha eternally blame,
Wha on *buts* an' on *ifs* rear their fabric o' fame;
Unto such I inscribe this most elegant sonnet,
Sae let them be croun'd in Rab Roryson's bonnet!

THE IRISH FARMER.

Air—"Sir John Scott's Favourite."

DEAR Judy, when first we got married,
Our fortune indeed was but small,
For save the light hearts that we carried,
Our riches were nothing at all:

I sung while I reared up the cabin,
  Ye Powers give me vigour and health !
And a truce to all sighing and sobbing,
  For love is Pat Mulligan's wealth.

Through summer and winter so dreary,
  I cheerily toiled on the farm,
Nor ever once dreamed growing weary,
  For love gave my labour its charm.
And now, though 'tis weak to be vaunty,
  Yet here let us gratefully own,
We live amidst pleasure and plenty,
  As happy's the king on the throne.

We've Murdoch, and Patrick, and Connor,
  As fine little lads as you'll see,
And Kitty, sweet girl, 'pon my honour,
  She's just the dear picture of thee.
Though some folks may still underrate us,
  Ah, why should we mind them a fig ?
We've a large swinging field of potatoes,
  A good driminduath * and pig.

---

* Driminduath is a general name in Ireland for the cow.

DEAR JUDY.

———

Dear Judy, I've taken a-thinking,
　The children their letters must learn,
And we'll send for old Father O'Jenkin,
　To teach them three months in the barn :
For learning's the way to promotion,
　'Tis culture brings food from the sod,
And books give a fellow a notion
　How matters are doing abroad.

Though father neglected my reading,
　Kind soul, sure his spirit's in rest !
For the very first part of his breeding,
　Was still to relieve the distressed.
And, late, when the trav'ller benighted,
　Besought hospitality's claim,
He lodged him till morning, delighted,
　Because 'twas a lesson to them.

The man that wont feel for another,
　Is just like a colt on the moor,
He lives without knowing a brother,
　To frighten bad luck from his door.

But he that's kind-hearted and steady,
  Though wintry misfortune should come,
He'll still find some friend who is ready
  To scare the old witch from his home.

Success to Ould Ireland for ever!
  'Tis just the dear land to my mind,
Her lads her warm-hearted and clever,
  Her girls are all handsome and kind.
And he that her name would bespatter,
  By wishing the French safely o'er,
May the de'il blow him over the water,
  And make him cook frogs for the core.*

THE HIELANDER'S INVITATION.

Air—" Will ye come to the bower ?"

WILL ye come tae the board I've prepared for you?
Your drink shall be guid, o' the true Hielan' blue.
Will ye, Donald, will ye, Callum, come tae the board?
There each shall be great as her ain native lord.

There'll be plenty o' pipe, an' a glorious supply
O' the guid sneesh-te-bacht, an' the fine cut-an'-dry.

---

* "Core," Scotch ; "Corps," French—Whole company.

Will ye, Donald, will ye, Callum, come then at e'en ?
There be some for the stranger, but mair for the frien'.

Thère we'll drink foggy Care tae his gloomy abodes,
An' we'll smoke till we sit in the clouds like the gods.
Will ye, Donald, will ye, Callum, won't you do so ?
'Tis the way that our forefathers did long ago.

An' we'll drink tae the Cameron, we'll drink tae Lochiel,
An' for Charlie, we'll drink a' the French tae the de'il.
Will ye, Donald, will ye, Callum, drink there until
There be heids lie like peats if hersel' had her will !

There be groats on the lan', there be fish in the sea,
An' there's fouth * in the coggie for freen'ship an' me.
Come then, Donald, come then, Callum, come then to-night,
Sure the Hielander be first in the fuddle an' the fight.

THE LAMENT OF WALLACE AFTER THE BATTLE OF FALKIRK.

Air—"Maids of Arrochar."

THOU dark-winding Carron,* once pleasing to see,
To me thou canst never give pleasure again ;

---

* " Fouth "—Abundance, plenty.

* *Carron.*—The part of this river referred to is in the parish of Falkirk, Stirlingshire. The battle of Falkirk took place on 22nd July, 1298, between the armies of Sir William Wallace and of Edward I., King of England, when the latter was victorious.

My brave Caledonians lie low on the lea,
    And thy streams are deep-ting'd with the blood of the slain.

Ah! base-hearted Treach'ry has doom'd our undoing,
    My poor bleeding country, what more can I do?
Ev'n Valour looks pale o'er the red field of ruin,
    And Freedom beholds her best warriors laid low.

Farewell, ye dear partners of peril! farewell!
    Though buried ye lie in one wide bloody grave,
Your deeds shall ennoble the place where ye fell,
    And your names be enrolled with the sons of the brave.

But I, a poor outcast, in exile must wander,
    Perhaps, like a traitor, ignobly must die!
On thy wrongs, O my country! indignant I ponder;
    Ah! woe to the hour when thy Wallace must fly!

In a letter to James Barr, dated 19th January, 1806, Tannahill says:—
"According to promise, I send you two verses for the 'Maids of Arrochar;'
perhaps they are little better than the last. I believe the language is too weak
for the subject; however, they possess the advantage over the others of being
founded on a real occurrence. The battle of Falkirk was Wallace's last, in
which he was defeated with the loss of almost his whole army. I am sensible
that to give words suitable to the poignancy of his grief, on such a trying reverse
of fortune, would require all the fire and soul-melting energy of a Campbell or a
Burns."

THE FAREWELL.

Air—" Lord Gregory."

—

ACCUSE me not, inconstant fair,
  Of being false to thee,
For I was true, would still been so,
  Hadst thou been true to me.
But when I knew thy plighted lips
  Once, to a rival's press't,
Love-smothered independence rose,
  And spurn'd thee from my breast.

The fairest flower in Nature's field
  Conceals the rankling thorn ;
So thou, sweet flower ! as false as fair,
  This once kind heart hath torn.
'Twas mine to prove the fellest pangs
  That slighted love can feel ;
'Tis thine to weep that one rash act
  Which bids this long fareweel.

OUR BONNIE SCOTS LADS.

OUR bonnie Scots lads in their green tartan plaids,
   Their blue-belted bonnets, an' feathers sae braw,
Rank'd up on the green war fair to be seen,
   But my bonnie young laddie was fairest of a';
His cheeks war' as red as the sweet heather-bell,
   Or the red western cloud lookin' down on the snaw;
His lang yellow hair owre his braid shoulders fell,
   An' the een o' the lasses war fix'd on him a'.

My heart sunk wi' wae on the wearifu' day,
   When torn frae my bosom they march'd him awa',
He bade me farewell, he cried, "Oh, be leal!"
   An' his red cheeks war' wet wi' the tears that did fa'.
Ah! Harry, my love, though thou ne'er shou'dst return,
   Till life's latest hour I thy absence will mourn:
An' memory shall fade like a leaf on the tree,
   Ere my heart spare ae thought on anither but thee.

ANACREONTIC.

——

Fill, fill, the merry bowl,
  Drown corrosive care and sorrow,
Why, why clog the soul,
  By caring for to-morrow?
Fill you glasses, toast your lassies,
  Blythe Anacreon bids you live;
Love with friendship far surpasses
  All the pleasures life can give.
    Ring, ring th' enlivening bell,
      The merry dirge of care and sorrow,
    Why leave them life to tell
      Their heavy tales to-morrow?

Come, join the social glee,
  Give the reins to festive pleasure;
While Fancy, light and free,
  Dances to the measure.
Love and wit, with all the graces,
  Revel round in fairy ring,

Smiling joy adorns our faces,
  While with jocund hearts we sing.
    Now, since our cares are drowned,
      Spite of what the sages tell us,
    Hoary Time, in all his round,
      Ne'er saw such happy fellows.

THE SOLDIER'S WIDOW.

THE cold wind blows,
  O'er the drifted snows ;
Loud howls the rain-lashed naked wood ;
  Weary I stray
  On my lonesome way,
And my heart is faint for want of food.
  Pity a wretch left all forlorn,
  On life's wide wintry waste to mourn ;
  The gloom of night fast veils the sky,
  And pleads for your humanity.

  On valour's bed
  My Henry died,
In the cheerless desert is his tomb :

Now lost to joy,
With my little boy,
In woe and want I wander home.
Oh ! never, never will you miss
The boon bestow'd on deep distress,
For dear to Heav'n is the glist'ning eye,
That beams benign humanity.

ONE NIGHT IN MY YOUTH.

Air—" The lass that wears green."

ONE night in my youth as I rov'd with my merry pipe,
List'ning the echoes that rang to the tune,
I met Kitty More, with her two lips so cherry ripe ;
"Phelim," says she, "give us ' Elleen Aroon ! ' "
Dear Kitty, says I, thou'rt so charmingly free !
Now, if thou wilt deign thy sweet voice to the measure,
'Twill make all the echoes run giddy with pleasure,
For none in fair Erin can sing it like thee.

My chanter I plied, with my heart beating gaily,
I pip'd up the strain, while so sweetly she sang ;
The soft melting melody fill'd all the valley,
The green woods around us in harmony rang.

Methought that she verily charmed up the moon !
Now, still, as I wander in village or city,
When good people call for some favourite ditty,
I give them sweet Kitty, and Elleen Aroon.

COGGIE, THOU HEALS ME.

DOROTHY sits i' the cauld ingle neuk,
Her red rosy neb's like a labster tae,
Wi' girnin', her mou's like the gab o' the fleuk,*
Wi' smokin', her teeth's like the jet o' the slae.
An' aye she sings "Weel's me," aye she sings " Weel's me,
Coggie, thou heals me ! coggie, thou heals me !
Aye my best frien' whan there's onything ails me,
Ne'er shall we part till the day that I dee."

Dorothy ance was a weel-tocher'd lass,
Had charms like her neebours, and lovers enow,
But she spited them sae, wi' her pride an' her sauce,
They left her for thirty lang simmers to rue.
Then aye she sang " Wae's me !" aye she sang " Wae's me !
Oh, I'll turn crazy, oh, I'll turn crazy !
Naething in a' the wide warld can ease me,
De'il tak' the wooers,—Oh, what shall I do?"

---

* '' Fleuk "—The flounder, a flat fish.

'Dorothy, dozen'd wi' leevin' her lane,
  Pu'd at her rock, wi' the tear in her e'e;
She thocht on the braw merry days that war gane,
  An' caft a wee coggie for company.
Now aye she sings "Weel's me!" aye she sings "Weel's me!
Coggie, thou heals me! coggie, thou heals me!
Aye my best frien' whan there's onything ails me,
Ne'er shall we part till the day that I dee."

ELLEN MORE.*

Air—"Mary's Dream."

THE sun had kissed green Erin's waves,
  The dark blue mountains tower'd between,
Mild evening's dews refresh'd the leaves,
  The moon unclouded rose serene;
When Ellen wandered forth, unseen,
  All lone her sorrows to deplore;
False was her lover, false her friend,
  And false was hope to Ellen More.

* The scene of this dirge is in the parish of Yarrow, Selkirkshire, where many
a mournful event has occurred, and been preserved in border minstrelsy.   Loch
Mary, or Saint Mary's Loch, is a well known lake, and the river Yarrow is also
equally well known.   Saint Mary's Chapel was situated on the north west side
of Saint Mary's Loch.

Young Henry was fair Ellen's love,
  Young Emma to her heart was dear ;
Nor weel nor woe did Ellen prove,
  But Emma ever seemed to share.
Yet envious still, she spread the wile,
  That sullied Ellen's virtues o'er ;
Her faithless Harry spurn'd the while,
  His fair, his faithful Ellen More.

She wander'd down Loch-Mary side,
  Where oft at ev'ning hour she stole,
To meet her love with secret pride ;
  Now deepest anguish wrung her soul.
O'ercome with grief, she sought the steep
  Where Yarrow falls with sullen roar ;
Oh, Pity! veil thy eyes and weep !
  A bleeding corpse lies Ellen More.

The sun may shine on Yarrow braes,
  And woo the mountain flow'rs to bloom,
But never can his golden rays
  Awake the flow'r in yonder tomb.
There oft young Henry strays forlorn,
  When moonlight gilds the abbey tower ;
There oft from eve till breezy morn,
  He weeps his faithful Ellen More.

GREEN INISMORE.

Air—" The Leitrim County."

———

HOW light is my heart as we journey along,
  Now my perilous service is o'er,
I think on sweet home, and I carol a song,
  In remembrance of her I, adore ;
How sad was the hour when I bade her adieu !
Her tears spoke her grief, though her words were but few ;
She hung on my bosom, and sighed, Oh, be true,
  When you're far from the Green Inismore !

Ah, Eveleen, my love, hadst thou seen this fond breast,
  How, at parting, it bled to its core,
Thou hadst there seen thine image so deeply impress't,
  That thou ne'er couldst have doubted me more.
For my king and my country undaunted I fought,
And braved all the hardships of war as I ought,
But the day never rose saw thee strange to my thought
  Since I left thee in Green Inismore.

Ye dear native mountains that tower on my view,
  What joys to my mind ye restore !
The past happy scenes of my life ye renew,
  And ye ne'er seemed so charming before.

In the rapture of Fancy, already I spy
My kindred and friends crowding round me with joy,
But my Eveleen, sweet girl, there's a far dearer tie
    Binds this heart to the Green Inismore.

THE WORN SOLDIER.

THE Queensferry boatie* rows light,
    And light is the heart that it bears,
For it brings the poor soldier safe back to his home,
    From many long toilsome years.

How sweet are his green native hills,
    As they smile to the beams of the west,
But sweeter by far is the sunshine of hope
    That gladdens the soldier's breast !

I can well mark the tears of his joy,
    As the wave-beaten pier he ascends,
For already, in fancy, he enters his home,
    'Midst the greetings of tender friends.

---

* *Queensferry boat.*—The Paisley Bard probably founded this song on the incident of having been ferried across the Firth of Forth from the one Queensferry to the other, and seen an old soldier on the occasion taking the same mode of conveyance.

But fled are his visions of bliss,
All his transports but rose to deceive,
He found the dear cottage a tenantless waste,
And his kindred all sunk in the grave.

Lend a sigh to the soldier's grief,
For now he is helpless and poor,
And, forced to solicit a slender relief,
He wanders from door to door.

To him let your answers be mild,
And, oh ! to the suff'rer be kind !
For the look of indiff'rence, the frown of disdain,
Bear hard on a generous mind.

POOR TOM, FARE-THEE-WELL.

Arranged by R. A. SMITH.

'MONGST Life's many cares there is none so provoking,
As when a brave seaman, disabled and old,
Must crouch to the worthless, and stand the rude mocking
Of those who have nought they can boast but their gold ;
Poor Tom, once so high on the list of deserving,
By captain and crew none so dearly were prized,
At home now laid up, worn with many years' serving,
Poor Tom takes his sup, and poor Tom is despised.

Yet, Care thrown a-lee, see old Tom in his glory,
  Placed snug with a shipmate, whose life once he saved,
Recounting the feats of some bold naval story,
  The battles they fought, and the storms they had braved.
In his country's defence he has dared every danger,
  His valorous deeds he might boast undisguised ;
Yet home-hearted landsmen hold Tom as a stranger,
  Poor Tom loves his sup, and poor Tom is despised.

Myself, too, am old, rather rusty for duty,
  Yet still I'll prefer the wide ocean to roam;
I'd join some bold corsair, and live upon booty,
  Before I'd be gibed by these sucklings at home.
Poor Tom, fare-thee-well ! for, by heaven, 'tis provoking,
  When thus a brave seaman, disabled and old,
Must crouch to the worthless, and stand the rude mocking
  Of those who have nought they can boast but their gold.

MOLLY, MY DEAR.

Air—" Miss Molly."

THE harvest is o'er, and the lads are so funny,
Their hearts lined with love, and their pockets with money,
From morning till night 'tis " My jewel, my honey,
  Och, go to the north with me, Molly, my dear !"

Young Dermot holds on with his sweet botheration,
And swears there is only one flower in the nation;
"Thou rose of the Shannon, thou pink of creation,
   Och, go to the north with me, Molly my dear!

"The sun courts thy smiles as he sinks in the ocean,
The moon to thy charms veils her face in devotion,
And I, my poor self, och! so rich is my notion,
   Would pay down the world for sweet Molly, my dear."

Though Thady can match all the lads with his blarney,
And sings me love-songs of the lakes of Killarney,
In worth from my Dermot he's twenty miles' journey,
   My heart bids me tell him I'll ne'er be his dear.

AH! SHEELAH, THOU'RT MY DARLING.

Air—"Nancy Verny."

AH, Sheelah, thou'rt my darling,
   The golden image of my heart;
How cheerless seems this morning,
   It brings the hour when we must part.
Though doomed to cross the ocean,
   And face the proud insulting foe,
Thou hast my soul's devotion,
   My heart is thine where'er I go!

When tossed upon the billow,
  And angry tempests round me blow,
Let not the gloomy willow
  O'ershade thy lovely lily brow;
But mind the seaman's story,
  Sweet William and his charming Sue;
I'll soon return with glory,
  And, like sweet William, wed thee too.
Ah, Sheelah, thou'rt my darling,
  My heart is thine where'er I go.

Think on our days of pleasure,
  When wand'ring by the Shannon side,
When summer days gave leisure
  To stray amidst their flow'ry pride;
And while thy faithful lover
  Is far upon the stormy main,
Think, when the wars are over,
  These golden days shall come again.
Ah, Sheelah, thou'rt my darling,
  These golden days shall come again !

Farewell, ye lofty mountains,
  Your flow'ry wilds we wont to rove;
Ye woody glens and fountains,
  The dear retreats of mutual love.
Alas, we now must sever.

Oh, Sheelah, to thy vows be true,
My heart is thine for ever;
One fond embrace, and then adieu !
Ah, Sheelah, thou'rt my darling,
One fond embrace, and then adieu !

PEGGY O'RAFFERTY.

Air—"Paddy O'Rafferty."

OH, could I fly like the green-coated fairy,
I'd skip o'er the ocean to dear Tipperary,
Where all the young fellows are blythesome and merry,
    While here I lament my sweet Peggy O'Rafferty.
How could I bear in my bosom to leave her,
In absence I think her more lovely than ever;
With thoughts of her beauty I'm all in a fever,
    Since others may woo my sweet Peggy O'Rafferty.

Scotland, thy lasses are modest and bonnie,
But here every Jenny has got her own Johnnie,
And though I might call them my jewel and honey,
    My heart is at home with sweet Peggy o' Rafferty.

Wistful I think on my dear native mountains,
Their green shady glens and their crystalline fountains,
And ceaseless I heave the deep sigh of repentance,
  That ever I left my sweet Peggy O'Rafferty.

Fortune, 'twas thine all the light foolish notion,
That led me to rove o'er the wide rolling ocean,
But what now to me all my hopes of promotion,
  Since I am so far from sweet Peggy O'Rafferty.
Grant me as many thirteens as will carry me
Down through the country and over the ferry,
I'll hie me straight home into dear Tipperary,
  And never more leave my sweet Peggy O'Rafferty.

YE FRIENDLY STARS.

Air—" Gamby Ora."

YE friendly stars that rule the night,
  And hail my glad returning,
Ye never shone so sweetly bright,
  Since gay St. Patrick's morning.
My life hung heavy on my mind,
  Despair sat brooding o'er me;
Now all my cares are far behind,
  And joy is full before me.

Gamby ora, gamby ora,[*]
How my heart approves me ;
Gamby ora, gamby ora,
Kathleen owns she loves me.

Were all the flow'ry pastures mine,
That deck fair Limerick county,
That wealth, dear Kathleen, should be thine,
And all should share our bounty.
But fortune's gifts I value not,
Nor grandeur's highest station ;
I would not change my happy lot
For all the Irish nation.
Gamby ora, gamby ora, &c.

THE DEFEAT.

FROM hill to hill the bugles sound
The soul-arousing strain,
The war-bred coursers paw the ground,
And foaming, champ the rein.

Literally--" I will sing."

Their steel-clad riders bound on high,
    A bold defensive host;
With valour fired, away they fly,
    Like lightning, to the coast.

And now they view the wide-spread lines
    Of the invading foe;
Now skill with British bravery joins,
    To strike one final blow.
Now on they rush with giant stroke,
    Ten thousand victims bleed:
They trample on the iron yoke
    Which France for us decreed.*

Now view the trembling vanquish'd crew
    Kneel o'er their prostrate arms,
Implore respite of vengeance, due
    For all these dire alarms.
Now, while Humanity's warm glow,
    Half weeps the guilty slain,
Let Conquest gladden every brow,
    And god-like Mercy reign.

Thus Fancy paints that awful day,
    Yes, dreadful, should it come;
But Britain's sons, in stern array,
    Shall brave its darkest gloom.

---

* Written during the last century when France threatened invasion.

Who fights, his native rights to save,
His worth shall have its claim;
The Bard will consecrate his grave,
And give his name to fame.

THE DIRGE OF CAROLAN.*

Air—"Ballymoney."

"YE maids of green Erin, why sigh ye so sad,
The summer is smiling, all nature is glad."
The summer may smile, and the shamrock may bloom,
But the pride of green Erin lies cold in the tomb;
And his merits demand all the tears that we shed,
Though they ne'er can awaken the slumbering dead;
Yet still they shall flow—for dear Carolan we mourn,
For the soul of sweet music now sleeps in his urn.

---

* [Carolan is the most celebrated of all the modern Irish bards. He was born in the village of Nobber, county of Westmeath, 1670, and died in 1739. He never regretted the loss of his sight, but used gaily to say, "My eyes are only transported into my ears. It has been said of his music, by O'Conner, the celebrated historian, who knew him intimately, that so happy, so elevated was he in some of his compositions, he attained the approbation of that great master Geminiani, who never saw him. His execution, too, on the harp, was rapid and

Ye bards of our isle, join our grief with your songs,
For the deepest regret to our memory belongs ;
In our cabins and fields, on our mountains and plains,
How oft have we sung to his heart melting strains.
Ah ! these strains shall survive, long as time they shall last,
Yet they now but remind us of joys that are past;
And our days, crowned with pleasure, can never return,
For the soul of sweet music now sleeps in his urn.

Yes, thou pride of green Erin ! thy honours thou'lt have,
Seven days, seven nights, we shall weep round thy grave ;
And thy harp that so oft to our ditties has rung,
To the lorn-sighing breeze o'er thy grave shall be hung;
And the song shall ascend thy bright worth to proclaim,
That thy shade may rejoice in the voice of thy fame;
But our days, crowned with pleasure, can never return,
For the soul of sweet music now sleeps in thine urn.

---

impressive, far beyond that of all the professional competitors of the age in which
he lived.   The charms of woman, the pleasures of conviviality, and the power of
poetry and music, were at once his theme and inspiration ; and his life was an
illustration of his theory ; for until his last ardour was chilled by death, he loved,
drank, and sang.   While in the fervour of composition, he was constantly heard
to pass sentence on his own effusions, as they rose on his harp, or breathed
from his lips ; blaming and praising, with equal vehemence, the unsuccessful
effort and felicitous attempt.   He was the welcome guest of every house, from
the peasant to the prince, but in the true wandering spirit of his profession, he
never stayed to exhaust that welcome.   He lived and died poor.—LADY
MORGAN.]

ADIEU, YE CHEERFUL NATIVE PLAINS.

Air—" The green woods of Treugh."

———

ADIEU, ye cheerful native plains,
　Dungeon glooms receive me,
Nought, alas, for me remains,
　Of all the joys ye gave me—
　　　All are flown !
Banish'd from thy shores, sweet Erin,
I, through life, must toil, despairing,
　　　Lost and unknown.

Howl, ye winds ! around my cell,
　Nothing now can wound me ;
Mingling with your dreary swell,
　Prison groans surround me :
　　　Bodings wild !
Treachery, thy ruthless doing,
Long I'll mourn in hopeless ruin,
　　　Lost and exiled !

RESPONSIVE, YE WOODS.

Air—" My time, O ye Muses."

RESPONSIVE, ye woods, wing your echoes along,
Till Nature, all sad, weeping, listen my song,
Till flocks cease their bleating, and herds cease to low,
And the clear winding rivulet scarce seems to flow.
For, fair was the flower that once gladden'd our plains,
Sweet rosebud of virtue, ador'd by our swains;
But Fate, like a blast from the chill wintry wave,
Has laid my sweet flower in yon cold silent grave.

Her warm feeling breast did with sympathy glow,
In innocence pure as the new mountain snow;
Her face was more fair than the mild apple bloom,
Her voice sweet as Hope, whisp'ring pleasures to come.
Oh, Mary, my love! wilt thou never return!
'Tis thy William who calls! burst the bands of thy urn!
Together we'll wander—poor wretch, how I rave!
My Mary lies low in the lone silent grave.

Yon tall leafy planes throw a deep solemn shade
O'er the dear holy spot where my Mary is laid,
Lest the light wanton sunbeams obtrude on the gloom,
That lorn love and friendship have wove round her tomb.

Still there let the mild tears of nature remain,
Till calm dewy ev'ning weep o'er her again ;
There oft I will wander—no boon now I crave,
But to weep life away o'er the dark silent grave.

YE DEAR ROMANTIC SHADES.

Air—"Mrs. Hamilton of Wishaw's Strathspey."

FAR from the giddy court of mirth,
  Where sickening follies reign,
By Levern banks * I wander forth
  To hail each sylvan scene.
All hail, ye dear romantic shades !
Ye banks, ye woods, and sunny glades !
Here oft the musing Poet treads
  In Nature's riches great :
Contrasts the country with the town,
Makes Nature's beauties all his own ;
And, borne on Fancy's wings, looks down
  On empty pride and state.

---

* *Levern banks.*—See Note on "The Flower of Levernside," page 175.

By dewy dawn, or sultry noon,
    Or sober evening gray,
I'll often quit the dinsome town,
    By Levern banks to stray.

Or from the upland's mossy brow
Enjoy the fancy-pleasing view
Of streamlets, woods, and fields below,
    And sweetly varied scene.
Give riches to the miser's care,
Let Folly shine in Fashion's glare,
Give me the wealth of peace and health,
    With all their happy train.

THOUGH HUMBLE MY LOT.

Air—" Her sheep had in clusters."

WHERE primroses spring on the green-tufted brae,
    And the riv'let runs murm'ring below,
Oh, Fortune! at morning, or noon, let me stray,
    And thy wealth on thy vot'ries bestow.
For, oh! how enraptured my bosom does glow
    As calmly I wander alone,
Where wild woods, and bushes, and primroses grow,
    And a streamlet enlivens the scene.

Though humble my lot, not ignoble's my state,
  Let me still be contented, though poor ;
What Destiny brings, be resigned to my fate,
  Though Misfortune should knock at my door.
I care not for honour, preferment, nor wealth,
  Nor the titles that affluence yields,
While blythely I roam, in the heyday of health,
  'Midst the charms of my dear native fields.

BONNIE WINSOME MARY.

Gaelic Air.

FORTUNE, frowning most severe,
Forced me frae my native dwellin',
Parting wi' my friends so dear,
Cost me many a bitter tear ;
But, like the clouds of early day,
Soon my sorrows fled away,
When, blooming sweet and smiling gay,
I met my winsome Mary.

Wha can sit wi' gloomy brow,
Blest wi' sic a charming lassie ?
Native scenes, I think on you,
Yet the change I canna rue ;

Wand'ring many a weary mile,
Fortune seem'd to low'r the while,
But now she's gi'en me, for the toil,
My bonnie winsome Mary.

Tho' our riches are but few,
Faithful love is aye a treasure ;
Ever cheery, kind, an' true,
Nane but her I e'er can lo'e.
Hear me, a' ye pow'rs above,
Pow'rs, of sacred truth and love!
While I live I'll constant prove
To my dear winsome Mary.

THE MANIAC'S SONG.

Set to Music by R. A. SMITH

HARK ! 'tis the poor Maniac's song :
  She sits on yon wild craggy steep,
And while the winds mournfully whistle along,
  She wistfully looks o'er the deep :
And aye she sings, " Lullaby, lullaby, lullaby !"
  To hush the rude billows asleep.

She looks to yon rock far at sea,
  And thinks it her lover's white sail ;
The warm tear of joy glads her wild glist'ning eye,
  As she beckons, his vessel to hail ;
And aye she sings, " Lullaby, lullaby, lullaby ! "
  And frets at the boisterous gale.

Poor Susan was gentle and fair,
  Till the seas robbed her heart of its joy ;
Then her reason was lost in the gloom of despair,
  And her charms then did wither and die ;
And now her sad " Lullaby, lullaby, lullaby ! "
  Oft wakes the lone passenger's sigh.

THE NEGRO GIRL.

Set to Music by MR. ROSS *of Aberdeeu.*

Y ON poor negro girl, an exotic plant,
  Was torn from her dear native soil ;
Reluctantly borne o'er the raging Atlant,
  Then brought to Britannia's isle.
Though Fatima's mistress be loving and kind,
  Poor Fatima still must deplore ;
She thinks on her parents, left weeping behind,
  And sighs for her dear native shore.

She thinks on her Zadi, the youth of her heart,
  Who from childhood was loving and true ;
How he cried on the beach, when the ship did depart !
  'Twas a sad everlasting adieu.
The shell-woven gift which he bound round her arm,
  The rude seamen unfeelingly tore,
Nor left one sad relic her sorrows to charm,
  When far from her dear native shore.

And now, all dejected, she wanders apart,
  No friend, save retirement, she seeks ;
The sigh of despondency bursts from her heart,
  And tears dew her thin sable cheeks.
Poor hard-fated girl, long, long she may mourn !
  Life's pleasures to her are all o'er ;
Far fled ev'ry hope that she e'er shall return
  To revisit her dear native shore.

I MARK'D A GEM OF PEARLY DEW.

I MARK'D a gem of pearly dew,
  While wand'ring near yon misty mountain,
Which bore the tender flow'r so low,
  It dropp'd off into the fountain.

So thou hast wrung this gentle heart,
  Which in its core was proud to wear thee,
Till, drooping sick beneath thy art,
  It sighing found it could not bear thee.

Adieu, thou faithless fair! unkind!
  Thy falsehood dooms that we must sever;
Thy vows were as the passing wind,
  That fans the flow'r, then dies for ever.
And think not that this gentle heart,
  Though in its core 'twas proud to wear thee,
Shall longer droop beneath thy art;
  No, cruel fair! it cannot bear thee!*

THE BARD OF GLENULLIN.

THOUGH my eyes are grown dim, and my locks are turn'd gray,
I feel not the storm of life's bleak wintry day,
For my cot is well thatched, and my barns are full stored,
And cheerful content still presides at my board:

---

* Mr. Ramsay gives the following note on the origin of this song:—

"Tannahill and Smith once went on a fishing excursion with some acquaintances. The two friends being but tyros soon grew weary of lashing the water to no purpose, and separated for a little, each to amuse himself in his own fashion. When Smith rejoined the poet, he was shown this song written with a pencil. Tannahill had been occupied observing a blade of grass bending under the weight of a dew-drop, and this trifling object had suggested to him the simile embodied in the song."

Warm-hearted Benevolence stands at my door,
Dispensing her gifts to the wandering poor,
The glow of the heart does my bounty repay,
And lightens the cares of life's bleak wintry day.

From the summit of years I look down on the vale,
Where Age pines in sorrow, neglected and pale ;
Where the sunshine of Fortune scarce deigns to bestow
One heart-cheering smile to the wand'rers below.
From the sad dreary prospect this lesson I drew,
That those who are helpless are friended by few ;
So, with vigorous industry, I smooth'd the rough way
That leads through the vale of life's bleak wintry day.

Then, my son, let the bard of Glen-Ullin advise,
(For years can give counsel, experience make wise) ;
'Midst thy wand'rings let Honour for aye be thy guide,
O'er thy actions let Honesty ever preside.
Then, though hardships assail thee, in virtue thou'lt smile,
For light is the heart that's untainted with guile ;
But, if Fortune attend thee, my counsels obey,
Prepare for the storms of life's bleak wintry day.

MY DEAR HIELAN' LADDIE, O.

Air—" Morneen I gaberland.

———

BLYTHE was the time when he fee'd wi' my faither, O,
Happy war the days when we herded thegither, O,
Sweet war the hours when he row'd me in his plaidie, O,
An' vowed tae be mine, my dear Hielan' laddie, O.

But, ah ! waes me ! wi' their sodg'ring sae gaudy, O,
The laird's wys'd awa' my braw Hielan' laddie, O ;
Misty are the glens, and the dark hills sae cloudy, O,
That aye seemed sae blythe wi' my dear Hielan' laddie, O.

The blaeberry banks, noo, are lanesome an' dreary, O,
Muddy are the streams that gush'd doun sae clearly, O,
Silent are the rocks that echoed sae gladly, O,
The wild meltin' strains o' my dear Hielan' laddie, O.

He pu'd me the crawberry, ripe frae the boggy fen,
He pu'd me the strawberry, red frae the foggy glen,
He pu'd me the row'n frae the wild steep sae giddy, O,
Sae lovin' an' kind was my dear Hielan' laddie, O.

Fareweel my ewes ! an' fareweel my doggie, O,
Fareweel ye knowes ! now sae cheerless an' scroggie, O ;
Fareweel, Glenfeoch ! my mammie an' my daddie, O,
I will lea' ye a' for my dear Hielan' laddie, O.

FROM THE RUDE BUSTLING CAMP.

Air—'' My laddie is gane.''

From the rude bustling camp to the calm rural plain,
I've come, my dear Jeanie, to bless thee again;
Still burning for honour our warriors may roam,
But the laurel I wished for, I've won it at home:
All the glories of Conquest no joy could impart,
When far from the kind little girl of my heart;
Now, safely returned, I will leave thee no more,
But love my dear Jeanie till life's latest hour.

The sweets of retirement, how pleasing to me;
Possessing all worth, my dear Jeanie, in thee!
Our flocks' early bleating will wake us to joy,
And our raptures exceed the warm tints in the sky!
In sweet rural pastimes our days still will glide,
Till Time, looking back, will admire at his speed,
Still blooming in virtue, though youth then be o'er,
I'll love my dear Jeanie till life's latest hour.

ALL HAIL! YE DEAR ROMANTIC SCENES.

Air—Mr. Hamilton of Wishaw's Strathspey.

ALL hail! ye dear romantic scenes,
　　Where oft, as eve stole o'er the sky,
You've found me by the mountain streams,
　　Where blooming wild-flowers charm the eye.

The sun's now setting in the west,—
　　Mild are his beams on hill and plain;
No sound is heard save Killoch burn,*
　　Deep murm'ring down its woody glen.

Green be thy banks, thou silvery stream
　　That winds the flowery braes among,
Where oft I've woo'd the Scottish muse,
　　And raptured wove the rustic song.

Killoch Burn.—The moor road from Paisley to Neilston over Fereneze Braes skirts the Killoch Burn and Glen at its Neilston termination, and the stream, dashing in several cataracts down the deep ravine and over the rocky channel, is certainly a romantic scene. Killoch farm at this place lies on the east side of the burn and glen, and Auchentiber farm on the west side.—*See note on "Epistle to James Scadlock."*

YE WOOER LADS WHA GREET AN' GRANE.*

Air—" Callum Brogach."

Y E wooer lads wha greet an' grane,
Wha preach an' fleech,† an' mak' a mane,
An' pine yoursel's tae skin an' bane,
  Come a' to Callum Brogach.
I'll learn you here the only art
Tae win a bonnie lassie's heart—
Just tip wi' gowd Love's siller dart
  Like dainty Callum Brogach.

I ca'd her aye my sonsie doo,
The fairest flow'r that e'er I knew ;
Yet, like a souple spankie grew,
  She fled frae Callum Brogach.
But sune's she heard the guinea ring,
She turn'd as I had been a king,
Wi'—" Tak' my han' or ony thing,
  Dear, dainty Callum Brogach ! "

---

* This song first appeared in Mr Ramsay's edition, and is there stated to have been copied from a letter written by the author to Mr. John Crawford, Largs, March 17, 1810.

† " Fleech "—Wheedle, flatter.

It's gowd can mak' the blin' to see,
Can bring respec' whar nane wad be.
An' Cupid ne'er shall want his fee,
    Frae dainty Callum Brogach.
Nae mair wi' greetin' blin' your een,
Nae mair wi' sichin' warm the win',
But hire the gettlin' for your frien',
    Like dainty Callum Brogach.

AN' WAR YE AT DUNTOCHER BURN?*

An' war ye at Duntocher † burn?
  An' did ye see them a', man?
An' hoo's my wifie an' the bairns?
  I ha'e been lang awa', man.

---

* The last four stanzas of this song first appeared in Mr. Ramsay's edition, where they are given with the following explanatory note :—

" This is one of the pieces of which only the first stanzas were understood to have been preserved. The remainder of the above has been recovered from a letter to King, 9th May, 1809, in which the author says : 'The above is written on a real occurrence, which fell under my observation, but I doubt the subject is not very well suited for a song ; therefore I am the more anxious to have your mind on it,—not in that loose, vague way which goes for little or nothing, but in —— I have shown you a pattern in my last.' "

† *Duntocher* is situated in Old, or West Kilpatrick parish, Dumbartonshire. Flax and Cotton spinning was commenced in Duntocher in the year 1807, and shortly thereafter Mr. William Dunn purchased the Duntocher mill about 1808. Water was the driving power of machinery in those days, and streams with water falls were coveted spots for the erection of mills for the spinning of wool and cotton. The writer of this note recollects of hearing Mr. Dunn state, in 1821, that he had been a blacksmith in the village of Johnstone, Renfrewshire.

This hedger * wark's a weary trade,
  It doesna suit ava', man ;
Wi' lanely house an' lanely bed
  My comforts are but sma', man.

An' how's wee Sandy, Pate, an' Tam ?
  Sit doun an' tak' your blaw, man ;
Fey, lassie, rin, fetch in a dram,
  Tae treat my frien', John Lamon' ;
For ilka plack ye've gien tae mine,
  Your callans shall get twa, man ;
O were my heels as licht's my heart,
  I sune would see them a', man.

My blessing on her kindly heart,
  She likes tae see me braw, man ;
She's darn'd my hose, an' bleach'd my sarks
  As white's the driven snaw, man.
An' ere the win's o' Martinmas
  Sough thro' the scroggie shaw, man,
I'll lift my weel-hain'd penny fee,
  An' gang an' see them a', man.

---

* " Hedger "—Heckler.

WHY UNITE TO BANISH CARE?*

Air—" Let us taste the sparkling wine."

———

WHY unite to banish Care?
Let him come our joys to share;
Doubly blest our cup shall flow,
When it soothes a brother's woe;
'Twas for this the powers divine
Crown'd our board with generous wine.

Far be hence the sordid elf
Who'd claim enjoyment for himself;
Come, the hardy seaman, lame,
The gallant soldier, robb'd of fame;
Welcome all who bear the woes
Of various kind that merit knows.

---

* A melancholy interest attaches to this piece. It was composed two days before
the poet's sad end. In reference to this, R. A. Smith, in one of several letters to
Motherwell, while editing *The Harp of Renfrewshire* (First Series), says :—
"Two days before his death he showed me several poetical pieces of a most
strange texture, and in the afternoon of the same day he called on me again,
requesting me to return him a song that had been left for my perusal. I had
laid it past in a music book and was unable to find it at the time. It was his
last production and he seemed to be much disappointed when, after a long
search, I could not procure it for him."

"Patriot heroes, doomed to sigh,
Idle 'neath Corruption's eye ;
Honest tradesmen, credit worn,
Pining under Fortune's scorn ;
Wanting wealth, or lacking fame,
Welcome all that worth can claim.

"Come, the hoary-headed sage,
Suffering more from want than age ;
Come, the proud, though needy bard,
Starving 'midst a world's regard :
Welcome, welcome, one and all
That feel on this unfeeling ball."

WHEN ROSIE WAS FAITHFU'.*

Written on reading the "Harper of Mull," a Highland story.

Set to Music by R. A. SMITH.

WHEN Rosie was faithful, how happy was I,
Still gladsome as Simmer the time glided by ;
I play'd my harp cheerie, while fondly I sang
Of the charms o' my Rosie the winter nichts lang.

---

* In the island of Mull lived a harper, conspicuous for nothing so much as his exquisite performance on that instrument, and his attachment to a lovely rosy-cheeked nymph, who was esteemed by the inhabitants of the island as the sweetest object ever formed by the hand of nature. As the harper was universally esteemed and admired for his sprightly appearance, and the affectionate

But now I'm as waefu' as waefu' can be,
Come Simmer, come Winter, 'tis a' ane tae me :
For th' dark gloom o' falsehood sae clouds my sad soul,
That cheerless for aye is the Harper o' Mull.

I wander the glens an' the wild woods alane,
In their deepest recesses I mak' my sad mane ;
My harp's mournfu' melody joins in the strain,
While sadly I sing o' the days that are gane.
Tho' Rosie is faithless, she's no the less fair,
An' the thought o' her beauty but feeds my despair ;
Wi' painfu' remembrance my bosom is full,
An' weary o' life is the Harper o' Mull.

---

simplicity of his manners, he soon gained the heart of his Rosie, and in a few weeks after he made her his bride. Soon after the nuptial ceremony was performed, he set out on a visit to some low country friends, accompanied by Rosie and his harp, which had been a companion to him in all his journies for many years. Overtaken by the shades of night, in a solitary part of the country, a cold and shivering faintness fell upon Rosie, and she sank almost lifeless into the harper's arms. His tartan plaid he unbound from his arm, and hastily wrapped it round her shivering frame, but the cold sweat still gathered on her check. Distracted and alarmed, he hurried from place to place, in search of fuel to revive the dying ember of life. None could be found. His harp lay carelessly on the grass. Its neglected strings vibrated to the blast. The harper loved it dear as his own life, but he loved his Rosie better than either. His nervous arms were applied to its sides, and in a few minutes it lay crackling on the heath. Rosie soon revived, and resumed her journey as soon as morning began to purple the east. Stepping down the sloping side of a hill, they were met by a hunter on horseback, who addressed Rosie in the style of an old and familiar friend. The harper, innocent himself, and unsuspicious of others, paced slowly down the hill. Wondering at his Rosie's delay, he turned round and saw the faithless fair seated on the hunter's steed. The horse flew swift as the wind. The harper, transfixed in astonishment, gazed at them. Then pacing heavily home, he sighing, exclaimed—" Fool that I was to burn my harp for her."

As slumb'ring I lay by the dark mountain stream,
My lovely young Rosie appear'd in my dream;
I thought her still kind, an' I ne'er was sae blest,
As in fancy I clasp'd the dear nymph tae my breast.
Thou fause fleetin' vision, too soon thou wert o'er !
Thou wak'dst me to tortures unequall'd before ;
But Death's silent slumbers my griefs soon shall lull,
An' the green grass wave over the Harper o' Mull.

BONNIE WOOD O' CRAIGIELEA.

Thou bonnie wood o' Craigielea,
Thou bonnie wood o' Craigielea,
Near thee I pass'd life's early day,
An' won my Mary's heart in thee.

THE broom, the brier, the birken bush,
Bloom bonnie o'er thy flowery lea,
An' a' the sweets that ane can wish
Frae Nature's han', are strewed on thee.
Thou bonnie wood, &c.

---

* The "Bonnie Wood o' Craigielea" was situated to the north west of
Paisley, on part of the estate of Ferguslie, which bounds the road leading to
Blackstoun. It was within a few minutes' walk of Tannahill's residence in Queen
Street, and was one of his favourite haunts. Its "dark green plantin' shade"
continued to be a resort of the weavers of the west end of Paisley until the
most part of the wood was cut down about forty years ago. The ground is still

Far ben thy dark green plantin's shade,
　　The cushat croodles am'rously,
The mavis, doun thy bughted * glade,
　　Gars echo ring frae ev'ry tree.
　　　Thou bonnie wood, &c.

Awa', ye thochtless, murd'rin' gang,
　　Wha tear the nestlin's ere they flee !
They'll sing you yet a canty sang,
　　Then, oh ! in pity let them be !
　　　Thou bonnie wood, &c.

Whan Winter blaws in sleety showers,
　　Frae aff the Norlan hills sae hie,
He lightly skiffs thy bonnie bow'rs,
　　As laith to harm a flow'r in thee.
　　　Thou bonnie wood, &c.

---

adorned with the "broom and brier." The song of the " Bonnie Wood o' Craigielea " was set to music by James Barr, Kilbarchan, an intimate acquaintance of Tannahill, to whom he addressed a poetic epistle, and refers as " Blythe Jamie Barr o' Barchan's Toun." Mr. Barr was a native of Tarbolton, and came when young to reside in Kilbarchan, where he was employed as a weaver. It was at this time he composed the tune. He was an accomplished player of the violin and flute, and taught instrumental music bands. About the year 1820, he removed to Glasgow, and commenced business as a tuner of pianofortes. From Glasgow he went with his family in 1832 to St. John's, New Brunswick, and followed the occupation of farming for upwards of twenty years, when he again returned to Glasgow, whence he removed to Govan, where he died on 24th February, 1860, at the ripe age of seventy-nine years. His wife died a year before him. Their last resting-place is marked by a tombstone in the burying-ground attached to the United Presbyterian Church of Kilbarchan.

* *Bughted.*—Winding.

Tho' fate should drive me south the line,
Or o'er the wide Atlantic sea,
The happy hours I'll ever min',
That I in youth ha'e spent in thee.
Thou bonnie wood, &c.

THE FIVE FRIENDS.[*]

Air—We're a' noddin'.

WEEL, wha's in the bouroch, an' what is your cheer?
The best that ye'll find in a thousand year.
  And we're a' noddin', nid nid noddin',
  We're a' noddin' fu' at e'en.

---

[*] The "Five Friends" were—James Clark of Campbellton, William Stewart of Glasgow, James Barr of Kilbarchan (see note to previous Song), R. A. Smith, and Tannahill himself.

R. A. Smith, in a communication to Motherwell, says in reference to this song :—"The little bacchanalian rant you are so anxious to know the history of was written in commemoration of a very happy evening spent by the poet with four of his musical friends. At that meeting he was in high spirits, and his conversation became more than usually animated ; many songs were sung, and we had some glee singing, but neither *fiddle* nor *flute* made its appearance in company, nor were any of us 'nid, nid, noddin'.' We were 'unco happy,' and had just such a 'drappie in our e'e' as enabled us to bid defiance to Care for the time being ; but the poet thought proper to embellish his song with the old chorus, 'We're a' noddin',' and rather than throw aside a lucky thought he chose to depict his ain bardship, 'as blind as an owl,' but I assure you this was not the case ; his bardship had all his faculties 'sitting lightly on him.' As the merry rhymes in question were never intended for the public eye, I hope you will not give a copy to any person."

'There's our ain Jamie Clark, frae the ha' o' Argyle,
W' his leal Scottish heart, an' his kind open smile.
And we're a' noddin', etc.

There is Will the guid fallow, wha kills a' our care
Wi' his sang an' his joke, an' a mutchkin mair.
And we're a' noddin', etc.

'There is blythe Jamie Barr, frae St. Barchan's toun,*
When wit gets a kingdom, he's sure o' the croun.
And we're a' noddin', etc.

There is Rab, frae the south, wi' his fiddle an' his flute;
I could list tae his strains till the starns† fa' out.
And we're a' noddin', etc.

Apollo, for our comfort, has furnished the bowl,
An' here is my bardship, as blind as an owl.
For we're a' noddin', etc.

HEY, DONALD! HO, DONALD!

THOUGH Simmer smiles on bank an' brae,
An' Nature bids the heart be gay,
Yet a' the joys o' flow'ry May
  Wi' pleasure ne'er can move me.

---

* The town of Kilbarchan.   † *Starns*—stars.

Hey, Donald! ho, Donald!
Think upon your vow, Donald;
Min' the heathery knowe, Donald,
Whar ye vow'd tae lo'e me.

MEG O' THE GLEN.
Air—" When she cam' ben she bobbit."

M EG o' the glen set aff tae the fair,
Wi' ruffles, an' ribbons, an' meikle prepare ;
Her heart it was heavy, her heid it was licht,
For a' the lang way for a wooer she sicht.
She spak' tae the lads, but the lads slippet by,
She spak' tae the lassies, the lassies war shy ;
She thocht she might dae, but she didna weel ken,
For nane seem'd tae care for Meg o' the Glen.

THE LASSIE O' MERRY EIGHTEEN.

M Y faither wad ha'e me tae marry the miller,
My mither wad ha'e me tae marry the laird,
But brawly I ken it's the love o' the siller,
That heightens their fancy tae ony regard.
The miller is crookit, the miller is crabbit,
The laird, tho' he's wealthy, he's lyart an' lean ;
He's auld, an' he's cauld, an' he's blin', an' he's bald,
An' he's no' for a lassie o' merry Eighteen.

THE LASSES A' LEUGH.

Air—"Kiss'd yestreen."

THE lassies a' leugh, an' the carlin flate,
But Maggie was sittin' fu' ourie an' blate,
The auld silly gawkie, she couldna contain,
How brawly she was kiss'd yestreen ;
  Kiss'd yestreen, kiss'd yestreen,
How brawly she was kiss'd yestreen ;
She blether'd it roun' tae her fae an' her frien',
  How brawly she was kiss'd yestreen.

COME HAME TO YOUR LINGELS.

Air—Whistle an' I'll come to you, my lad.

COME hame tae your lingels, ye ne'er-do-weel loon,
You're the king o' the dyvours,* the talk o' the toun ;
Sae soon as the Munonday mornin' comes in,
Your wearifu' daidlin'† again maun begin.
Guidwife, ye're a skillet,‡ your tongue's just a bell,
Tae the peace o' guid fallows it rings the death-knell ;
But clack till ye deafen auld Barnaby's mill,
The souter shall aye hae his Munonday's yill.

---

* *Dyvour.*—A lazy sort of person who hangs about the street, unwilling to
work.

† *Daidling.*—Trifling.   ‡ *Skillet.*—The small bell of the town-crier. A
scold's tongue.

THE SOLDIER'S FUNERAL.
Air,--" Holden's Dead March."

N OW let the procession move solemn and slow,
While the soft mournful music accords with our woe,
While Friendship's warm tears round his ashes are shed,
And soul-melting Memory weeps for the dead.
Kind, good-hearted fellow as ever was known !
So kind and so good every heart was his own ;
Now, alas ! low in death are his virtues all o'er ;
How painful the thought, we will see him no more !

In camp or in quarters he still was the same,
Each countenance brighten'd wherever he came ;
When the wars of his country impell'd him to roam,
He cheerful, would say, all the world was his home.
And when the fierce conflict of armies began,
He fought like a lion, yet felt as a man ;*
For when British brav'ry had vanquish'd the foe,
He'd weep o'er the dead by his valour laid low.

Ye time-fretted mansions ! ye mould'ring piles!
Loud echo his praise through your long vaulted aisles ;
If haply his shade nightly glide through your gloom,
O tell him our hearts lie with him in the tomb !

----

* " They bore as heroes, but they felt as man."
Pope's Homer.
" He thought as a sage, while he felt as a man."
Beattie's Hermit.

And say, though he's gone, long his worth shall remain,
Remember'd, belov'd, by the whole of the men :—
Whoe'er acts like him, with a warm feeling heart,
Friendship's tears drop applause at the close of his part.

MARJORY MILLER.

LOUDER than the trump of fame
  Is the voice of Marjory Miller;
Time, the wildest beast can tame,
She's eternally the same :
  Loud the mill's incessant clack,
Loud the clink of Vulcan's hammer,
  Loud the deep-mouth'd cataract,
But louder far her dinsome clamour !
  Nought on earth can equal be
  To the noise of Marjory.

Calm succeeds the tempest's roar,
  Peace does follow war's confusion,
Dogs do bark and soon give o'er,
But she barks for evermore.

Loud's the sounding bleachfield horn,
But her voice is ten times louder !
Red's the sun on winter morn,
But her face is ten times redder !
She delights in endless strife,
Lord preserve's from such a wife !

NOW WINTER IS GANE.

Air,—" The fair-haired child."

*　　*　　*　　*　　*　　*

YE mind when the snaw lay sae deep on the hill,
When cauld icy cranreuch hung white on the tree,
When bushes were leafless, and mournfully still
Were the wee birds o' sweet Woodhouselee :
When snaw show'rs were fa'ing,
And wintry winds blawing,
Loud whistling o'er mountain and meadow sae chill,
We mark'd it wi' sorrowin' e'e ;
But now since the flowers
Again busk the bowers,
O come, my dear lassie, wi' smilin' good-will,
And wander around Woodhouselee.

BRAVE LEWIE ROY.

An old Gaelic Air.

BRAVE Lewie Roy was the flower of our Highlandmen,
Tall as the oak on the lofty Benvoirlich,
Fleet as the light-bounding tenants of Fillin-glen,*
Dearer than life to his lovely *neen voiuch.*†
Lone was his biding, the cave of his hiding,
When forc'd to retire with our gallant Prince Charlie,
Though manly and fearless, his bold heart was cheerless
Away from the lady he aye loved so dearly.

O HOW CAN YOU GANG LASSIE.

Air—The bonniest lass in a' the warld.

O HOW can you gang, lassie, how can you gang,
O how can you gang sae to grieve me !
Wi' your beauty, and your art, ye hae broken my heart,
For I never, never dreamt ye would leave me.

---

* *Benvoirlich and Fillin Glen.*—The readers are referred to the note on the "Braes of Balquhither." The high mountain of Benvoirlich is 3300 feet above the level of the sea, and is situated in the parish of Comrie, in the neighbourhood of the braes of Balquhither. Fillin Glen, named after one of the saints of the Culdees, Saint Fillin, is also situated in the parish of Comrie.

† Beautiful maid.

I'LL LAY ME ON THE WINTRY LEA.

Air—Waly, waly,—old Set.

I'LL lay me on the wintry lea,
 An' sleep amidst the wind an' weet,
An' ere another's bride I be,
 O bring tae me my winding sheet !

What can a hapless lassie do,
 Whan ilka freen' wad prove her foe,
Wad gar her break her dearest vow,
 Tae wed wi' ane she canna lo'e ?

FAITHLESS NANNIE.

FULL eighteen Simmers up life's brae,
 I speeded on fu' canny, O,
Till sleeky Love threw in my way
 Young, bonnie, fair-haired Nannie, O.

I woo'd her soon, I wan her syne,
 Our vows o' love war mony, O,
An', O what happy days war mine,
 Wi' bonnie fair-haired Nannie, O.

DAVIE TULLOCH'S BONNIE KATIE.

DAVIE TULLOCH'S bonnie Katie,
  Davie's bonnie blythesome Katie,
Tam the laird cam' doun yestreen,
  He socht her love, but gat her pity.

Wi' tremblin' grip he squeez'd her haun',
  While his auld heart gaed pitty-patty;
Aye he thocht his gear an' laun'
  Wad win the love o' bonnie Katie.

Davie Tulloch's bonnie Katie,
  Davie's bonnie blythesome Katie,
Aye she smil'd as Tammie wil'd,
  Her smile was scorn, yet mixt wi' pity.

O LADDIE, CAN YE LEAVE YE.

O LADDIE, can ye leave me!
  Alas! 'twill break this constant heart!
There's nought on earth can grieve me
  Like this, that we must part.
Think on the tender vow you made
  Beneath the secret birken shade,
And can you now deceive me!
  Is a' your love but art?

THOU CAULD GLOOMY FEBERWAR.

———

THOU cauld gloomy Feberwar,
  O gin thou wert awa',
I'm wae to hear thy sughin' winds,
  I'm wae to see thy snaw;
For my bonnie brave young Hielander,
  The lad I lo'e sae dear,
Has vow'd to come an' see me,
  In the spring o' the year.

———

NOW, MARION, DRY YOUR TEARFU' E'E.

———

NOW, Marion, dry your tearfu' e'e,
  Gae break ye're rock in twa,
For soon ye're gallant sons ye'll see,
  Return'd in safety a'.
O wow, gudeman, my heart is fain!
An' shall I see my bairns again,
A' seated roun' our ain hearth-stane,
  Nae mair tae gang awa'?

AWAY, GLOOMY CARE.*

AWAY, gloomy Care, there's no place for thee here,
   Where so many good fellows are met;
Thou would'st dun the poor bard ev'ry day in the year,
   Yet I'm sure I am none in thy debt.
Go, soak thy old skin in the Miser's small beer,
   And keep watch in his cell all the night;
And if in the morning thou dar'st to appear,
   By Jove, I shall drown thee outright.

THE POOR MAN'S LAMENT FOR THE DEATH OF HIS COW.

HOW gay rose this morning, how cheerful was I,
No care on my mind, and no colud on the sky;
I dreamt not ere night that my sorrows should flow,
Bewailing the fate of my poor drimindo.*

AWAKE, MY HARP, THE CHEERFUL STRAIN.

AWAKE, my harp, the cheerful strain !
   Shall I, the first of Erin's warrior band,
     In wasting sorrow still complain?
   The first to dare stern Danger's bloody field,
     Shall I to silly, changeful woman yield?

---

* This and the following seven Fragments were first published in Mr. Ramsay's edition.
     † *Drimindu.*—A name for the cow.

No,—raise, my harp, the cheerful strain,
What is a rosy cheek, or lily hand !
Since thus she scorns, I'll scorn again.

THE SOLDIER'S ADIEU.

THE weary sun's gane doun the west,
The birds sit nodding on the tree,
All Nature now inclines for rest,
But rest allow'd there's nane for me :
The trumpet calls to War's alarms,
The rattling drum forbids my stay;
Ah ! Nancy, bless thy soldier's arms,
For ere morn I will be far away.

O WEEP NOT, MY LOVE.

O WEEP not, my love, though I go to the war,
For soon I'll return rich with honours to thee;
The soul-rousing pibroch is sounding afar,
And the clans are assembling in Morar-craiglee :
Our flocks are all plunder'd, our herdsmen are murder'd,
And, fir'd with oppression, aveng'd we shall be ;
To-morrow we'll vanquish these ravaging English,
And then I'll return to thy baby and thee.

SING ON, THOU SWEET WARBLER.

SING on, thou sweet warbler, thy glad e'ening song,
   And charm the lone echoes the green woods among;
As dear unto thee is the sun's setting beam,
   So dear unto me is the soul's melting dream:
The dark Winter frowning, all pleasure disowning,
Shall strip thy green woods and be deaf to thy moaning;
But dark stormy Winter is yet far away,
   Then let us be glad, when all Nature is gay.

LONE IN YON DARK SEQUESTER'D GROVE.

LONE in yon dark sequester'd grove,
   Poor hapless Lubin strays;
A prey to ill-requited love,
   He spends his joyless days:
Ah! cruel Jessie, couldst thou know
   What worthy heart was thine,
Thou ne'er hadst wrong'd poor Lubin so,
   Nor left that heart to pine.

THE BANKS OF SPEY.

SCENES of my childhood, your wanderer hails you,
Wing'd with rude storm, though the Winter assails you,
Bleak and dreary as ye are, ye yet hae charms to cheer me,
For here, amidst my native hills, my bonnie lassie's near me;

'Tis sad to see the wither'd lea, the drumly flooded fountain,
The angry storm in awful form, that sweeps the moor and mountain;
But frae the surly swelling blast, dear lassie, I'll defend her,
And frae the bonnie banks o' Spey* I never more shall wander.

KITTY O'CARROL.

YE may boast of your charms, and be proud, to be sure,
As if there was never such beauty before ;
But ere I got wedded to old Thady More,
I had dozens of wooers each night at my door,
With their " Och dear! O will you marry me,
   Kitty O'Carrol, the joy of my soul !"

MY DAYS HAE FLOWN WI' GLEESOME SPEED.

MY days hae flown wi' gleesome speed,
   Grief ne'er sat heavy on my mind,
Sae happy wi' my rural reed,
   I lilted every care behind;
I've been vext and sair perplext
   When friends prov'd false, or beauty shy ;
But, like gude John o' Badenyon,
   I croon'd my lilt and car'd na by.

---

* *Spey.*—The author introduces this sonnet as the "scenes of my childhood," but it must have been written for another person. The Spey is one of the principal rivers of Scotland, celebrated for the rapidity of its course. It derives its name from a small loch called Spey in Inverness-shire ; and after flowing a course of 120 miles, with all its windings, and receiving the water of tributary streams, it falls into the Moray Firth at Garmouth.

APPENDIX.

Paisley Burns Club.

The following argument for the formation of a Paisley
Burns' Club by Tannahill may be taken as a specimen of the
poet's prose composition.   William Maclaren and the poet
seem to have been the chief promoters of the Burns Club,
the former having been the first president, and the latter the
first secretary.   The argument is entirely the holograph
of the poet, and also the accompanying resolution to form
the Club.

ARGUMENT.

"That man is the only creature capable of enjoying an
eminent degree of felicity is a truth so evident and so
generally admitted that it were foolish to labour for its
proof.   An indulgent Nature, ever attentive to the happiness of her offspring, has enriched the world with men of
superior intellect, who by the splendour of their genius, the
fascinating charms of their writings, have, like the sun,
which dissipates the vapours of the night, dispersed the
dark clouds of ignorance, have taught the vacant hours of
life to steal on with uninterrupted felicity, and thus in an
eminent degree contributed to the happiness of manhood.
Shall we, then, suffer such characters to pass unnoticed ?
No.   Ye illustrious benefactors of the world ! we will
cherish, we will celebrate your memories ! your virtues are
already engraven on our hearts, and the tears of honest
gratitude shall bedew your tombs ; posterity will imitate
and applaud the deed, and your proud names shall roll on
through an eternity of years.

"Animated by these reflections, a number of the admirers of Robert Burns met on the 29th January, 1805, in the Star Inn, Paisley, to celebrate his memory, when a beautiful bust of the bard, painted by an eminent artist, was exhibited from the window. The company, amounting to nearly seventy, sat down to supper, after which the president (William Maclaren) addressed the company, and proposed "The Memory of our immortal Bard, Robert Burns."

"The toast was drunk with enthusiasm, after which the following Ode (written for the occasion), was read to the company.*

Among the many toasts drunk in the course of the evening were the following :—"May the genius of Scotland be as conspicuous as her mountains;" "May Burns be admired while a thistle grows in Caledonia;" "May Scotia never want the sword of a Wallace, nor the pen of a Burns." The night went off with uninterrupted harmony; and the company, resolving to meet annually on the same occasion, appointed the following gentlemen to conduct the business of the ensuing year:—

> WILLIAM MACLAREN.
> WILLIAM ANDERSON.
> CHARLES MARSHALL.
> PATRICK M'LERIE.
> ROBERT MORGAN.
> ROBERT LANG.
> ROBERT A. SMITH.
> WILLIAM STEWART.
> JAMES TANNAHILL.
> WILLIAM WYLIE, West Street.
> JAMES SCADLOCK, Abbey Close.
> WILLIAM GEMMIL.
> JOHN KING.
> ROBERT TANNAHILL."

The meetings of the Club continued to be held with considerable regularity up till 1836, when, at a preliminary meeting—Mr. Robert Lang in the chair, and Mr. John Crawford acting as clerk—"It was agreed that the 31st Anniversary of the Bard should be celebrated on the evening of Monday first in the Saracen's Head Inn, at 8 o'clock." The next minute is dated 18th March, 1874 (an interval of

---

* See page 55.

thirty-eight years). It states that the 31st anniversary was celebrated in pursuance of the preceding meeting.

"Paisley, 18th March, 1874.

" The thirty-first anniversary was celebrated in pursuance of the preceding minute. I was in the chair; Mr. Alexander Borland was croupier. Mr. Gavin Browning (who was chairman at the celebration of the 30th anniversary), Mr. John Auld, writer, Mr. Joseph Fleming, writer, were, I recollect, among those present. There might be from twenty to twenty-five gentlemen in the company. The meeting was held, not in the large hall, but lesser hall, upstairs. Mr. Granger, a nephew of Mr. Thomas Granger, civil engineer (who was then engaged surveying the line of the Paisley and Renfrew Railway) attended the meeting. He was an exquisite singer, and contributed largely to the delight of the meeting by his songs.

"JOHN CRAWFORD."

Since 1836, no meeting of the club has been held ; but it is proposed to resuscitate the club at the anniversary in 1875.

First Epistle to James Scadlock, page 86.

" Your ' Spring's ' a precious evergreen,
Fresh beauties budding still ;
Your ' Levern banks ' and ' Killochburn,'
Ye sing them wi' sae sweet a turn."

James Scadlock. -- He was born in Paisley in 1755, and died at Grahamston, on the Levern, in the parish of Neilston, on 4th July, 1818. He was a flower-designer, and afterwards an engraver at Fereneze Printfield. He sketched the ticket of admission to the membership of the Paisley Croft Society, and it bears his name as draughtsman. The Society was formed in 1761 by the weaver feuars of the Croft in Paisley, from William, 7th Earl of Dundonald, in the sixth decade of the 18th century, and both Tannahill and Scadlock became members of the society. The ticket commences with the motto—

"In unity we all agree."

Then follows a coat of arms—the armorial bearings of the

weavers. A shield with a cheveron, *argent*, charged with three cinquefoils, and three cats' heads, each with a shuttle in the mouth, in dexter and sinister chief, and base, *azure*. The *crest*, a cat's head, with a shuttle in the mouth, with a cap made of coops or pirns. There are also two oval pictures on the ticket, one with a widow and three orphan children, and the other containing the figure of Justice with sword and balance. There is also inscribed on the ticket—

" ERECTED IN 1761.

THE PAISLEY CROFT SOCIETY.

HERE POVERTY AND SICKNESS

CAN CLAIM RELIEF."

James Scadlock was also a poet, and he wrote the volume referred to in the Epistle, " The Scottish Exile," " Levern Banks," " Killochburn," and other songs, which were published in 1818.   It may be acceptable to present a few of his verses to the reader, which made the heart-strings of Tannahill thrill.   In one of these he sings—

> " The sun's now setting in the west,
> And mild's his beams on hill and plain ;
> No sound is heard, save Killoch burn
> Wild murmuring down its woody glen."

Again in another, of his songs—

> " Hark ! the winds around us swell,
> Raving down Glen Killoch dell,
> Where aft wi' thee, my bonnie Bell,
> I've wander'd blythe and cheery."

And again in another, to the air of " Ewe Buchts Marion,"

> " Will ye go to Glen Killoch, my Mary,
> Where the burnie falls over the linn,
> Its murmurs are dear to me, Mary,
> When borne on the soft breathing win'."

Second Epistle to James Scadlock, then at Perth, June, 1804, page 96.

> Alang the banks of classic Tay,
> *   *   *   *
>
> Think on our walks by Stanely tow'r,
> And sage Gleniffer brae ;
> *   *   *   *

Think on our walks by sweet Greenlaw,
*   *   *   *
And think on rural Ferguslie.
*   *   *   *
Yon mentor, Geordie Zimmerman,
Agrees exactly with our plan.

Tay.—The classic Tay is one of the principal rivers in Scotland, and Tannahill reminded his friend, then residing in the fair town of Perth, in musing on its banks, to remember their walks of solitude in places around ancient Paisley, endeared to them from their youth.

Greenlaw.—Scadlock was brought up in the Abbey Close of Paisley, and of course his walks were on the east or Newtown side of the river Cart. Greenlaw path and Arkleston road would be the walks of solitude in that district. *Easter Greenlaw* belonged to Mr. Charles Ross, surveyor, who, in 1760, built a house thereon in the Ionic order of architecture. He made a nursery on his lands for fruit and forest trees, and for evergreen and flowering shrubs. He published a map of the county of Renfrew, besides other county maps, and "The Traveller's Guide to Lochlomond in 1792." *Wester Greenlaw* belonged to Robert Corse, Esq., merchant. In 1780 he built a splendid mansion on Greenlaw hill, after the Corinthian order, and its elevation was given in William Semple's plan of Paisley, published in 1782. This house, now possessed by John Morgan, Esq., is one of the finest looking mansions in Paisley at the present day.

Geordie Zimmerman.—The familiar Scots orthography of one of the Christian names of this foreign author is characteristic of a Paisley weaver. Johann Gorg von Zimmerman, the celebrated author of a treatise on *Solitude*, was born at Brug, in Switzerland, in 1728, and died at Hanover, in 1775, aged 67.

Epistle to William Thomson, page 101.

"Amang the braes of Overton."

Overton.—Places with this name are numerous ; one almost in every landward parish. Among so many places it is difficult to fix on the right one without particular and well corroborated information. Persons supposed to have the most correct knowledge of matters regarding the Poet were applied to on the subject, and each of them gave

different Overtons. The writer, with these conflicting statements, was placed in a dilemma which to choose, when
there was opportunely handed to him an envelope containing a letter, which, on his opening, he found on it an address
in the well-known hand-writing of Tannahill, "Mr. Thomson, Overton, near Beith." That authentic document,
dated 1st May, 1807, at once settled the right place, and it
was neither of the places supposed by others. The letter is
well composed, and has been preserved in this volume.
William Thomson, an old friend and a member of the same
social club with the poet, had obtained subscribers to the
first edition of Tannahill's poems, and the letter accompanied
the 29 volumes sent to Mr. Thomson.

Will M'Neil's Elegy, page 115.

" To visit auld I-Columb-kill,
    *   *   *   *   *
He clamb the heights of Jura's isle.
    *   *   *   *   *
He rang'd thro' Morven's hills and glens,
Saw some of Ossian's moss grown stanes."

* *Will Macneil.*—William M'Neil was a surgeon in West
or Old Kilpatrick, and survived Tannahill several years.

† *I-Columb-Kill.*—The illustrious island of Iona, which
was once the luminary of Caledonia, from whence were sent
the benefits of knowledge and the blessings of religion
among savage clans and roving barbarians. Iona is known
by four names,—1st, *Innis-nan Druidhneach*—the Isle of
the Druids; 2nd, *Ii*—the Island by way of eminence; 3rd,
Ii-Cholum-chille—the Isle of Colum of the Cell; and 4th,
Ii-shona—the Blessed or Sacred Isle. Iona was the burial-
place of the kings of Scotland until 1056, when Malcom
(III.) Canmore succeeded to the throne. In the end of the
12th century, or beginning of the 13th century, some Cluniac
monks from Paisley landed in Iona, and erected the
Cathedral. The edifice was cruciform, and dedicated to
Saint Mary. The capitals of the columns are carved with
grotesque figures, still very sharp, and well preserved.
Besides these quaint delineations, there are several dragons
with tails ending in scrolls and foliage. In that portion of
the Isle, are to be seen the romantic remains of Monasteries

both of monks and nuns, Cathedral, Chapels, Colleges, and Oratories,—ruins of ancient grandeur, piety, and literature, surrounded by the old sanctuary of the dead, with their mouldering tombstones of Scots, Irish, and Norway kings, Lords of the Isles, chieftains, and bishops, priests, abbesses, nuns, and friars.

Morven.—Tannahill was a great admirer of Ossian's poems, and must have particularly studied his poem of "The war of *Inis-thona.*" Morven, or Morvern, in Argyllshire, bounded on the south by the Sound of Mull, is a modern parish composed of the two ancient parishes of Killcomkill and Killintag, which were united about the time of the Reformation. It includes the greater part of the Lordship of Morvern. *Killcolmkill*, the church of Saint Columba in Morwarne ; a small portion of the ruins of the church and the burying ground remain. This district was at one time considered the land of Morven, as stated in the poems of Ossian, and generally believed in the days of Tannahill, but investigations since that period have dissipated the land of song. Professor Wilson, in his poem of " Inismore," a Dream of the Highlands, writes of this parish—

> " Morven and Morn, and Spring and Solitude !
> In front is not the scene magnificent ?
> *　　　*　　　*　　　*　　　*
>
> Morven and Morn, and Spring and Solitude !
> A multitudinous sea of mountain-tops."

Woodhouselee.—This place is in the parish of Glencross, Edinburghshire, the seat of the Tytler family ; and Ramsay, in his " Gentle Shepherd," says the parish is a place

> " Where a' the sweets o' spring an' simmer grow."

Connell and Flora.
" O will you go to Garnock side."

* *Garnock.*—This river rises at the base of the hill of Staik, in the Parish of Lochwinnoch, Renfrewshire,—a hill 1200 feet above the level of the sea, and which flows through the Parishes of Kilbirnie, Dalry, Kilwinning, and Irvine, where it falls into the Firth of Clyde. This place is near the district of country where the poet's mother was brought up with her uncle at Langcraft, Lochwinnoch. The only places worth visiting on the Garnock river are the romantic falls called the Spout of Garnock and its windings round Glengarnock Castle.

PROCEEDINGS

AT THE

CELEBRATION of the CENTENARY

OF

ROBERT TANNAHILL.

PROCEEDINGS.

On Wednesday, 3d June, Paisley celebrated the centenary of the birth of Robert Tannahill, under the most favourable auspices, —equally as regards the weather, and also in respect of the enthusiasm which was evinced throughout the town. Early morning saw numbers of the inhabitants and shopkeepers earnestly at work finishing the decoration of their respective premises, and, on every hand, congratulations were exchanged that the weather was of the most brilliant description. The celebrations included a public procession through the various principal thoroughfares of the town to the Braes of Gleniffer, followed in the evening by a public banquet in the Abercorn Rooms, a musical soiree, and numerous other indoor social gatherings. The General Committee who had been entrusted with the erection of the floral arches, and making the other arrangements for duly celebrating the auspicious event, did their work well, and received the commendations of the public generally. There were seven arches composed of evergreens and flowers, and in height about thirty feet, erected at various points throughout the town, besides others erected at Glenfield by Mr. William Fulton, near his works there. This gentleman deserves the warmest thanks for the ready and liberal manner in which he placed at the disposal of the committee the grounds of his beautiful estate at Glen, and through which he had specially cut a new road to enable the processionists to climb the heights and pic-nic on the hallowed spots so frequently visited by the poet.

THE DECORATIONS.

As we have mentioned, the decorations throughout the town in honour of the occasion were alike profuse and tasteful. Not the least effective were those witnessed at the railway station, at County Square, on which, for several days, the employés, under the superintendence of Mr. W. Auchterlonie and Mr. Beattie, had been busily at work. From the castellated towers of the main building floated flags and banners, and over every available space were hung festoons of evergreens and flowers, while the parapet walls were surmounted with massive fire-clay vases from the works of Messrs. Speirs, Gibb & Co. There was an arch over the entrance to the station, along the entrance road to which was spread a long line of evergreen festooning. Over the buildings of the County Prison, flags of various nations floated, and the house fronts in County Square were bedecked with evergreens, flags, and flowers in profusion. Among the other decorations, the Fountain Gardens afforded a gay spectacle, enhanced by a display of flags. At the house of Dr. Taylor in St. James Place, which was tastefully decorated, there was placed in front an oil painting of Tannahill. Along Old Sneddon there was almost a continuous line of garlands of flowers, &c., reaching from house to house on either side. In Incle Street, several very pretty designs were to be seen. In Gauze Street, the more attractive decorations were those at the Abercorn Hotel and Mr. Snodgrass's shop. A fine array of flags was also stretched across the street from the windows of Mr. Auchter- lonie's residence to the opposite side. The neighbourhood of the Cross was beautifully arrayed, — the Commercial Hotel particularly presented an imposing appearance. The City of Glasgow Bank was draped with crimson cloth and festoons of evergreens. In Moss Street, the most noticeable features of decora- tion were a floral archway at Meeting-house Brae, and a banner stretching across the street at the Theatre Royal with the inscription, "To Paisley's honoured dead." In the High Street, Messrs. Parlane & Naismith had tastefully bedecked the front of their premises, and the fronts of the premises occupied by Mr. Richardson, Mr. John Gibb, the North British and Washington

Inns, 39 High Street, were gaily attired. The house of Christopher North was very prettily decorated. Perhaps the most beautiful feature in decorations in this street was outside the house of Mr. David Semple, F.S.A. He had placed the letters "R. T." made of flowers of large size on the front wall of the house, while the windows were artistically festooned with choice flowers and shrubs. At Messrs. Risk & Marshall's premises some very tasteful devices were displayed, made of ornamental shavings, and relieved with drapery. Castle Street was adorned with flowers and evergreens from end to end. In Lady Lane, Mr. W. Robin, builder, had erected in front of his works a beautiful bust of the poet, and several other smaller busts of eminent persons. In Broomlands, Mr. John Dunlop, Mr. James Moodie, Mr. J. Scott, Gordon & Barclay, and Mr Peter Wallace, had all beautiful devices and arrangements. In George Street, the more noticeable features of decorative art were in front of the premises occupied by Mr. James Wills, Mr. W. Foulds, and especially at Messrs. David Speirs & Co.'s warehouse. Along the whole of the Causeyside to the head of that street the decorations were continued, and espccially did Stanley Place appear conspicuous. The Neilston Road and Carriagehill were alike tastefully decorated. As a whole, the decorations were of a most tasteful and beautiful character, and gave a convincing proof that the inhabitants of Paisley had entered with earnestness into the spirit of the celebration of the centenary of the poet's birth.

THE PROCESSION.

The *Glasgow News* thus describes the procession :—Like every branch of the arrangements, the procession proved a thorough success. It was formed into order in St. James' Street, which from nine o'clock till eleven was crowded with spectators. The first of the processionists to appear on the ground were the carters, in big bonnets, little bonnets, and all kinds of bonnets, with all kinds of knots, varying in hue from turkey-red to the most delicate ginger. They were all, of course, dressed in riding costume, and some of them came out "awfu' strong." To beguile the time a few of the equestrians, evidently with the view of cutting in more senses than one, "a dash," rode their neighing

steeds up and down, much to the delight of the assemblage.
The animals were all gaily comparisoned, not a few of them
having bells tinkling at their glossy necks ; and as they pranced
here and sidled there, or stepped proudly up the street, you
might have easily mistaken them for their betters. Common dray
horses as they were, they looked in their holiday ribbons quite
above their stations ; and even the ponies, mettlesome, pretty,
and skittish, seemed impressed with the importance of the
event, and neighed and danced as if they felt morally bound
to exhibit some outward satisfaction. By the way, it should be
mentioned that the fleshers, well dressed and some with aprons,
were also mounted on chargers, and followed the carters. The
second party to arrive in St. James's Street was the Fire Brigade,
enveloped in their helmets, which raised quite sympathetic feelings in the hearts of the crowd. The men were seated on one of
the engines, embowered amid green leaves, and as grim and determined as if they were bent on extinguishing the Cart, were
that classic stream to break into conflagration. Paisley must
be congratulated on the possession of such a heroic corps. It
is not every community that can hope to retain the services of
men with heads capable of sustaining such a heavy pressure as
that imposed by a helmet on a June day, with the temperature
at 80 degrees in the shade. But by the time you are com-
miserating with Brigade, who, by the way, were in the very
whitest of duck trousers, a host of trades, bristling with emblems,
has arrived. Superintendent Sutherland, of the police force, who
has the marshalling in hand, has a busy time of it, but gradually
order is gained ; the bands have fallen in at the head of their
respected detachments ; "the triumphal" car (which wears a
very dejected look in consequence of the shrivelled evergreens
with which it is busked) moves off in front of the carters ; the
music bursts out simultaneously ; there is a plunging and rearing
in front ; and then all march off in regular succession. Next
the horsemen are the Fire Brigade, and the following is the
order of the other bodies :—

Marshall.
Provost, Magistrates, and Town Council, in carriages.
One Hundred and Fifty Carters.

Fleshers.

Firemen.

Carriage with Mr. Thomas Coats.

Representatives of the Press.

Band.

Tannahill Club Committee.

Band.

Gardeners.

Band.

Freemasons and Oddfellows.

Band.

Glenfield Workers.

Band.

Trades' Council.

Weavers and Elastic Weavers.

Band.

Slaters, Shoemakers, Joiners, Clothlappers, and Bricklayers.

Band.

D y e r s.

Band.

Tailors and Lithographers.

Band.

Engineers and Moulders.

Band.

Coats's Workers.

Band.

Good Templars.

Nothing could in its way have been gayer than the procession on its way through the town. The brilliant sunshine, the picturesque decorations on every hand, the spirit-stirring music, and the innumerable flags, emblems, and coloured mottoes carried by the tradesmen, made up a scene that for effectiveness has never been surpassed in the ancient town. A few of the trade emblems were clever in their way. The Glenfield workers, for instance, displayed some beautiful strips of many-coloured cloths, and they maintained, on a device that was carried high, that they were "Second to None." On a large banner, which required the aid of two or three men to hold aloft, the admiring crowd was informed in gilt letters that "Nothing on earth remains but fame." The workers turned out about 330 strong, and were headed by five lusty pipers of the 105th Glasgow Highlanders. The tailors, as was to be expected, set the fashion as regards dress. There were about 200 of them in all, and a number of them appropriately wore aprons made of artificial fig-leaves. The Gleniffer Flute Band (Stevenson Street) headed the ornamentors of the human frame. The followers of St. Crispin, preceded by the Beith Rifle Band, carried a few emblems of their calling, such as awls, lasts, &c. The bricklayers showed a model stalk-vent, and told all and sundry through the medium of a motto the fact that "We join to protect." The joiners, about 150 strong, elicited for their models the warmest admiration. They carried very neatly-constructed crowns, a miniature bound door, a skylight, and two benches, with a couple of men planing some wood at a rate so furious as to suggest the idea that the whole success of the centenary depended on their efforts. The clothlappers likewise showed several automata, evidently impressed with a similar opinion. The motto of the trade, a very apposite one, was—"The harder pressed the firmer pressed," and a tiny bale of goods ready for shipment was shown in illustration. The slaters were pathetic, but not very lucid. They carried a banner with the following inscription:—"We give honour to him who, though dead, yet speaketh," likewise a model cottage roofed with slates so disproportionate in size as to very naturally excite in the breasts of humane people a hope that the inmates of said dwelling had gone out for a walk, or had permanently removed ·from such a dangerous structure. The dyers, as usual, from time immemorial, or from the date of the first trades' demonstration, were epigrammatic;

their emblem was—"We dye to live, and live to die."   They turned out to the number of 150, headed by the North Quarter Brass Band, and carried two banners and a small bale of shaded wool.   The weavers, as might have been expected, turned out most largely, several hundreds joining in the procession.   Their simple but beautiful motto—"Weave truth with trust"—was in keeping with their whole demeanour.   The prominent emblems were a Tannahill plaid and a Jacquard loom.   You can easily point out a Paisley weaver; his meek and thoughtful aspect stamps him at once as a driver of the loom; and on Wednesday no greater contrast was presented than between the weavers and the engineers—the latter bustling and jolly, and apparently as full of "steam" as the little engine they carried, which was working away like fury.   A number of equally ingenious devices were exhibited by them.   But, turning from the men of metal to the men of flowers, we must refer, before leaving the trades' display, to the exceedingly pretty bower which was carried in front of the gardeners.   In the centre of it stood a little table, on which were spread what was supposed to be all the delicacies of the season, with many fruits that were not in season ; but the gardeners, like the poets, must be allowed great license.   Coming now to the bodies who did not represent trades, there were first, the Freemasons.   Deputations were present from various lodges in the neighbourhood, among them being representatives from Lodge No. 347, Rutherglen ; Beith St. John's, Kilwinning, Lodge No. 157 ; Renfrew County, Kilwinning, Lodge No. 370 ; Union and Crown (Barrhead), No. 307 ; St. Mirren (Paisley), No. 127 ; Coatbridge, No. 177 ; Clydesdale, No. 556 (Glasgow) ; Shamrock and Thistle, No. 275 ; and Roman Eagle, No. 160 (Edinburgh).   About seventy members of Odd-fellows' Lodges in Paisley, Glasgow, Govan, and Greenock Rifle Band preceded them and the Freemasons. The lithographers had a press at work, and were throwing off a sheet, containing a portrait of Tannahill and other emblematic figures, and the following lines by Mr. William M'Lean :—

> " Each touch he gave to Scotia's lyre
>   Sent forth a song sublime

To live, and other bards inspire
   Throughout revolving time.
The strains he sung have made us prize
   Our native woods and braes ;
Our hills and glens before us rise
   Whene'er we sing his lays.

When 'Gloomy Winter ' leaves the scene,
   An' 'downy buds ' appear,
An' o'er Gleniffer's dewy green
   The lav'rock warbles clear,
We'll wander 'mang the bonnie braes,
   Or stray by Craigielea,
An' ilka scene that greets our gaze
   His monument shall be.

The mavis singin' in sweet strain
   His mellow hymn at e'en,
Brings bonnie 'Jessie o' Dumblane '
   In fancy to the scene.
An' ilka bird on ilka tree,
   An' flower by rippling rill,
Brings floating tae the memory
   The sangs o' Tannahill."

Such are a few of the particulars of the various bodies composing the procession. It is impossible to give the exact number of persons that took part in it, but we do not overstate the mark when we say that there could not have been less than 2,500.

The first street that the procession entered was Moss Street ; and the most prominently decked house in the portion which was traversed by the cortege was that of Dr. Taylor. Here all the windows were tastefully festooned, and beneath the centre casement was a capital oil painting of Tannahill. On the opposite side of the street, on the top of a low-roofed building, a band of daring youths had established themselves ; and, looking right up the same thoroughfare, you could see a similar sight on the railway bridge, varied only by the greater amount of danger which attached to the airiness of situation. Turning then into Sneddon Street, which is in a perfect eruption of bunting, you find every window crammed with women, whose household duties in most cases seem to have so monopolised their attention during the morning that they have not found time even to wash their faces. Bashfulness, however, does not appear to be one of their characteristics, and half-a-dozen greasy aprons or so are waved towards the procession in general, in answer to several cries addressed to them from the street to "Jine in." Several short stoppages occurred here and in South Croft Street and Incle Street, which afforded a little time to admire the decorations. There was scarcely a house which did not in some way or other contribute to the general rejoicing ; and the same may be said of the whole town. Gauze Street was noticeable for the "bits" of poetry which it exhibited, and the number of lads who preferred the tops of lamp-posts to *terra firma*. As a specimen of the former, we had—"We'll meet beside the dusky glen," and "Ambition courts promotion"—from the "Lass o' Arranteenie." Old Smithhills Street presented on either side a neat and pleasing appearance, and here, near the George Hotel, the procession passed under the first of seven arches erected along the route. The strips of red cloth which depended from the windows of many of the tenements lent a rich aspect to the scene, which was pleasantly varied by a judicious display of flowers. At the Cross the turn out of people was very large, the square being densely packed. The decorations here were quite brilliant, flags and streamers and variegated cloths waving from many of the windows in the large drapery and upholstery warehouses. A little above the Cross was another arch, very handsomely got up, bearing on the top the following lines :—"Tannahill, 1774. We may weel say, alas ! for our ain scant o' grace, that we reck'd not his worth till he died." To describe the particulars of the display in High Street would be impossible ; suffice it to say that from top to foot the thoroughfare was brilliant in the extreme. We must, however, notice the house of Mr. Semple, whose appreciation of Tannahill led him to edit notes in the centenary edition of the works of the poet. On either side of the door, in large letters, were the initials "R.T.," while the whole of the windows were elegantly wreathed with flowers. Coming into Wellmeadow Street, the same earnestness to do honour to the memory of the sweet singer was visible, and on one of the dwellings a more than ordinarily enthusiastic householder had stuck up—"All honour to Seestu's gentle Bard." But let us hurry on to Castle Street. Passing under another arch erected at the entrance, you near the supposed birthplace of the poet, and as you approach the lowly cot you instinctively raise your hat. Substantially, however, it remains the same as it was one hundred years ago— the same "one storeyed biggin'." The present occupant, not insensible seemingly to the merits of the man who "once dwelt there," put up a flag and a few scraps of bunting. Of course, it is known that on the anniversary of the birth of the poet, two years ago, a memorial-stone was inserted in the front of the building, bearing the inscription—

> "Here Nature first waked me to rapture and love,
> And taught me her beauties to sing."

Entering George Street, going westwards, you pass beneath another arch, on which there is boldly standing out the word "Craigielea ;" then turning up Queen Street you find the workshop of the poet, a little thatched place, which was busked in honour of his memory, and presented on its windows several verses taken from one of his poems. Little need be said of the remaining portion of the route. Broomlands Street, the east end of George Street, Causeyside Street, and Neilston Road were interesting enough. The Good Templars joined the procession at this point. At the entrance to Neilston Road was another arch, bearing on one side the words "Stanely green shaw," and on the other "The Braes o' Gleniffer." The drive down Falside up to the Braes was beautiful, and the road was literally thronged with pedestrians of all ranks. The procession passed through a fine arch draped with tartan, and festooned with folds of cloth of various colours. In the keystone of the arch was a fine bust of Tannahill, encircled with a wreath of laurel, and on either side there were columns ornamented with flowers. Passing through this arch the procession entered the Glenfield estate by an avenue of beech and plane trees, beautifully shaded.

GLENIFFER BRAES.

Sometime before reaching Gleniffer Braes, we begin to get some idea of the locality made famous by the Poet. Glimpses of hill and dale break upon the eye as we wend towards Mr. Fulton's lovely estate of Glen; and when, at last, we turn off the road leading to Barrhead, into the sylvan lane which winds along the lower fringe of the Braes, we suddenly find ourselves entering the quiet meditative world of nature, where one is inclined to be silent, feeling sure that it was hereabouts that Tannahill many a time and oft wandered and pondered, and found the genius which impelled him to sing so sweetly. After the heat and flying dust of the streets, it was like getting into a cool, green fairy-land, which the exquisite brightness and balminess of the day rendered still more fairylike. Both sides of the avenue are sheltered by great-armed trees, which fling over our heads the grateful shelter of their leaves. It must, we are sure, have been with feelings of thankfulness that the sweltering thousands with their flowing banners and blowing trumpets entered within the precincts of this umbrageous region. Taking in the sinuosities of the march through the·town, the processionists must have marched at least three long miles. But no lack of courage or sign of faltering was visible. Everybody "swat," but it may be said that it was a poetic sweat, considering the earnest purpose of the demonstration. Thoroughly in harmony with the enthusiasm of the people was the reception which had been prepared for them. Like Sir Walter Vivian, mentioned in the prologue to the "Princess," Mr. Fulton —

> " All a summer's day
> Gave his broad lawns, until the set of sun,
> Up to the people."

But not only did the genial Lord of the Manor throw open his gates to the poetic idolators, but he made very thoughtful and handsome provision for their comfort in the construction of a new road from a point near his mansion along the middle distance of the Braes, to another point from which the multitudes could easily find their way to the airy table-land prepared for speakers and singers. More even than this, however, Mr. Fulton had constructed at various points of the march a number of beautiful floral arches, which were enriched by appropriate poetic inscriptions. These preparations must have cost Mr.

Fulton several hundred pounds—surely a solid proof of the genuineness of his sympathy. Leaving the processionists to wind upward along the new road, we chose an older, and, though a more hidden, yet a more delightful way to reach the Braes, knowing that we should be in time to catch them before they reached the destined height. Our path led us into the Glen, the poet's "dewy dell," which, although small in extent and compass, is yet big enough to contain a world of beauty, and witching enough to inspire a poet with immortal bursts of song. It is not space or bulk, but quality, that strikes the imagination of the poet into sweet or mighty harmonies. The character of this Glen is not rugged, nor is it made vocal by a raging torrent. Being well, but not over-wooded, it is mildly and exquisitely sylvan, and contains a few dim recesses which, as one pauses to listen to the melodious ripplings of the burn below, bewitch the fancy, and carry it into endless poetic mazes. Wandering in this beautiful region, one is at no loss to understand how it must have affected the gentle spirit of Tannahill. The most poetic passages of his songs might have been inspired by the subdued loveliness of its scenery. Of course, it must be somewhat altered since Tannahill's time. It is now artfully laid out with fine walks and rustic stiles ; and here and there the traveller unexpectedly finds a seat whereon to rest his weary limbs, or indulge the spirit of meditation. Crossing the burn, and ascending a little way, we come to a beautiful spring—"Tannahill's Well" it is called—where the water, pure as crystal and cool as ice, falls into a white granite fountain, from which the visitor may quench his legitimate thirst, and, in doing so, thank Mr. Fulton for what may be called his poetic considerateness in converting this "dewy dell" into one of the finest possible memorials which could be dedicated to Tannahill. A young bird's flight farther on, the ear is touched by the sound of falling water ; and you have only to go round a jutting elbow of the hill, and downward a few easy paces, when lo ! a dim mysterious Linn, into which falls, especially on a summer's day, a gauzy veil of water, making a mild noise, more like many whisperings than one clear voice. Taking the glen as a whole, it would be difficult to imagine a finer haunt for lovers and

poets. On this particular day it was all sweetness and brightness, as if Nature, conscious of the genial worship with which
her poetic child was being honoured, had prepared her part of
the unpurchasable festival. The yellow broom hung out her
innumerable banners of gold; everywhere the hawthorn burst
into white glory, and breathed forth the most delicious
exhalations; overhead the larks chanted as if the world had just
been created; and above the larks bent an almost cloudless blue
sky, with its suggestions of infinite sweetness, and purity, and
beauty.

At length Gleniffer Braes is reached, and yonder march the
banners and the drums and the trumpets towards the high
trysting-place. It was altogether a brilliant procession, and a
stranger might have imagined that some king was going to be
crowned. Nor would he have been altogether wrong; for although Tannahill was a mild monarch in the region of song, yet
in some essential sense he was one; and certainly no king could
have received a crown of honour on a more commanding throne.
From the plateau on which the head of the procession stopped,
could be seen a splendid variety of scenery stretching out from
the beautiful landscapes of Gleniffer and "Stanely greenshaw"
to the misty magnificence of Benlomond. Having reached the
appointed platform, upon which a select group was gathered, a
band played a selection of Tannahill's music; while by-and-by
a select choir sang, in capital style, a number of the poet's
songs, including "Thou Bonnie Wood o' Craigielea" and
"Jessie, the Flower o' Dunblane." On the platform were Provost
Murray, Bailies Masson, MacKean, Clark, and Scott; Councillors Fisher, Cochran, Lewis, M'Gown, Halden, Ker, Watson,
and Armour; Messrs. Thomas Coats, John Lorimer, P. Comyn
Macgregor, James Caldwell of Craigielea, R. Ronald, J. Reid,
Robert Russell, Robert Hay, J. S. Mitchell, D. Campbell, J.
Robertson, William, Joseph, and James Fulton, Peter and
John Currie; Councillor Wellstood, Ex-Councillor Murray, and
Mr. W. W. Kennedy, Edinburgh; Mr. James Wallace, Glas-
gow, &c. In front of the platform was a choir organised for the
occasion, and under the leadership of Mr. M'Gibbon. The choir
having sung "Thou Bonnie Wood o' Craigielea,"

Provost MURRAY addressed the assemblage.   If, he said, there is anything of which a nation and a community have great reason to feel proud, it is the fact of having given birth to a man of genius whose name the world will not willingly let die— (hear, hear)—a man of genius who has not only reflected credit on his native town, but added to that national treasury of science and art which form after all the richest glory and praise of any nation.   It is therefore with peculiar feelings of satisfaction that I, as the head of the community of Paisley, have this day witnessed so thorough an appreciation of the merits of poor Robert Tannahill.   (Cheers.)   It shows to me, beyond all question, that the Scottish mind is still, as of old, thoroughly imbued with the love and spirit of poetry, and that there are still among us the elements for producing great men in that department of literature.   (Cheers.)   We have this day visited the humble abode where the sweet singer first saw the light of heaven.   We have passed that humble dwelling where he pursued his daily toil, and we are now on the spot of his favourite haunts, where he gratified that intense love of Nature which is evident in all his works, and from which he drew that inspiration which produced those imperishable lyrics which will never cease to call forth the feelings of Scotchmen wherever they are sung.   (Cheers.)   The minstrel's harp is now unstrung.   The sweet singer's voice is now mute and silent. That heart once pregnant with celestial fire is now cold and unfeeling.   But Nature never dies.   Those hills and scenes are still renewed to us from year to year with all that perennial fresh- ness, forming to us, as they did to him, a true and never- failing source of poetry.   (Cheers.)   We are here in the haunts of the poet—on the Gleniffer Braes,—in the neighbourhood of the "dewy dell" and Stanely's turrets, which certainly are not at present "covered wi' snaw," and at no great distance is the bonnie wood of Craigielea.   (Cheers.)   I trust that among the crowds that are here to pay this ovation to the memory of Tannahill we may have some latent talent that may a hundred years hence lead to the commemoration of some son equally gifted, who will reflect additional honour on our native town. (Cheers.) Tannahill, though dead, yet speaketh,

and it will be far better than any feeble words I can utter that he
should discourse these songs of his which have been wedded to
such delightful music.   (Cheers.)

The choir then sang " Gloomy winter's noo awa'," after which

Mr. P. C. MACGREGOR moved a cordial vote of thanks to Mr.
Fulton of Glenfield, for the kindness he had shown to the Committee of the Procession, and the homage he had that day paid
to the memory of Robert Tannahill.   Mr. Macgregor was about
to proceed, but was interrupted by the loud and prolonged
cheering with which his closing words were received, and further
by the choir starting, and the vast assemblage joining in singing
" For he's a right good fellow."

" Jessie, the Flow'r o' Dunblane " having been sung by the
choir,

Bailie MASSON said—We have had a very enthusiastic and
successful demonstration on the haunts of our sweet singer,
Tannahill ; and I am sure that hundreds who have never been
here before will feel inspired by the beauty of the scenery and
the associations surrounding Gleniffer Braes, to come back again
—and you are welcome.   The centre round which we have
gathered has been our worthy Provost, and I beg to propose a
very hearty vote of thanks to Provost Murray—(applause) ;—for
besides the Laird of Glen, there is another right good fellow.

The choir and company again took up the refrain.

Councillor COCHRAN moved for a hearty vote of thanks to Mr
R. F. M'Gibbon and the choir.   (Applause.)

" God save the Queen " having been sung by the choir, the
multitude then dispersed themselves over the grounds ;   while
the Provost, Magistrates, and Councillors, with other friends,
proceeded to Glenfield, where during the day numbers partook of
luncheon through the hospitality of Mr. Fulton.   It had been
announced that the procession would be reformed at 4 o'clock,
and the interval was agreeably occupied in various ways.   Numbers visited the well and the linn ; and many engaged in dancing
to the strains of bands or flutes and pipes.   Groups here and there
enjoyed their pic-nic, while the tents were thronged with cus-
tomers.   The processionists returned to town about five o'clock,
separating from the County Square to their respective head-

quarters. The order, sobriety, and good conduct by which they were characterised, were the theme of commendation.

THE BANQUET.

In the evening a banquet was held in the Abercorn Rooms, at which covers were laid for 120 persons. Immediately at the back of the chairman's seat was erected a colossal bust of Tannahill, the work of Mr George E. Ewing, sculptor, and which he has intimated his intention of presenting to the Public Museum. Provost Murray occupied the chair, and was supported by Mr W. Holms, M.P., Sheriff Cowan, Mr Thomas Coats, Bailie Masson, Rev. Dr Hately Waddell, Mr James Arthur, Rev. James Brown, Dr Taylor, Mr George E. Ewing, and James Reid, secretary. The croupiers were Mr James Caldwell, Craigielea, supported by Bailie Fisher, Mr James R. Lamb, Mr Matthew Hodgart, Mr John Cook, and Mr J. Fullarton; Mr Wm. Hector, Sheriff Clerk, supported by Major Fullerton, Mr Tannahill, great nephew of the poet; Mr A. C. Holms, Sandyford; Mr Wm. Cross, Mr Gordon Smith, and Mr Robert Macfarlane; Mr P. Comyn Macgregor, supported by Dr Donald, Mr James R. M'Nair, Mr James Forbes, Mr Walter King, Mr W. Gardner, and Mr Alex. Boyd. Amongst the company were Mr Robert Russell, Mr R. L. Henderson, Mr Robert Barclay, Mr R. Watson, Mr Wm. Foulds, Mr R. F. Dalziel, Mr T. R. Cameron, Mr A. R. Campbell, Mr. R. A. Ronald, Mr A. Craig, Mr James A. Mackean, Mr Charles Warrington Lang, Mr R. Rowand, Mr J. R. Macgregor, Mr R. Armour, Mr John Ker, Mr J. M'Gown, Mr Robert Hay, Mr D. S. Porteous, Mr W. Craw, Captain Wallach, Mr Thomas Reid, Mr Andrew Gilmour, Muirhead, Neilston; Mr Hugh Calderwood, Mr Alexander Semple, Mr Richardson, Glasgow; Mr James Cook; Mr William B. Watson; Mr James Gibson, Mr Murray, Edinburgh; Mr J. K. Crawford, Mr Andrew Brown, George Place; Mr Wm. Stewart, Glasgow; Mr M. Blair, Mr James Hamilton, of Johnstone, Mr M. Hodgart, Mr John Snodgrass, Mr Robert Paterson.

The CHAIRMAN intimated that letters of apology for absence had been received from the Earl of Glasgow; Sir Michael Shaw-Stewart, Bart., lord lieutenant of the county; Sir Robert

Napier, Bart., convener of the shire ; Sir James Watson, Lord Provost of Glasgow ; Mr. Crum-Ewing, ex-M.P. for Paisley ; Colonel Mure, M.P. ; the Rev. Dr. Walter C. Smith ; and Mr. James Ballantyne, of Edinburgh.

The toasts of "The Queen" and "The Baron of Renfrew and the other members of the Royal Family" having been duly honoured, the CHAIRMAN gave "The Navy, Army, and Reserve Forces," coupled with the health of Captain Wallach, who replied.

The CHAIRMAN next proposed "Both Houses of Parliament." The House of Commons might now, he remarked, be literally said to be a representation of the people, based, as it was, upon household suffrage. And although the House of Lords might have a more restricted constituency—in fact, it represented an exclusive order—they knew that the House was graced by the presence of men of the greatest eminence as statesmen, and that in their deliberations—in sometimes, perhaps, checking hasty and undue legislation, and in giving deep consideration to the best interests of the country—they had displayed an immense amount of ability. (Applause.) He coupled the toast with the health of Colonel Holms, member for Paisley. (Applause.)

Colonel HOLMS, M.P., responding, said—My experience of what has well been termed the first legislative assembly in the world has been so brief that I have not yet fully appreciated the enormous influence which it exerts, or thoroughly understood the vast amount of work which it is called upon to perform. Nothing is too great and nothing too small for its consideration. The regulation of cab fares or our relations with mighty empires alike come under its cognisance. A few months ago, as you are well aware, a change occurred—a change so important that we might characterise it as a revolution—a change which transferred political power from one party to another; and in no respect was that change more marked than in the *personnel* of the House of Commons. Instead of Gladstone, with his restless impetuosity, joining (like Achilles of old) in every fight, we have Disraeli, with his marvellous power of silence—(hear, hear)—rarely speaking, and scarcely ever interfering in any departmental debate—invariably, I may say, leaving his fighting to be done by his lieutenants. So sudden—and, I may say, to the surprise of Whig and Tory alike—was the transition that the present Government had little time to arrange great measures for the present session. The public did not expect much ; and their expectations have been confirmed by the declaration made by an eminent member of Government to the effect that the policy of the Ministry was one of silence and consideration. (Laughter.) Amply they have fulfilled that policy in so far that, up to the present moment, with the exception of some routine measures, we have had brought before us by the Government itself very few bills indeed. The most important of those submitted to the House has been the Licensing Bill ; and, as regards Scotland, the Conveyancing and Land Transfer Bill and the Patronage Bill. (Hear, hear.) But if, on the one hand, Government has not taken the initiative in many measures of importance, on the other hand, private members have been by no means idle. Up to the Whitsuntide recess, apart from those measures inaugurated in the House of Lords, and which, by-the-by, will come down for consideration to the Lower Chamber, no fewer than 114 bills have been laid on the table of the House of Commons. Of those, 24 have been passed, rejected, or withdrawn. In such a meeting as this, when we are met to do honour to one of the greatest lyric poets of any age or country, it would be out of place for me to venture to give an opinion upon any of those measures, especially as I see around me gentlemen of every shade of politics ; but let me say this, it appears to me that, instead of our having too little legislation this session, the danger rather is that we shall have too much. For instance, we have before us at the present time five game-law bills and seven licensing bills. It seems to me that we are in danger of having hasty and ill-considered measures brought before us; and with what result ? Why, that next session we shall be called upon to pass some other measures to amend or define those which received our sanction this year. Another danger to which I would call your attention is that of centralisation. For my own part, I deprecate exceedingly anything that will interfere with our ancient system of municipal self-government. To our system of municipal government we owe it that we are so self-reliant and so independent a people; and we are so tolerant of government, that we are so law-abiding. I trust, therefore, that we shall do all in our power to prevent the evil of centralisation, which I see increasing every day—not, I would say, on the part of any particular Government, because I think the same danger was to be apprehended under a Liberal Government as it is under a Conservative one. The toast comprehends not only the House of Commons, but the House of Lords. I think we are exceedingly fortunate in having, upon the whole, a well-constituted Second Chamber. (Applause.) When you look abroad and find the difficulties which other countries have with respect to the formation of a Second Chamber, we may consider ourselves extremely fortunate in having a House of Lords, from time to time recruited by men of eminence from various professions amongst the Commons. And we cannot ignore the fact that the House of Lords, of late years especially—as, for example, when these great measures were passed connected with Ireland—showed a very great amount of debating power. They rivalled certainly the House of Commons in that respect. As long as the House of Lords will be guided by the public opinion which is so well expressed by our daily press, and which is also directly represented in the House of Commons, so long will it continue to receive the respect of the people of this country. I have only to add that while we reformers—and I count myself among the number—think there are many things in our Constitution which might be reformed—indeed, the varying phases of our ever-advancing civilisation call continually for certain alterations and modifications, I must, on the other hand, say that we ought to be proud of our constitutional system of Government. (Applause.) I know of no country in ancient or modern times which has given to its people that inestimable blessing of liberty to speak, to write, and to act with the utmost freedom compatible with allowing the same privileges to others as our own; and therefore I think that that Constitutional system of government is worthy of our most loyal and hearty support and all the enthusiasm which you have shown in responding to the toast this evening. (Applause.)

The CHAIRMAN then gave the toast of the evening, "The Memory of Tannahill." He said—It has been said, and not without some degree of truth, that Paisley neglected poor Robert Tannahill when alive, and that she has failed in her duty to his memory in that there has not hitherto been erected any suitable monument to perpetuate a name which has reflected so much honour on the place of his birth—any visible expression of respect and admiration which his townsmen entertain of the sweet singer whose charming lyrics have for ever rendered classic many of the scenes and surroundings of their native place. But, gentlemen, the proceedings of this day show that these feelings of respect and admiration are neither dead nor dormant in the hearts of the people of Paisley, and only wait a fitting opportunity to find expression. (Applause.) If we might be allowed to suppose that the spirits of the departed ever revisit this sublunary scene, if we could fancy the gentle spirit of our native bard to have this day been hovering over the scenes of his earthly existence, he must have felt some recompense for any coldness or neglect he experienced in life, and been convinced that he had a better and a nobler monument in the hearts of the people of Paisley than that of

Storied urn or animated bust—

(applause)—and that in the universe of respect for his memory and admiration of his genius, which the recurrence of the centenary of his natal day has evoked, there is a proof that his name is one that the world

Will not willingly let die—

(applause)—that his songs have really become part of the national inheritance—the expression of those deeper feelings of the human heart which only find their adequate utterance in the language of true poetry. In introducing the toast of the evening, I feel that it would be but a poor compliment to the memory of the man we have met to honour were I to attempt to make him an object of hero worship. The modest, retiring spirit of the man would have shrunk from such a thing in life; and nothing could be more incongruous as a tribute to his memory. The facts connected with Tannahill's life were few. His short, alas ! too short, existence was singularly uneventful, and even-tenored.

With a character so retiring, and even shrinking, it is not to be expected that there could be anything marvellous or exciting to notice. The family from which the poet sprang on the paternal side belonged to Ayrshire, but his mother's family to Renfrewshire. His father was probably drawn to Paisley, and to the trade of weaving, by the prosperous state of the silk gauze manufacture here, which was the cause of attracting many young men from the surrounding districts, from the highly-remunerative character of the employment. He was thus essentially a poet of the working-classes—born of humble but respectable parents. His whole life was passed at the loom. Of course, I am not old enough to recollect the poet, but I had the pleasure to know intimately for many years his younger brother Matthew, with whom I have spent many an agreeable hour ; and, judging of the poet and the family from which he sprang from what I know of one of its members, I can scarcely realise a finer example of the Paisley weaver of the olden time—intelligent, well-informed, highly moral, and in that distinguished by all the real graces of character that adorn and dignify our common humanity, apart altogether from the merely meretricious and adventitious conditions of rank and social position. (Applause.) It is needless that I shall dwell on any of the incidents of the poet's life. When we recall his birth, his apprenticeship to the weaving, his residence in Lochwinnoch, where he could not summon courage to approach Wilson the ornithologist, who, by a rather strange coincidence, was also resident in that village ; his short sojourn in England ; his return to his native town to see his father die, and the filial tenderness that distinguished him in resolving to remain at home to cheer, comfort, and support his widowed mother, and the tragic and melancholy close of his life, we may be said to sum up the events of his too brief existence. It is very natural that we should wish to know something of the every-day life and the minutest features of a man of genius like Tannahill; and fortunately in the letters of R. A. Smith, one of his closest and most intimate friends, we have some most interesting glimpses of the poet. In fact they are so life-like that we can almost fancy that in the mind's eye we see him sitting at his loom in Queen Street with the little desk and the ink-bottle within reach, ready to note down the thoughts as they occurred, for it appears that many of his best pieces were composed in this way—in fact, while he was weaving those textile fabrics that were to adorn the bodies of the fairer portion of creation, he was weaving at the same time songs of love and female beauty that were to render his name immortal. (Applause.) Or we see him taking down his broken and mended flute to gratify his exquisite taste for melody. Or again, we see him, after the toils of the day are over, solitary or in company with some kindred spirit, wandering forth to visit the braes o' Gleniffer, the bonnie woods o' Craigielea, or any other of those favourite retreats, from the scenery of which he drew the inspiration that waked his lyre to tuneful numbers. (Applause.) Or, if the weather was unpropitious for his out-door walk, we see him spend his Saturday half-holiday with his friend, R. A. Smith, in reading and reviewing what pieces he had composed during the week ; and singing and playing any new music which his friend had composed. His simple tastes and unobtrusive habits were, therefore, very much in unison with his uneventful life. This is scarcely the place to attempt any criticism of the genius and works of Tannahill. While we cannot claim for him the power and versatility of Burns either in pathos or passion, he excelled him in his fine poetic feeling for the beauties of natural scenery, and few, indeed, have swept the Scottish lyre with so delicate a touch. Yes, Tannahill was a poet ; and all real poets are of Nature's own making ; and even Allan Cunningham, who I regret to think, failed to do justice to poor Tannahill, could not " hesitate to admit him to the fellowship of the born spirits of lyre verse." Perhaps the greatest tribute of contemporary genius to the merits of Tannahill as a song writer was the visit paid to him by the Ettrick Shepherd not long before his death. Hogg made a somewhat romantic pilgrimage in days when travelling was a very different affair from what it is now, to enjoy the fellowship of one gifted like himself with the voice of song. (Applause.) I have already alluded to one of the marked features of Tannahill's poetry—his intense feeling for natural beauty—and, in common with many of the Scottish poets of humble rank, this feeling is often developed to excess. This was especially marked in one of his most beautiful songs, "Jessie, the Flower of Dunblane," where the human feeling is almost hidden by the luxuriance of the poetic description, although the fault is so splendid that we can scarcely wish it removed. But Tannahill often shows a mental susceptibility to the emotional influence of Nature, and makes the cheerful and gloomy features of the external world correspond with and express the pleasures and pains of our human experience. This is finely illustrated in the finest of all his poems, "Keen blaws the wind ow'r the braes o' Gleniffer "—

> The trees are a' bare and the birds mute and dowie :
>   They shake the cauld drift frae their wings as they flee,
> And chirp out their plaints, seeming wae for my Johnnie—
>   'Tis Winter wi' them, and 'tis Winter wi' me.

(Applause.) Gentlemen, it has been remarked that there has always been diffused among the people of Scotland of the humbler ranks of life not only a poetical taste, but a considerable poetic faculty. Tannahill has contributed to preserve and keep alive a feature in the national character which we must all wish to see conserved, and it is therefore that I have had the greatest pleasure in witnessing and participating in the proceedings of this day, because these are a proof to me that the feeling which I have alluded to still influences to no small extent the character of our country. (Applause.)

The toast was cordially pledged.

Mr. JAMES CALDWELL, in proposing the toast of " Fillans and Henning," said—Your attention has been directed on the present occasion more particularly to poets and poetry ; but I am sure you will be not the less willing on that account to do homage to the memory of those who have distinguished themselves in the sister art of sculpture. The thoughts that animated the chisel of a Phidias, or the pencil of an Apelles, were akin to those which inspired the pen of a Homer and a Virgil ; and their embodiment in the marble has had equal influence in educating mankind in the good and the beautiful. I have therefore much pleasure in rising to propose, for your acceptance, a toast to the memory of John Henning and James Fillans. (Applause.) Born in the neighbouring county of Lanark, exactly two years before the untimely death of him whose birth has been the cause of our present meeting, Fillans came to Paisley in early boyhood. It was doubtless the artist's spirit that led him to adopt the trade of a stone mason as being closely allied to the art in which he afterwards became celebrated, and it is interesting to know that some of his earliest efforts may still be seen in four carved heads and the figure of a horse which adorn the fronts of houses in Paisley. These and other productions fortunately attracted the attention of those who perceived in them the germs of future greatness, and by timely encouragement he was led to greater efforts, until he established himself in London, that great centre of attraction to the young enthusiast. Here he attracted the notice of Chantrey, who was so struck by his abilities, that he employed him to execute commissions that he himself had received, but was unable to overtake. No higher testimony of the abilities of Fillans need be sought than this mark of approval and confidence by one of the greatest of modern sculptors. Among the ideal works of Fillans which will perpetuate his name may be mentioned the alto-relievos of "The Birth of Burns," and "The Madonna and Child"—subjects widely different in their character, and yet both happily and successfully treated, showing the varied scope of his genius. His statue of Sir James Shaw, in Kilmarnock, met with universal approbation; but perhaps his greatest work, whether it be regarded as a likeness or an embodiment of the general character and spirit of his subject, is the bust of Christopher North—(applause)—that was placed in the Paisley Coffee-Room in the year 1848, and which was so well described in the lines of a local poet :—

> " How like a lion, in quiescent might,
>   The noble-soul'd old Christopher appears !
> The mental glory of internal light
>   Smiles beautiful amid his ripening years.
>   No petty meanness, no flesh-shapen fears,
> O'ercast the noble firmness of his face :
>   His brow a dome of thought majestic rears ;
> His eye a thousand fancies seems to trace ;
> His flowing locks swim o'er a neck of grace,
>   And all the aspect of his form is power,—
> A manliness that time cannot displace,
>   Free and unbending as in youth's gay hour.
> The heathens had their gods ; so, Scotland, thou
> May'st trace as proud a form in living Wilson, now."

(Loud applause.) Four short years after this interesting event, Fillans died at the early age of forty-four, respected by all who knew him ; but his works will endure, and his name be honourably mentioned among the sculptors of our native land. (Applause.) Of John Henning, we can speak as of one of ourselves. He was born and reared in Paisley, and his attachment to his native town never forsook him during a long and successful career. The genius of Henning began to develope itself while working at his father's bench in High Street, where he frequently amused himself by carving with his chisel busts of his fellow-workmen. Adopting art as a profession, he settled for a short time in Glasgow, whence he went to Edinburgh, where he became intimately acquainted with Jeffrey and Brougham, and other eminent men who, in the early part of the present century, were rendering the metropolis of Scotland illustrious in literature and art. From Edinburgh he gravitated towards the centre, and found the field of appreciation of genius in the great metropolis, where he attracted many of the leading men of the day, and even Royalty itself, and soon attained a position second to none in the particular department of art to which he had devoted himself. Here he commenced and completed, after twelve years' close application, the great work of his life,—the restoration of what are popularly known as the Elgin Marbles,— (applause),—which, as you are well aware, are the remains of the frieze that adorned the Parthenon. These remains of the works of the greatest Grecian sculptor were broken and mutilated, and to supply their defects required a genius only inferior to his from whose hands they originally came. Henning had in him that rare combination of unfaltering industry, high sense of beauty, and accuracy of eye, without which he could never have achieved this great masterpiece, which from its attractive character has been copied and re-copied in every conceivable style, and spread throughout the world with an educating and elevating influence which it would be difficult to over-estimate. (Applause.) Well do I remember seeing the old man entertained to a public dinner by his fellow-townsmen in the hall of the Saracen's Head Inn, now nearly thirty years ago, for it was in the year 1846. Provost Murray, who had then only recently been elevated to the municipal chair, which he has now so long and so ably filled—(applause)—presided on the occasion, and discoursed in eloquent terms of Henning and his genius. Close beside him sat Henning, with his thin grey hair and clear piercing eye, and those who heard him will not readily forget how feelingly he spoke of his early days and youthful companions, or the effect on the meeting when he said that, after so long an absence, he felt as if he "stood alone like a pilgrim in a desert," and that "throughout all his wanderings he could, with heartfelt, soul-stirring affection, say, 'Paisley, I love thee still.'" I now ask you to join with me in drinking to "The Memory of Henning and Fillans."   (Loud applause.)

The Rev. Dr. HATELY WADDELL gave "The Memory of Christopher North."   He said—He certainly felt extremely obliged to the committee who had charge of the day's arrangement for having honoured him with such a position at this entertainment.   The day's proceedings had been agreeable, auspicious, and triumphant ; and it was a great honour to be permitted to take any part in them at all ; but to be privileged to address this audience and to propose "The memory of Christopher North," was really an honour he had neither expected nor anticipated. (Applause.)   The only difficulty that lay in his way was this, that there were so many points characteristic and peculiar in that wonderful man that deserved to be spoken to and spoken of, in the hearing of the people of Paisley, that he did not know which of them to select.   Christopher North was, to use a common phrase, so many-sided a man, that one did not know which side to look to.   He appeared to be like one of those portraits that used to be popular in the last generation, which was always looking at you in any part of the room where you were.   And the difficulty was still further increased when the speaker who was to propose his memory, was limited to a mere after-dinner speech.   The difficulties were increased in this way, there are so many things for which Christopher North was remarkable, and so many things the very opposite of these for which he was not remarkable, that you do not know very well how to balance and divide them.   His life was a kind of literary, political, intellectual, moral, and social antithesis, not to say paradox, from beginning to end. The man was different from all other men, and yet was in himself unique. He was, for example, well known at Oxford as one of the most accomplished athletes, one of the finest boxers, one of the swiftest runners, and one of the most astounding leapers ; and yet he was not an Englishman. He was one of the most devoted and accomplished anglers, and wrote upon angling with perhaps more taste and effect than anyone else ; and yet he was not Isaac Walton. He was one of the most distinguished students at Oxford, and passed an examination the like of which had not been known in the memory of man ; and yet he was not to be called a mere Oxford dun or a literary prig. He was a most accomplished critic; his essays on Homer, in fact, in a literary point of view, have been unsurpassed ; and yet he was not Francis Jeffrey. He was a most admirable essayist, full of genius and humour ; and yet he was neither Addison on the one hand, nor Lord Bacon on the other, nor Lord Macaulay in more recent times. He was perhaps the most popular and influential of editors in Great Britain—I might say in Europe ; and yet he was not an editor like Sir David Brewster. He was a most profound and diversified metaphysician, a most assiduous and popular professor ; and yet he was neither Adam Smith nor Sir William Hamilton. He was the author of most beautiful semi-religious, sunshiny, dreamy poetry, and of beautiful religious novels—for example, " The Elder's Death-bed " and the story of " The Female Martyrs ; " and yet he was neither a clergymen, nor, I think, was he even an elder. (Laughter.) He was a most intense politician ; and yet he was not a revolutionist. He was a most attractive and eloquent orator ; and yet he was not an orator " as Brutus is." He was the author of " Noctes Ambrosianæ " — (applause) — and yet he was not William Shakespere. He had a finer, richer, and more powerful command of the Scottish language than any man living in Scotland at the time; and yet he was neither Robert Burns nor Walter Scott. He was all these, you observe, and yet he was not all these ; and that is the strange part of the man's intellectual character, so to speak—his peculiar idiosyncrasies. But what I wish to say that, being all these, he was neither emperor nor king, nor prince, nor baron, nor baronet, nor knight, but only a native of Paisley. (Applause.) "And what for no?" (Applause and laughter.) "Olivia, my dear," as the Vicar of Wakefield's wife said to her daughter, "hold up your head when you have men like Tannahill, Christopher North, and all the rest of them." Applause) I think you perceive the application of that. (Laughter.) Now, it is a difficulty with me on which of these points I can best address you. If it had been my unhappy lot to address a circle of the prize-ring, then I know whose name would have brought out a round of applause. If I happened to be present in a company of students, I think I would have to mention nothing more than the name of Christopher North to ensure three rounds and one in addition. (Loud applause.) Coming down to a company of editors, there was no company of editors in Europe or America who would not receive with editorial enthusiasm a fitting tribute to the memory of their fellow labourer. (Applause.) After some further remarks, the rev. doctor concluded by saying—And in this complex character, concrete in him, but capable of analysis for a whole hour, if you would like me to do it, in this aspect I propose to you the memory of your great townsman, "Christopher North,"—the boast of Oxford and the pride of Edinburgh, and worthy to be compared with any of the great men that can be named for the last three hundred years. (Loud applause.)

Mr. GORDON SMITH gave "Wilson the Ornithologist." Wilson, he remarked, was one of those men of whom the people of Paisley were proud, and justly proud, not only because of the valuable contributions which he made to science, but because of the position which he occupied in literature as a poet. He did not know that Wilson could ever have been so distinguished as an ornithologist if he had not first graduated as a poet. (Hear.) He had no doubt whatever that on the Braes of Gleniffer he had first received that stimulus which subsequently led him to do such great service to science. The people of Paisley—indeed, the people of Scotland—were well acquainted with his writings; they knew well what his contributions had been to literature and to poetry. He did not know that there was anything in the language much more dramatic and powerful than Wilson's "Wattie and Meg;" and he did know that many of his sayings and minor pieces were highly cherished by those who had the truest appreciation of genuine poetry. (Applause.) As an evidence of that, the people of Paisley had resolved many years ago to perpetuate Wilson's memory by the erection of a statue. (Laughter.) Well, that was a matter upon which he should not enter; but he expressed the hope that many months would not elapse until they were assembled to inaugurate the statue in question. (Applause.)

Sheriff COWAN, in proposing the toast of "William Motherwell," said—It was a happy thought which led the committee, in arranging for the celebration of to-day, to contemplate a visit not only to the birthplace and the home of Tannahill, but also to the green braes of Gleniffer, which were the haunts that he loved and the home of his muse. And this day so bright and joyous, so full of poetry and music has fitly ushered in—

" The merry summer months of beauty, song, and flowers,
    The gladsome months that bring thick leafiness to trees."

Responsive to the poet's invitation—

Up, up, my heart, and walk abroad, flink cark and care aside,
Seek silent hills, or rest thyself where pleasant waters glide"—

you left the dusty town behind, and wended your way to the green hillside, and found, as the same poet says—

" The grass was soft, its velvet touch was grateful to the hand,
And like the kiss of maiden love, the breeze was sweet and
    bland ;
The daisy and the buttercup were nodding courteously,
It stirred their blood with kindest love to bless and welcome
    thee."

(Applause.) It has been deemed by the committee well that in celebrating the centenary of a poet whose name shall be dear to his country so long as there are gloomy winters to wear away, and bonnie woods of Craigiclea to flourish green again, we should remember other names of which Paisley has just reason to be proud. The poet whose verses I have ventured to quote is one of these, and I do not think I am far wrong in supposing that you will not be slow to acknowledge the claims of William

Motherwell to be remembered to-night. (Applause.) Occupy-
ing as he did, with credit to himself and advantage to the public,
for a good many years, the position of Sheriff-Clerk Depute in
Paisley, he had the opportunity of obtaining a varied acquaintance with men and things, and of studying in the dim recesses
of the Sheriff-Clerk's office those old deeds and documents which
probably led him to a love for antiquarian studies. Yet he was
no mere lawyer or learned Dr. Dryasdust ; and in his leisure
hours he turned with delight to the more congenial pursuits of
literature.   Even in early years he seems to have been a poet,
and his merits as a true and vigorous prose-writer were early
acknowledged, While in Paisley, he published an interesting
volume which is still much prized,—the *Paisley Magazine*. He
also became editor of the *Paisley Advertiser*, and in 1829 he removed from Paisley to become editor of the *Glasgow Courier*.
These, however, do not constitute his claim to be remembered
to-night, but rather his services to literature. In 1819, he
edited, with critical and historical notes and a valuable introductory essay, the *Harp of Renfrewshire*. This was the precursor
of a more valuable work, *Minstrelsy, Ancient and Modern*, the
able and valuable introductory dissertation to which at once gave
him an acknowledged position among literary men. (Applause.)
The service which he rendered by this publication to the
ballad literature of his country is one which, I am per-
suaded, will be increasingly felt as time advances.   He was
no reckless innovator or moderniser, but a true lover of the old-
en ballad; it was his delight to search out, in the true spirit of
an antiquary, what was really old, and preserve it for the lovers
of poetry.   But Motherwell was himself a poet of no mean order.
In the reproduction of Norse legends, he carved out for himself
a path to fame which had never been attempted before, and in
which, so far as I am aware, he has found no imitators. His
imitations, too, of legendary ballads are some of them of great
merit and spirit ; while what perhaps constitutes the most pleasing part of his poetry are the little simple lyrics which he wrote.
Of these, the sweetest and best is the well-known address to
Jeanie Morrison. He was a true poet who wrote that, and it
were well for all of us if, as we advance in life, we could say, as
he said—

> "The fount that first burst frae this heart
>   Still travels on its way,
> And channels deeper as it rins
>   The luve of life's young day."

On these grounds I ask you to drink to " The Memory of William Motherwell."

Rev. JAMES BROWN, in proposing the next toast, " Alexander Smith," said—If this were a meeting at which we were expected to weigh impartially the value of the contributions to our literature made by the different men whose memory we are honouring I feel that I could not fairly undertake to speak of Alexander Smith. Even as it is, I find it difficult to introduce his name in the style appropriate for after-dinner talk. To me—and I have reason to believe to some others at these tables—that name starts a spirit—the spirit of the vanished past. It awakens tender memories of a lost friendship, which was one of the most valued possessions of our lives. To those who enjoyed that friendship it must always be a secondary question what precise place will be assigned to the works of Alexander Smith by the authoritative critics of the future—

> " To have the deep poetic heart,
>   Is more than all poetic fame ;"

and we who knew and loved the man can testify that he had most surely the poet's heart. Even casual acquaintances will remember the peculiar richness of his voice, and how, when he read and spoke, " his hollow oes and aes " made "deep-chested music." But there was an inner circle who owned that they were in contact with a nature peculiarly rich and mellow. To walk and talk with him had much the same effect as a day in the fields and woods in earlier autumn, when there is in the very air a sense of wealth and fulness, and when as yet there is no sickly tint on flower or leaf. The wine of his life was of a generous vintage, and had that peculiar flavour which nobody can precisely describe. I speak not thus in tone of apology, as if I were setting the richness of his nature against the poverty of his work. He was unquestionably greater than all he wrote, and yet I affirm that his writings have taken and will maintain no mean place in our literture.   It is more than twenty years since his "Life-Drama" was given to the world. We can all remember how the respectability of Glasgow rubbed its eyes, and slowly awakened to the fact that a true poet was walking in its streets and drawing patterns in one of its warehouses. We remember the somewhat tardy but not ungenerous verdict of the London press. The carping criticism of the *Athenæum's* smart man, with his charge of plagiarism advanced with the manifest design of showing how widely read he was, would have been forgotten were it not that *Punch* came to the rescue and reduced the charge to an absurdity. The "City Poems" which followed some years later, more than maintained the reputation the "Life-Drama" had won; and his third volume of verse, "Edwin of Deira," only comparatively failed, because it appeared immediately after the publication of the "Idyls of the King," and because those who did not reflect that it must have been written before its author had seen the Idyls, chose to pronounce it an echo of the Laureate's verse. I am not so blinded by friendship as to deny that in his earlier poems especially, there are many faults which no one was more ready to condemn than he. But I do assert the presence of undoubted power—of true poetic fire. I do not claim for Alexander Smith an equal place beside the poet whose fame we are celebrating to-day; but in your comparative estimate, I ask you to remember that he had not, even though he had professed equal power, the same chance of immortality as Tannahill. It is the lyrist who is always the likeliest to live in a nation's memory. But for "Gloomy Winter's noo awa'," "Jessie, the Flower o' Dunblane," "Bonny Wood o' Craigielea," and some half dozen of the most exquisite songs ever sung at Scottish firesides, I venture to say that we would not have been keeping holiday under green arches and gay banners to day. It is something that, as Alexander Smith has given us nothing to sing, he is still read among us. We have more than one copy of most of his works in the Free Library, and I found yesterday that all but a mere fraction of them were out in the hands of readers. (Applause.)   In the estimate of the future, it will probably be acknowledged that Smith displayed higher power in his prose

than in his poetry.   On the pages of "Dreamthorpe," the genius
of the old essayists of the Augustic age in England seems to have
revived.   And certainly, if we except the pictures of the great
Wizard in his "Lord of the Isles," there is nothing descriptive
of the grandest of the western islands and of the awful glories
of Coruisk equal to what we find in the "Summer in Skye."
Most of us read "Alfred Haggart's Household" under the dis-
advantage of its appearing in a monthly serial, and were more
interested in identifying the characters and scenes in "Greys-
ley," than in marking the exquisite simplicity and quiet power
of what, if you read it again in its connected volumes, you will
own to be one of the happiest, most life-like pictures of a Scottish interior that artist ever drew. All his work was done within a few years.   He did not pass the age fatal for poets.   At
thirty-seven, when Burns and Byron fell, Smith died, and, as
he says of Hugh Macdonald,—"Since his removal, there are perhaps some half dozen persons in the world who feel that 'the
strange superfluous glory of the air' lacks something, and that
because an eye and an ear are gone, the colour of the flower is duller
and the song of the bird is less sweet, than in a time they can remember."   Smith was not, like Tannahill and the Wilsons, a native
of Paisley. Perhaps even on this day when we are celebrating the
peculiar glories of St. Mirren, you will own it to be no disad-
vantage to have first breathed in Ayrshire, and to have drawn
inspiration from the nursery of even a mightier singer than
Tannahill.   And though Smith was not born here, it is undeni-
able that his early residence in this town served to direct the
current of his thoughts and to give its own peculiar bent to his
genius.   It would not be difficult to show that what was most
distinctive of his song was to a great extent the product of his
Paisley life.   I know no town where you have so many striking
combinations.   With one memorial of hoar antiquity, one
remnant of mediæval beauty, the aspect of the town is, or rather
was—for I speak of a time before the Provost had framed his
Gas and Burgh Bills—(laughter)—wholly unromantic, or had
only such romance as is associated with the doing of a day's
work in grimy loom shops.   Yet, on the one hand, there lies,
but a few miles away, the great city, the roar of which almost

breaks our stillness, and the gleam of whose night fires serves to relieve our gloom; and, on the other hand, there lie at our very doors the finest stretch of country and the grandest table-land in the west. It is but a step to "Gleniffer's dewy dell" and to "Newtown Woods," where still "lav'rocks fan the snaw-white clouds." (Applause.) The very water that gurgles from our pipes speaks to us of "Stanely Shaw," and in ten minutes the factory worker can be in sight of the "lofty Ben Lomond." I can trace their influences on every page of Smith's prose or verse. The murmurs of leaves and streams mingle continually with the roar of streets. The lights of Gleniffer sunsets blend curiously with the gleam of Glasgow furnaces. The chimney stalk and the "crested hill" stands side by side in his chambers of imagery. He was thoroughly *en rapport* with our busy time, but he had ever "a pant for woodland din." The poetry of the city and the field are interwoven in his prose. (Applause.) Mr. Chairman, you will remember that the last time Alexander Smith appeared among us was a at farewell dinner given to your gifted son before he crossed the Atlantic. It is in harmony with the tone of the meeting in which we are honouring poets and poetry, to recall the fact that within the last few days Professor Murray has given to the world one of the most genial, comprehensive, and appreciative volumes on the songs and ballads of Scotland, which it has ever been my privilege to read. (Applause.) Gentlemen, I give you "The Memory of Alexander Smith," the man we knew and loved. (Loud applause.)

Mr. P. COMYN MACGREGOR of Brediland said—I was always proud that I was a native of Paisley, but never prouder than to-day, and what Paisley man could look upon the toast list I hold in my hand and not feel proud? The toast list is unique, and contains the names of eight distinguished sons of the past, all clustered nearly within a century, whose memories the world will not willingly let die; and Paisley claims them all as her own, and specially proud I am to claim the last in our list of that glorious octumvirate, Hugh Macdonald, for just as the mountains of the Dee first inspired the muse of Byron, so the Braes of Gleniffer first inspired the muse of Macdonald. I cannot at this moment remember any other town that could have produced such a muster-roll of imperishable names, all in a sense contemporaries, and most of whom had met each other. Born in Bridgeton, Glasgow, he came as a young man to Paisley, where at Colinslie Printworks he worked for years, and there his rambling tastes over hill and dale were developed. With a brief intervening sojourn in Bridgeton, where he tried his hand at, to him, the uncongenial business of a grocer, for which Nature seemingly had not destined him—he was too big a man for that, he spent many years in Paisley in the printing works of Robert M'Arthur & Co., and Harrow, M'Intyre, & Co., Colinslie, principally the latter. It was when there that he was seized with an unconquerable longing to see Professor Wilson, who was then—I am speaking of 1846 or 1847—in the blaze of his popularity. See the author of the *Isle of Palms* he must —shake the hand of him who had revelled in the *Noctes* he had resolved, and he accomplished both. There were no cheap trains in those days, and Macdonald was a poor man, but a resolute one. Early one June morning, ere the sun had travelled far, he was on the road to Glasgow, and on the evening of that day he entered Edinburgh, footsore and weary. Next morning, his courage failed him. How to approach the mighty Christopher— that was the question. He went early to the grave of the poet Ferguson, and there sat musing for hours, and in that reverie he gave the finishing touches to a lyric he had on the anvil, "The Birds of Bonnie Scotland." He carefully wrote a copy of the lyric as corrected, and called on the Professor, with it as his introduction. He was at once admitted, the song was criticised in a friendly spirit, and Macdonald received words of encouragement which had a great effect on his after career. How true of himself the stanza—

> " O for the time when first I roamed
>   The woodland and the field,
> A silent sharer in the joy
>   Each summer minstrel pealed.
> Their nests, I knew them every one,
>   In bank, or bush, or tree,
> Familiar as a voice of home
>   Their every tone of glee."

And, after describing a host of his favourite birds he concluded
with the somewhat sad stanza :—

> "Sweet warbling birds of Scotland,
>   I loved you when a boy.
> And to my soul your names are link'd
>   With dreams of vanished joy.
> And I could wish, when death's cold hand
>   Has stilled this heart of mine,
> That o'er my last low bed of earth
>   Might swell your notes divine."

When at Colinslie, Macdonald was a regular contributor of
poetic snatches to the *Glasgow Citizen*, conducted then as the
Daily *Citizen* is now by Mr. James Hedderwick. Many incidents
occurred while Macdonald was in Paisley, worthy of notice, but
to one only will I refer, as it was the turning point of his career.
I refer to it with pain, because I will have to speak some hard
words in reference to a big-hearted man whom I sincerely respect.
But, having been entrusted with this toast, the memory of Hugh
Macdonald, on this auspicious day for Paisley, a man I knew so
well and loved so dearly, I must be true to my trust. About
the year 1847, *Chambers' Edinburgh Journal* was in the height
of its popularity, and it had the field very much to itself.
However it was at this time menaced by a rival production
called *Hogg's Weekly Instructor*. On 20th November, 1847,
the 143d number was published, the first article in which was
on Robert Burns, and bore the name of George Gilfillan, then
and now a minister in Dundee. Wherever *Hogg* penetrated,
that article was read with astonishment and indignation. In it
our national poet was foully assailed, and the bitterest invective
was hurled at him. It was said of him that in his latter days
in Dumfries his mouth had become an open sepulchre full of
uncleanness and death, his eloquence had become "a hideous
compost of filth and fire," and the article concluded by saying
"that death never did a more merciful act than when he closed
the lips of Robert Burns." Sensible people wondered whether
Gilfillan had gone crazy. For since the masterly defence of
Burns by Professor Wilson, few had been foolhardy enough to
take up the cuckoo song and repeat the oft exploded scandals
that had been trumped up against the peasant bard. On Christ

mas day of 1847 a reply to Gilfillan appeared in the *Glasgow Citizen*; it was an article characterised by manliness of conception and vigour of diction, defending Burns from the attack, and in a tone of lofty scorn a cursory but scathing criticism on some of Gilfillan's own literary productions. The editor, in a note, stated that the article was from the pen of Hugh Macdonald, a name hitherto unknown in prose literature. The article produced a great sensation, and every one asked, who is Hugh Macdonald? Gilfillan was stung into a reply, and on 1st January, 1848, a long letter appeared in the *Citizen* from him. He seemed galled, angry, and was certainly nasty, and without his usual skill he showered on Macdonald his wild blows like wintry rain. He called him "*A* Mr. Macdonald," "an unknown scribbler who knew nothing of Burns' writings;" and in reference to Macdonald's remarks on Gilfillan's *Gallery of Literary Portraits*, he says, "If he had read the writings he abuses, he might have known that I have not yet commenced my 'Gallery of Demons,' nor yet my 'Gallery of Dunces;' but I promise him, that when I do, his name shall not be forgotten in one or in both." The following Saturday Macdonald made a triumphant rejoinder, in which his whole heart welled out in defence of his beloved Burns, and the Gilfillan battery was silenced. Mr. James Hedderwick was so impressed with the ability as a prose writer of his former poetic correspondent that he soon removed him from the printing table at Colinslie, and put him on the literary staff of the *Citizen*, where he continued till the starting of the *Morning Journal*. During his career on several Glasgow newspapers, much of his writing is, of course, lost. Such, indeed, is the general fate of newspaper writers. Articles hastily written, and generally on subjects of floating interest, the newspaper editor does not write. Enough, however, has been produced in a permanent form to keep Hugh Macdonald's name before the world—"Rambles round Glasgow," "Days at the Coast," and his Poems, when collected, will constitute three volumes, and the basis of his permanent reputation; and if Sappho lives in virtue of a single song, and has made herself immortal by one such outpouring, they are enough, though but a small part of his literary work. The "Rambles round Glasgow" is one of the freshest, most life-like pictures of the various scenes described which it is possible to conceive. It is here that the author avails himself of those rich stores of botanical knowledge which he had garnered up. in his early days, and that intimate acquaintance with natural history which lends such a charm to his writings. How refreshing to read his "Days at the Coast," where he guides us into many a lovely, many an impressive, scene. As we read, we sniff in fancy the sea-breeze, and smell the red heather—so natural, so life-like are his descriptions. Perhaps the best specimen of his poetry is the beautiful little poem, *The Flower Lovers' Song.*   I am sorry to detain you, but I would like just to give you a few lines of it :—

> "When Spring frae the blue-lift in beauty comes smiling,
>   And stern icy winter gangs frowning away ;
> While blythe sings the mavis the bright hours beguiling,
>   And woods a' are busking in leafy array ;
> Coltsfoot and Celandine
>   Wee gowden Starnies shine,
> And sweetly the primrose and violets blow ;
>   Forth over hill and glen,
>   Far frae the haunts of men,
> Joyously wandering, we flower-lovers go."

There is an incident connected with the subject of my toast of which I would like to say a word ere I conclude. Most of you will remember, on the road to the Pecsweep Inn, just before the steep ascent to the Braes commences, there is at the roadside a little natural fountain trickling from a green bank, at which everybody stops to drink. Macdonald had been walking on the Braes, and after describing the flowers unknown to the rich flat below, the bracken, the heather, the myrtle-leaved blacberry, the delicate wild pansy, the fairy blue bell, and the graceful bedstraws white and yellow, he too stops at the little well to drink—the well whose water is always deliciously cool and clear. But, hark, he speaks. "Full many a crystalline draught are we indebted to this tiny well. Oft in our rambles over these Braes, alone or in company with valued friends, have we come for rest and refreshment to this secluded but commanding spot. Many are the blythe groups we have seen circled around it, while each individual in turn dipped his beard into its stainless bosom. Fair faces, too, have we seen mirrored in its waters, while rosy lips have met substance and shadow on its cool dimpled surface. Were we a rich man we should gift thee a handsome basin, thou well-loved little fountain; but silver and gold have we none, so thou must even content thyself with a humble poet's honest meed of praise." I will read one or two stanzas of the poem in question, called "The Bonnie Wee Well":—

> " The bonnie wee well on the breist o' the brae,
> Seems an image to me o' a bairnie at play;
> For it springs frae the yird wi' a flicker o' glee,
> And it kisses the flowers while its ripples they pree.
> The bonnie wee well on the breist o' the brae
> Wins blessings on blessings fu' mony ilk day;
> For the wayworn an' weary aft rest by its side,
> And man, wife, and wean a' are richly supplied.
>
>   *   *   *   *   *   *   *   *
>
> The bonnie wee well on the breist o' the brae,
> Where the hare steals to drink in the gloamin' sae grey,
> Where the wild moorlan' birds dip their nebs and tak' wing,
> And the lark weets his whistle ere mounting to sing."

Well, some friends of Macdonald, headed by the late Mr. William Johnstone, Glasgow, arranged to erect "a basin" at the "bonnie wee well," and made an appeal to the landowners of Renfrewshire, which was cordially responded to by the Earl of Glasgow, Sir Michael Shaw Stewart, Colonel Campbell, and others. The basin has assumed the form of a monument and is now ready, and in the studio of Mr. Mossman, on whose ability it reflects great credit. Mr. Johnstone, on his deathbed, entrusted me with the sad duty of seeing his intentions, as to the monument, carried out. Several things have caused delay, among others, perhaps my busy life, and this day's proceedings. I trust, however, that ere long the monument will be placed "on the breist of the brae." (Applause.) But I must draw to a close. Hugh Macdonald, like others spoken of to-night, died young, in the midst of his aspirations. How he would joyfully have joined the thousands on Gleniffer Braes to-day is known to his friends, and how little did he think that ere this glorious

Centenary day his spirit would be fled.   I thought of him this day when on Gleniffer Braes.   From his grave he seemed to say, in the beautiful words of Coleridge—

> "Bloom on, ye amaranths! for whom ye may,
> For me ye bloom not."

The unexpected news of his death fourteen years ago saddened many a heart.   To think that the Rambler was dead?   Dead? No, men like our octumvirate never die; their bodies may be laid in the dark and silent grave, and loving friends may sprinkle cypress on their monuments, but the spirit which animated them, their vitalising power, that individuality which made them kings among men is immortal—I speak not now of that immortality which is the Christian's sheet anchor in the hour of trial; the believer's hope when the days of darkness come; an immortality common to all mankind; I speak rather of that lesser though still glorious immortality reserved to the sons of genius; an immortality which inspires the soldier on the battle field and has made England not tell the sailor boy in vain that she expects that he will do his duty—the immortality of Fame; and in this sense Hugh Macdonald still lives.   He lives in those animated pictures of land, lake, and mountain scenery which will make his works perennial classics; he lives in those groves which have been made vocal by his song; he lives—and when they are better known he will more largely live in those lyrics which have inspired in many a bosom emotions which no one need blush to own; he lives in those wood notes wild which waken up a song in the saddest heart; he lives in his intense nationality—he was the most Scottish of the Scottish; he lives in his idolatry of Burns—an idolatry endorsed and intensified by the genius of the land, who on a recent centenary occasion imperishably bound around the poet's brow the lilac-leaved crown that shall live for ever; he lives in his glorious and manly defence of Burns; and meet it was that he who by one immortal song sanctified for ever the poor man's cot, should have his fair fame protected from all that bigotry and fanaticism could heap upon it, by the pen of one, a working man himself; he lives, in spite of his unfinished life.   Yes—

    "Let fate do her worst, there are relics of joy,
      Bright dreams of the past, which she cannot destroy ;
      Which come in the night-time of sorrow and care,
      And bring back the features that joy used to wear.
      Long, long, may my heart with such memories be fill'd,
      Like the vase in which roses have once been distilled
      You may break, you may ruin, the vase if you will,
      But the scent of the roses will hang round it still."
—(Loud applause.)

Mr. WILLIAM CROSS gave "The Minor Poets of Paisley."

Mr. ROBERT HAY in proposing "The Memory of R. A. Smith," spoke thus—The Bard of Avon has well said—

    "As when a well graced actor leaves the stage,
      The eyes of all are idly fixed on him
      Who enters next, thinking his prattle to be tedious."

I feel that I am in the position of "him who enters next." Those who have preceded me have spoken so eloquently that I hesitate to intrude. Still it affords me an opportunity of joining my fellow-townsmen in celebrating the Centenary of our own loved bard Tannahill, who, born and reared in "oor ain guid toon" poured forth these lyrics, so true to nature, which the world will not willingly let die, and which have shed a lustre on the place that gave him birth, and delighted am I at being favoured with the privilege of calling upon you to pledge the memory of one who was Tannahill's bosom friend, whose strains he has wedded to music so sympathetic and appreciative that all feel that poet and musician were one in thought, feeling, and imagination. Poetry and music in all ages have been close companions, and exercised potent sway over all hearts. While, take them apart, they are powerful ; united, they are irresistible, and stir the hearts and move the feelings of mankind. The celebrated poets of olden time, the echo of whose fame falls on our ears through the vista of the past, like the lullaby of waters, were masters of the lyre, and gave colour and force to the imperishable thoughts that their genius conjured into existence. The Æolian Lyre may be of beauteous form, and attract admiration from its elegance, but it is only when the airs from Heaven pulsate upon its strings that music is evoked, and the ears of listeners are enthralled. So the finest lyrics that ever poured from the warm heart of the poet, only attain their force and completeness, and exercise their full power when linked to music's heavenly strains. Nothing gave Tannahill greater pleasure than, as he sauntered along, to hear his songs chanted by the fair. Then was his cup of happiness filled to the brim. Beautiful, however, as his lyrics are, they would not have acquired the same popularity or produced the same effect upon his countrymen had immortal music not been wedded to immortal words. And he, who greatly aided in the work for Tannahill was R. A. Smith, the subject of my toast. R. A. Smith, though born in England, was to all intents and purposes one of ourselves. His father was a Paisley man who removed to Reading to better his circumstances and there wooed and won an English lass. Both of them were musical, and their son, born on 16th November, 1780, was reared in an atmosphere of music, and his powers fostered from his cradle by the melodies of England and Scotland. He easily played the violin, and oftentimes noted down street melodies that pleased him as he passed along. In 1800 the family removed to Paisley, and soon his admirable voice and exquisite musical taste caused his company to be courted. Paisley has ever been distinguished for its musical taste, and I question if there is any town in broad Scotland that has, for its size, so many musical associations. It has been spoken of as a " nest of poets" let me add that it is also an "aviary of singing birds." In 1807, R. A. Smith was appointed precentor to the Old Abbey, and there formed and trained a choir which obtained more than a mere local celebrity, from the admirable manner in which they performed the psalmody of the Church along with anthems and other sacred pieces. In 1823 Smith removed to Edinburgh, and became, through the influence of Dr. Thomson, the leader of music in St. George's Church, and did for its choir, as for the Abbey one here, by making it a model one for other choirs to follow. On January 3, 1829, nineteen years after the decease of his friend Tannahill, death took away all that was mortal of R. A. Smith. The sacred music of Scotland is much indebted to R. A. Smith. Before his time the psalm music of Scotland had fallen to a low ebb. Musical execution was bad, and many of the melodies and harmonies were poor. R. A. Smith did much to remedy this.   He published numerous editions of sacred music with the tunes remodelled and harmonised anew, and composed himself very many tunes, which, to this day, are sung with great acceptance, and of which "Invocation," "St. Mirrens," "Selma," "St. Lawrence," &c., are apt illustrations.   To his qualities as a man and as a friend, those who knew Smith bear hearty witness. He was singularly modest and unassuming in his deportment, and his death was lamented by all who loved music, and by many who felt that they had lost in him a brother and a friend. But specially in connection with Tannahill should his name be held by us in remembrance.   The sweet strains he has composed for Tannahill's songs are the evident productions of a pure mind and cultivated taste.   Some of these we have heard this evening, and to many, if not to us all, they are familiar.   So long as the songs of Tannahill shall endure, so will the melodies of R. A. Smith.   Beautiful as are the spots in the vicinity of our town, their charms are hallowed and made famous by the sweet lyrics of Tannahill and the matchless strains of R. A. Smith.   (Applause.)

The other toasts were "The Ladies," "The Chairman," and "The Croupier."

FESTIVAL IN DRILL HALL.

A soiree in honour of the occasion took place in the Drill Hall at eight o'clock.   The large hall was beautifully decorated with flowers, evergreens, and appropriate mottoes.   There were about 900 persons present.   Mr. Thomas Coats of Ferguslie occupied the chair, and on the platform were Colonel Holms, M.P. ; Bailie Clark, ex-Bailie M'Kean, Councillors Halden, M'Gown, and Cochran ; P. C. M'Gregor, Brediland ; Rev. Jas. Brown; James Wallace, Braehead ; R. L. Henderson ; Sheriff Cowan ; David Semple, F.S.A.; John Brown of Mossvale Villa ; Joseph Fulton of Glen ; Captain Wallach ; Mr. Finlayson of Merchiston ; Councillor Boa, Kinning Park ; Wm. M'Oscar, Kilbarchan ; Thomas Fraser, Belfast ; Drs. Richmond and Donald ; Messrs. Louis Hoeck, James Robertson, J. R. Fraser, J. Lorimer, James Reid, R. Russell, James Smith, T. Wilkie, J. M'Kay (secretary of the Weavers' Society), John Hart, and R. Skimming.

After tea,

The CHAIRMAN said he had received letters of apology for unavoidable absence from Messrs H. E. Crum-Ewing, James Dodds (London), Rev. James Dodds (Abbey), Dr. Wallace (Glasgow), Rev. Wm. Graham (Edinburgh), Wm. Wotherspoon, James Clark (Camphill), Mr. Fraser (Johnstone), Mr. W. L. Mair (Edinburgh), and Sir Peter Coats.

Mr. COATS then said—We are met here this evening to pay a tribute of homage and respect to the memory of our bard—Robert Tannahill—(applause)—whose sweet lyrics have cheered the hearts and enlightened the cares of many of this town and elsewhere for now three-quarters of a century—(applause)—and I am sure the same pleasure and gratification will be afforded to succeeding generations. (Cheers.) If there is anyone to whom we ought to be grateful, certainly it is to one who can wile away the dull, tedious hours with such beautiful songs as we have had from our incomparable Tannahill. (Applause.) Like many here, Tannahill was bred to the loom; and, being master of his own time, had much leisure to devote to the muse, of which we know he was a very successful wooer. Many of the subjects of his muse are in the surrounding hills and glens and burns and braes in our neighbourhood, where I have no doubt many youthful lovers will resort. (Cheers.) Few of Tannahill's contemporaries are now alive, but I understand there is one still present with us—Mr. John Hart. He was well known to Tannahill, and enjoyed his friendship. I may also say that my father, who was of the same calling, knew Tannahill well, and I have heard him describe him as a quiet, retiring man, very fond of his favourite pursuit; and often has he seen R. A. Smith and Tannahill together at the loomside adapting music to the poet's verses. Smith was one of his earliest companions, and his counsellor and friend to the last. Many things can be said of Tannahill even by gentlemen who are present, and therefore I will not detain you longer, more especially as I think we cannot do greater homage to the bard than to sing some of his beautiful songs. (Loud applause.)

Colonel HOLMS, M.P., said—Mr. Chairman, ladies, and gentlemen, I thank you most heartily for having given me this opportunity of being present on an occasion of which Paisley may well be proud. (Cheers.) There is something deeply interesting in the life of a man of genius living in a great period of the world's history. Such a man was the poet Tannahill, and such an age was that in which he lived. (Applause.) In the very year in which he was born an event occurred which, perhaps, more than any other event during the last century has moulded the history of the English-speaking race. In that year this country, by taxing her American colonies without giving them the right of representation, roused a resistance which led, as Edmund Burke in one of his most celebrated speeches predicted, to the separation of these colonies from the mother country—(applause)—and the establishment of the New World Republic, which in wealth and enterprise rivals the most favoured nations of Europe. (Applause.) He lived in an age of mighty men destined to play a great part in the world's history. Napoleon and Wellington, Walter Scott and Robert Burns, were boys when he was born. James Watt and Adam Smith were then in the prime of life. He had for his contemporaries Pitt and Fox, Burke and Sheridan; among the poets, Byron and Campbell, and Southey and Moore. I need not occupy your time with telling you of the galaxy of illustrious men of literature, science, and art who flourished then. Suffice it to say that during the latter part of the 18th century and the beginning of this century, warriors, statesmen, poets, and philosophers dazzled the world by the brilliance of their victories, their eloquence, their genius and their learning. (Applause.) And yet, after 100 years have passed away, the memory of Tannahill is as dear to every Scotchman and, I venture to say, dearer than ever to every man and woman in Paisley. Whence this undying fame? Whence is it that Paisley is moved to-day as it has seldom been moved even in times of the highest political excitement? Whence is it that men and women have for Tannahill such affection, and how is it they hold his memory in such respect? Other authors have written voluminously—other poets have sung in more ambitious strains—other men have made a greater figure in their day and generation; but of few men, however illustrious, can it be said that after so long a lapse of time their fame has been continually increasing. (Cheers.) Tannahill was gifted in the very highest degree with that genius which creates a fellow-feeling, which gives expression in simple but poetic words to those thoughts which are common to humanity—which, in fact, link the lips of one to the hearts of many. (Cheers.) I have read in the life of Tannahill that when away from home he derived the most exquisite pleasure from hearing a country Scotch girl singing, "We'll meet beside the dusky glen by yon burnside." (Cheers.) Little could he foresee that generations of Scotchmen and Scotch-women would have their labours lightened and their happiness increased by singing those songs of exquisite beauty with which we are all so familiar. (Cheers.) When I look around this vast assembly I am led to think—What makes a country really great? Not merely material prosperity, but rather that halo of glory with which its great men invest it. Sir Walter Scott, as with the wand of a magician, has rendered classic almost every castle, almost every keep, every mountain-pass and every headland of our native land ; and he has shed a fresh lustre on the history of our country. What would Ayrshire have been without Robert Burns? Would Bannockburn be as famous in story if he had never penned "Scots wha hae"? (Cheers.) Would we have appreciated the simple virtues of the Scottish peasantry if he had not given to the world "The Cottar's Saturday Night?" What a wealth of pleasure, what a treasure of thought, would have been lost to mankind, had he never written these songs which have immortalised his name. And so it is with the poet Tannahill. "Craigielea," "Newtonwood," "Stanely Shaw," "Gleniffer Braes," are doubly dear to us, because there Tannahill wandered, and there from his habitual musings sprang those originalities of thought which have inspired some of the sweetest lyrics in any country. (Cheers.) Of Tannahill it may well be said that he never wrote a line which will die, or that we could wish to blot out. Such a man, however humble, is an honour to his birthplace. His thoughts—embodied in undying song—are an inheritance of which we, the people of Paisley, may well be proud. They tend to raise us above the dull routine of common life ; they give us a higher and deeper insight into the beauties of nature ; they inspire us with a deeper love of country, while they tend to elevate and purify those sentiments and affections which are common to all the conditions of life. (Cheers.) And let me only add that it is because we, his fellow-townsmen, fully appreciate not only his genius but his worth and true nobility, that we this day endeavoured to do fitting honour to his memory. (Cheers.)

Mr. JAMES WALLACE, Glasgow, having been called on, in the absence of Mr. Mair, advocate, delivered a short address, in the course of which he urged the desirability of erecting a monument in memory of Tannahill.

The CHAIRMAN said he was sorry that Mr. Fraser of Newfield was unable from indisposition to be present, but his son had kindly consented to occupy his place.

Mr. JAMES ROY FRASER, after a few introductory remarks, read the following speech, which his father had prepared for the occasion :—Sixty-eight years ago I went to be an apprentice to a Paisley weaver, Alexander Renfrew, who took a small farm near Glenfeoch, the scene of one of Tannahill's songs. He for many years kept a stock of six apprentices. Songs, chiefly Burns's, were daily sung by the boys, to the rattling accompaniment of the shuttle. Some impure ones unhappily got in among us, and never can I forget the bad effect they produced on our young sensitive minds. The influence of songs, poetry, and music on the young is irradicable. How often through life have I ardently wished to forget them, but in vain. Music is the chosen memory of the human heart, and careful should we be of what we store it with. I could then sing a snatch of Tannahill's song, "My dear Hieland Laddie, O?" It always affected my young mind powerfully, and created in me an ardent desire to obtain the whole of it. As soon as I had enough money, I went to Paisley and bought his then recently published book. In about two weeks thereafter I had the whole volume committed to memory, and my mind greatly improved and instructed by its many wise precepts and grand moral truths. The other apprentices speedily learned many of the songs, which were daily sung individually, or by all of us together. We felt Tannahill as a great moral power over us, and to our lively apprehensions a very great man.

> "Thus song and music rouse the mind to think,
>   The heart to feel, as all true hearts should do ;
> To exalt our being, and enlarge our joys ;
>   And every form of evil to eschew."

All the boys learned Tannahill's "Soldier's Return," with which they were all charmed. It is a dramatic piece in three acts, with six representative characters. Each of the boys appropriated one of them ; and when the weather was not propitious, we betook ourselves to the barn, and acted the piece to our own great satisfaction, delight, and benefit. Most of you will remember that many of Tannahill's pieces are, like Burns's gill-stoup productions, tinged with a strong Bacchanalian flavour, but sometimes in very guarded language. In these days there could be no song without the smell of whisky. When Burns sent his "A man's a man for a' that" to his publisher, he said—"Here is a song containing neither love nor wine ; and, according to the critics, it can be no song." I will now relate to you a little instructive incident—a mere boyish romance—about drink. Influenced by Tannahill, and probably by Burns's gill-stoup productions, we determined to taste of the whisky ecstacy that Tannahill says exalts the soul. Our plan was quite original. Smuggling was then very common. We daringly determined to try it. There was plenty of barley in the barn, and we soon contrived to convert a bushel of it into malt. The father of one of the boys had a small still, used in distilling herbs for medicinal purposes. We soon got it. We prepared a fire in a sequestered spot among surrounding brambles and brushwood. On it we erected the still ; and, oh ! what rapture when we saw the mountain dew trickling from the nozzle of the worm. We did this frequently like fairies in the middle of the night, glorying in our triumph, besides being greatly amused, tickled, and even instructed by the interesting philosphy of the distilling operation. So much, gentlemen, for the dangerous influence of Bacchanalian songs, on young, wild excitable minds—aye, on any mind. But poetry, especially lyrical, belongs not to the whisky barrel, but to the finest forms of pure sentiment, truth, virtue, and good principles. A clearer perception of the great moral purpose of the two superlatively fine arts, Poetry and Music, will we hope

ere long put an end to their prostitution, in spreading a delusive
charm around the maddening bowl and the drunkard's drink.

> " The painter's tints may be profane,
>   Polluted be the poet's strain,
>   But she, sweet Music, never stamps a stain
>   On mind or heart. "

You all know Tannahill's sweet song, "The Lass o' Arranteenie,"
with its simple, fine melody by his bosom friend, R. A. Smith.
The poet had at one time visited this grand romantic spot, situated near the mouth of Loch Long, on the western side. It was
then a ferry station and a public inn. Walter M'Farlan was the
ferryman and innkeeper, and his only daughter, Jeanie, the lass
of the song. My parents and this man (both Highlanders) were
well acquainted. In about the year 1800 my father paid a visit
to Arranteenie, taking me along with him. Jeanie was there,
very young like myself, and my constant companion, little dream-
ing that in future years her name would be set like a jewel in
one of your poet's songs. Sweet creature, she led me like an
innocent angel up among "the rocks and woody glens" of that
place, in search of blaeberries, wild fruit, and wild flowers. The
scene was indeed " 'mong Nature's wildest grandeur." It was
the first time I had ever beheld such natural beauty and magnificence. It was my first grand lesson in the school of old august
Nature, never to be forgotten. In future years I visited Arranteenie twice. The first time Jeanie was in full-blown woman-
hood, sweet, graceful, pretty, her face greatly fernitickled, and
her manners simplicity itself. I sang to her among the rocks
and woody glens of our young days "The Lass o' Arranteenie ; "
—but time will not permit me to enlarge on this most interesting
romantic scene. On my last visit, thirty years ago, I found she
was married to a blacksmith, and was then living at the head of
Lochgoil. My family sang habitually the finest of Tannahill's
songs throughout Great Britain, a part of Ireland, and the New
England States of America. Tannahill's songs and poems are
entwined around the very meshes of my soul ; and proud am I
to be enabled, even at this late hour of my life, to bear this pub-

lic testimony to their and his intrinsic worth.   When my family, more than twenty years ago, gave an evening to aid in raising a monument to your Wilson, the ornithologist, (saving for that purpose above £20), I appealed to the audience for a similar compliment or honour to be conferred on Tannahill. Now is your time.   It is impossible to let it pass.   The honour of Paisley—of you, sons of daily toil—is now at stake.   Pure, patriotic, national song-writers are the most influential and valuable instructors of the national mind.   A beautiful song, with beautiful music, once known and sung by the people, is far more influential than a thousand commonplace prose volumes in forming, influencing, refining, and improving the national character. Burns and Tannahill are national luminaries that will shine for ever.   Like Venus in the heavens, they will ever shed on us, and on generations yet unborn, their beautiful silvery radiance. In truth, poetry is the most potent and grandest teacher in the world.   It presents love, beauty, truth, and nature in their sweetest, most silky, and sublime forms.   It is the grand intellectual glass, through which we see to the very best advantage everything interesting and lovely, above, around, beneath us. A true poet born in our midst is a heavenly boon above all price. Even "tho' poorith cauld" (as in the case of Tannahill) be his lot, his influence gradually, irresistibly increases, like the sun rising out of its eastern chamber, above all depressing, conventional forms, estimates, and ideas ; and makes the very richest and proudest among us glad to bend the knee at his honoured, humble shrine. The great, the unique public compliment paid by you to-day to your own poet will be justly ranked by millions throughout the world as the most beautiful feather in the cap of Paisley, and raise your town and character a hundred per cent in public esteem.   Such a peculiar compliment, got up with so much public zeal, skill, ability, and taste, to the humble poet, with not one attractive point about him, except his sterling worth and genius, is, I suspect, unparalleled in the history of any people.   Is it too much to say, if the stamp of immortality be not already impressed upon his fame, you have this day completed the impression.

Shade of the Poet, dost thou hear
  What I've now said of thee ;
How you inspired my youthful soul
  With song and melodie ?

Old as I am, my heart's yet warm,
  Once kindled by your fire ;
Old as I am, my mind's yet fresh,
  Your genius to admire.

Long as it is since first I read,
  Enraptured, your fine songs,
My heart cries out that unto you
  Deep gratitude belongs.

The flame you kindled e'er shall burn,
  And not till death expire ;
The mind you roused to mental life
  Till death will you admire.

Ye men—ye patriots of this town—
  Let Glasgow not you shame ;
What it for Burns intends to do,
  To your bard do the same.

The ploughman bard, in sculpture grand,
  In Glasgow soon you'll see ;
Your weaver bard, in sculpture fine,
  In Paisley soon must be.

See ! see him on yon hill of graves !
  Striking his golden lyre ;
Gazing on grand Gleniffer Braes,
  His heart and soul on fire.

Gleniffer Braes ! the world wide
  Will then resound your praise,
When to his worth, and yours as well,
  A Monument you raise.

—(Loud applause.)

Mr. LORIMER proposed a vote of thanks to the pianists, and Councillor HALDEN a like compliment to the speakers.

Bailie MACKEAN proposed a vote of thanks to the Festival Committee, coupled with the name of the secretary. (Applause.)

Mr WILKIE replied.　He said—on behalf of myself and the other members of Committee, I beg to acknowledge your thanks, and at the same time thank you for your presence here to-night. This festival has not been the least successful of this day's demonstrations, of which it may be said :—

> Paisley's honoured Tannahill,
>   Her native bard supreme,
> Wing'd his praises near and far,
>   Where living millions teem ;
> Wak'd the beauties of his songs,
>   And made his name her theme,
> Proudly whisper'd, " 'Twas thy loom
>   That wove my wreath of fame."

Bailie CLARK said—We have now come to the last proposal, and I believe the most important of all.　I quite endorse the remark of Mr. Wilkie, that this meeting of ours has been not the least successful of those held to-day.　I really do believe it has been the most successful.　I am sure, moreover, that the enjoyment afforded here has been of a very satisfactory nature. This very happy meeting has been presided over by our esteemed friend, Mr. Coats, of Ferguslie.　He has acted his part well, and to him we ought to accord a very hearty vote of thanks. (Loud applause.)

The CHAIRMAN said—I assure you this night has been to me one of unalloyed pleasure.　From the time the centenary celebration was taken in hand by the committee, I went into the matter heartily, and did all I could to forward the movements that were necessary to bring it to a happy conclusion.　I was to-day on the Braes o' Gleniffer, and I never saw a more enthusiastic gathering than that on the classic ground.　Indeed, I think a brighter day has never been seen in Paisley.　(Great applause.)　It has given me very much pleasure, and I esteem it a high honour, indeed, to occupy the position of your chairman.　Tannahill's songs have undoubted charms, both in our native town and elsewhere, but they have had a double charm to-night.　I think, however, that those parties who take an interest in the productions of the bard might popularise them to even a still greater extent by organising choirs to sing them occasionally. I thank you for the way in which you responded to the proposal of Bailie Clark. (Applause.)

During the evening a number of songs were sung by Miss Gow, Mr. Hamilton Corbett, Mr. M'Lean, Mr. Muir, Mr. Lee, Mr. Willison, and Mr. Walker. Prominence was, of course, given to the compositions of Tannahill, and all the efforts of the artistes were hailed with enthusiasm.

TROGLODYTE CLUB.

The members of the Troglodyte Club dined in honour of the occasion in the Terrace Tavern. The hall was beautifully decorated, and there was a crowded attendance—upwards of forty members having assembled. Mr. John Crawford, writer, in the chair, and Mr. Hugh Smith, croupier.

The CHAIRMAN, in proposing " The Health of Her Majesty, the Queen," said—On no occasion could the Troglodyte Club drink the health of Her Majesty with more fervour and devotion than on the present, because we are met not only to celebrate the fifty-fifth anniversary of her birth, but likewise the hundredth anniversary of the birth of our townsman, Robert Tannahill. On the one hand, Victoria, Queen of Great Britain and Ireland, and Colonies thereunto belonging, the greatest sovereign on earth; and on the other, Robert Tannahill, the humble Paisley weaver and song-writer,—receiving the combined homage of the people of Paisley, joined in one joyous celebration,—entwined in one wreath—monarchy and the muse, sovereignty and song, divine poesy and worldly policy blended in delightful unison. Her Majesty loves Scotland. She loves the poetry and the songs of Scotland. She knows how superior the lyric poetry of Scotland is to the doggerel ribald popular poetry and songs of England. I do not imagine that Her Majesty has never heard of Tannahill. On the contrary, I should say she knows his history and melancholy fate ; and that "Jessie, the Flower o' Dunblane," "Gloomy Winter's noo awa," "Bonnie Wood o' Craigielea," "Loudon's bonnie woods an' Braes," and several of Tannahill's beautiful, songs, are not unknown nor unsung at her Highland home at Balmoral. Her Majesty will naturally be interested in the proceedings of this day, and will be eager to see the account of them in the papers of to-morrow or next day. I beg to give "The Health of our good Queen Victoria." (Applause.)

Drank with all the honours, followed by the Queen's Anthem.

The CHAIRMAN next said—If, in these days, Paisley is celebrated as the birthplace of poets, in the early period of its history it was the birthplace and also burial-place of kings. The founders of the Stuart race, through whom the Baron of Renfrew derives his title as heir-apparent of the British throne, repose within the precincts of the auld Abbey ; those precincts being therefore consecrated ground, not to be touched by the profane hand of the spoiler,—not to be sold for sordid greed of money, no old buildings within them to be demolished in a spirit of ruthless savagery, and in ignorance seemingly that archæology is not limited to old manuscripts or parchments, but embraces architectural remains as well, which, when read by the enlightened or spiritual eye, reveal the past as clearly as any mere written record, and therefore to be preserved with the same care and reverence. (Hear, hear.) Every true antiquarian, if he has aught of a poetic soul within him, remembers—

> " There is not a mountain pass,
>   Nor castle hoary,
>   Nor e'en a blade of grass
>   But tells a story
>   Of marty'rd saint and warrior slain,
>   And deathless fame and matchless glory ; "

and would count it an act of the grossest desecration, worthy, truly, of "minstrel's malison," to obliterate from the face of his native land those distinctive monuments of her past eventful history and struggles of our forefathers for freedom and independence—that civil and religious freedom we, their ungrateful and degenerate sons, now enjoy. In former times Paisley used to be honoured with royal visits. James IV. and his consort, we have recently been told, frequently visited the Abbey, and were entertained by Abbot Schaw, and, as is well known, James VI. visited the Place of Paisley in 1617, on his return to Scotland after being fourteen years in England. On none of these occasion, however, did their Majesties cross the Cart or go into the Burgh, the Bailies and Council having made a "puir mouth" in the case of James VI., and sent a message that they could not entertain His Majesty with that "sumptuousness" due to royalty, and therefore the duty devolved on the Master of Paisley. Two hundred and fifty years, therefore, have elapsed since Paisley was countenanced with a royal visit. Seeing that by the determined perseverance of our Provost and Bailie Mac-Kean, the Hausmann of Paisley—(a laugh)—a royal road is now opened to the Abbey, and that the Burgh funds are reported in a flourishing condition, would it not be a proper thing to invite the Baron of Renfrew, along with the Baroness, to pay a pilgrimage to the shrine of the founders of the royal race whence they are descended? Were they thus to honour Paisley, I think I may venture, in name of the Troglodytes, to assure them of a right loyal and loving welcome from every son and daughter of Seestu. Mr. Croupier and gentlemen, I beg to give "The healths of the Baron and Baroness of Renfrew, Duke and Duchess of Edinburgh, and the rest of the Royal Family." (Applause.)

Drank with all the honours.

The CROUPIER then gave, "Army, Navy, and Volunteers."

Song by Mr. Peacock, "Should mighty Gaul invasion threat."

The toast was acknowledged by Captain Peacock.

"Her Majesty's Ministers," "The Lord Lieutenant of the County," "The Members for the County and Burgh," "The Magistrates and Council of Paisley," and "Clergy of all Denominations," were given *in cumulo*, and responded to by Bailie Cochran.

The CHAIRMAN then said—The hundred years comprised in the period betwixt the birth of Tannahill and this day, specially set apart in his honour, have been productive of more wonderful events bearing on human progress than any former similar period in the history of the world. The mere enumeration of the political revolutions, social ameliorations, discoveries in science, inventions in art, additions to literature in philosophy, history, fiction, poetry, and song, would fill a large volume—not to speak of the increase of population, extension and improvement of agricultural growth, of manufactures, and mining, and fisheries, and commerce, and augmented wealth of the nation. If one name more than another distinguishes the period, so far at

least as material progress is concerned, it is the name of James
Watt in connection with the application of steam power to
almost every industrial purpose, but especially to locomotion or
transit by land and sea. Comparing 1774 with 1874, and con-
templating what steam power has effected in, the intervening
period both at home and abroad, the mind is literally over-
whelmed. In 1774, no railways, nor steam navigation, no gas,
no water—that is, no supply by gravitation—no electric tele-
grams, nor photographs, nor penny postage, nor savings banks,
nor sewing-machines, nor lucifer matches even, nor numberless
variety of other inventions subservient to facility of production
and human wants and comfort. In the world of literature,
Burns had not burst like a meteor ; nor had Walter Scott,
nor Francis Jeffrey risen in the horizon. There was no
Edinburgh Review or *Blackwood's Magazine* in Scotia's
capital then ; nor Alexander Wilson, nor John Wilson, nor
Robert Tannahill, poet, in provincial Paisley ; nor had either
Goudie, Kennedy, or Motherwell came on the stage as the
editors or conductors of the *Advertiser*, or first newspaper ever
published in Paisley. The history of these hundred years, if
written, not in wearisome detail, but dashed off in something of
the style and with the genius and power of Carlyle's " French
Revolution," would be a grand epic poem. For sixty-four years
out of the hundred, Tannahill has slept in his silent grave. But
in the midst of the variety and importance of the achievements
in arts and arms,—scientific discoveries and mechanical inventions projecting humanity on its onward course, and extending the dominion of mind over matter ; and rivalries and com-
petitions, and noise and strife of the living world, his songs—
attuned to the music of his twin brother and inseparable companion and friend, R. A. Smith—have taken strong hold of the
hearts of his countrymen. His fame has extended till it has
culminated in the ovation of this day—an ovation greater than
victorious general, king, or emperor ever received ; because a
tribute to the power of the spiritual or mental over the mere
material or mechanical in human life. I do not mean to take
up your time by any dissertation on the genius and character of
Tannahill. It would only be going over ground often be-

fore trod in Paisley. You are all familiar with his songs ; and these will be infinitely better illustrated by those brethren gifted with the power of song, by whom they will be sung this evening, than by any prosaic observation of mine. Besides, some may feel their souls stirred within them, and may long to give utterance to their feeling and thoughts on so inviting—so inspiring—a theme ; and it would not become me to stand in their way. All I shall say is that we cannot value too highly the rich inheritance left us by Tannahill in his songs. Many competent judges have declared them superior to those of Burns. In sweetness and tenderness Tannahill may excel, but surely not in power and energy. Surely it is no disparagement to Tannahill to say he never could have written "Scots wha hae" or "A man's a man for a' that," or many other famous soul-inspiring songs of Burns. A certain writer, professing to give an account of the poets of the West of Scotland, recently brought a wholesale charge of drunkenness against Macfarlane, Motherwell, Tannahill, and others, who, he said, all died in poverty through having been given to drink—that drink was the bane of the poets of Scotland. I cannot speak as to Macfarlane, but as to Motherwell and Tannahill there could not have been a more reckless or unfounded charge. The weakness of Tannahill's constitution precluded him from anything like excessive indulgence. It was repugnant to his feeling. Not that he was an ascetic. On the contrary, in a letter to a friend, published in his memoir by P. A. Ramsay, he says, " A night spent in moderate social enjoyment is life to me. But the roar of bestial intoxication is what I never could and never shall be able to bear." Tannahill never was a drunkard ; and I avail myself of my privilege, as chairman this night, to pronounce the imputation inconsiderate and reckless—in short, a lie. (Applause.) His intoxication was of another kind. He had a thirst for nature, and drank largely of the inspiration she yields her votaries.

> " O how enraptured my bosom does glow,
>   As calmly I wander alane,
>   Where wild woods and bushes and primroses grow,
>   And a streamlet enlivens the scene.

> " Though humble my lot, not ignoble by fate,
>   Let me still be contented, though poor ;
> What destiny brings, be resigned to my state,
>   Though misfortune should knock at the door.
> " I care not for honour, preferment, or wealth,
>   Nor the titles that affluence yields,
> While blythly I roam, in the hey day of health,
>   'Mid the charm of my own native fields."

The spirit of Christian contentment, and the feelings of the lover of Nature, and true poet, never were finer described. This will be a white day in the calendar of Paisley. In honouring Tannahill, Paisley honours herself. The glorious anthem sung this day by 10,000 human voices on the Braes of Gleniffer, under the open canopy of heaven—Stanely Green Shaw in the fore-ground, and the lofty Ben Lomond in the distance, the name of Tannahill inscribed on every intervening and surrounding spot made classic by his genius—is a resurrection unto life ; and the weaver poet of Scotland is now ranked amongst the immortals. I beg accordingly to give " The Immortal Memory of Tannahill." (Great applause.)

The toast was drunk with the greatest enthusiasm.

Song by Mr. M'Nee,—"Jessie, the Flower o' Dunblane."

Mr. R. HOWARD LANG then proposed "The Memories of R. A. Smith, Tannahill's companion and friend and composer of the music of his song ; and of P. A. Ramsay, biographer of both Tannahill and Smith."

"The Memory of Burns" was given by Mr. Wingate.

Song,—" Robin was a roving boy."

"Shakespeare, Milton, Wordsworth, and the poets of England ; and Moore and the poets of Ireland" was given by Captain Peacock.

Song,—" Bonnie wood o' Craigielea," by Mr. Peacock.

" Longfellow and the poets of America," by the Chairman.

Song,—" Be kind to Auld Grannie," by Mr. M'Nee.

" Alexander Wilson, (ornithologist) ; John Wilson (Christopher North) ; Goldie ; Kennedy ; Motherwell ; David Webster, author of 'Tak it man, tak it ;' John Lorimer, author of the 'Kiltie Lads ;' and 'Paisley poetry and literature." "The memory of Andrew Park, author of 'Silent Love,' and of many admirable songs, such as 'Hurrah for the Highlands,' 'We'll row thee o'er the Clyde,' and 'Scotland I love thee;' Henning, Fillans, Ewing, and the Fine Arts;" "Kindred meetings in town engaged in celebrating the centenary." "Paisley Bodies o'er a' the world;" "The Strangers;" "The Ladies;" "Chairman, and Croupier," were proposed and drunk in succession, intermingled with songs and recitations by Messrs. M'Neil, M'Lachlan, Galt, Park, Peacock, Lamb, Harl, and others, all given in splendid style.

Special bumpers were called for to "The Laird of Glen" for the great interest he had taken in the day's proceedings, and in throwing his grounds open to the thousands of admirers of Tannahill who had visited the Braes of Gleniffer this day; also to "Mr. M'Oscar," author of "The Ghost," a Kilbarchan poem. These toasts were proposed respectively in eloquent speeches by Mr. Peacock and Mr. Stewart. In like manner "The health of Mr. Peter M'Neil" was drunk as the practical man of business on whom had devolved all the arrangements that tended to the success of the meeting.

After responding to the toast, Mr. M'Neil sang "My pretty Jane."

The Health of the author of "A Nicht wi' the Troglodytes," and Poet-Laureate of the club, was given by the chairman; in responding to which that gentleman recited an original ode in memory of Tannahill, as follows :—

The Poet needs must sing :
  The soaring lark
That makes the welkin ring,
  When dies the Dark,
With happy heart-beats, thrilling, full, and strong,
His bliss holds by the tenure of his song.

The poet needs must sing :
  The bubbling well
Breaks from dark prisoning,
  And leaps to tell,
In liquid murmurings and ripples bright,
Of freedom's joys—glad life, and air, and light.

The poet needs must sing :
    The vagrant breeze,
That fans, with cooling wing,
    The drooping trees,
Is softly whispering a sweet refrain,
To Nature's many-voiced, melodious strain.

The poet needs must sing :
    The wild-flowers raise
A silent worshipping
    Of incense-praise,
And blossom music in harmonious dyes,
With God-ward homage in their upraised eyes.

The poet needs must sing :
    O Tannahill !
When bird, and breeze, and spring,
    And flow'ret, fill
The ear of Day with harmonies divine,
A higher, nobler ministry is thine !

The lav'rock heavenward springs,
    And, as he towers,
Life's quit-rent song out-flings,
    In pattering showers
Of throbbing rapture—Tannahill, 'tis thine
Its fleeting sweetness, in thy song to shrine !

Nested 'mong daily care,
    Thy heart was strong
To leave life's hillside bare,
    On wings of song,
The common daylight of our thoughts to fill
And glorify with music, Tannahill !

The little wayside well,—
    In stones and earth
Low-cradled, yet can tell,
    Of humble birth
Ennobled by such worth and purity,
As, gentle Tannahill, we find in thee !

Scooped by life's dusty way,
    Thy pure, cool spring
Of song. our toilsome day
    Aye rest will bring ;
While in the limpid depths, we fondly trace
The mirror'd beauties of fair Nature's face.

The westland breezes bring,
    From verdant leas,
Soft airs, and, cooing, sing
    Among the trees,
Æolian melodies, our hearts that thrill
Again, in thy sweet numbers, Tannahill !

Cool, from the sunny hill
  And dusky glen,
They stir thy song, and fill
  The hearts of men—
Hot with o'erdriving in life's growing strife—
With the calm pulses of a sweeter life.

The wildflower bloom and scent—
  A choral strain
Of hue and odour blent,
  After soft rain—
With simple grace and dewy freshness fill,
To keep thy memory fragrant, Tannahill !

"The Health of Mine Hostess of the Terrace " was given in acknowledgment of the excellent dinner provided, which had called forth unqualified approbation from every one.

The meeting, after the ceremonial of admission of a new member—the standing orders having been suspended—broke up, having spent a delightful evening, replete with poetry and song in harmony with the spirit of the occasion.

MASONIC DINNER.

The Masonic brethren of Paisley and of other towns celebrated the event by dining together in the Globe Hotel. About eighty were at table. Bro. Alex. M'Leod, R.W.M., 129, presided, and Bro. James Anderson, R.W.M., Renfrew County Kilwinning, 370, discharged the duties of croupier. Amongst those present were Bros. W. Brown, D.M., 129 ; H. S. Edmonds, S. W., 129 ; T. J. Bustard, J. W. ; M'Pherson, Secretary, 129 ; Carswell, P.M., 129 ; Goldie, Treasurer, 370 ; Marshall, S.W., 370; M'Gregor, P.M., 156 ; Wheeler, Glasgow ; W. Guy, P.M., Houston ; George Peter, R.W.M., 153; and James Banks M'Neill, 362. After dinner, the Chairman proposed "Her Majesty and the Royal Family," "The Grand Lodge of Scotland," "The Grand Lodges of England and Ireland, and their respective Grand Masters," "The Army, Navy, and Reserve Forces." In proposing the toast of the evening, "The Memory of Tannahill," the Chairman alluded to the great event of that day, remarking that it would have been a pity if the Masonic brethern of Paisley had not specially assembled to do honour to Paisley's greatest poet. It was highly incumbent upon the brethren not only to join with the municipal body and the trades of the town in marching to Gleniffer Braes, consecrated by the genius of the bard, but to meet, as they did now, to drink to his memory. (Applause.) It was the general belief of the craft that Tannahill was one of the sons of light, having been initiated at Kilbarchan. It was, therefore, all the more their duty that the celebration of the centenary of Tannahill should be recorded in the Masonic annals of Paisley.

The toast was enthusiastically pledged.

The other toasts were—"The Provost, Magistrates, and Council of Paisley," by Mr. Carswell; "The Provincial Grand Lodge of Renfrewshire, East," by the Chairman, Br. Oliver M'Gregor replying; and "The Town and Trade of Paisley," by Mr George Fisher.

An agreeable evening was spent.

THE ODDFELLOWS.

The Alexander Wilson Lodge of Oddfellows, after their return from the Pic-Nic, assembled in the hall in New Street, where "The Memory of Tannahill" was cordially pledged. Other toasts were given, and a very happy evening was spent.

THE CENTENARY CHOIR.

The gentlemen composing the choir which sang at the Braes, with a few of their musical friends, held a social meeting in the Globe Hotel. Mr. John Tyre was in the chair, and proposed "The Memory of Tannahill," which was received with enthusiasm. Other toasts were given by Lieut. Fleming, U. S. Navy, Mr. D. Hunter, Mr. T. Davidson, Mr. Mure, Mr. M'Ewan, and Mr. Charles Hayes.

CASTLE STREET CALLANS.

The Castle Street Callans and friends met in the Hay Weighs Inn, King Street. Mr. Robert Henderson occupied the chair, and Mr. Neil Darroch discharged the duties of croupier. The toast of the evening was proposed by the chairman, and responded to with cordiality. A number of appropriate toasts followed, and Tannahill's songs were sung by several members of the company.

THE "AULD TOLL CALLANS."

The celebration of the Centenary of Tannahill by the "Auld Toll Callans," took place in the Commercial Hotel, Cross, at seven o'clock, when a goodly number of the brotherhood assembled. Mr. W. M'Lean occupied the chair, and Mr. A. Johnstone officiated as croupier. "The Memory of Tannahill" and "R. A. Smith" were given and responded to.

VICTORIA BOWLING CLUB.

The members of the above club, with their wives and friends, met in Anderson's Hall to celebrate the Tannahill centenary. Mr. Archibald M'Fadyen occupied the chair, and Mr. Robert More and Mr. J. Young were the Croupiers. "The Memory of Tannahill" was given by the chairman, and enthusiastically pledged. Other toasts were also given.

TEMPERANCE INSTITUTE.

The members of the Temperance Institute, Orr Square, held a soiree in their own hall—Mr. Robert Easton in the chair.

PAISLEY HOPE LODGE, I.O.G.T.

On Thursday evening, the members of the above Lodge held an open meeting to celebrate the centenary of Tannahill. The chair was occupied by Bro. W. Alexander, P.W.C.T., who, after a few remarks on the object of the meeting, introduced Bro. P. K. Millar, L.D., "Robert Tannahill" Lodge, who gave an address on the leading features of the poet's life ; and as the various songs were sung, contributed a running commentary on each illustration.

JOHN DUNLOP LODGE OF GOOD TEMPLARS.

The members of the choir of the John Dunlop Lodge, No. 28 I.O.G.T., and a few friends, met in the large hall, 25 High Street, to celebrate the centenary with a supper—Mr. T. J. Melvin in the chair. Mr. Alexander Eadie, Mr. James Fergus,

Mr. Robert Hawson, and Mr. James M'Murray, croupiers. After the cloth was removed, the chairman delivered a suitable address, referring to Tannahill and other local celebrities.

DALRY.

The members of the Dalry Junior Burns Club met in the Burns Tavern, in honour of the poet. The chair was occupied by Mr. A. M'Intosh ; Mr. John Blair acting as croupier. A few hours were spent in a very harmonious way, the evening's proceedings being interspersed with a number of the poet's songs.

DUMBARTON.

The centenary of the birth of Tannahill was commemorated here on Wednesday evening last by a number of the natives of Renfrewshire. The hall of the Elephant Hotel was engaged for the occasion. A goodly number assembled, all evidently deeply interested in the proceedings. The chairman, Mr. Currie, gave the toast of the evening, which was cordially received.

THE PRESS ON THE CENTENARY.
(From the Evening Citizen of 1st June).

The eighteenth century's prolific production of men of genius has led to numerous centenary festivals in the nineteenth. Of these a Scotchman most readily calls to mind the tribute paid to the memory of Burns in 1859, and the more recent commemoration of the hundredth anniversary of Scott's birth—two celebrations which, it is to be hoped, Scottish memory will link in future with the rejoicings of which Paisley is on Wednesday to be the scene. It is true that, while the Burns anniversary festivities were world-wide, and the Scott celebration at least national, what we are now considering is only a local festival : yet he who is capable of appreciating Scott and Burns can surely find a place in his heart for Tannahill. For, if not a great poet —if forced to be content with a secondary rank in the literature of his country—this sweetest singer of the many sweet singers to whom his native town has given birth was endowed with no mean portion of poetic fire, and put his talent to the best and

purest use. His townsmen must ever hold him chiefly in remembrance as one who added by his exquisite fancies new charms to
each scene of his lonely rambles ; while, at the same time,
apart from mere local interest, they can unite with every lover
of poetry in enjoying the purely abstract beauties of his verse. If
it is only a dweller by the Cart who can appreciate to the full
the poet's glowing descriptions of Gleniffer braes, of Glenkilloch,
or of Craigielea, yet he must be indeed dull and cold of fancy
who, with a volume of Tannahill in his hands, and even
without having ever set his eyes on one of those charming
scenes, cannot picture an imaginary Gleniffer, Craigielea, and
Glenkilloch for himself. The stranger to the locality who reads
our poet's lyrics—so simple, yet so passionate in their adoration
of nature—need have no difficulty in conjuring up the scenes
which they celebrate ; and, as he gazes upon this mental landscape, he may seem, perchance, to see a solitary figure crossing
the field of his vision, and recognise it as that of the sad minstrel of the spot. For poor Tannahill, in spite of the unaffected
joyousness of some of his songs, was one of the most melancholy
of men. Proud and poor ; greedy of fame, yet shrinking from
notice ; sickly and consequently fretful—his life from our first
glimpse of it till its tragic end knew but little sunshine. In
this respect he has something in common with his great master,
Burns, whose more robust nature, however, prevented his feeling
misfortune so acutely. Tannahill's habit of mind was much more
feminine than masculine. He was staunchly independent ;
but his independence was sensitive and retiring, not aggressive
like that of Burns. This slight contrast of the two poets has
been suggested by the rather ambitious comparisons of some of
the Paisley bard's fellow-townsmen. In reality the two stand
strongly opposed as well in their natures as in their poetry.
It is not intended here, however, to enter deeply into either of
these points. While Tannahill is a poet of nature Burns is
essentially the poet of human nature, and in this the great differ-
ence between them lies. While over-estimation of their hero is to
be deprecated, no one can fail to sympathise with the enthusiasm
of the Paisley folks, or think that Wednesday's speeches,
banners, and arches will have aught but a worthy object. It

is well that the anniversary occurs during a month more favourable to the description of festival than does that of Burns. The season of his birthday is admirably fitted for a cosy club reunion, but a "blast o' Januar' wind" would be hardly an agreeable adjunct to an open-air *fete*.   Let us hope that the weather will be propitious on Wednesday, and that the sun will shine and the sky smile as they aught in that "leafy month of June" which in our sterner climate takes the place of the southern poets' May.

PAISLEY WORTHIES.

(From the Daily Mail of 4th June.)

It was Rowland Hill, if we mistake not, who, in the journal of one of his northern tours, described Paisley as the Paradise of Scotland.   This eulogium by the witty evangelist was not extorted by the scenery on the banks of the Cart, but by the religious character of the population.   Among the celebrated men produced by Paisley, there has certainly been a goodly portion of divines—such men as Boyd of Trochrig ; Adamson, who rose to the dignity of an Archbishop ; Smeton, who became the Principal of a College ; Witherspoon, who is generally honoured by the prefix of President ; James Buchanan, who succeeded to the Theological Chair at Edinburgh, of which Thomas Chalmers was the first occupant ; and James Hamilton, who followed Edward Irving in the Scotch Church in Regent's Square, and who was perhaps the most winsome representative of modern Presbyterians who ever crossed the Tweed.   The gallery of local worthies, thus seen to be strong in able theologians and preachers, includes not a few names illustrious in the fields of science and art—Wilson the ornithologist, and Wilson, of Woodville, being the most noted of her scientific sons, while Henning and Fillans and Noel Paton are the most brilliant of the many artists produced by this prolific mother of great men. The bookworm does not forget that Watt, the painstaking compiler of the "Bibliotheca Britannica," and T. K. Hervey, one of the early editors of the *Athenæum*, were both Paisley men. In the early morning of Time when Greece was the world, we are told that every artist, but especially such as worked in wool, invoked the help of Minerva. The weavers of Paisley must surely have got to be on good terms with that goddess, for she not only assisted them at the loom, but has given to them many a niche in the temples of literature and art. Especially prolific has Paisley been in poets. As one who was himself at least half a Paisley man, the late Alexander Smith, has somewhere remarked, the town famous for its shawls has for the last fifty years or more been an aviary of singing birds—the abode of poetic inspiration, just as Comrie is the abode of earthquakes. Smith did not exhibit his usual kindliness when he sketched the native bards of his own day, and it was asserted at the time that he had drawn on his fancy for some of his facts ; but be this as it may, we cannot doubt that many even of the numerous minor poets of the place contributed in some degree to raise the general culture of the population, and assuredly Paisley has no cause to feel compromised by a company of singers which includes Alexander Wilson, who, in his " Wattie and Meg," showed a graphic fidelity of touch, and a humour which Burns alone could excel ; that other Wilson, whom we delight to think of as Christopher North, whose best poetry is to be found in prose compositions, which Scotland at least can never cease to read with delight ; William Motherwell, who, if born in Glasgow, still owed to Paisley the training of his youth, and who, alike for pathos and masculine vigour, deserves to be ranked among the greater minstrels of his country ; and poor Robert Tannahill, who, alone of all these men, died in the town where he was born, and who must be regarded as *par excellence* the Paisley poet. It was meet that honour should be done to his memory on the centenary of his birth by those who dwell in the place that must for ever continue to be haunted by his pensive shade. Tannahill cannot be called a great poet, but his harp was all his own, and the notes which he struck were sweet and true. He was no mere echo of the great master, who had risen in that neighbouring shire from which his parents came ; and if he lacked the vigour of Burns, and was utterly destitute of humour, his songs were yet characterised by qualities which, within their own sphere, are equally attractive. In particular, he deserves credit for the minute fidelity of his sketches of nature—a

w 2

will be sung over the world while a Scot has an accent left in his throat. "Jessie the Flower o' Dunblane" will continue to have her praises celebrated as wide as the sound of Her Majesty's drum. When shall we lose the ring in our ears of "O, are ye sleeping Maggie?" "London's bonnie woods and braes;" or, better still, that pretty song, fresh and sparkling as a dew-drop, "The Lass o' Arranteenie"? The man who wrote these songs, if he had done nothing else, earned his centenary from Paisley.

The curious thing is that, granting the advantages of Paisley and its surroundings, such a well of poesy should have gushed up in the bosom of a common weaver, hardly wrought, and in humble circumstances. Tannahill was but a "wabster"—one of those poor creatures whom Burns in his lordly strength as ploughman pictured as "coming frae Kilmarnock." But he had industry although he was a poet. One of his biographers mentions that he did not permit his writing to detract from his work. He had a small writing apparatus fixed by the side of his loom, and, as the verses came up to his thoughts, he secured himself against forgetfulness by committing the rough draft to the sheet beside him. To this plan of dividing his work he is said to have referred with triumph when any of his friends accused him of turning his time to profitless use. How a man who has written some of the lines which have come from Tannahill's pen could have received them under such conditions is a marvel, but het Power which evolved "the mossy rosebud down the howe" came down, no doubt, on the brain of the poor weaver, and inspired it with the power of moving fingers capable of striking the Scottish Harp, and drawing forth tones which still touch the hearts of his countrymen.

The Paisley "bodies" are almost Highland in the "shoulder-to-shoulder" feeling they exhibit on certain occasions. Yesterday they gathered to a man, apparently, and they certainly did honour to the event which gave rise to their demonstration with a warmth of feeling which does credit to their soundness of heart. There was just over the proceedings a sufficient shade of sentimentality to be strictly appropriate, and there was all the heartiness which became the townsmen of Tannahill.

NOTE.

[We publish the following, which speaks for itself.—Ed.]

"Moss Street, Paisley, June 5, 1874.

"Mr. Matthew Blair,

"Dear Sir,—Can you furnish me with any information from recollections regarding the life or character of Robert Tannahill, from remarks made or conversations with your grandfather, Mr. Matthew Tannahill. If you recollect anything of interest, would you please communicate by Monday, and oblige, yours, &c.,

"Alex. Gardner."

———

"104 Causeyside, Paisley, June 8, 1874.

"Mr. A. Gardner,

"Dear Sir,—I thank you for this opportunity of placing on record from recollection a few statements made by my grandfather, Matthew Tannahill, regarding his brother Robert.

"After the death of my grandmother, I was sent to sleep in the house with grandfather, and during several years spent the evenings in company with him.

"He made many references to his brother Robert, which I fear cannot be recalled to memory, not having taken any notes. I remember a vivid description he gave of a visit he and Robert paid to an uncle in Ayr. They travelled all the way from Paisley on foot; stayed over a night or two, and walked back to Paisley. They made frequent excursions to Largs. Robert had an intimate acquaintance in Largs, named John Crawford. My grandfather worked more than a year in Largs when he was a young man. On one occasion, I had a young friend spending the evening with grandfather, when he repeated a song composed by Robert, which has never been printed. The subject was the marriage of an old man to a very young woman in Plunkin (Orchard Street). It was comprehensive, sharp, and conveyed a valuable moral lesson.

"One night, during our conversation, he referred to the illness of his brother Robert.   As far as I can recollect, his statement was as follows:—'Robert and I were near the present site of St. George's Church (George Street was not opened to Causeyside at the time); he looked up to the sky, and made a strange remark about some imaginary object he saw.   I turned to him saying, 'Ha'e ye gane by yersel', Bob.'   My grandfather always spoke in the most affectionate terms of his brother, and from that hour to the hour of his death, some days afterwards, he believed him to be in no way responsible for his actions.   The poet died of a disease to which all mankind is exposed, and for the results of which we are no more responsible than the man who drops from a window in the delirium of a fever, or the sailor who falls from a yardarm during the violence of a storm.

"About forty years ago Mr. Edward Morris, a temperance lecturer, came to Paisley, and during his lecture referred to the death of Robert Tannahill as an example of the baneful influences of drink.   After the lecture, he was met by several of Robert's intimate friends, who assured him that his statement was without foundation, and entirely at variance with truth.   He afterwards lectured in many parts of this country, but never afterwards referred to Tannahill in connection with drink.   I state this circumstance on account of reports which have been mentioned regarding the character of Robert Tannahill which are not true,—not that I love temperance less, but because I love truth more.

"My grandfather was most grateful for any kindness done to the memory of his brother.   The Rev. J. B. Dickson lectured on his works about eighteen years ago in the Old Low Church. When I came home and gave his criticism of

> 'Even valour looks pale o'er the red field of ruin,'

and

> 'Yon cauld sleety cloud skiffs alang the bleak mountain,'

the tears rolled down the old man's cheeks.   When Queen Victoria and Prince Albert reviewed the Volunteers of Scotland in Holyrood Park, in the year 1860, the band of the Royal Archers

played her Majesty off the ground into the Palace to the tune set
to the words of 'Loudon's bonnie woods and braes.' This circumstance produced much gladness amongst the friends at the
time. But after the unprecedented honour shown to the memory
of Robert Tannahill on Wednesday, 3d June, an honour which
a monarch might covet, if the relatives are not grateful to the inhabitants of Paisley to the latest days of their lives, they are
unworthy of the family with which they are connected.—I am,
&c.,

" MATTHEW BLAIR."

SONNET.

He was no climber on the giddy heights
Of poesy, where few can dare to stand ;
Nor did he search through dreamy days and nights
To find in human souls some strange new land.
He lived familiar with the sounds and sights
That rise, from city streets and country soil,
Around the footsteps of the sons of toil.
But on these common things he threw such lights
Of beauty, and from them drew so sweet a song,
That hearts and homes awoke to the glad voice
Which, rising upwards, moved them to rejoice.
Would that on him had gladness lasted long !
And still his thoughts come cheering us this day,
Clear, warm and healthful as the Summer's ray.

M. R.

3rd June, 1874.

Printed by Alex. Gardner ; Bound by D. Carswell.